Praise for Joanna

'If you hear someone snorting beside the pool this summer, they'll be reading this' *Grazia*

'Scotland's answer to *Bridget Jones's Diary*' ***Daily Record***

'A fearless approach to sex and romance' ***List Magazine***

'Very very naughty and lots of fun' ***Sun***

'A very naughty but nice read that will have you gasping one minute and laughing out loud the next'
Abby Clements

'Raunchy and hilarious . . . you'll be laughing all the way to the beach!' ***Scottish Sun***

'Hilariously funny, and very sexy (you may blush!), it's a fantastic feel-good read' ***No. 1 Magazine***

'An absolutely hysterical main character that you can relate to and page after page of pant-wettingly hilarious scenes . . . Without a doubt this is the best and funniest book I have read so far this year. I can't wait to see what Joanna Bolouri does next!' ***Novelicious***

'Sexy, smart and scandalous, I'd recommend to anyone with a taste for adventure' **Victoria Fox**

Also by Joanna Bolouri

The List
I Followed the Rules

Wishing You a Happy Christmas!

To: ~~Robert~~ Evan

From: Emily &

the Most Wonderful Time of the Year

JOANNA BOLOURI

Quercus

First published in Great Britain in 2016 by

Quercus Publishing Ltd
Carmelite House
50 Victoria Embankment
London EC4Y 0DZ

An Hachette UK company

A CIP catalogue record for this book is available
from the British Library

PB ISBN 978 1 78429 912 5
EBOOK ISBN 978 1 78429 913 2

10 9 8 7 6 5 4 3 2 1

Typeset by CC Book Production

Printed and bound in Great Britain by Clays Ltd, St Ives plc

For Mum

CHAPTER ONE

'Tell me, have you met anyone nice?'

For the past two years, my mum asks me this question every time I call her.

Every. Single. Time.

Since I broke up with my last long-term boyfriend, Tomas Segura, the railway engineer (a half-Spanish, half-boorish man-child whom I now affectionately refer to as Tomas the Wank Engine), she's been crippled by the fear that I, Emily Carson, may be the only one of her three idiot children never to get married. To her, marriage is everything. Family is everything. Being alone is not an option, especially not for a thirty-eight-year-old childless English teacher, who should really consider freezing her eggs before they shrivel up and die – her words, not mine, and she'll continue to repeat them just in case I missed it the first few thousand times.

'I mean, really, Emily. Don't you think that two years of being single is long enough? One day, you'll wake up and you'll be my age and you'll wish you hadn't been quite so picky. You're running out of time. When I was your age, you were eighteen *and* I had twin eight-year-olds.'

'Do we need to have the "I'm not you, I am a completely different person" conversation again, Mum?' I sigh, wondering why I put up with this, and the answer is, because it's Sunday.

Sunday at six p.m. is the time when I allow her judgemental voice to travel the 411 miles by phone from the Scottish Borders to my flat in London and directly into my ear; well, unless I forget to call her, in which case she'll hound me until I answer her call and then ask me if I'm dead. Am I dead and am I still single? In her eyes, both are equally catastrophic.

Normally, my standard response of 'No Mum, I haven't met anyone nice' is met with a sinister sigh of disappointment or a rant on how my brother, Patrick, succeeded in finding himself a delightful girl, despite the fact he's lacking in any kind of social skills.

'Christ, he can't even eat with his mouth closed and *he* got married. And your sister can barely write her own name, but she managed it!'

This woman drives me to distraction, so much so that, despite having started this conversation with her in my bedroom, I now appear to be standing in my bathroom, staring at my own exasperated reflection in the mirror. I spot a grey hair in my brown pigtail and pluck it quickly before her bony hand reaches through the phone and does it for me.

'Jesus, Mum,' I gasp, moving the phone to my other ear while I inspect the rest of my hair, 'do you like any of your children? Iona is dyslexic, not brain-dead – of course she can write her own name, she's a bloody solicitor . . . I know what you mean about Patrick, though; it's like sitting across from a llama. You'd never believe those two were twins, they're so different. Anyway, to answer your question, I have some news and—'

'All I'm saying is there's someone for everyone and –'

Oh good, she's going to tell me what I need to do now.

'– what you need to do is—'

'Mum,' I quickly interrupt, 'I know what you're going to say, but I'm trying to tell you that—'

'– consider men you wouldn't normally consider. That's what I did with your father and—'

'I MET SOMEONE ALREADY! Christ, let a girl get a word in. Did you get that? I. MET. SOME. ONE.'

There's a short-lived silence while she processes this information and I smugly think, That's shut you up, hasn't it, Mother dear? I've snagged myself a new man and he's impressive as fuck, before she finally blurts out, 'Met who? A MAN?!'

'No, Mum, a badger.'

'What? How? When did this happen?'

If it were anyone else, I'd tell them that, eight months

ago, I met Robert at a wine bar in Soho. A vision in Armani, he'd sent over cocktails to our table, along with his 'I'm a fancy marketing director' business card, with his private mobile number scrawled on the back, and then he left with a smile before I even had the chance to size him up properly. All I knew was that he was tall, handsome and apparently mysterious, so of course I googled him to make sure he wasn't in the Interpol database before texting him to say thanks for the drinks. He replied almost immediately and from there it took less than two weeks to discover he was forty-five, very well spoken, worked weekends, wore Tom Ford eau de parfum and had a salary almost as huge as his penis, and less than a month to fall head over heels in love with him. If this were anyone else, I'd tell them that I'm successfully managing to hide my craziness on the outside, but internally I've already decided to double-barrel my surname when we marry and would prefer to get hitched in Scotland, though I'm open to an extravagant ceremony at Kew Gardens followed by a honeymoon in Barbados, where it'll be so romantic he'll feel compelled to propose all over again.

Yes, if I were having this conversation with anyone else, I'd tell them that, for the first time ever, I'm in a proper, grown-up relationship with a responsible, serious man who might help me become a responsible, serious woman – not the current version of myself, who still thinks it's appropriate to wear her hair in pigtails at the age of thirty-eight. I'd tell them that I'm completely smitten. And then I might mention his penis again. But this *is* my mum and, as it does with most mothers, information always leads to interrogation, so instead I say, 'His name is Robert Shaw and—'

'Like the actor? I don't believe you.'

'You don't believe what? That Robert Shaw is his name or that I'm seeing someone? Shall I take him into the woods, cut out his heart and send it to you?'

'Don't be silly. Tell me everything! Is he wonderful? What does he do for a living?'

Ugh, I'm going to have to share something, but her words make me grin. 'Yes, he is rather wonderful. He works in mark—'

'EEK! I'm so happy for you, darling.' She's not even listening. That sentence could have finished 'Marks and Spencer's Prisoner Reform Programme' and she wouldn't have heard a thing over the sound of her own relief.

'Hang on a sec, your dad's just come in from the garden . . . William! . . . WILLIAM!'

She muffles the mouthpiece with her hand because she still believes that doing this will undo the creation of both sound waves and ears, despite the fact that she's yelling at 12,000 decibels.

'WILLIAM! Emily met someone. Yes, a man. I know . . . What? I don't know . . . I'll ask . . . Your dad wants to know when we can meet him.'

My expression in the mirror has changed from one of frustration to one of unbridled horror. As much as I love my parents, they're completely deranged. On paper, they seem relatively ordinary: my accountant dad comes from a long line of Conservative-supporting, wealthy public schoolboys, inheriting a rather large farmhouse – a place I undoubtedly wouldn't have grown up in had his own father known he was a closeted left-winger who despised the Tories. He met my mother, Jennifer (an only child and former beauty queen, crowned 'Miss Beltane' in 1974), when she was seventeen. According to them, it was love at first sight, and they married two years later, shagging their way into parenthood as they went. However, off paper, they are very different. They are, in fact, cocktail-guzzling, boundary-lacking, politically incorrect monsters who live to pry and feed off the screams and mortification of their own offspring. They are the only couple I've ever known who I can honestly say are perfectly matched.

She's breathing excitedly down the phone like some sort of pervert and I know she's waiting for an answer, but all I can think is, Meet him? Bloody hell, first she doesn't believe me and now she wants proof of life? No way. No chance. I try to remain calm.

'But we've only been going out a few months! It's a bit soon, no?'

'Months? And you're only telling me now?' she replies, sternly. 'Exactly how long have you been seeing each other?'

'Since April . . .'

I hear her gasp. 'You've let me worry about you all this time! Thinking you're hundreds of miles away and lonely. How could you keep this hidden from me?'

'Jesus, you don't need to know everything the minute it happens!'

'Of course I do, I'm your mother, and, after eight months, it's appalling that we haven't met him. Is there a reason you don't want us to meet him?'

'You're seriously asking me that?'

Me, alone with my family, is one thing, but when an outsider manages to infiltrate their lair, it's utter carnage. For example, when Tomas and I visited one Easter, we'd only been together for twelve weeks. Dad got pissed on champagne cocktails, then hid the rest of the booze and made us all dance to 'Gangnam Style' to get it back. Patrick refused, but later caved in and had to do the routine all on his own to earn his beer. This was followed by the game 'Who am I?', where we all wrote a famous person's name on a sticky note and stuck it to the head of the person on our right. Iona chose Inigo Montoya for Tomas (just so she could make him say the whole *Princess Bride* speech in a Spanish accent) and Dad chose porn star Ron Jeremy for me, complete with a drawing of a cock and balls, added by Patrick. Tomas stared at the badly drawn comedy knob on my forehead for ten minutes before I gave up and then died a little inside when I saw the answer. Finally, they made us sleep in my old room, which Pacino (their 120-pound Great Dane) now calls his own, and Pacino made it clear he had no plans to sleep anywhere else except in bed with us. When we left the next day, tired and emotional, Tomas announced that he'd never met such an awful bunch of '*inadaptados*' in his life, which of course led to a massive, heated argument, as, while they might be misfits, no one is allowed to slag off my family except me. We broke up two years later when he left me for a redhead called Kristen, who works behind the Chanel counter in Selfridges, but I'm totally convinced my unhinged family were the catalyst for his infidelity.

But Robert is completely different to Tomas. Robert is considered. Robert is cultured. Robert has an important job which requires him to fly business-class all over the world. Robert enjoys the more refined things in life, like Grey Goose in quiet cocktail bars, single malts and bespoke suits. If I took him to meet my family, they'd spend five minutes with him before writing *London Twat* on a sticky note and letting the dog dry-hump him while they all danced to 'Blurred Lines'.

'When can you meet him? Oh, I don't know, Mum; let me think . . . How about *never*? Oh, wait, I'm busy on never, how about NOT IN A MILLION YEARS?! That work for you?'

'We were thinking more of Christmas. You'll be staying for four days, anyway, and the whole family will be here.'

'I know they will, that's why the answer is—'

'We're not taking no for an answer. I'm so excited. Does your sister know? I must call her. Bye, darling!'

She hangs up and I'm left staring at myself in the mirror, the realisation of what's just happened slowly dawning on me.

CHRISTMAS? That's only two weeks away! Oh, fuck. Oh, fucking fuck.

CHAPTER TWO

When I decided to leave the rent-free comfort of my parents' home at twenty-four, they were horrified. Not only that I'd want to move away, but that I wanted to live in London, of all places, which, according to them, is a city where people hate each other for fun and profit, and where the poor are forced to shack up with bearded strangers in tiny, overpriced flats.

'I'm sharing with two other teachers. It'll be fine,' I say in my best reassuring voice. 'I have a good job offer and I'm not stupid. I'm twenty-four, for God's sake. I need to stand on my own two feet.'

'You mean you need to get away from us,' Mum snarls, hands on hips. 'I don't understand it. Your brother and sister are perfectly happy here.'

I look across at the twins, both engrossed in their mobile phones, ignoring each other and everyone else. 'They're fourteen, Mum. Their lives revolve around *Family Guy* and wishing they had bigger body parts. Don't take it so personally. This is what children are supposed to do. We grow up, move out and we start our own lives.'

'But London?' Dad chimes in. 'It's the other end of the country. Couldn't you have chosen Edinburgh or Glasgow?'

I could have, I thought. But that's within 'popping in' distance. I need enough mileage to avoid unexpected family ambushes at ten a.m. on a Sunday. I plan to have a lot of sex in London.

Dad starts pacing. He does that when he's in fixer mode. 'At least let us rent you somewhere in a better area,' he says. 'I have a friend who—'

'No offence, Dad, but it's hard to stand on my own two feet when you're renting them a flat and deciding where they should live.'

He stops pacing and sits down, defeated.

My mum's hands haven't left her hips, but I don't think I've ever seen her look so dejected. 'The twins will miss you,' she says quietly. 'We all will.'

I walk over and hug her. My parents may not understand my need to leave, but they don't have to; they just have to accept it. She hugs me back so tightly, softening my resolve and causing a lump in my throat. 'I promise I'll visit on school holidays,' I whisper. 'There's Easter, Christmas, summer . . . I'm a teacher – we get loads of time off.'

She nods, sniffing back tears and snot, while my dad grips my hand and smiles. 'You need anything, you call. Anything.'

Three weeks later, I was waving them off at Waverley station, ready to start my new life, feeling confident that going it alone was absolutely the right thing to do.

'Is my topknot too high? I feel like a pineapple.'

'You look like one. And stop using my fucking Body Shop shower gel, pretty boy. If I wanted us to smell the same, I'd just stop washing completely.'

Meet Toby and Alice – my flatmates. They hate each other. In fact, they despise each other with a passion that erupts the minute they wake up in the morning and continues all day long, but frequently changes from hatred to lust when they get drunk and furiously shag each other in the living room when they think I'm asleep.

'Morning, children,' I say sleepily, pulling up a chair at the kitchen table. 'Toby, your hair is fine.'

'Good morning, Miss Carson,' they chime in unison.

I grin and pour myself some coffee before yawning with such force my jaw cramps. 'Jesus, I'm fucking exhausted. Our thoughtless, idiot neighbour was shagging someone who made the weirdest noises last night. They were at it for hours – I've hardly slept a wink. I swear, between this, his Xbox and the never-ending parties, I'm going to end up doing time for assault.'

'That's the price you pay for having the big bedroom,' Alice replies. 'We can swap, if you like – I'll take hot-neighbour sex-sounds over Toby's snoring any day.'

'I have allergies,' Toby protests meekly in his soft Northern accent. 'I can't help it. I'll also offer to swap rooms, though, while we're at it.'

'No chance,' I say, opening the bread bin. 'I earned that room and I'm the oldest. I honestly don't know how his roomies put up with it – unless they're also having group sex on the other side of my wall . . . Anyone want toast?'

Alice nods, despite the fact she's already cramming an excessively scorched toast triangle into her mouth.

'No, ta,' replies Toby. 'I have quinoa and granola flakes here. I'm good.'

I glance over at Alice, who is glaring at Toby, desperately attempting to wolf down the remains of her toast so she can call him a pretentious wanker, but the moment passes.

Placing four slices of bread into our temperamental toaster, I hover around beside it, ready to press the eject button before it burns to death and I'm forced to eat Toby's cereal. I grab the jam from the fridge, noticing that Alice has stuck three new sparkly Christmas cards to the door and tied tinsel around the handle. Last night's conversation with Mum suddenly bounds back into my brain and I hear her say, *We won't take no for an answer.* Robert's already told me he visits his parents at Christmas; it might be too short notice to change his plans. But if I don't bring him, they'll think he's a dick for not coming . . . and if he doesn't want to come, they'll still think he's a dick and then I'll be thrown pity looks the whole time I'm home because I'm the woman with the dick boyfriend, instead of the plain old woman with no boyfriend. I don't know which is worse. I'm just going to have to fake my own death. Or murder them all.

Luckily, Alice interrupts my increasingly destructive train of thought.

'I have to go in early this morning, Em. John Bowman's wife had the baby,' she says to me, sticking her knife into a tiny pot of marmalade. 'I'm covering his art classes this week. If Pauline fucking Leeland gives me any shit, I'm going to shove an easel up her arse.'

'For a teacher, you're very intolerant of children, you know,' Toby sniffs. 'They all have potential.'

'What the hell would you know about being a teacher?' She laughs, waving her sticky knife in the air. 'You work in a pet shop. You talk to hamsters and goldfish all day.'

'The pet *boutique* is part-time,' he replies defensively, spooning more cereal into his mouth. 'Once I get my modelling portfolio up to scratch, you'll be eating your words.'

'I'd rather eat my words than eat that nonsense cereal, mate.'

I pop up my toast and drop the hot slices on to a plate. 'A baby! Just in time for Christmas – that's lovely! What did she have?' I reply, trying to diffuse the argument, but Alice is still taunting Toby.

'Aww, Toby, did someone once tell you you had

potential?' she cackles, completely ignoring me. 'Never mind, eh?'

'Oh, piss off, Alice.'

'Jesus, guys, it's only seven a.m. Can you both give it a rest?' I sigh and pick up my plate, trudging off back to my room. It would be nice to have a living room to chill out in, but our landlord thought it would be much more profitable to turn it into a third bedroom (now my bedroom), so we're all forced to endure each other in the kitchen at mealtimes. Before I've even reached the end of the hall, I can hear kissy noises and what sounds like Toby's bowl hitting the kitchen floor. Monsters.

I've been in this flat for fourteen years and, despite their weirdness, they're still my favourite flatmates. The first two strangers I shared with in my twenties were Joseph and Darren, both history teachers, who farted continuously for three years and were the messiest pair of piss heads I've ever met. After them were Sharon and Edith, who shared a passion for Botox and *Coronation Street*, and selfishly left me to live with their significant others. Luckily for me, Alice, my Australian colleague, was looking for a place last August and snapped up Sharon's room, shortly followed by Toby, who, to be fair, was mainly welcomed into the fold because of his rather beautiful face.

Once I'm back in my room, away from the humping housemates, I sit on my beautiful red velvet snuggle chair, my most prized and comfortable possession, and continue to eat my breakfast. I don't have to leave for another forty minutes, so I have time to reflect on how splendid my rented flat-share life is. Sure, it would be nice to walk around naked in places other than my bedroom, but it's large and bright with its very own en suite, which was professionally fumigated after Joseph moved out. The walls are annoyingly thin, however, and I'm often forced to endure the nocturnal sounds of my thoughtless neighbour, Evan bloody Grant, the twenty-something, music-blasting, loudly shagging, party-throwing ball-bag who shares a bedroom wall with me and whose headboard must be one thrust away from complete obliteration. Regardless, I'm reasonably happy here, especially as the landlord throws in free Wi-Fi and I'm close to the Tube – a must in London. It's pointless having a car here, as there's no parking, but back home, my beautiful, blue BMW convertible is tucked up in my parents' garage, awaiting my return.

I know that, at thirty-eight, I should be living alone by now, but unless I get a £40,000 pay rise, there's no way I could afford to fly solo in London. Before I met Robert, I must admit, London had been losing the appeal it once had when I was in my twenties and had no need to plan any further ahead than the weekend. I got offered the head of English position in a high school in Newton Mearns, near Glasgow; the current headmaster is my old school friend, Gordon, who Facebooks me occasionally when he's sozzled. For a while, I considered it; I could afford an actual whole house, live quietly near the countryside, see farm animals for free and drive my much missed car on a daily basis, instead of standing next to exceedingly sweaty commuters every morning. But now that Robert's in the picture, my plans to drive with the top down past some sheep have been put on the back burner. He's a city man through and through. Christ, I'm hesitant to ask him to my parents' house for Christmas, never mind broach the subject of moving to Scotland with me.

Just as I'm getting ready to embark on the eight-minute walk to the Tube station, my phone starts to ring in my pocket.

'Morning, darling. Am I forgiven?'

It's Robert, back from his weekend business trip – a trip which he refused to let me accompany him on, despite my assurances that it was the best idea I'd ever had.

'Let me think . . .' I reply, pulling on my jacket. 'No.'

'You wouldn't have enjoyed it,' he insists. 'I hardly got a moment to myself.'

'I would have amused myself during the day!' I reply. 'We could have had dinner in the evening, maybe taken—'

'Emily, when we do go to Rome, I intend to spend every minute with you, not be holed up in the office while you hop on an open-top bus tour,' he replies. 'I want to stroll with you through the Piazza Navona, kiss you at the top of the Spanish Steps, watch you make a wish at the Trevi Fountain: all the things I can't do when I'm working.'

God, that's romantic. I'm practically swooning. 'Well, you could have said that, instead of just refusing point-blank!' I reply. 'I just wanted to spend a bit of time with you. That's all.'

'What can I say? I'm an idiot,' he responds, softly. 'But I promise I'll take you to Rome, and we'll stay at the Waldorf Astoria and make love all night on Egyptian-cotton sheets, not in some stuffy business hotel my company pays for. You're worth more than that.'

'Robert, I'd be happy in a cheap little B & B—'

'Nonsense,' he interrupts. 'Nothing but the best for my girl. So, if I'm forgiven, let me take you to dinner tonight. There's a little French place just opened near Angel.'

'How super!' I reply, like some sort of jolly fucking hockey sticks schoolgirl, which, despite growing up with posh parents, I'm anything but. However, Robert is soooo well spoken, and every word that falls out of his mouth screams *I WENT TO PUBLIC SCHOOL*, that my Scottish east-coast accent seems coarse in comparison. I bet Robert's parents take brandy in the drawing room and discuss important world events, unlike mine, who make screwdrivers in the living room while they dance to old repeats of *Top of the Pops*.

'Excellent,' he replies. 'I'll pick you up at seven. Love you.'

'Love you too. See you tonight.'

I throw my mobile into my bag and immediately start planning my outfit as I head towards the front door. I'll wear the blue maxi . . . No, the black Karen Millen dress I got last week. Yes, I'll put my hair up, wear my red heels and then dazzle him with my sophisticated charm and wit. Then, after he's had his third whisky, I'll drop the C bomb and hope it doesn't explode in my face.

There are two notoriously slow lifts in our building, the one to the right being the better-smelling of the two, as Mr and Mrs Holborn, who live on the fourth floor (along with their incontinent Yorkshire terrier), tend to use the left one several times a day. I press the button and wait, scrambling around in my bag to make sure I have my Oyster card. We live on the seventeenth floor, which Alice describes as 'the penthouse' when she sneakily rents out her room on Airbnb on weekends she's not there. It's an old ex-council high-rise block, now mainly owned by private landlords, excluding Mr and Mrs Holborn, who've been there since time began. I press the lift button again and glance at my watch, tutting quietly. Behind me, I hear the sound of my neighbour's door loudly slam closed and my tuts become noticeably louder.

'Good morning, Emily.'

'Morning, Evan,' I reply coolly. Jesus, that boy can't even close a door quietly.

'Busy day ahead?'

'Hmm.'

'Yeah, I hate Mondays too. I can barely string a sentence together until I get my morning Starbucks . . .'

'You seem to be managing just fine.'

Either I'm not very proficient in hostility or he just doesn't care, because he's still blabbering on.

'Like the jacket. Red suits you.'

Why is he still talking? Why does he think that complimenting my tailored long-line coat (which, admittedly, is worth complimenting) will make me want to converse with him? It's his fault I only got four hours' sleep last night.

'Good weekend?'

I can feel him staring at me as I ignore him.

'Oh, bad weekend? What happened?'

My reluctance to engage with him doesn't seem to faze him. He's enjoying this.

'I know. You forgot to record the *Antiques Roadshow*, didn't you? No, don't tell me, I'll get it . . . You lost a bed sock, right? Oh, no, did someone rip your knitting?!'

Knitting? How fucking old does he think I am? I throw him a *piss right off* look.

'You're mad at me, aren't you?'

I cave. 'Yes, as it happens, I am. You're aware of how thin our bedroom walls are. I had to suffer the sounds of you and whoever the hell it was unfortunate enough to agree to come home with you last night.'

He grins. 'That was Cassie. In my defence, I've never heard anyone squeal like that before either.'

I scowl and continue looking at the lift doors, praying

for them to open. 'Just have a bit of bloody consideration, that's all I ask. Like your flatmates – those girls seem to manage it.' I pointlessly press the lift button again. Twice.

'They work nights at the Royal Infirmary and sleep during the day; sometimes it's like living with vampires, instead of nurses. Between you and me, I thought they'd be much more fun.'

'Oh, you poor thing. How dare they not live up to their stereotype. How awful for you.'

He hangs his head. 'You're right. I'm sorry. I'm a dreadful human being, one who should be . . . Hang on – if our walls are so thin, how come I never hear you?'

'Because, unlike you, I don't—'

'Get any?' He laughs.

'What? That's none of your business!' This boy is unreal. Doesn't he have anyone else to annoy?

'Maybe uptight Scottish women don't have sex?'

My head quickly spins around. 'I am NOT uptight! I just happen to have respect for my neighbours,' I reply, omitting the fact that Robert has never spent the night in my flat. We always have sex at his place.

The doors open and, although I'm tempted to wait for the next lift, I'm aware I'll miss my train. We walk in and stand side by side in awkward silence. This doesn't last long.

'Did you dye your hair? It looks darker than last week.'

'Will you stop commenting on my appearance?' I insist,

sweeping my recently coloured hair over my shoulder. The box said *mocha brown*, but really it's more of a dark chocolate. 'It's none of your business. Look somewhere else . . . And another thing—'

My rant is cut short when a man in a camouflage jacket steps in, the music from his headphones *dush-dush-dushing* as he presses the already illuminated ground-floor button. I move to the left and continue the rest of the ride down silently fuming while Evan smirks to himself. A few seconds later, the doors open and camouflage man gets out first. Just as I'm leaving, Evan leans in and whispers, 'And the winner of Most Uptight in a Lift goes to . . .' before strolling off towards the door, leaving me alone in the lift, giving him both middle fingers behind his back and mouthing, 'Fuck you!' while Trevor, the concierge, looks on in amusement.

My train journey from Liverpool Street to East Acton takes roughly thirty-two minutes in the morning, compared to fifty minutes by bus, and minus the inevitable traffic jams, congestion charge, road rage, wankers in Audis and cyclists I'd have to battle if I drove. I find standing on the train and avoiding eye contact while stealthily watching for people who may be about to leave their sitting position and allow me to make a move I like to call 'THAT'S MY SEAT NOW, BITCHES!' much more tolerable.

Still feeling tired and completely wound up by Evan, I stick my headphone buds in and press *shuffle* on my iPhone, hoping the sounds of Chvrches will inject me with some much-needed oomph. Just as the doors close, a young woman wearing an eighties-style camel trench coat rushes in and stands beside me. As we move off, I see her, out of the corner of my eye, trying to pick off the numerous strands of blond hair which have stuck fast to her shiny pink lipgloss, and I feel her pain. I stopped wearing lipgloss years ago for this very reason; however, my mum likes to think it was due to her incessant cries of, *No one will kiss you wearing that gloopy shit on your mouth!*

I arrive at East Acton, where a ten-minute walk past some red-brick houses leads me to Acton Park Secondary School, the place I've worked for the past thirteen years. From the outside, the old brown brickwork makes the building look dreary, and the interior is only marginally better. It comprises three levels of classrooms, with dark-brown, wooden balconies looking on to the assembly hall and cafeteria, which I'm pretty sure resembles that of the nearby prison. However, we've been promised a modest refurb over the Christmas holidays, which no doubt will be a lick of white paint and some classroom blinds that actually work, but there's also been talk of closure for quite some time. Another reason the job offer in Newton Mearns is appealing.

I pretend not to see Paige and Charlotte smoking near the entrance, because I'm too tired for an argument with girls who insist on using the term 'innit' at the end of every sentence; instead, I make my way through the car park towards the main doors. I have twenty-five minutes until my first class, and my second coffee of the day awaits me in the teachers' lounge. I wonder if Alice managed to prize her lips from Toby's and make it in early. I scurry past the office and say a quick 'Good morning' to Lizzie, one of the administrators who tries to sell me Avon every chance she gets. As I get to the door of the teachers' lounge, my phone starts to ring. It's my sister, Iona. I know she's calling because Mum's told her about Robert and she has a million questions ready to fire at me, but she'll have to wait. No one comes between me and my coffee.

CHAPTER THREE

'Settle down, everyone. Pamela, take your seat and put your phone away.'

My sixth-form class are rowdy today. There's still ten days before we stop for Christmas break, but it's obvious they plan to do fuck all, regardless. Half of them are still chattering away as I take a huge pile of unmarked mock exam papers out of my drawer and place them beside the tiny fake Christmas tree on the corner of my desk. I don't normally bother with decorations, but this was my attempt to make the classroom look festive, along with five silver strings of tinsel Sellotaped to the top of the whiteboard and a wreath, which, until recently, hung on the classroom door and I suspect was pinched by Pauline fucking Leeland. There are 645 students enrolled at Acton Park Secondary and Pauline wreaks more havoc than the other 644 combined.

As my laptop powers up, I sit on the front of my desk, shushing the remaining chatterboxes.

'Now, as we've been studying *Doctor Faustus* this term, we're going to watch the film adaptation this morning—'

There's a faint groan, presumably because they're being forced to watch something that wasn't created by Marvel or Adam Sandler.

'And I'll be asking you, in groups, to compare and contrast with the original play itself.'

Another groan. Eye-rolling. The faint sound of someone pocket-munching crisps.

'And, if you stop being so miserable, I'll bring in popcorn and something suitably inappropriate next week.'

Now I have their attention.

'Like what, miss? *Fifty Shades of Grey*?' Kevin Cole shouts from the back of the room, obviously pleased with himself for bringing up something vaguely sexual in class.

'I said inappropriate, Kevin, not shite. No, I'm thinking something with just enough swearing or violence to get me into trouble with your parents. Deal?'

The groans change to giggles and nods of agreement, so I find the film online and they reluctantly settle down to watch Elizabeth Taylor and Richard Burton ruin a perfectly good play. It's not necessary that they watch it, but I plan on getting as much marking done as I can today so I can relax on my date with Robert.

Thirty minutes into the film and my bag starts to vibrate. I check my phone and there's a text from Iona – *You have a man??!* – and a missed call from Kara, my recently married, closest friend. This means she's back from her honeymoon, but, more importantly, it means she might have got me something from duty-free. She is the last of my childhood friends to get hitched and, of course, when Mum found out, she was less than thrilled.

'I just met Maureen Bastami in John Lewis. Why didn't you tell me Kara was getting married?'

'I don't know, Mum . . . probably because of the conversation we're about to have?'

'And she's marrying John Lyon, the plastic surgeon. How can you still be single and that mono-browed child you went to school with lands herself a millionaire? Maureen asked if you were married and I didn't know what to say!'

'Well, "No" would be the appropriate response. Kara is beautiful, funny and kind – that's the reason she's getting married. Her teenage brows have nothing to do with it. Also, she has her own money and—'

'Maybe John Lyon has a friend? What you need to do is—'

'Jesus, I'm hanging up now, Mum.'

Life in the Scottish Borders wasn't particularly diverse, so when half-Iranian Kara moved from Sheffield and joined our school in second year, I thought she was the most beautiful, interesting girl I'd ever seen and firmly planked my pasty-skinned arse down beside her in the lunch hall. Her dad, a chemist, and her mum, a pastry chef, were proper, sensible parents, unlike mine, who'd throw impromptu parties on a Wednesday night and dance barefoot in the garden. Even at thirteen, she knew exactly who she was and what she wanted from life, while I wasn't even sure what I wanted for lunch, but despite our differences, we quickly became inseparable, even going to the same university, where she studied dentistry and I went into education. The year I moved to London, she jetted off to Dallas to specialise in cosmetic dentistry, where she met Kent-born John Lyon at a conference and fell madly in love. I was thrilled when she followed him back to London, because being anywhere your best friend isn't, sucks.

I send both Kara and Iona quick replies, telling them I'll call them later, before getting back to my marking and the sounds of Kevin Cole repeatedly sniffing and blowing his nose into a hanky. As I go through their mock exam papers, I feel proud. The majority of the kids have really applied themselves this year, and it shows. I worked hard and so did they. I may not have the most well-paid or glamorous job in the world, but I wouldn't want to do anything else.

I spot Alice in the teachers' lounge at lunchtime, looking weary and sipping on a large mug of tea. She's wearing a pair of skinny jeans and a T-shirt, with a picture of Minnie Driver's face on the front, under the scruffy black cardigan she keeps in school during winter, which, to Alice, is any day colder than twenty-five degrees.

When I came in here this morning, there were a few tasteful Christmas decorations, but it's obvious that someone who really adores Christmas lurks among us. 'You all right?' Alice asks, motioning for me to sit beside her before the head of history, Kenneth Dawson, plonks himself down and forces her to make polite-yet-excruciating conversation. I quickly take the seat and he makes his way over to the table near the window.

'You lifesaver,' she whispers. 'He had egg salad sandwiches. I don't need that shit near me. You not eating?'

'Nah, I'm not that hungry. Besides, I'm having dinner with Robert tonight. I intend to stuff my face.'

'Good plan.' She nods. 'I'm meeting my friends for drinks, so I'm lining my stomach with biscuits.'

'Is this your handiwork?' I ask, looking around the room. 'I imagine this is what Liberace's house would look like at Christmas, if Liberace suddenly lost his fucking mind and just started throwing tinsel at the wall until the police intervened.'

'Very funny. The place needed brightening up and we had masses of decorations in the store cupboard. I know how much you hate Christmas, so I'll keep it to a minimum at home, but in here, you have no power over me. In here, it's going to be festive as fuck.'

I head over to the recently boiled kettle and make my third coffee of the day from the oversized tin of freeze-dried cheap crap we all pay a quid a week for. Well, except Kenneth, who carries a pouch of Carte Noire in his jacket pocket and doesn't share.

'It's not that I hate Christmas,' I reply, carefully sitting down again with the hot cup. 'It's just that my family always go over the top, in every respect. Most people celebrate Christmas Day and Boxing Day, but in our house our celebrations last four days. We arrive on the twenty-fourth and leave on the twenty-eighth.'

Alice splutters her tea. 'Four days? What the hell do you do for four days?'

'Survive,' I reply. 'Well, we drink and we eat and we exchange horrible gifts; we talk and eventually someone cries. Oh, and the day after Boxing Day, my parents invite their friends over, so there's usually dancing and falling and bitching and at least nine full hours devoted to the subject of why I'm not married.'

Alice smiles. 'Sounds pretty normal, to be fair. Excessive, perhaps – but normal. At home, we usually all head to the beach. I prefer it here. I like a snowy Chrimbo.'

I shake my head. 'There's nothing normal about my family. We're all as damaged as each other . . . and this year they want me to bring Robert.'

She stops sipping her tea. 'Oh, really . . . ? And does Rabbie want to go?'

'It's Robert—'

'I know, I'm just practising my Scottish accent.'

'You sound like Shrek, and Shrek doesn't sound Scottish. Anyway, I'm asking him tonight. Think he'll say yes?'

'He's quite . . . well, reserved,' she says diplomatically.

'Perhaps a four-day family gathering is a bit much for someone who's never met them?'

I nod. 'Oh, I agree, but they're not taking no for an answer. Besides, they know he exists now. If I don't bring him, I'll look like a loser. They'll never let me hear the end of it.'

'What if you just don't go? Stay here for Christmas?'

'That's worse,' I reply. 'The only valid excuse for missing Christmas at the Carsons' is death, imprisonment or maybe a hostage situation. I told you – they're not normal.'

'Won't Robert be visiting his own parents?' she asks.

'Yes. I'm just hoping that his are more reasonable than mine. Anyway, what are you getting up to? Anything exciting?'

'Definitely not coming to your house.' She giggles. 'Christmas in Oz would be nice, but I can't afford to go home this year. I think our neighbour is having a party. I might pop in.'

'Who? Evan? I almost pummelled him this morning. Arrogant little shit. Called me uptight.'

'I wouldn't say you were uptight,' Alice replies, sliding her finger down the middle of her second KitKat. 'Boring, perhaps . . .'

'What?!'

'Come to think of it, boring's not the right word either. I don't know; you're just not as carefree as you used to be. You're more focused.'

'I'm exactly the same as I've always been! Aren't I?'

She uncrosses her legs and turns to face me. 'OK, remember that time you confiscated that joint from Gary Morris and we got stoned in my room, watching cats jumping on toddlers on YouTube?'

'Yes.'

'And when you split with Tomas, you built a duvet fort in your room and stayed there for two days, doing vodka-jelly shots and singing Whitney Houston songs?'

'Forts make everything better.'

'And when Toby moved in, you invited everyone in the building to a welcome party?'

I giggle. 'Can't believe how many people turned up.'

She nods. 'But, recently, you're all, "I really should think about getting an ISA" and "I'm having a TED-talk marathon this weekend" and "No, you can't borrow my iPad—"'

'So I'm boring because I won't let you borrow my iPad?'

'Well, it was a factor in my decision-making.'

'You dropped my Kindle in the bath! You're not allowed anywhere near my iPad.'

I glance at the clock on the wall; lunch is nearly over and so is this conversation.

'Look, I won't let Toby borrow my iPad either.'

'Understandable – I wouldn't let Toby borrow my pen.'

'And, sure, *maybe* I'm a tad more sensible; it doesn't make me boring or uptight.'

'Evan thinks it does.' She squishes her empty biscuit wrapper into a tiny ball.

'Well, Evan is a halfwit.'

'I seem to remember you feeling slightly different when he moved in.' Alice smirks. 'In fact, I remember you calling him – now, what was it? Oh, yes – "a big ride".'

It's true. The day Evan moved in, I helped him carry a box into his flat, and, while he thanked me for my help, I thanked the Lord for making men who look like him.

I shrug. 'I cannot be held responsible for my hormones. Besides, that was before he became the bane of my existence.'

She nods. 'He is hot, though. I would.'

'Hotter than Toby?'

'What?! Of course,' she replies, completely flustered. 'Toby is a hipster idiot. Not remotely hot.'

The bell rings, finally ending my conversation with a now-extremely-red-faced Alice.

'We'll continue this later,' I say, going to place my coffee cup in the sink. 'You both think I button up the back.'

'What does that even mean? Stop being so Scottishy.'

'It means I'm not stupid. You make a cute couple. Just, for the love of God, refrain from shagging in my bed while I'm gone.'

'Well, it's about time someone *did* shag in your bed, Emily . . .' she says quietly as I walk towards the door.

'I heard that.'

I hear her laugh as I close the door behind me. Bloody hell. Am I the only one who's not concerned about my bedroom's lack of action? Actually, Robert not staying over isn't entirely a bad thing. He likes to talk during sex and the last thing I need is Alice, Toby or – God forbid – Evan hearing him. Even I don't want to hear him.

I finish up at five p.m. and walk back with Alice towards the Tube station. It's cold enough for snow, but instead we have frosted pavements and icy blasts of wind to contend with. It's already dark, but the quiet streets are well lit and, if anyone decides we look like easy prey, I take comfort in the fact that I can run faster than Alice.

She gets off at Notting Hill Gate to meet her friends, wishing me luck with Robert later. She thinks he'll say no. She thinks his idea of Christmas bliss is dismissing the servants and reading quietly beside a roaring fire, pausing occasionally to give thanks for the new silk pyjamas he's currently wearing at eight p.m. When she calls him 'Downton Rabbie', I laugh more loudly than I should. Yes, he's a little old-fashioned, but I'm almost certain that he'll cast aside any reservations he has and do this for me. I am his girlfriend, after all.

Toby isn't home when I get back, so I start getting undressed in the hallway, aware that I only have forty-five minutes until Robert picks me up and therefore every second counts. As I intend to re-create the Gemma Arterton updo I saw in *Grazia* last week, I don't plan on washing my hair; however, Toby has stolen my shower cap yet again and I'm forced to wrap my hair in a Tesco carrier bag. Multitasking, I get in the shower and brush my teeth with my left hand while shaving my legs with my right, nicking my ankle bone in the process, then hop out and slather myself in body lotion, which will hopefully dry as I'm doing my make-up. Robert is always bloody early and hates being kept waiting. He believes that *lateness is weakness*, and at some point, when we're married, I'm going to tell him what a stupid statement that is.

I've just applied my second coat of mascara when the buzzer goes. Six fifty-five p.m. – early, as predicted, but I'm ready to go. Cheerily announcing that I'm on my way down, I take one last look in the mirror. I look hot: sophisticated, but also sexy enough to ensure that he'll be powerless to resist any request I make.

Once in the hallway, I reluctantly take the left-hand lift, as I don't want to keep Robert waiting and the lift on the right is showing no signs of being at my floor any time soon. I have some Very Irrésistible Givenchy perfume in my handbag, which I spray liberally as soon as I enter, praying that it's a quick descent to the ground floor. As the doors open, I see Robert, with his back to me, chatting to the concierge; thankfully, he doesn't turn around in time to witness me clumsily trip over absolutely nothing. Trevor obviously did, because he's smirking. That fucker doesn't miss a trick.

'Hi, Robert; ready to go?' I say, placing my hand on his shoulder.

He turns and kisses me on the cheek. 'Yes, I'm starving. You look great!'

'Oh, this old thing?' I reply, glancing down at my dress. 'It's been gathering dust for a while. Forgot it was even there.' What a fucking liar. This brand-new dress has been hanging inside a garment bag since I bought it. I look at it daily and I might have even kissed it once. When you save for a month to afford a dress, that dress is *everything*.

'For you,' he says, handing me a bunch of red roses.

I grin. Robert thinks flowers are a waste of money, but he knows how much I love them.

'They're perfect,' I reply, inhaling their perfume. 'Trevor, can you keep these for me until I come home?'

Trevor nods and takes the roses into his office, while I take Robert's arm as we make our way outside.

We climb inside Robert's Mercedes and start our drive towards the restaurant. He's been listening to Nickelback and, for some reason, thinks it's acceptable to leave it playing when there are other people in the car, but I let it slide, as I have more important things to worry about. Nickelback, though. Really?

'So was your weekend productive, then?' I ask chirpily, to show him I'm not sulking anymore. 'I sent you a couple of texts; didn't you get them?'

'Afraid not,' he replies. 'Phone reception wasn't great.

Work was work, you know – usual nonsense. I won't bore you with it. How about you? Good weekend?'

'It was fine,' I reply, clearing my throat. 'In fact, I had an interesting phone call with my mother. Well, I say interesting, it was more stressful than—'

'We're here.'

I look out of the window. We've pulled up across the street from the recently opened Durand's, named after French chef Chloé Durand, famous for her long list of celebrity customers and equally famous racing-driver boyfriend, Hugo.

'That was quick! We could have walked!' I say, unbuckling my seat belt.

Robert switches off the engine and turns to look at me. 'I didn't buy this car to walk, darling. Now, you were saying?'

'What?'

'Your phone call?'

'Oh, it's nothing,' I lie. 'This looks lovely. Shall we go in?'

'In just a second,' he replies before leaning in and kissing me. Robert's lips are thin and his kisses delicate, almost courteous, like those no-tongue kisses from movies in the fifties, before someone has to board a train in an awesome hat. After a few seconds, he squeezes me on the knee and says, 'Let's go. I don't want to be late.'

I wouldn't mind being late, I think. I've just been kissed and food is now the last thing on my mind. I want to forget dinner and have him drive me directly into bed, or at least throw me into the back seat, but he's already opened his car door and now a big cold gust of air has just blown up my skirt and cooled my jets considerably.

I throw my wrap around my shoulders as we cross the road, walking straight into a crowd of disorderly office workers, who are one Jägerbomb away from a police caution. Robert mumbles something about 'sodding Christmas parties' and we navigate our way through the drunks and into the warmth of Durand's.

We're seated, by the waitress, in the centre of the cosy, busy restaurant. The tables are covered in white linen, with small, green, spikey holly centrepieces and heavy silver cutlery; a large, minimally dressed gold-and-white Christmas tree stands in the corner. Robert orders some water for the table and then opens the wine list.

'How about a nice bottle of Chardonnay?' he enquires, skimming down the page. 'That suit you?'

'Yes, but if you have the car, there's no need to get a bottle. I can order by the glass.' I glance down at the menu, skipping past anything snail- or frog-related.

'Nonsense; Vic, from the office, is collecting the car shortly. He'll drop it home for me. Let's have a bottle of the Chablis. I think it'll go well with the trout.'

Generally, when choosing wine, my thought process goes like this:

Is it on offer?

What's the percentage?

Fuck it – let's get two.

'Anything is fine with me,' I reply, feeling relieved that he's drinking and might, therefore, be more susceptible to my Christmas request.

Robert orders the wine and excuses himself to use the bathroom, while I continue looking at the menu, eventually deciding on the pork with a truffle jus, and feeling a little disappointed there are no croque-monsieurs available. I could eat those all day long. Sometimes, I feel sorry for chefs. They waste hours planning intricate menus and dishes, using obscure ingredients, and then people like me show up, yearning for what is essentially a cheese toastie.

When Robert returns to the table, I notice that his suit, his shirt and his face all remain crease-free, despite his having just finished work. He looks remarkably fresh and very handsome. I can easily see myself growing old with him, maybe having kids. This man knows exactly what he wants from life and it's refreshing. There's a lot to be said for an older man. Sure, younger men like Evan may be very easy on the eye, all dirty blond, blue-eyed and toned, but Robert is handsome in an astute, groomed, Jon Hamm kind of way, and—

'Emily?'

'Yes?'

'I asked if you were ready to order? You were miles away, there. Everything all right?'

I hadn't heard a word. 'Sorry; I'm here. Just been a long day. Yes, I'm having the Hamm, thanks.'

'The ham?'

'Pork! The pork.'

He calls the waitress back over to order and I smile sweetly, all while I imagine myself drop-kicking Evan fucking Grant directly into the sea.

One hour and eleven minutes later and we're deep in conversation. We've discussed my work, his work, that time he went snorkelling in Tahiti and his ex-girlfriend cried when she got too close to a fish, and how that man on the other side of the room really, really looks like Benedict Cumberbatch, whom I adore, but Robert thinks is overrated. We've ordered another bottle of wine and played footsie under the table, and now I feel deliciously tipsy and ready to bring up the subject of Christmas.

'Soooo, Christmas be soon, then!' Maybe too tipsy. And possibly a pirate. 'I mean, *is* soon. Very soon, in fact.'

'I know,' he replies, straightening his cutlery. 'Are we doing presents this year?'

'This year? Well, it's our first one together, so I'd say yes.'

Are we doing presents? What kind of stupid question is that? I feel a little hurt. I've already bought him a black Armani shirt, which went straight on to my credit card, as I'd blown my budget on this dress.

'Oh, of course. Sorry. Ignore me – I don't know what I was thinking. Sorry; carry on.'

'So . . .' I continue, desperately thinking of a way to shoe-horn my request in. 'Are you having a work's Christmas do? I'd love to meet your colleagues!'

'We had it last week,' he replies. 'Now, don't pout, it was an average three-course meal for staff only. My colleagues are all boring, anyway.'

Ooh. Robert is a sucker for my pout; he can't stand to see me unhappy. 'Well, they might be, but I'd at least like to meet some of them,' I say, miserably. 'You do realise it's been eight months, and I don't recall having met any of your friends or colleagues.'

'You met Geoff,' he replies quickly. 'You remember. We bumped into him at the Ivy.'

'The guy you waved at as we were leaving?! That hardly counts. We're a couple, Robert. We should be doing couple things . . . with other people . . .'

'Like what?' he asks. 'What does your pretty heart desire?'

Here goes: 'Oh, I don't know – like having dinner parties with friends, or lunch dates, or . . .'

He nods. 'Well, I'm sure we could arrange someth—'

'Or Christmas with my family?'

'I beg your pardon?'

'We could spend Christmas with my family – in the Borders.'

He's looking at me like I've just invented a whole new language, but I keep going.

'Four fun-filled days in Scotland. Whaddya say?'

He puts down his glass of wine and smiles, but he looks uncomfortable, and my heart is in my throat. Finally, he speaks.

'I don't think that's possible for me. I'll be working on Christmas Eve, and then I'll be—'

'So I'll wait for you and we can drive up after work. I'll drive; you can relax.'

'Things are too up in the air at the moment and—'

'It would mean a lot if you came – they'd love to meet you!' I'm not giving up here. God, I'm just like my mother. 'And we can visit with your parents when we get back,' I continue, trying desperately not to grab him by the collar and explain that there hasn't been a Christmas in three years where I wasn't the black sheep, and he could put an end to this misery by doing me a solid, bro.

After a brief silence, during which he seems to be staring at my right shoe, he says, 'Sure. Why not? If it makes you happy, then Christmas in Scotland it is.'

I give a little shriek and kiss him hard on the mouth to prevent any kind of immediate retraction. 'Oh, thank you! This is going to be so much fun!'

He nods and takes another sip of wine. I can tell that he's as unsure of that last statement as I am.

'My family can be a tad unconventional, but whose family isn't, right? They're harmless, really; more eccentric than weird . . .' I should definitely shut up now, before I talk us both out of it.

Robert signals to the waiter. 'Let's get the bill.'

Ugh, too late – he's planning his escape. 'Oh. Sure. OK. You don't want dessert?' I ask. 'Because I saw lavender ice cream on the menu and we can plan how—'

'I'm not hungry for ice cream, Emily.' He leans in and discreetly moves his hand under the table. 'My appetite lies elsewhere.' I feel his hand slide up the inside of my thigh. He's either incredibly horny or incredibly eager to change the subject. Both are fine by me.

'I'll get the coats.'

We hail a black cab outside, which takes us to Robert's flat in Vauxhall while we make out like teenagers in the back seat: hands everywhere, clumsy fumbling and no consideration for the frowning taxi driver, who's undoubtedly seen much worse. Once we get inside and close the front door, Robert's mouth never leaves mine, even as we make our way to his bedroom. We kiss along the short hallway with the fake brickwork and the black iron coat-stand, then left past the living room with the LCD fireplace positioned below the oversized television, finally stumbling into his uncluttered white bedroom with the queen-sized bed and floor-to-ceiling window with a view over the Thames, which never fails to delight me.

'I do adore you,' he whispers, nuzzling into my neck as his hands explore beneath my dress. I reach around towards his crotch. He groans. 'You're like my little Scotch pixie.'

Pixie? I'm five feet nine.

'It really isn't wise to refer to a Scottish person as *Scotch*,' I whisper, 'especially not when they have their hand on your dick.'

He laughs and spins me around. 'Ooh, feisty. Are you feeling naughty, Emily?'

Oh, God – here comes the talking. He's so wonderful and attentive in every other way, I don't have the heart to tell him that I think he sounds ridiculous. I don't have the heart to shit all over something he obviously enjoys. So, instead, I just nod.

'I know you are, because those red shoes . . . I know why you wore them . . .'

Because I'm stylish as fuck, that's why.

One quick tug of the side zip and my dress is on the floor. Ugh – my beautiful dress. I'm aware that asking for a timeout while I hang it up on the back of the door might be a passion killer, so I gently kick it to the side, hoping that it won't fall foul to any flying bodily fluids. Now Robert's unzipping his trousers while he admires my underwear – a red and black Victoria's Secret set with a lace trim and bow at the back. He probably thinks I always dress like this; little does he know that I spent the earlier part of the day hairy legged and in mismatched, greying bra and pants, leggings and a tunic with a shoddily sewn hole in the armpit.

I lie back on the bed, propping myself up by my elbows while he removes the rest of his clothes, mumbling something as he struggles with his socks about bending me over. He removes his white boxer briefs and I see, quite clearly, just how worked up he's got himself, but before I can comment, he's on me, pulling at my underwear and insisting I leave my shoes on for reasons which are muffled when his face disappears between my legs.

I've slept with Robert at least thirty times since we started dating and there's only two things that bother me: the talking (obviously) and the fact that he's rubbish at foreplay. I've explained to him that, with a knob that huge, it means the difference between great sex and a trip to A & E, but I have the feeling we're going to have to have that talk again. However, I'm not going to let a little thing like internal bruising stand in the way of my double-barrelled, exotic-honeymoon happiness with this handsome, employed, stable man.

It's almost one a.m. when I call a taxi. I could have slept over, but it's a school night and I can't be seen arriving at work in an evening dress and red heels, which I'm now very grateful are patent leather and wipe-clean. Robert is still in bed, ready to sleep, but keeping himself awake until I leave. I stand by the window, brushing my hair, gazing out on to the dark river.

'You're so lucky to have this view,' I say. 'It's bewitching.'

'I quite agree,' he replies behind me. 'That arse of yours is something else.'

'Ha! I'm serious! I miss a breathtaking view. I look on to traffic and grubby windows from my flat. You know, I grew up surrounded by fields, hills and a sky you could clearly see stars in at night. Not sure anything can compare to that – even this view.'

'Oh, come on. This is London.' He laughs. 'There is nowhere better. We have architecture. We have glamour. We have the MI5 building. We can see where the spies live.'

My phone begins to ring. 'That's my taxi. Well, once you've visited Scotland, you'll see what I mean. You'll love it, I'm sure.' I leap over to the bed and kiss him goodbye.

'Doubtful.' He winks. 'It's full of Scotch people.'

'Behave!' I laugh, playfully slapping his legs. 'Call me tomorrow.'

'Och, aye!' he replies, just as I'm closing the bedroom door, and I yell, 'Why can no one ever do a decent Scottish accent?!'

Robert's building is far superior to mine in every way. For a start, the lift arrives at lightning speed and smells like it's been cleaned recently. It has private underground parking, and let's not forget about the concierge who calls me madam and sits behind a plush desk, not in some pokey office which resembles an emergency-room reception and smells like old Pot Noodle. I'm not entirely sure whether Robert or his company own the flat, but either way, at London prices, it'll be nothing less than hideously expensive. For the rent I pay to share a flat, I could have a mortgage on a three-bedroom bungalow with front and back gardens and a driveway, in Newton Mearns. Not that I've been researching it or anything.

I collect my roses from Trevor and make my way upstairs, smiling to myself. I can hear the faint sound of Toby's television as I walk into the flat. Alice's biker boots haven't been kicked off haphazardly at the front door, so I assume she hasn't made it home yet, unlike me. Shutting my bedroom door behind me, I peel off my clothes and vow to shower vigorously in the morning, but, for now, I'm literally shagged out. I run some water in the en-suite sink for my flowers, then throw on an old T-shirt, set my alarm and gratefully climb into bed, pulling the duvet around me.

As I let my eyes gently close, I run over the day's events in my head. Despite Robert's misguided xenophobic jibes at the end, it was a splendid day, but, most importantly, he's agreed to come home with me for Christmas! I am victorious! I have never felt more festive in my . . . What the hell is that? I sit up in the darkness and listen closely to the gentle thud, which is growing louder and louder, as are the familiar squeals I remember from last night. You have got to be fucking kidding me. I need to sleep! I grab a shoe from the floor and hammer loudly on the wall, three times, yelling, 'SHUT THE FUCK UP!' at the top of my lungs, before grabbing some cotton balls and shoving them into my ears as tightly as I can. I swear, I am going to kill that boy.

CHAPTER FOUR

I feel myself being shaken into consciousness by Alice, who's mouthing something at me. Removing my make-shift earplugs, she informs me that it's almost half seven and I've slept through my alarm, causing me to spring from my bed with a force normally reserved for grey-hounds at a racetrack. This is the exact reason I don't wear earplugs. No time to shower, I wash myself quickly by the sink, then grab some clean underwear from my bedside table, while Alice informs me that she's made me a coffee and we have to leave in fifteen minutes.

'He's a dead man,' I mutter, pulling some black trousers from the wardrobe. 'I'm going to rip off his face and wear it . . . No, I'm going to strangle him with his own—'

'Who are you talking to?'

I spin around and see Toby grinning back at me. 'What? No one, I'm just planning next door's demise. Fuck, I'm so late; can you hand me that red blouse . . . ? No. Christ! That's pink, Toby; the red one's at the end!'

He hands me my top and scurries back towards the door. 'You're mean when you sleep in. Good luck with your assassination; just don't get caught.'

'I don't care if I do,' I reply. 'I bet I'd sleep like a baby, in prison. I bet murderers and bank robbers make less noise than fuck-face next door.'

I'm still ranting as Toby leaves the room and disappears back into the kitchen, where my wrath won't follow him. I snatch my make-up bag from my dresser, planning to make myself look a little more presentable when I get to school. With two minutes to spare, I meet an impatient Alice by the open front door.

I'm ready for a showdown should Evan appear at the lifts, but he doesn't. I assume he's either fast asleep or right-swiping girls on Tinder who have no idea that they're likely to be considered collateral damage when I firebomb his flat.

I watch Alice pull her woolly hat over her head and button up her coat. She looks as exhausted as me.

'What time did you get in this morning?'

She considers this question for a moment and frowns. 'Stupid o'clock. We went back to Daisy's flat after the bar closed and she had chocolate Baileys. I think I drank all of it. If I vomit on the Tube, don't leave me.'

'I'll be too busy smelling of sex to notice . . . Oh, by the way, I asked Robert.'

'Asked him what?'

The lift doors open and I let her go in first, while I wait for the penny to drop.

'OH, YEAH! CHRISTMAS!'

There it is.

'He said yes, didn't he? He must have, otherwise you'd be in a doubly foul mood.'

'He did!' I reply excitedly. 'I am officially taking my boyfriend home for Christmas. Now all I need to do is speak to my family and ensure they'll be on their best behaviour.'

She laughs. 'Chances of that happening?'

'Hmm. Slim to fuck all.'

'It'll be cool,' she says, giving me a nudge. 'Stop worrying.'

She's right. I need to get a grip. I need to approach this in a positive, adult manner. All I can do is make sure they understand how important Robert is to me and ask that they play nice.

Once outside, we cautiously make our way along the slippery pavements towards the Tube. The temperature seems to have plummeted to 'fucking Baltic' and everyone I see is wrapped in layers of wool, and miserable. However, the cold air starts to clear my head and I begin to calm down and think more rationally.

'Robert isn't Tomas, right?'

'Um, right,' Alice agrees, holding on to my arm as she carefully steps over some black ice. 'Tomas was much shorter.'

'And Robert probably has to deal with difficult people

on a daily basis, so handling my family will be a piece of cake for him,' I continue.

'Good point . . . and – who knows, Emily – maybe they'll really like each other? You're assuming the worst. They might all get on like a house on fire. They might like him more than they like you.'

'I hadn't considered this. But YES! This could happen!' I now find I have a spring in my step.

'Big patch of ice ahead, Em.'

'Ooh! Maybe my dad and brother will take Robert for a beer at the local? We could take long country walks.'

'*Emily*, watch—'

'Maybe, *just maybe* this will turn out to be the most wonderful time—'

Alice lets go of my arm, just as my feet leave the ground and I hit the deck with a massive *thwack*. A passing woman makes an *ouch* sound on my behalf.

'Fuck – are you all right?!'

I look up at Alice, who's trying to assess my injuries before she starts laughing. 'This is a sign,' I say as she helps me to my feet. 'It's an omen!'

'No, Emily, it's not an omen. It's ice and gravity. You sure you're OK? That was spectacular.'

'I think I've broken my arse.'

She links her arm in mine and helpfully assists me, until the feeling returns to my bottom and I can walk unaided. Even as we reach the school gates, she's still laughing. I, on the other hand, have a horrible feeling that this is just a taste of what festive fuckery awaits me over Christmas. I'm doomed.

My backside finally thaws out by lunch and, after demolishing a ham roll from the canteen, I decide that now is as good a time as any to call Iona and catch up, because today cannot possibly get any worse. The teachers' lounge is too busy, so I scuttle back to my classroom. Putting my feet up on my desk, I await the soothing, calm tones of my sister's voice.

'Finally! What the fuck, Emily?! I've called you ten fucking times!'

Or maybe not.

'Nice to speak to you too, Iona.'

Iona's telephone manner leaves a lot to be desired. Actually, her manner in general can be less than pleasant. She's bossy, snooty, impatient, and has a perturbing dislike for people who openly shop at Primark.

'So?' she huffs. 'Who is he? Fill me in.'

'Yeah, all right; calm down, Craig David. Are we not going to chat first, before my inquisition?'

'Nope. I'm going into a meeting in five minutes. Talk.'

'No pressure, then? Fine. His name is Robert. He's from London—'

'Employed?'

'Yes, he works in marketing and—'

'Drives?'

'Mercedes.'

'Fine. Any kids?'

'No . . . Iona, are you working through a checklist?'

'What? No.'

She totally is.

'OK, no kids. That's good.'

'Why is it good?'

'Because other people's children are infuriating.'

'You're infuriating.'

'Mum says he's coming for Christmas. You sure about that? You know what Mum and Dad are like.'

I laugh loudly. 'Iona, I know what *all* of you are like, and this is why you have to promise to be nice. I really, *really* like him. He's incredible and—'

'Wait, he's nothing like Tomas, is he? I didn't like him.'

'Really?! I'd never have guessed,' I reply dryly. 'No, he's completely different. Much taller.'

'I hope so. You've never been great at picking boyfriends.'

I'm about five seconds away from repeatedly banging my head on my desk. My tumble on the ice earlier wasn't as painful as this.

'Look, just promise me that you'll behave,' I plead. 'You *and* that husband of yours. He's just as hypercritical as you are.'

Graham and Iona met at Edinburgh University, where they were both members of the bridge club and shared a mutual interest in salsa. You couldn't make this shit up. While she hates Primark, he has an overwhelming disdain for IKEA . . . and fat people . . . and buskers, crowd-funding, Facebook, reality television, tattoos, children and cats. He's a real gem.

'Oh, Graham can't make it this year. The company is merging with some American lot, so he'll be out there for the week.'

'And you're not going with him?'

'Oh, God, no. The flights are far too long, and, besides, I'm looking forward to spending time with my big sister.'

It takes me a second to remember she's talking about me.

'So you'll be nice to him? It's important to me.'

'Look, I have to run, Emily, but I'll see you and your mystery man on the twenty-fourth.'

'He's not a myst—'

She's hung up. I feel more drained than ever now. She hardly listened to a word I said, so I'm not feeling hopeful that she'll do what I asked, *and* I still have to have the don't-be-mean-to-my-boyfriend talk with my brother and my parents. It'll have to wait until tomorrow. For now, all I want is to eat the Dairy Milk in my bag, get through the rest of today unscathed and take a long hot shower before curling up in bed with Netflix, and if Evan Grant so much as sneezes too loudly, I'm going to get my sister to checklist him to death.

The afternoon's lessons fly in and the kids are surprisingly well behaved, considering they're now counting down the minutes until they stop for their break. To be fair, though, they're never that belligerent in my class, and I assume this is because I am awesome. I finish up at half four and, as I stroll towards Alice's classroom at the back of the building, I send Robert a quick text to see when he's free this week. I pop my head in and see Alice rolling up paper as she dances around to music playing from a tiny radio on her desk.

'Oi, Beyoncé. Ready to go?'

'Two minutes and I will be!' She doesn't stop dancing, even as she pulls on her jacket and hat.

'I want your energy,' I moan. 'I've been ready to go back to bed since I woke up.'

'Starbucks?' she asks, flicking off the light switch with her elbow. 'I could really go a brownie right now. Or one of those frangipane bars.'

'No, coffee,' I reply. 'I don't want to risk sabotaging the coma I plan on slipping into shortly. Hot chocolate might be good, though.'

Given earlier events, I tread carefully as we walk to the Tube, giving us time to peer surreptitiously through the illuminated windows of the neighbouring homes, some of which have had their Christmas trees up for weeks now.

'Do you think they enjoy Christmas?' Alice laughs, as we pass a small garden swamped with flashing snowmen and fairy lights. 'It's hard to tell.'

'My parents put a life-size Santa by the front drive every year. It's really old and creepy. Looks more like the Krampus. That thing used to give me nightmares. Even the dog is scared of it.'

'If you don't text me a photo of that, I'll never forgive you.'

'I will,' I reply. 'I'm sure, if you look closely, you'll see Robert in the background, understandably fleeing.'

'Look! Number seven has one of those wanky fibre-optic trees. They must hate Christmas. Who the hell buys a tree you can't decorate?'

'My brother,' I respond, grinning. 'He doesn't hate Christmas; he just likes anything gadgety. He also has one of those robot vacuum-cleaner things and a remote-controlled wife.'

'What? Can you send me a picture of her too?'

'I feel bad for saying that; Kim's great, in all fairness. She's just a tad "stiff" until she's had a drink.' God, I can never be bitchy and just own it. I always feel shitty afterwards.

'What does she do?' Alice enquires.

'Erm, she does something science-y, like stem-cell research or harvesting personalities, I'm not entirely sure . . . Ugh, why am I being so unkind? What's wrong with me?'

'It's Christmas stress,' Alice replies. 'I'm not judging. And, I've been thinking.'

'Yes?'

'Robert coming to yours for Christmas – it's a big deal,' she continues. 'You've been together for a while and now he's meeting the family . . . Next, he'll be proposing . . .'

'Let's not get ahead of ourselves here,' I reply, giggling. 'But, I *know*, right? He's even talking about taking me to Rome and kissing me on some steps, or something.'

She laughs. 'I predict big things for your future, Miss Carson, but I'm telling you straight – if my bridesmaid's dress is ugly, I'll be less than thrilled.'

We stop for brownies and hot chocolate at Liverpool Street station, where I hatch a plan to ensure I get some rest this evening, and that plan involves buying two extra brownies that sadly won't be eaten by me. Alice leaves to do some Christmas shopping and I gratefully march myself back home. I still have a few things to get, but not tonight. Tonight is all about me, but first, there's just one little thing I have to take care of.

As tempted as I am to knock on Evan's door with an axe, I decide that the best course of action will be to deal with him in a calm and civil manner, in the hope that he'll be gracious enough to grant me one night's undisturbed sleep. I smooth down my hair, put on my best smile and knock on his door firmly but politely. A few seconds later, I'm greeted by Stephanie, who really does look like she's just woken up inside a coffin. She's not happy.

'Hi! Is Evan home?'

Before she can answer, she gives the biggest, widest yawn I've ever seen. I feel like I'm in an Aphex Twin video. Eventually, her face returns to her starting grimace and I get the feeling that, if Evan *was* home, she wouldn't have had to answer the door.

'No.'

'Right. Can you tell him that I'm looking for him?'

'Who are you?'

'Seriously?' I stare at her resting bitch face in astonishment. How can she not know who I am? She even borrowed our fucking kettle last month. 'I'm Emily ... Your neighbour ... Kettle lender ... None of this rings any bells?'

'Oh, right.' She nods slowly. 'Emma. Will do.'

I become aware of an unfamiliar feeling creeping over me. I think it might be empathy for Evan. She closes the door before I get the chance to correct my name, and I have no choice but to return home with a handbag full of brownies and no conflict resolution to ensure my evening of peace.

I head straight for the kitchen, where Toby is cooking tortellini with pesto and pine nuts, one of the only dishes he makes which doesn't involve kale or the use of his trusty spiraliser.

'How's it going?' he asks, wiping his hands on some kitchen roll.

I pull out a chair at the table and plonk myself down wearily. 'Not bad, thanks,' I reply, taking one of the brownies from my handbag. 'Oh, I've got a wee present for you. It's organic and gluten-free and everything.'

'Cheers, Em!' he exclaims, popping it on the worktop. 'I'll have that later.'

'Just my way of saying sorry for being so bad-tempered this morning. I wasn't quite myself.'

'You want some pasta?' he asks, gesturing to the cooker. 'There's loads.'

'I was hoping you'd say that. I'm too tired to cook.'

He leans in and gives me a hug. 'Look, go and have a shower and get chilled and I'll put a plate in your room.'

I was hoping he'd say that too. 'Toby, you're my hero. If you weren't twenty-two and I wasn't an old hag, I'd insist you marry me straight away.'

He beams. 'You're not an old hag – not even close. Your boyfriend is a very lucky man.'

'He is, isn't he?' I agree, with a wink. 'Do we have any of that white wine left?' I'm getting up to investigate when I hear a knocking sound at the front door.

'Want me to answer it?' Toby asks, turning down the hob, but I shake my head.

'No, it'll be for me. I'll go.'

I throw my bag over my shoulder and walk up the hall, slightly surprised that Stephanie remembered to give him the message. I bet he called every 'Emma' he knows before she mentioned it was his neighbour. I pull open the door and try to look happy to see him.

'Hello, Evan.'

He takes a step back from the door. 'Are we going to fight? Because, if we are, I should warn you – I know karate.'

'No, quite the opposite.'

'Good, because I do not know karate. What's up?'

'I have something for you.' I reach into my bag.

'Is it a gun?'

'Wrong again,' I reply, trying not to let him see my smirk. 'This is for you.'

He looks confused. 'It's a cake. Why are you giving me cake?'

'It's a brownie . . . In fact, it's more than a brownie. It's a peace offering,' I explain. 'It's a last-ditch attempt to appeal to your better nature.'

'I'm intrigued,' he replies, smugly folding his arms. 'Go on.'

'The thing is, I'm tired, Evan. And tonight I have plans to rectify this. Tonight I have plans to sleep for at least ten hours, peacefully. Uninterrupted. Straight through. Without—'

'I get it.'

'And I will give you this brownie in exchange for your silence.' I hold it out at arm's length and wait.

'You're very weird,' he replies, taking the brownie and examining it. Then he says, 'But what if I don't like brownies?'

'Who doesn't like brownies?!'

'Lots of people. I'm not saying that I *don't* like them, I'm just asking what would happen if I didn't? What would you offer me then?'

This boy is now balancing precariously on my last nerve. 'What? I don't know! A cookie? A beer? A meal? A—'

'OK, a meal,' he interrupts. 'That could work.'

'Ugh, fine. I'll order you a pizza or whate—'

'No, Emily – a meal with me . . . I will agree to keep it down this evening, if you agree to have dinner with me.'

Huh? I stare at him in disbelief.

'You're not serious.'

'Totally serious.'

'I have a boyfriend,' I reply. 'His name is Robert.'

'Well, he can't come.'

I have never met anyone so cocky in my entire life. I grab the brownie back off him.

'I don't date younger men and I prefer to dine at places where they don't accept student discount or serve Happy Meals.'

'Ouch.' He laughs. 'I'm not a student, *and* I'm older than you think. Go on, guess my age.'

This is becoming surreal. 'What? I don't know . . . fourteen?'

'Nope, twenty-nine – last week. See – older.'

I just stand there, shaking my head. 'The answer is still no, Evan. I have a boyfriend.'

'Yes, you've said that . . .'

'And I'm too old for you.'

'How old are you?'

'But, more importantly . . .' I continue, completely avoiding his question. 'Oh, wait – what was the last thing? Oh, yes – I don't like you!'

He frowns. 'You like me enough to give me a brownie.'

I can physically feel my last nerve twang. It's now glaringly obvious that my clever plan isn't going to work, so I rip open the packaging and bite the surprisingly dense brownie in half. I hadn't quite thought this through. I feel it cement in between my teeth as he stares at me in amusement.

'There's a "biting off more than you can chew" joke in there somewhere.'

As he starts laughing, the remainder of the brownie flies from my hand and hits his left shoulder with a dull thud.

'You're the reason people don't like brownies,' he mumbles, brushing the crumbs away.

Further down the corridor, I hear the lift doors ping open. A young woman, around twenty, wearing a woolly hat with teddy-bear ears, emerges looking rosy-cheeked, and she's heading in our direction. This must be the squealer. Evan hasn't spotted her yet, as he's still too busy laughing at his own joke. Let's see how funny he thinks this is:

'But you told me you *loved* me!' I exclaim loudly. 'I thought we would be MARRIED!'

I always believed I'd be excellent in a period drama.

Evan stops brushing down his coat and looks at me like I've just gone completely insane, until a voice behind him says, 'Evan? Everything all right?'

Then he understands, and, if looks could kill, I'd be dead fifteen times over.

He hurriedly swings around to face her. 'Cassie! How are you, babe?'

I surreptitiously suck the rest of the brownie from between my teeth while he tries to gain control of the situation.

'Everything's fine,' he continues, ushering her towards his front door. 'Ignore her; she's not well. Let's get inside.'

'You broke my heart, Evan!' I cry. 'How could you do this to me?!'

He turns back around to face me, but surprisingly he doesn't look angry. He looks intrigued. His girlfriend, on the other hand, looks utterly horrified.

'Evan, what the hell is going on here?' Cassie now has her hands on her hips, but it's hard to take her seriously when she has a teddy bear's head for a hat.

'Hang on,' he says, placing a reassuring hand on her arm. He takes a few steps towards me, but I stand my ground defiantly. We're close – within smelling distance – and he smells . . . like fresh air and this morning's after-shave. I'm suddenly reminded that I haven't showered since yesterday. Dammit.

'Are you finished?' he asks quietly. His mouth forms a little smile.

'Nope,' I whisper back. 'You should have taken the brownie.'

'I'm going inside now,' he murmurs, 'but this is far from over . . .'

Before he can say any more, I dramatically push him away, yelling, 'I'm empty inside, Evan! I have nothing! I am a shell!' I bury my face in my hands and start to wail so loudly that Toby appears at our door. 'What's going on? Emily, are you OK?'

I nod pathetically and pretend to compose myself, sniffing. 'I'll be all right, Toby – in time. Just get me away from him.'

Evan stands there, open-mouthed, as Toby escorts me back inside. I hear Cassie exclaim, 'What the actual fuck, Evan?' as I close the door behind me, throwing in an extra-loud sob for good measure.

'Care to explain?' Toby asks with a confused smile on his lovely face.

'I'm not sure I can,' I reply. 'Let's just say, I expect he'll think twice before messing with me now.'

Toby doesn't look convinced, but he's too polite to say. Instead, he points to my bedroom. 'Your pasta's in there. Wine, too.'

I thank him and retreat into my room, feeling disgustingly pleased with myself. The pasta is slightly cold, but it's a meal I didn't have to cook, so I happily wolf it down before taking a long, hot and decidedly overdue shower. I triumphantly sing along to Hozier, hoping that, if I sing loudly enough, I might invoke the man himself and he'll appear in the shower beside me.

When I eventually climb into bed, I'm relaxed to the point of floppy. I manage to watch two episodes of *Jessica Jones* before my tired eyes demand I stop and I comply. While I set my alarm, I notice that Robert has sent me a goodnight text with an invite to dinner on Friday, and I respond with two little kisses, which is all my fatigue will allow. The fact that I haven't heard one single peep from next door hasn't gone unnoticed, and I'm soon fast asleep, delighted in the knowledge that Evan Grant has met his match.

CHAPTER FIVE

'. . . and then the monkey stole his sunglasses! He dropped them eventually, when John offered him a banana. It was hilarious!'

My best friend, Kara, has been talking about her honeymoon for the past one hour and six minutes. In her defence, I did ask her to 'tell all' the moment we arrived at our favourite diner, Poppy's, for a catch-up meal, but I didn't expect her to tell me, well, everything.

'I mean, the best thing about going to Mexico in December is that it wasn't horrifically hot. I remember when we went to Cyprus during the summer and it was so humid and sticky, we physically stuck together during sex – like Velcro. I had friction burns for our entire stay.'

'Thanks for planting that image in my head,' I say, screwing my face up. 'I could have existed quite happily never knowing this. I'll forgive you this time, but only because you bought me Chanel.'

She smiles at me, her perfect teeth appearing even

whiter against her suntan. 'I'm having a coffee. You want?'

She waves over at our waitress and, even though she's appropriately dressed for the cold weather, she's showing just enough skin to make me envious as hell. I sit in front of her, pasty – with a tinge of green – replying that I'd like a cappuccino, please.

'I don't think I've ever had a tan like that,' I moan. 'I just burn and freckle.'

'Well, being half Iranian helps,' she replies, flicking her long dark-brown hair over her shoulder for effect. 'I may tan, but just remember, in order for me to step outside in a bikini and get that tan, I have to wax my entire fucking body. All of it. It's not pleasant.'

The waitress clears away our dinner plates and Kara orders the coffee while I try discreetly to loosen my trousers.

'I'm definitely going to try and get a holiday next year,' I say. 'Anywhere warm will do.'

'You must go to Cancún,' Kara insists. 'It's so beautiful – you'd love it.'

'On my salary?' I laugh. 'Yeah, I was thinking more of Benidorm.'

'Aren't you running that school by now?' she asks. 'You've been there long enough. Oh, I badly need to pee. Back in a sec.'

She rushes towards the toilet, almost knocking over the waitress, who's returning with our coffee. Hurriedly, she places a bowl of grubby-looking sugar cubes on the table, so I ask for some sweetener instead. I take out my phone and send Robert a little text. I haven't heard from him today – he must be busy, as he's always first to text. As I wait for Miss Pissy-Pants to reappear, I think about her last statement, and she has a point. I've been doing the same job at the same school for years and I haven't made any major steps to further my salary or my career. Is this normal? Am I stuck in a rut?

Kara returns in front of the waitress, who hands me a bowl of little yellow Splenda packets.

'Where were we?' Kara asks, eyeing up the sugar cubes suspiciously.

'Holidays,' I reply. 'How I can't afford to go anywhere that costs more than my rent.'

She frowns. 'Your boyfriend must be rolling in it; demand he take you somewhere lavish.'

I empty a packet of sweetener into my coffee. 'I could,' I say, stirring slowly until the little frothy heart melts away, 'but I'll wait until we get Christmas out of the way first. He's coming home with me, you know.'

She stares at me over her cup. '*Home* home? Like Scotland, home?'

'Yep.'

'With your parents?'

'Uh-huh. They insisted.'

I look down the little wooden menu on the table,

wondering if they have any of those pecan pastries I love so much.

'That's amazing!' she shrieks, unexpectedly. 'I love your parents. They're mental. I used to adore their Christmas parties. Dancing in the garden . . . sneaking champagne into your bedroom . . .'

'Vomiting over the Krampus . . .'

She snorts into her Americano. 'Ha ha, yes! You think Robert will be able to cope? I mean, I've only met him once, but he doesn't strike me as the wearing-a-paper-hat-and-getting-completely-shit-faced-with-loads-of-strangers type . . .'

'I'm currently in the process of pleading with my family to behave,' I reply. 'I'm hoping for a miracle.'

We both reflect on this for a moment.

'I'm screwed, aren't I?' I sigh.

She shrugs. 'Maybe not. Look, if he loves you, he'll put up with your family. Between you and me, I cannot stand John's mother, but I only have to see her once or twice a year and, well, she'll be dead one day. Anyway, he's my boyfriend – it's not such a huge sacrifice.'

'Husband,' I interject.

'What? Oh, shit – yes! Husband! God, I'll never get used to that. It makes me feel so fucking old.'

'We'll be forty in two years, Kara. We are old.'

'Nonsense,' she disagrees. 'We will never be old – even when we are.'

At ten p.m., I kiss Kara goodbye and promise to call her

over Christmas, when she'll be entertaining both John's mother and her own parents, and may require my dulcet tones to talk her down off the ledge. She heads left towards the Tube, while I turn right and begin the short walk back to my flat. It might only be Wednesday, but the streets are still heaving. It feels like a weekend, but, in the last week before Christmas, every night feels like a Saturday night, especially in London. I'm surrounded by late-night shoppers, weary-looking office workers, half-cut executives, tourists and everyone in-between, all avoiding eye contact and desperate to be somewhere warmer. I stop at a twenty-four-hour shop to buy some bagels and milk for the morning, as Alice goes through it like a newborn baby.

Alice is still up when I get back, summoning me into her room, where she's propped in bed, reading, wearing a faded Rolling Stones T-shirt and a cardigan.

'You all right?' she asks. 'How's your mate?'

'She's great. Honeymoon sounded amazing. What are you reading?'

She holds up her book so I can see the cover. 'Amy Poehler. It's hilarious. I'll lend it to you when I'm finished.'

It's my fucking book.

'Oh, and before I forget, we're out of milk,' she continues, disappearing behind the book again, making it obvious that this one-sided conversation has come to an end.

Iona was right – other people's children *are* infuriating.

Having a coffee so late perhaps wasn't the best idea, as

now I'm wide awake. I approach Toby's door for a chat, but I can hear him on his mobile, so I keep walking and end up in the kitchen, which smells like burnt bacon and bleach. Kettle on, I rummage around in the cupboards, looking for a stray biscuit while throwing out various tins and spice jars which are centuries out of date. How can we have three jars of unused, expired saffron strands, but not one bloody custard cream? These people have their priorities all wrong.

Tea in hand, I carry it carefully back to my room with plans to watch something grim, dark and subtitled, possibly Danish and definitely involving a murder and impressive knitwear. I throw my work clothes into the laundry basket, lazily wipe off my make-up and remove my iPad from its charger, bringing it into bed with me.

At midnight, I turn out my lights and it occurs to me that, for a second night, there hasn't been any disturbance from next door. This is unheard of. I press *pause* on my programme and listen, just to be sure. No music, no talking, no Xbox gunfire, no humping sounds – nothing. This is so unlike Evan. As I close my eyes, I begin to wonder whether my plan actually did work, or if something more sinister is afoot. Perhaps sweet, bear-headed Cassie brutally slaughtered Evan? Perhaps she dumped him? Perhaps I went too far. Perhaps . . . Perhaps they're both plotting to murder me in my sleep and I should go and double-check that I locked the front door when I came in.

I go and do this.

At half past twelve, I'm still not asleep. My pillow muffles the screams of frustration which follow, because I'm furious that Evan Grant has the ability to keep me awake, even when he's being quiet.

CHAPTER SIX

I awaken early on Friday morning to the first sprinkling of snow, which has delicately covered London like a posh, lace tablecloth. Throwing open my curtains, I marvel at how bright and aesthetically pleasing my normally dull, grey street has become. Everything, from the snow-topped cars and wheelie bins to the patches of fresh, untrodden snow, delights me in a way that only the prospect of a white Christmas can. With less than a week before I travel back to Scotland, I'm finally excited.

After reading the lovey-dovey text Robert sends me every morning, I pull on my dressing gown and scurry to the kitchen, where Toby has already filled the kettle and is singing along to Adele on the radio.

'Wow, you know *all* of the words, Toby. I'm impressed,' I say, looking in the fridge for something to spread on my bagel.

'Shame you don't know all of the notes!' cackles a voice from the bathroom.

And so it begins.

Alice comes bounding out of the bathroom in her Rolling Stones T-shirt and baggy red pyjama bottoms. 'Morning, people,' she chirps. 'Did you see the snow? Anyone want to build a snowman?'

'I don't think there's enough snow, Anna,' Toby replies nonchalantly, and I snigger from behind the fridge door.

'Glad all that time spent alone in your room watching *Frozen* finally paid off, Toby,' she snaps back.

They continue bickering while I find some cheese spread at the back of the fridge. The sell-by date was yesterday, but I'm willing to risk botulism, salmonella or even death for this red-onion bagel.

'I'm going to watch the carol singers in Spitalfields tonight, if anyone's up for it?' Alice announces. 'Roasted chestnuts and merriment? Anyone? I think they're having some sort of a cappella battle.'

'Aww – I would, but I have plans with Robert,' I answer. 'Shame; that sounds like fun.'

'Well, I'm up for it,' Toby replies. 'Persuade Robert to come along. He can throw them a shilling for their troubles.'

I watch in dismay as both Toby and Alice high-five each other. They seem to have found common ground at my expense. Bastards.

'You both have the wrong idea about Robert,' I insist. 'He's perfectly down to earth.'

'Oh, don't be so touchy,' Alice replies as I savagely hack my bagel in half. 'It's just that standing in the cold with the Shoreditch crowd on a Friday night doesn't seem like his bag.'

'What time does it start?' I ask, slamming down the toaster lever.

'Eight p.m.'

I stamp off into my bedroom, grab my phone from the floor and text, *Carol singing in Spitalfields tonight! Meet me here at half seven. Dinner after. Don't drive. Love you x*

I return to the kitchen just as my slightly burnt bagel pops up. 'Done,' I say, flinging it on to a plate. 'We'll be there.'

'Excellent news!' Alice announces, pouring herself some cereal. 'I knew today was going to be a good one. Oh, and I'm getting my hair cut after work, so I'll just meet you there.'

I smile and nod as I spread the cheese on to my bagel, half expecting to hear my phone beep with a reply from Robert asking if we can just stick to the original plan, which no doubt involves three courses, soft music, fine wine and my footwear. In fact, I don't get a reply until half past four in the afternoon, while I'm still in class, working. It reads, *Sure. See you then.*

It's not the energetic response I was hoping for, but it'll do. I'm in the middle of replying when an anonymous call cuts in and I swipe *answer* without thinking.

'Hey, sis. How are you?'

'Patrick! Is that you? Your voice sounds strange.'

'I'm in the shower. You're on speaker.'

'Do you want to call me back when you're not naked, you little weirdo?'

For some reason, I am the person Patrick always thinks to call when he's in the middle of something. I've lost count of the calls we've had while he's in his car, walking round the supermarket, playing golf and even on the toilet.

'Dad mentioned you're bringing someone for Christmas. Just wanted to see if you've completely lost your fucking mind.'

'Quite possibly,' I reply. 'But it beats yet another year of snarky comments, lectures on how I'm not getting any younger and being the only one who shares their childhood bed with the dog.'

He snorts.

'And you and Iona are just as bad as Mum and Dad.'

I hear the water being turned off and what sounds like the swish of a shower curtain. 'That's harsh,' he protests. 'I am nothing like them.'

'Patrick, last Christmas, at the party karaoke, you changed the Shirley Bassey song "Big Spender" to "Big Spinster" and dedicated it to me.'

'Oh, come on, that was—'

'And you tried to hook me up with your mate, Ross, from school, because you thought that someone who'd spent two years in prison for fraud was a worthy suitor for your sister.'

'In his defence, everyone on that trading floor was—'

'And anyone I have brought home in the past has point-blank refused to return because you're all nuts. All of you.'

'You're talking about the Spanish guy, right? He was a prick, anyway. Look, it's our job to weed out the shite ones. Nothing but the best for my big sister. We did you a favour, there.'

It's glaringly obvious that not one member of my family is going to take any responsibility for their actions. 'Look, Patrick, all I'm asking is that you go easy on Robert because I love him and I don't want anything to screw this up for me.'

'Wow. The L word, eh? I'm expecting great things now; he'd better not disappoint.'

And once again, I'm close to self-harming in my class-room. 'Fine, Patrick, whatever. I need to go, anyway. Give my love to Kim. I'll see you next week.'

I hang up and my phone takes me back into my unfin-ished text with Robert. Telling him I'll see him soon, I flick off my classroom light and begin my journey home.

I arrive back to an empty house and a note on the kitchen table from Toby, saying that he's gone to get some food with friends and will join us at the carol concert later. I'm starving, myself, but as we're planning on a late dinner, I resist the urge to work my way through an entire tube of

Pringles, eating only three before begrudgingly replacing the lid. I still have an hour to kill before Robert arrives, which gives me time to shower and change. And maybe have another Pringle.

Playing the Polyphonic Spree loudly, just to piss off Evan (if he's still alive), I change into my favourite blue tea-dress, the one I was wearing the night Robert approached me in the Soho bar, and curl the ends of my hair, most of which will be hidden under my pompom hat. If he thinks I'm standing around, in snow, wearing high heels, however, he's very much mistaken. Pulling on my black leather knee-high boots with the furry lining and my cosy hooded parka, I'm ready to embrace the cold, and also my boyfriend.

As the lift doors open on the ground floor, I see Robert on his phone, deep in conversation. He spots me and waves over, gesturing that he'll only be a moment. While I'm dressed in mismatched layers of padding and fur, Robert looks like he's been dressed by Christian Dior himself: a long grey wool coat, black leather gloves, perfectly groomed hair (no silly hat) and polished size-eleven shoes, which look like they've only ever walked on velvet carpet. Christ, he looks like he's going to the opera. Alice was right – he's going to hate this.

'Sorry, darling,' he says, placing his phone in his inside pocket. We hug, but all he successfully manages to squeeze is my padding. 'I hope you have something naughty on under all that,' he whispers.

'Emily!'

Startled, I turn around. It seems that, while I've been busy hugging my boyfriend, Evan Grant has been busy *appearing from fucking nowhere*. He isn't dead, after all. We share a brief moment – one that only we're aware of – and it's in that moment we both realise that I'm screwed.

'Is this the man I've been hearing so much about?!' He doesn't wait for me to reply; instead, he holds out his hand towards Robert and says, 'Evan. Pleasure to finally meet you . . . I mean, she said you were handsome, but WOW.'

OhmyGodohmyGodohmyGod. What is he doing? My heart rate has just gone through the roof and it's entirely possible that I might have a stroke.

Robert politely shakes his hand, glancing at me with a 'You know this person?' look on his face, before replying, 'Thank you. I think. You live in the building?'

I want to pull Robert by the sleeve and make a run for it, but I'm stuck, frozen to the spot.

'We're neighbours!' Evan replies enthusiastically. 'We share a wall. We share a lot of things, in fact. Emily was there when I broke up with my girlfriend.'

Yikes. I unstick. Flight mode has kicked in. 'Robert, we have to go!'

'Really? Shame. Where are you off to?' Evan asks, smiling.

I keep my mouth shut. There's no way I'm divulging any—

'Oh, just some carol-singing event at Spitalfields,' Robert reveals.

Agh! He knows *everything* now. *Abort! Abort!*

'Shut up,' Evan replies. 'I'm heading there too. What a coincide—!'

'OK, have a nice night!' I interrupt, leading a rather bewildered Robert towards the front door. I look back and see Evan waving us off, while my eyes shoot a thousand imaginary daggers at his head.

We stroll towards Spitalfields market, taking the long way round in case Evan reappears beside us and links arms, like we're all heading to the Emerald City. I can tell that Robert is thinking about Evan because, after that display, who wouldn't be?

'Your friend is certainly animated,' he eventually says. 'Known him long?'

'Not really,' I reply casually.

'Never dated him?'

'*What?* HA! Me?! No, never.' Christ, get a hold of yourself, Carson. 'He's gay. So, no.'

'Didn't he say you were there when he broke up with his girlfriend?'

Ah, fuck.

'Nope, pretty sure he said boyfriend,' I lie. 'And I only saw them arguing in the hall . . .' My mind shoots back to Cassie in her hat. 'I think he likes bears.'

Robert shrugs. 'Well, he seemed quite chummy with you.'

I giggle – not only because my nerves are completely shot, but also because I'm dating someone who uses the word 'chummy'.

I squeeze Robert's arm. 'No, we're not even really friends. Acquaintances, if anything. Hang on – are you jealous?!'

'Hardly,' he replies. 'Just curious ... Look – isn't that your flatmate?'

I turn to where Robert is pointing and easily spot six-foot-three Toby, waving over at us. His great big friendly smile is very welcome right now. As we get closer, I see that, wrapped around his waist, there is a significantly smaller woman, gazing up at him adoringly.

The old market area is jam-packed and noisy as hell. The carol singing hasn't started yet, but everyone is in high spirits, wearing sparkly tinsel scarves, carrying mistletoe, craftily swigging mulled wine from hip flasks and taking selfies to show their Facebook friends how fulfilled and varied their lives are – *#blessed*. We push our way through until we reach Toby. 'Hey! Alice not here yet?' I ask. 'You remember Robert, Toby?'

Toby and Robert have only met once, when Robert made the mistake of coming to our flat via the smelly lift and Toby made him some God-awful fruit tea while I got ready. An experience he swore he'd never put himself through again.

Toby shakes Robert's hand. 'How's it going? Yeah, Alice is on her way.'

Now we're looking at Toby's friend, but she's still staring up at him and ignoring us.

'Introduce us, then, Toby?'

'Sorry, wow, yeah – this is Becca. Becca – Emily and Roberto.'

Roberto? Methinks Toby has had a smoke.

Becca pulls her gaze away from Toby, but doesn't remove herself from around his waist. She's like one of the koala pencil-huggers I had in primary school. We exchange pleasantries, but I can tell that she doesn't give a shit who we are. She's here for the Toby.

'So how did you two meet, then?' I ask, wondering whether Becca just superglued herself to him while he wasn't looking.

'Tinder,' he replies with a wink. 'Turns out there are some normal people on there, after all.'

'I wouldn't know,' I say, which Toby knows to be untrue, but Robert doesn't.

Truth is, I spent almost a year on Tinder, meeting and dating some of London's biggest arseholes. There was the man who lied about his age by fifteen years, the man who lied about his face by fifteen years, the man who promised to call, then didn't, the man who became obnoxious when I didn't want to call him, and all the other men who either bored me to death or I bored them by not having the life experience or body of a twenty-two-year-old. And then I met Robert. No swiping, no signing up, no expectations. He was just there at a bar, and so was I.

'We went gin-tasting on our first date.' Becca's voice brings me back to reality. 'I don't even like gin, but I thought he was hot.'

Doesn't like gin? What kind of monster are we dealing with here?

'And what do you do, then?' She's staring intensely at Robert, trying to size him up.

'I'm in marketing,' he replies. 'You?'

'Beauty therapist.'

'Yes. Well, of course you are,' he replies, before turning to me. 'Would you like a coffee?'

I don't know if I'm more stunned at his obnoxious answer or the fact that Becca seems to be taking it as a compliment. I ask for a latte and he happily frees himself from our little circle. Toby is still high as a kite and un-aware that a conversation even took place.

'Hey, dipshits! Hasn't it started yet?'

'Alice!' I'm so happy to see her, I almost kiss her. 'What a fucking night I've had so far, mate. Seriously, I'm ready for the bin.'

'Where's your fella?' she asks, looking around.

I point towards the coffee van, where he's taking his sweet time.

'Ah, yes. Christ, it's busy, isn't it ... Emily, who is that person hanging on to Toby?'

For someone who claims not to be interested in Toby, Alice is really rubbish at hiding her obvious interest in him.

'Becca. They met on Tinder,' I reply quietly. 'She's a beauty therapist.'

'Is she, now?'

'Toby's stoned, though,' I continue. 'Not even sure he knows she's there.'

'I'm not worried.'

'Um, I didn't say you were.'

'Good. I'm going to say hi to him. Oh, look – there's Evan.'

'If Toby wants to . . . What? Where's Evan?'

'Right here,' he replies in my left ear. 'Miss me?'

Panicked, I quickly glance towards Robert, who's still waiting in line, and then over at Alice, who's struck up a conversation with Toby, much to Becca's annoyance.

'Ugh! Here you are again! Are you stalking me, Evan?'

'Of course not.' He frowns. 'I'm with friends. I told you I was coming here.'

'Imaginary friends don't count.'

He points towards the middle of the crowd. 'See those three blokes in Santa hats?'

They're hard to miss. Burly-looking rugby types, wearing polo necks tucked into their jeans.

'I see them,' I reply. 'Are they as charming as they look?'

'No idea,' he sniffs. 'I'm not with them. I'm with the two nerdy-looking guys beside them.' He waves over at two skinny, scruffy-looking men, one of whom is cleaning his glasses on the other's scarf. 'We're celebrating tonight. Big day at work.'

'Good for you. I don't care. Why don't you go back and join them?'

He doesn't. Instead, he pulls some gloves from the pocket of his leather jacket and puts them on. 'Cassie sends her best, by the way – her best being her middle finger and a request for us both to go and fuck ourselves.' It's obvious he's fishing for an apology.

The carol singers have just taken their places and a hush has fallen over the patient crowd.

'Look, Evan, I don't normally lose my temper, but you have to see it from my point of view ... The constant noise ... I was tired ...'

The first lines from 'Silent Night' float out into the air. Evan smirks at the irony. I look behind me to track Robert's progress and discover he's on his way back.

'I'm apologising, Evan,' I say through gritted teeth. I'll say anything to make this smirking fool piss off. 'Can we just move on?'

'I'll consider it,' he says, watching Robert walk towards us. 'One question before I go, though.'

'Fine. What is it?' I whisper, aware that everyone is being much quieter than we are.

He slowly moves in closer, then subtly motions towards Robert.

'My question is ... *This* guy? *Seriously?*'

'Oh, get lost, Evan.' I push him gently so he backs away, but he's still talking. A woman in a bright-green bobble hat shushes us.

'Do you think he stirred your coffee with his silver spoon?'

'Oh, grow up.'

'I mean, I know you have age hang-ups, but what is he? Like, fifty?'

'Goodbye, Evan,' I growl quietly, and he laughs as I turn my back on him, chirping, 'See you later, neighbour. Say hi to your dad for me.'

With seconds to spare, Robert returns, coffee in hand. If he spotted Evan, he doesn't say anything, he just wraps an arm around me. I cosy into him and sip slowly, trying to enjoy what should be a romantic, wintery storybook moment; it's dark, people have fake candles and there are happy revellers singing about peace on earth, for God's sake! I will not let that little ratbag rattle me. I'm determined to end this day on a high. I almost get there too, until I hear a familiar voice shout, 'Get your face off my boyfriend, bitch!'

Me and Robert, and everyone else within a two-mile radius, turn to witness Toby and Alice kissing like their lives depend on it, and an irate Becca, at the coffee van, being angrily shushed by the lady in the bright-green hat.

CHAPTER SEVEN

By the time the carol concert ended, Becca had been removed by security, while Toby and Alice have removed themselves, no doubt heading back to the flat, leaving Robert and I to have dinner in a nearby generic chain Italian restaurant.

From the look on Robert's face, I can tell that it's not exactly what he had in mind for dinner this evening, or maybe it's just standing in the cold with people who probably shop at Lidl that has him rattled. Either way, he doesn't look comfortable.

The waiter shows us to a table near the back of the busy, brightly lit room, beside a table of six women, all over sixty and all clearly enjoying each other's company. I look at their faces and I'm reminded of that certain glow that exudes from women who've found their tribe. It's like a force field. It's radiant.

'Was bingo closed?' Robert scoffs quietly.

My heart sinks. Why did he have to say that? I glance over at the table, hoping that his words didn't penetrate the force field, but the woman sitting closest is already scowling at him. I smile meekly and pick up a menu from the middle of the table, telling him not to be so mean. 'Snobbery isn't an attractive trait,' I advise him, but he's too busy trying to find something to his liking on the three-courses-for-twenty-quid menu. A better woman would have made him apologise. A better man wouldn't have made the remark in the first place.

Our waiter returns, informing us that his name is Mike, and the soup of the day is Italian bean, and they're out of calamari. Robert orders the penne with wild mushrooms and I choose the crab ravioli.

'Can I get you some bread or olives for the table?' Mike asks for the hundredth time that day.

'Both,' Robert replies. 'And a bottle of the Pinot. Quick as you can, there's a good chap.'

I graciously thank Mike and hand him back my menu, hoping that he'll only spit in Robert's food and pardon mine. I didn't quite realise just how abhorrent Robert's manners could be; in fact, I don't think he has a clue either. Taking him out of his overpriced boys'-club comfort zone has certainly been an eye-opener.

Moments later, the wine, bread and olives arrive. I hungrily dive straight for the bread, politely declining the olives because olives can fuck off.

'Are you all right this evening?' I ask Robert, softly. 'You don't seem yourself.'

'I'm fine,' he replies, watching me dip my bread in some chilli oil. 'Not long until you stop for Christmas break? It seems like you teachers are always on holiday, though.'

'Four days,' I reply. 'It can't come quickly enough. And, despite the annual leave, we work hard!'

He picks up the bowl of olives and sniffs them before putting them back on the table.

'You should try this bread,' I say, changing the subject. 'It's delicious.'

He complies, taking a small wedge of ciabatta from the basket.

'I spoke with my brother today,' I continue. 'He's looking forward to meeting you – they all are. I was thinking that we should drive u—'

'Ah, yes ... about that . . .' he interrupts. 'I've been meaning to talk to you. I don't— Oh, good – food's here.'

Mike sets our dishes down and offers us black pepper, which Robert accepts.

'I don't think I'm going to be able to make it,' he continues, signalling to Mike to stop grinding. 'I'll be working Christmas Eve and—'

'So we'll drive up later! It's no problem.'

'No, I don't want to mess up your plans.'

'Or you can drive up when you've finished and meet me there. I'll send their address to your phone – hang on.'

He takes a forkful of pasta and watches me quickly type my parents' address into a text and press *send*.

'There. Or you could get the train to Edinburgh and I'll pick you up.'

The message arrives on his phone, but he doesn't look. Instead, he takes my hand and says, 'Maybe next time. I just have so much on. You go and have fun.'

This cannot be happening. I remove my hand from his and stab at my ravioli. 'Look, we can just go for a couple of days. Overnight, even?'

He shakes his head. 'Jesus, Emily. I can't go. OK? I shouldn't have agreed to it. I'm sorry.'

'But I've told everyone you're coming, now!' I despair. 'They're expecting us. Why is it so hard to find a couple of days to spend Christmas with me and my family?'

He's staring at the table. He isn't speaking. Fuck, has someone secretly warned him about my family? He takes a gulp of wine.

'Because I'll be spending Christmas with my own family, Emily.'

'So we'll do half with yours and half with mine!' I exclaim. 'That could work. I'd love to meet your family. Parents love me, and—'

'You're not hearing me, Emily. I have a family.'

I roll my eyes. 'I am hearing you; I'm just trying to work out a way that . . .'

And then I hear him. I hear him and it hits me like a

freight train, knocking the breath from my body and the heart from my chest. It takes me a moment to find the words I need.

'How many kids?'

He looks a little taken aback. 'Two. A boy and a girl.'

'Wife or girlfriend?'

'Wife. Ten years. Look, it's complicated.'

I take my napkin from my lap and throw it on the table. I feel sick. 'Oh, God, I'm a mistress. I'm a *fucking mistress*. How could you do this to me? No, wait. How could you do this to *them*?!'

'Emily, I never meant to hurt you. I never meant to fall in lo—'

My napkin takes a second journey from the table to his face. 'Love? Is that what you were going to say? Are you for real?' I swallow. There's a cry stuck in my throat that won't come, but something has to give, so I laugh. It's a nervous laugh. It's a dumbfounded laugh. It's one of those laughs that could easily turn into a raging sob at any moment and even I am not sure which way it's going to go. I grab my bag. 'You don't get to say that to me, Robert; in fact, you don't get to say anything to me ever again. Save the *L* word for your wife and kids, you piece of shit.'

I lift the half-empty wine bottle out of the cooler and march through the restaurant, still laughing. My laughter continues until I reach the main doors and find myself outside on the pavement, shaking. I take a huge swig from the wine bottle and a sob catches the back of my throat. Let the bawling commence.

'You OK?'

The Uber driver glances at me in his mirror as I silently nod, rummaging around in my bag for a tissue or anything that could be a suitable substitute. Robert has left three messages in the time it took me to scuttle around the corner, hide, down the rest of the wine and procure a taxi. I don't care what he has to say. Does he honestly think he can explain his way out of this?

'Explain what?'

Oh, great – not only am I a sobbing mess, but I'm thinking out loud in front of strangers. 'Nothing,' I reply, wiping my mascara with an old Tesco receipt. 'I'm just over here, on the left.'

I clamber out into the cold once again and hurry into my building. I feel numb. No, scrap that, I feel stupid – stupid and pathetic – and, worst of all, now I have to explain to my family that my lying-bastard bullshit-radar appears to be broken and I'll be returning home alone this year. I can hear the interrogation now.

How could you not have known?

Does his wife know?

Oh, Emily, you never get it quite right, do you?

How could you be involved with someone so despicable?

He has children? Oh dear god, Emily, think of the children!

I open the door to my flat and step into darkness. I call out to see if Toby and Alice are home, but there's no reply. I wonder where they vanished to. I throw down my bag and take off my coat, grateful that I'm home alone. I don't want to explain why I'm crying. I just want to go to my room, pull my duvet over my head and hide until New Year. But, in order for this plan to work, I'll need more booze. I'll need *all* of the booze.

I don't even bother turning on the lights as I walk to the kitchen, swiping the bottle of Jim Beam I keep beside the microwave. Only, Alice appears to have drunk my Jim Beam and replaced it with a shitty supermarket bourbon, hoping I won't notice. Yes, I might not have been observant enough to notice that my boyfriend was married, but I'm not a complete fucking idiot. Shot glass in hand, I vow to avenge Jim's disappearance, but now is not the time. Now is the time for getting utterly and completely wasted.

After three shots, I realise that this cheap bourbon isn't too bad and has significantly improved both my state of mind and my ability to construct an amazing fort out of my snuggle chair, a kitchen chair, some pillows and my duvet. I turn on my Bluetooth speakers and click the Spotify app on my phone. What am I in the mood for? Lana Del Rey? Ugh, too intense. Nirvana? Too angry . . . I need something cheesy. Something light and upbeat.

Backstreet Boys? Oh, hell, yes. I intend to dance that man right out of my mind.

Before 'Backstreet's Back' has even finished, I'm out of my fort, out of my dress and out of breath. I'm either incredibly unfit or incredibly drunk, but I don't let this stop me, for next up on the playlist is 'The Call' and . . . What the hell is that banging noise? I stop bouncing and listen. There it is again – a relentless thumping on the wall. I pause the music and hear a voice shouting, 'Turn that shit off!'

Oh, you have got to be kidding me. Evan fucking Grant is complaining about *my* noise levels? 'BITE ME!' is my reply, and not only do I turn the music back on, but I turn it up. Let's see how he likes it, for once. And maybe I'll just sing along too, so he doesn't miss any of the amazing lyrics.

His wall-banging continues for another minute and then it stops. Victory is mine! Maybe now he understands what he's put me through for the last year.

The doorbell rings.

And rings.

And.

Rings.

I know it's him and I know he's not going to stop ringing that fucking bell until I answer the door. I pull on an old T-shirt and storm down the hallway on unsteady feet before throwing open the front door.

It's Robert.

Man, I was *not* expecting that. He looks miserable.

Good.

'Please, Emily. We need to talk. We can't leave things like . . .' Hearing the music, he suddenly stops and peers behind me. 'Are you alone?'

I close the door over slightly. 'Yep, alone and absolutely shit-faced. Now, get away from my door; you're not welcome here.'

'If you'd just let me come in, I can—'

'No, thank you. Come in for what? You've ruined my night and you've ruined Christmas. I've heard enough from you, now OFF YOU FUCK!'

Am I shouting? God, my mouth feels dry. Am I even wearing underwear?

He moves closer and puts his hand on my cheek. 'My feelings for you are real. Let me come in and we can talk. You shouldn't be alone.'

'She isn't alone. Sorry I took so long, Emily.'

A surprised Robert watches in disbelief as Evan manoeuvres around him and hands me some beer.

'Nice T-shirt, Emily.' Evan grins. 'Why don't you put those in the fridge?'

'We're trying to have a conversation here!' Robert barks, totally confused by what's happening.

Evan stands between us. 'I'm sure you can finish it tomorrow, when she's not crying, shouting and half dressed in the hallway, mate.'

Although my reaction time is highly impaired, I get what he's trying to do.

'You put them in the fridge, Evan, I'll be through in a sec.'

As he disappears into the house, I turn back to Robert, who looks furious. 'Just an acquaintance, eh, Emily? Oh, I see what's going on here.'

'You don't get to assume anything, *Rabbie*, and I'd rather have a beer with Jack the Ripper than spend one more second on my doorstep talking to you. Go home to your wife. Go and talk dirty to her. See if she'll let you defile her fucking shoes, because I am done!'

He starts to say something, but I close the door because I can't listen to him anymore. If I keep listening, he might say something that will change my mind about hating him, and I'm not ready to do that yet. I decide that the best course of action is to sit on the floor.

'You OK?' a voice calls from the kitchen.

'Yes, I'm fine,' I yell back.

'Emily?'

'What?'

'I *really* need to know about the shoes.'

'You can go now.'

I hear the clink of a bottle top, then Evan appears in the hallway. 'I'm only kidding. Kind of. Do you need to talk?'

'No,' I reply, looking up at him. 'I need to have another drink. Are you wearing a beard?'

He stoops down and helps me up. 'I think you've had enough for now.'

'You can't tell me what to do. You're not my real dad.'

He laughs loudly. 'Look, I will go – once you've had some water. And turned that fucking music off. Boy bands, Emily? I thought better of you.'

I push past him, stumbling towards my room. 'I am going to continue my little pity party, Evan. Join me or go home – your choice.'

I go back into my room and locate my shot glass. Spotify has shuffled on to Dionne Warwick and I rush to change it, knowing that my heart might just burst otherwise. I continue on my nostalgic cheese quest, moving on to New Kids on the Block. I'm halfway through the dance routine to 'Hanging Tough' before I even notice that Evan is in the room, swigging from a beer and carrying a bottle of water.

'This isn't healthy,' he says, watching me with both abject horror and amusement. 'I'm staging an intervention.'

Before I can protest, he's sitting on the floor, scrolling through my playlist, shaking his head. New Kids go off and the Weeknd goes on.

'Ugh, you have terrible taste in music,' I snarl, ignoring the water and pouring myself another shot.

He holds out his hand for the bourbon bottle. 'Um, it's your playlist that we really should discuss at some point. It's like a cry for help.' I hand him the bottle, which he sniffs first before knocking back a mouthful, then shuddering. 'So, are you going to tell me what happened with your boyfriend, or am I going to have to guess?'

'It's really none of your business,' I reply, snatching the bottle back.

'He's married, isn't he?'

'Am I the only one who didn't know?'

'I heard the word "wife" while you were arguing.'

'Oh, fucking good for you, Sherlock,' I slur, balancing on the edge of my bed. 'Yes, he appears to be with wife and child – no, *children* – but, worst of all . . . he fucking ruined Christmas.'

'Like the Grinch? I noticed there weren't many decorations in here – did he *steal Christmas*, Emily?'

I laugh and slump from the bed to the floor. 'It was all planned out! He was supposed to come home with me! He was supposed to be the reason my family didn't hound me about my life this year. For once, it was actually going to be the most wonderful time of the year, instead of the shit-show it always is.'

'Why do your parents hound you about your life? What's wrong with it?'

I clink the bottle off my front tooth. Jesus, I can't even see this bottle properly, never mind drink from it.

'I'm thirty-eight, Evan! I have room-mates! I have no children or savings or matching fucking dinner plates! I've lived in London for years and I don't even have a whole house or a relationship to show for it.'

He's quiet for a moment. 'You're thirty-eight?'

'Oh, shut up.'

'Anything else you'd like to moan about?'

'Yes. I have terrible neighbours.'

Evan raises his bottle and grins. 'All of this may be true, but you do have excellent taste in indoor camping. That's worth something.' And, with that, he shuffles himself into the fort. 'You should build these professionally. Hurry up and bring the booze.'

I crawl in beside him and place a cushion under my head. When I woke up this morning, I never imagined that, by eleven p.m., I'd be single, drunk and huddled inside a makeshift fort with my rotten neighbour.

He looks down at me. 'Emily, I don't care what anyone says about you. I think you're great.'

'Who said . . . ? Oh, very good . . . I am pretty great, though.'

'And now you say something nice about me.'

I laugh. 'Like what?'

'Well, I did save you from the bad man, so I guess I'm like your hero now.'

I shake my head. '"Save" is a bit strong. You helped to diffuse a situation with my boyfriend. Sorry – ex-boyfriend.'

'Shoe Boy has a nice ring to it.' He takes a long swig from his bottle. 'Now, did the dirty talk involve the shoes, or was it a—'

'Stop that!' I insist.

'Stop what?'

'Being a dick! Stop prying.'

'Not prying. Just curious.'

'Well, go home and be curious in your own . . . home.' Ugh, the booze is limiting my vocabulary. It's a bad sign. I crawl back out of the fort and turn the music up. 'If you insist on staying here, then you have to dance,' I inform him. 'And drink. Them's the rules.'

He gets to his feet and downs a shot of bourbon. 'Isn't that music a bit too lo—'

'DANCE!'

'Fuck's sake, you're bossy. Fine, but as long as I can . . .'

The next thing I remember is waking up alone, with the hangover from hell, back inside the fort. Beside me, a bottle of water and an iPod missing at least thirty songs.

CHAPTER EIGHT

'Was that Robert I heard leaving this morning?' Alice peers over her glasses as I slope into her room, watching me assume the foetal position in bed beside her. 'Because, if it was, he's eaten your lemon yogurt.'

'Nice try,' I say quietly. 'Just buy me another; I don't care.'

She laughs and reaches behind her back, then continues to eat my yogurt. 'Feeling delicate? I take it things went well, then?'

I'm too fragile for this conversation right now. All I can taste in my mouth is old bourbon and what appears to be regret. I bury my head under her duvet, hoping she'll drop it.

'Looks like he's making an effort for you, anyway. The carol concert . . . Meeting the family . . . Your mum will be thrilled – she'll be picking out hats and everything. I'm thinking a summer wedding . . .'

'He's already married, Alice. He has a fucking wife and kids. We didn't even make it through dinner.'

She puts down the yogurt. 'No! Are you shitting me? How is that even possible?'

'I didn't ask,' I reply, 'but I imagine that his week-end-work excuses are bullshit.'

'So he lives in London during the week and commutes back at weekends?' she muses. 'I wonder if his wife suspects.'

'I have no idea.'

'I bet she does suspect. Women always know when their men are being sneaky fuckers.'

I fling the cover back from my face. 'Well, *I* didn't! I seemed to miss that *completely*!'

I disappear back under the duvet, where her pity-face can't follow me. I feel her hand gently stroke my hair.

'What an arsehole. I'm so sorry . . . I know you had high hopes for him. If you need to have a cry, I'm here.'

'Thanks.'

I'm too dehydrated to cry – though I'm pretty sure, if I did, my tears would be forty-per-cent proof and flammable. I hear her resuming yogurt duties.

'But, hang on, if you and Robert didn't make it through dinner . . .'

Here it comes.

'Then who did I hear leav—?'

'Evan,' I say from under the duvet. 'It was Evan.'

She pulls the covers off my face. 'WHAT? Evan? How did that even . . . ? You didn't . . . did you?'

'I have no idea,' I reply, trying to sit up. 'I remember being drunk . . . and then Robert came to the door . . . and Evan showed up and made him go away. And then we hid in my fort.'

'Your fort? How drunk were you?'

'Maximum drunk. What time did you hear him leave?'

'We got home around three a.m. and it wasn't long after that.'

'Wait! You and Toby kissed. Let's talk about that instead.'

'This isn't about us,' she responds. 'Let's focus on you.'

'Fine, but you know I'm coming back to this when I feel better, right?'

'Oh, I know . . . but Evan, though. What the hell happened?'

I try to establish a timeline, but it's hazy. 'I'm not entirely sure. I'll talk to him later,' I reply, attempting to stand up. 'I need more water. Do you have a spare drip?'

I grab one of the two-litre bottles of water from the fridge and take it back to my room, where I rummage quietly in the bathroom for some paracetamol. I take two and drag my duvet from the fort, climbing back into bed. My phone beeps. Twice. I know it'll be Robert and I am in no fit state to deal with him. I switch it off and throw it under the bed. I hope his weekend at home is as miserable as mine.

Toby pops his head in at lunchtime, just as he's leaving for work. He's wearing a red scarf the length of an anaconda and asks if he can get me anything. What I really want is my Scottish hangover cure – some Irn Bru and square sausage with tattie scone – but this is London and he'd miss work trying to locate these items.

'Do we have any crisps?' I ask him. 'I think I need junk food.'

'I have dried banana chips,' he replies, 'or some rice cakes?'

'Is there anything that isn't from Holland and Barrett?'

He shakes his head. 'Oh, Alice keeps Kettle Chips in her room. That any good?'

'How do you know what's in her room?' I reply, peering at him.

He flushes pink and smiles. 'Shall I bring you some?'

'No,' I reply. 'Not some. All. Bring them all.'

Seconds later, he appears with two full packets of plain crisps and half a packet of cheese-flavoured ones.

'You may have saved my life,' I gush, taking them under the covers with me. 'You're a national treasure.'

He slinks back out of the room as I devour Alice's stash. Feeling a bit better, I find some John Oliver videos online and make myself some hot, sweet tea. My room smells like an old man's pub and I'm forced to open the window slightly, letting the cold December wind blast through while I remain snuggled under my duvet, where I can pretend that everything's OK. I know that, when I come out, I'll have to deal with Robert, Evan, my family, and the disgusting film that's covering my teeth, but I'm not ready. I'd like the world to go away, for today at least.

I don't quite manage an entire day of sleep, waking at ten p.m. in a pitch black, freezing room. Feeling a modicum better than this morning, but still nowhere near Bristol fashion, I can only think of one thing: food. Closing my window, I venture through to the kitchen to make my second-favourite comfort food, after crisps: toast. Stacks and stacks of warm, soft, buttery toast.

Upon discovering that there isn't even *one* slice of bread in the house, not even the heel of the loaf, I have what can only be described as a gargantuan fucking tantrum. It's completely unnecessary, yet spectacular. Dishcloths are thrown, chairs are knocked over, pots are banged and the fridge door is slammed shut with a force that makes the magnet-held Christmas cards fall and scatter at my bare feet.

Luckily, for them, Alice and Toby are nowhere to be found, because only idiots who date married men are at home, losing their shit over processed white carbs on a Saturday night. Storming back into my room, I grab my phone and turn it on to text the bread thieves. If they're not here to witness my wrath, then they'll feel my text-rage, with what may just be an endless stream of poo emojis. My phone powers up.

You have 17 missed calls.

You have 12 unread text messages.

In my fury, I'd forgotten why I'd switched my phone off in the first place, and now I'm left staring at Robert's many attempts to contact me since last night. Sighing, I sit myself down on my bed where I start deleting his text messages. I catch glimpses of his explanations, his apologies, his bullshit, but I don't linger on any of them for too long. They're separated . . . They're together for the children . . . He loves me . . . He seems unable to spell 'necessary' . . . He's sorry . . . All erased. I don't listen to any of his voicemails, pressing *delete* before he gets the chance to pollute my ears. I make the grand, albeit pointless gesture of deleting him from my contacts; I know his number off by heart and I know that, before the weekend is over, he'll have texted me again, anyway. But still. Fuck him.

I return to the kitchen table as the light from my phone screen fades. This time last week, I was telling my mother how wonderful things were, and now I have no boyfriend, no plus-one for Christmas, no idea what happened with Evan last night and, most tragically, no toast.

And tomorrow is Sunday. Tomorrow is the day when my voice will travel the 411 miles from London to the Scottish Borders and directly into my mother's ear, informing her that I've made a mistake. It seems I haven't met anyone nice, after all.

CHAPTER NINE

The sight of Kara at my front door this morning is a welcome one. She's skipped her Sunday morning hot-yoga class in order to bring me tea, sympathy and a breakfast baguette from the café on the corner.

'You didn't have to come over,' I say, taking the small paper bag from her hand while she removes her coat. I peek inside. 'Does this have bacon in it?'

'Bacon, sausage and ketchup. I'd have got you mushrooms, but he'd run out.'

'I'm not sure if I love you or my breakfast more. Come through to the kitchen. The others are still in bed.'

Kara follows me in, commenting on how nice the place looks, which we both know is a fib. Alice describes it as 'retro' on Airbnb, but really that's code for 'may contain asbestos'. It seems whoever lived here in the 1960s was Artex crazy, ensuring every wall and ceiling was suitably naff and bumpy. Unwilling to remove or plaster over it, the landlord arranges to have our Braille-covered hallway painted every now and again; last year, he took a break from the usual boring white and covered the walls in a lovely cream shade I like to call 'Baby Sick'. With the exception of my en suite, renovations to the flat have been minimal, but we all do our best to make it look cosy, adding our own little unique finishing touches. Alice likes arty postcards and scented candles, I like fairy lights and fresh flowers, and Toby likes to leave his shoes strewn all over the hall.

Kara sits herself down at the table. 'I want to know everything,' she says, blowing on her hot tea. 'And then I'll decide whether to maim or kill him on your behalf.'

'Not much more to say,' I reply. 'Like I said in my text, he's married and we're over.'

She watches me as I bite into my baguette and allows me that initial moment of pleasure, where mouth meets bacon and the world seems a little better, before pouncing again.

'This is what happens when you date someone who doesn't use Twitter or Facebook. It's obvious that they're hiding something. And to dump you at Christmas! Well, I've never—'

'Mo. Ah dunt hem!' I reply quickly. I may have a mouthful of pig, but I couldn't let that one slide.

'What? Oh, you dumped him?'

I quickly swallow what's left in my mouth. 'Yes! I chose to end it. He was the dumpee; I was not dumped!'

'OK, I don't—'

'I was the dumper. Not him. Me.'

'—suppose it really matte—'

'In Mexico, they'd call me El Dumpo.'

She splutters her tea. 'Ha ha, fine. I hear you. I have to say, I thought you'd be in a worse mood.'

I shrug and continue eating. 'I'm mostly fine,' I assure her. 'I'm sad, but I feel stupid. I wanted this to work so badly that I let my bullshit radar down. The signs were there, I just didn't see them. I mean, he asked if we were doing presents this year! Who the hell says that to someone they've never had a Christmas with?! And working every weekend? Conferences around school holidays? Ugh, I'm smarter than this.'

Kara leans across the table and hugs me. 'Please don't blame yourself. It's not your fault he's a lying shitebag.'

'What do I tell my family? I'm going to look like a pathetic loser. Dammit, Kara, I really thought he was the one.'

She reaches under the table, retrieves one of the Christmas cards that fell from the fridge and hands it to me. 'Make something up … Say he had to work … or that he's dead. Anything.'

'So he's a wanker who won't make time for his girl-friend's family or he's just a dead wanker.' I stick the card back on the fridge before Alice sees it's missing.

'You could always spend it with us?'

I put my head in my hands. 'Why is this my life?'

Suddenly, a half-naked Toby appears at the kitchen door. 'Morning. I thought I heard voices. Hi, Kara. You all right?'

Kara sits up straight and gives Toby her very best smile. 'I am,' she replies. 'How's the glamorous world of modelling?'

'Slow,' he replies, scratching his stomach. 'London Collections' castings are next month; hoping to get some work from that.'

He brushes past my head to get to the fridge, taking some orange juice out and drinking straight from the bottle.

'Gross, Toby,' I moan. 'Don't put that back in the fridge. It's full of spit now.'

'Sorry, Mum.' He smiles and takes the bottle back to his room, while Kara chuckles.

'God, I do sound like his mum,' I say, placing my head back in my hands. 'He's only twenty-two. I'm bloody old enough to be his mother.'

Kara stops smiling. 'That means so am I. Jesus, how depressing. Talking of mums, John's arrives tomorrow and I still have a million things to do before she gets here. You OK if I shoot off?'

'Of course,' I reply. 'I should get dressed, anyway. Thanks for coming over, though – appreciate it.'

I can hear Alice and Toby messing around as we walk up the hall towards the front door. Kara stops to listen.

'Are they . . . ?' she whispers.

'Yep,' I mouth back.

'Since when?!'

I signal for her to move to the front door. 'About a month after Toby moved in,' I whisper. 'It became unofficially official on Friday.'

She opens the door and steps outside. 'That's not good,' she informs me, shaking her head. 'Living with a couple is the worst. They'll either be shagging or fighting or planning, and you'll always feel like a spare prick. Trust me. Anyway, I'm off. Try to enjoy your Christmas; don't let that worm ruin it for you.'

She kisses me on both cheeks and I watch her walk towards the lift, letting her words sink in. She's right, of course – she always is. I'm going to be the third wheel. Not only will I be privy to their usual fights, I'll also have to put up with cuddling, kissing, sex noises and, worst of all, their bloody happiness. I'm not ready to be happy yet.

I move back inside the flat, managing three steps up the hallway before I hear a knocking on the door. I backtrack and tug it open again, expecting to see Kara, but instead I'm greeted by the grinning face of Evan Grant.

'So we need to talk about the other night.'

My stomach flips. Oh, God, what did I do? It's all so hazy after the dancing.

'Yes, I've been meaning to talk to you about that,' I reply quickly. 'Look, if something happened . . . I don't remember. I'd had a lot to drink and—'

'Woah, there!' he interrupts, holding his hands up. 'You were blasted. I might be a lot of things, but I'm not *that* guy. Jesus.'

I feel my face go red. 'OK; so what, then?'

He looks irritated, but continues. 'About your proposal.'

'My what? What proposal? Oh, please tell me I didn't fucking actually propose.' I stare blankly at him and he stares right back.

'Your idea . . .'

Nope. Nothing.

'You . . . I have to say, your morning hair is amazing. Does it always stick up like that at the side?'

My hand leaps up, feeling the left side of my head.

'Other side.'

I smooth down the right side and wonder why Kara let me sit there looking like a maniac. 'Evan, what the hell are you on about?' I reply in a fluster. 'Just spit it out!'

'Christmas!' he exclaims. 'You asked me to come to your house for Christmas!'

I laugh out loud in astonishment. 'What? That's absurd!'

He nods. 'Totally absurd,' he replies, 'but it doesn't make it less true.'

My eyes shoot up and to the right, trying to remember something. Anything. There is no way in hell I'd ask him to come home for Christmas. 'You're lying, I would never . . .'

Just be him for four days. They've never met Robert. You could totally be him . . .

Uh-oh.

You will literally save my life . . . I'll pay you! One month's rent . . .

He sees the look on my face change from vacant to panic.

'With me, now?'

'Fuck. No. Wait . . . Fuck. Forget I said anything. That was clearly the booze talking.'

He smiles. 'Maybe, but I could do with getting out of London for a few days – breathe in some Scottish air. I'm up for it—'

'There is nothing to be up for, Evan! *Pay* you to pretend to be my boyfriend for four days? I wouldn't do that in a million years.'

He pulls out his phone and does a series of quick swipes. 'Um, you already did.'

And, sure enough, there on his online banking screen is a credit from Emily Carson for £650. I want to vomit. I am never, *ever* drinking again.

'Transfer that back to me, *immediately!*' I exclaim, thrusting the phone back into his hand. 'This is insane!'

'Well, it's not the oddest proposition I've ever had . . .'

'Enough! Read my lips, Evan: IT IS NOT HAPPENING.'

I flounce back inside, slamming the door shut behind me. I hear Alice enquire if everything's all right and my mouth replies, 'Everything's fine,' but it couldn't be further from the truth. I feel like an idiot for the second time this weekend and all I want to do is scream.

The lovebirds finally surface from Alice's room around dinner time, no doubt to refuel for their next sex marathon. I should cut them some orange slices, rub their shoulders and squirt water bottles into their stupid smug faces.

'It's Mother Hubbard in there,' I tell Toby, who's opening and closing the same three cupboards, hoping food will miraculously appear. 'I'm doing an online shop later. Make a list, if you want in, but I need the money up front. I'm unexpectedly skint this week.'

'Cool,' he replies, giving me a thumbs-up. 'I'll do it in a mo.'

'Don't buy that organic reduced-sugar ketchup again,' Alice insists, tying her hair back. 'It's fucking awful. Tastes like actual tomatoes.'

Toby sighs. 'I know healthy eating is a bizarre concept for you, but you really should rethink your diet.'

'You should rethink your hair.'

'Oh, please stop!' I yell. 'I'm not in the mood to listen to th—'

The sound of my phone ringing makes me jump. Oh, fuck – it's Sunday. I forgot. How could I forget?

'You going to answer that, grumpy?' Alice enquires. 'Or are you just going to keep frowning at it until it stops?'

'The latter. It's either my mum or Robert. I don't want to speak to either of them.'

Alice grabs it from the table. 'Hello? Hi, Mrs Carson! Yes, it's Alice . . . I'm fine; how are you?'

I hold my hand out to collect the phone, but she keeps talking.

'Yes, Emily's here . . . Her boyfriend? Well, I—'

I wrestle the phone from her and scurry out of the kitchen. 'Hi, Mum. How are you?'

'I'm fine, Emily. How's the new man?'

God, that didn't take her long. I feel every part of my body clench. I'm not prepared for this. Must. Stall.

'What about me?' I deflect. 'Aren't you going to ask how your eldest and favourite child is?'

'Of course. How are you?'

I take a deep breath. 'Well, to be honest, I'm—'

'Dad's just been to the cash and carry for drinks,' she predictably interrupts. 'We've bought loads extra in for your Robert. Does he drink gin? Dad bought you some of that pink gin you love.'

'Oh, right. Great . . . but, as I was saying, there's been a—'

'Oh, did you hear?' she interrupts *again*. 'Iona's husband isn't coming. Some work nonsense.'

'Really?' I play dumb. I'm not getting involved. I have my own mess to explain.

'Yes. I mean, who abandons their wife at Christmas? It's despicable. Your dad called him a "complete tosser", and you know how much your dad hates to swear.'

My dad swears, roughly . . . oh . . . every nineteen seconds – as does my entire family.

'Any decent man would put his family first,' she continues. 'Can you imagine Robert choosing *anything* over you at Christmas?'

Just his wife. And kids . . .

'We'll have a word with her properly when she gets here. Anyway, what were you saying?'

I'm panicking now. I can't use the 'Robert has to work' excuse now, can I? And if I go with Kara's 'Robert is dead' excuse, she'd only want to come to the fucking funeral and tell me I'm wearing the wrong shade of black. Agh! I'm going to have to tell the truth.

'Look, Mum,' I say, steeling myself. 'There's something I have to tell you about Robert and you're not going to like it, but—'

'Oh, God, don't give me any more bad news. What is it? He's not allergic to dogs, is he?'

'What? No.'

'Because I'm not keeping Pacino in the conservatory overnight – he gets lonely.'

'This is not about the dog, Mum, it's that he's—'

'You're worrying me now. Oh, Emily, he's not a fucking vegetarian, is he?'

'No, if you'd let me—'

'Well, what is it, then? Emily Carson, I'm about to have a—'

'He's much younger than me!'

I scrunch up my face and slap my hand against my head.

What is wrong with me?! After a moment of silence, she clears her throat.

'How much younger?'

'Um . . . nearly ten years,' I reply, my eyes still tightly scrunched. 'I just thought you should know.'

I await her reaction, but instead I hear her muffle the handset.

'William! WILLIAM . . . Emily's got herself a toy boy . . . I'll ask . . .' She returns, full volume: 'Your dad wants to know if cougars can still drink gin.'

I tell them both to piss off, but they're too busy laughing to hear me, so I hang up. It appears the theme of this year's Christmas insults has been decided.

I look towards the wall I share with Evan and take a deep breath. I guess there's only one thing left to do. I march down the hall and out of the front door, where I soon find myself at Evan's front door, getting ready to grovel. Before I can knock, Stephanie stomps out, followed by Evan's other room-mate, Ling.

'Is Evan around?' I ask, smiling civilly.

Stephanie adopts her usual helpful-as-fuck manner by ignoring me, but Ling nods and gives him a shout.

I thank her and stand nervously, waiting for him to appear, which he eventually does – in his robe.

'I was just going for a shower.'

He has chest hair. I pictured him smooth. It's confusing.

'I came to apologise.' God, I can't stop looking. It's

darker than I imagined. Not that I imagined anything. Oh, God, Emily, get on with it.

He folds his arms and smiles. 'What are you staring at?'

'Nothing . . . Well, I totally took you for a shaver. But, there you are. Hairy.'

'I am man, Emily,' he replies in his best caveman voice.

I divert my eyes to his face. 'Look, it seems I just told my mother that Robert will definitely, one hundred per cent, be there for Christmas. Dad's bought gin, you see.'

'Ah. You need my help now.'

'I do.'

'Well, in that case, the answer is . . . no.'

'What? Why not?'

'Because you're right, it was a stupid idea. Now, I have the shower ru—'

'Oh, come on! I already paid you and everything!'

'Now I just feel cheap . . .'

I can feel the fear setting in and I start to panic. 'What'll it take, Evan? What will it take to make you say yes? Name it.'

He ponders this for a moment, probably longer than he needs to. I can hear the shower running in the background. If all else fails, I'll drown us both.

'What does Robert drive?' he asks.

'A Mercedes.'

'Then I want a Merc to drive up in. That's what it'll take. A big shiny car.'

'That'll cost a fortune! I thought we'd take the train. I can't afford to rent a Mercedes!'

'Oh, I'm sure the big wad of cash your dad slips you every Christmas will cover it.'

I take a step back. How the hell did he know that? I don't think even Mum knows about that.

'You really don't remember anything we spoke about on Friday night, do you? Anyway, I'm wasting water, here. Do we have a deal?'

'Fine,' I reply through gritted teeth.

'Excellent!' he exclaims, putting his hand up for a high five. 'Let's have a pre-match chat tomorrow . . . Wait – will we need to practise kissing? Your family will expect to see kissing, right?'

'Ugh, you're a pig, Evan.' I about-turn and, as I trudge back to my flat, I hear him call.

'Robert. You're a pig, *Robert*.'

Closing my front door behind me, I head straight for my bedroom and flop on to the bed. My head is spinning. Even if Evan can play a convincing marketing executive, how the hell am I going to play a convincing girlfriend when all I want to do is strangle the little bastard? We have a lot of work to do if we're ever going to pull this off.

CHAPTER TEN

While the north of the country is being battered by snow storms, it seems that London is now melting instead, ruining shoes and causing major spray from traffic as it whizzes through piles of brown slush. I'm out of the house an hour earlier than normal with a plan to throw myself into some marking before class begins and ruins my day. As the school closes tomorrow, I'm determined to try and limit the amount of work I need to take home with me over Christmas. I asked Alice if she wanted to come in early with me, but was answered with a loud 'Get fucked!' from the other side of her bedroom door.

The Monday-morning Tube is standing-room only and even my best attempts to hunch my shoulders, stick out my belly and feign a look of morning sickness aren't enough to make anyone give up their seat. I'm not surprised. In London, you could commando-crawl your way on to a train with broken legs and a ruptured arse and no one would voluntarily shift from their precious spot. I hold on to one of the handrails and position myself directly in front of a woman who has a small gift-wrapped present, which reeks of Secret Santa, hanging out of her handbag. We used to organise a Secret Santa at the school, until the presents started getting increasingly offensive. The final straw was Kenneth Dawson's gift, of 2012: a plain white mug which said *I'm a twat* on the underside. Someone from the education authority requested that the person responsible apologise, but Alice never did.

I reach into my pocket and pull out a small piece of white paper. Evan has kindly provided me with his mobile number, written on the back of a Boots receipt and shoved through my letterbox late last night. Not only are we going to have to chat about our upcoming festive fraud, but also about his hair-product choices. Holding the receipt between my teeth, I fish around in my bag for my phone, hoping that the train doesn't suddenly jerk, sending both me and the contents flying. I then enter his number into my contacts and save, but not before sending a quick text: *I need your licence details for car insurance. Oh, and Boots from 1930s called. They want their Brylcreem back.* Puerile, maybe, but I snigger quietly as I place my phone back in my bag and zip it firmly shut.

I have so much to get organised before Thursday. In my head, I start mentally packing for the trip. *Presents, warm jumpers, new nightdress – no, scrap that – reinforced stainless-steel pyjamas, make-up bag, tangle teaser, fancy party-wear, those diamond earrings Robert gave* . . . My heart suddenly drops. Robert gave them to me on my birthday. I was really looking forward to showing them off. It then occurs to me that Robert hasn't texted me since that night, and it bothers me. It shouldn't, but it does. As much as I despise him, there's a tiny part of me that needs to believe I was special and not just a fling, that I meant something to him, that he risked everything to be with me because I'm extraordinary. But I'm not extraordinary. I'm a thirty-eight-year-old single woman with snow slush on her tights and a heart that feels a little more hollow every day.

The train comes to a halt at East Acton and I clamber past the other commuters to get out. I need some fresh air. By the time I reach the school gates, my feelings of sadness are rapidly turning into very healthy feelings of anger. Fuck him, I think as I trudge towards the main doors. Fuck him and his expensive flat and his bespoke suits and his airs and his pomposity. The truth is, Robert risked everything because he's a middle-aged, weak, inadequate, walking cliché, and there are a million others like him. I might not be extraordinary, but neither is he. In fact, he's worse. He's unreservedly average.

'I printed off my licence information for you.' Evan hands me a sheet of A4 and I glance over it, expecting to see some penalty points for speeding or a disclaimer that he's only entitled to drive a tricycle. He sits down beside me at the kitchen table, taking an apple from the fruit bowl.

'That's Toby's apple,' I inform him. Evan looks at the apple closely, then back at me.

'No, you must be thinking of another apple. This is my apple. I've had this one for years.' He bites into it and I try not to smirk. He has a fucking answer for everything. 'Oh, when you're booking the Merc, try and get one with heated seats.'

'Anything else? A minibar? Morgan Freeman's voice on the satnav?'

He grins and continues chomping away on Toby's apple. 'Have you had any thoughts on how we should play this charade? What's my character's motivation?'

'To stay alive over Christmas.'

'Apart from that. Tell me what I need to know about Robert, or rather what they already know.'

I put down his driver information. 'Thankfully, they don't know much about him, but I'll run through the main points.'

I reach across to the fridge and grab the packet of yellow Post-it notes we keep there to label food.

'OK. Firstly, his surname is Shaw, which is also the name of an actor, so google him in case jokes are made.'

'I know who Robert Shaw is, Emily. "Here's to swimmin' with bow-legged women . . ." *Jaws*, Emily. He was in *Jaws*.'

'I know –' I didn't – 'and he works in marketing. Director. I can't change that, as I've already told my sister and she remembers everything. You can choose which field, though – pick something boring so they won't press you for more info.' I write *research marketing* on the first yellow note and stick it to his T-shirt.

'Is this really necessa—'

'Nope.'

'Fine.'

'Next, we've been together since April. We met at a bar in Soho. You sent over a drink with your business card and I called you the next day.'

'Wow – I'm really lame,' he replies, while I press the next note – *business card and cocktail pickup* – firmly to his forearm.

'I'll be wearing diamond earrings on Christmas Day,' I continue. 'You bought them for my birthday, when we stayed at the Beaumont.'

'So I'm lame and unimaginative?'

'It was lovely!' I protest. 'We laughed a lot that weekend. That was when I knew he was . . .' I stop myself before my eyes well up and I crumble.

'It's OK,' Evan reassures. 'You're allowed to be sad, you know. He did a shitty thing.'

'What's your idea of a romantic birthday, then?' I continue, brushing off his comment. 'A Haribo jelly-ring and a quick fumble in a Premier Inn?' I write *Beaumont and diamonds* on the third sticky and shove it over his mouth. He mumbles something in return.

'And, lastly – my family. Be warned: they're like a pack of wild dogs. They will surround you, sniff you, locate your weak spots and then pounce. It might be best to play dead. If my mother had to pick her favourite child, it would be the dog; my sister is a snob, my brother is immature and my father will make you dance, at some point. Also, they're aware of the age gap and have already started making cougar jokes. Be prepared to be called a toy boy, jailbait and whatever else they come up with before we arrive.'

I take my final Post-it note and write *Beware the Carsons*, sticking it to his forehead.

'So that's about it,' I conclude. 'I'm sure you have lots to research. I'll be in touch if I think of anything else.'

He just sits there, covered in stickies, with a half-eaten apple in one hand.

'Was there something else?'

He takes the note off his mouth and grins. 'Look, I'll have no problem pretending to be Robert, but there is one thing we haven't discussed.'

'The sleeping arrangements? Yes, I know. You can just take the floor, or we'll shove a pillow between—'

'No,' he interrupts. 'What kind of couple are . . . were you and Robert? Tactile? Hands off? Public displays of affection? How would you have acted in front of your parents?'

'Oh.' I think about this for a moment. It's a fair question. We weren't hand holders, that's for sure, and most of our affection was shown in cars or in the privacy of his flat. It all makes sense, now that I know his situation.

'Still with me?' Evan asks. 'It can't be that difficult a question, surely?'

'No, it's just . . . Never mind. We'll act like two people who are madly in love, yet respectful of our boundaries in my parents' house.'

'Oh, for God's sake.' He starts laughing. 'Look, Emily, if I'm your boyfriend, the man you might some day marry, you're going to have to act like you're into me. You're going to have to throw me loving looks, stroke my arm, let me whisper in your ear and, most importantly, kiss me.'

I scrunch up my face.

'Yes, Emily, if you don't kiss me like you truly mean it and without making that face, the game will be up.'

'I'll cross that bridge when we come to it,' I reply quickly, standing up. 'Now, if you don't mind, I have a lot to do.'

He peels off the remaining Post-it notes and puts them in his pocket. 'Fine. I'll be in touch if there's anything else I need to know before Thursday.'

I open the door, desperate to get him out of the house, and I see Alice scurrying back down the hallway and into her room.

'I see you!' I yell in her direction. Oh, just brilliant. I

hide my face in my hands. I bet she heard everything. How the fuck am I going to explain this?

I don't notice Evan leaving until I hear the front door close behind him. Two seconds later, Alice's grinning face appears. 'Put the kettle on, Em; I want to know everything.'

CHAPTER ELEVEN

The last day of term arrives with a bang. Almost half of my students haven't shown up and the other half are high as a kite in anticipation of their early finish and two-week break. My routine is simple: prise teenagers off the ceiling, play film to pass the time, distribute chocolate and glare at anyone who takes the piss out of my good nature. When that bell finally does ring, my colleagues and I will wish our darling students a wonderful Christmas and a Happy New Year, before heading to the teachers' lounge, turning on some music and making our first official festive season coffee – Irish. Today should be a day where two fingers are stuck up to everyone who doesn't get a fortnight's holiday from work, but I'm preoccupied with the fact that, in two days, I'll be arriving chez Carson with a man who's only slightly less irritating than thrush.

The twenty Year-Eleven students who bothered to show up today were given the choice of watching either *World War Z* or *The Great Gatsby*, so predictably I can now hear

Brad Pitt on the screen behind me as I tap away on my iPad keyboard, attempting to remain focused on the next few days.

Clicking *Book Now* on the car-rental website, I wave goodbye to the £500 it's just cost me to hire a black Mercedes C-Class for four days, including insurance, parking assist and heated seats. As much as it pains me to admit it, Evan was right about the whole car thing. I've already told Iona what he drives and does for a living; if we'd turned up in a Fiat, eyebrows would have been raised and questions asked.

My phone vibrates in my bag and, although I'm not entirely surprised to see a message notification from Robert's number, it still manages to make my stomach churn. I eat three chocolate coins before I open and read.

This can't be over, Emily. I love you. Tell me what u want me to do and I'll do it.

I then eat a further three coins before replying.

I want you not to be a lying, cheating, sneaky-as-fuck married bawbag who just ruined everything. Can you do that? K, thx. Bye.

Not a perfect response, but it'll have to do.

At interval, I nip down to the teachers' lounge, where I spot Alice talking to Herr Weber, the only high-school German teacher I've ever met who is actually German. Despite the fact he's still sporting his dodgy Movember moustache, he's very attractive – a sentiment shared by many of the female staff, who refer to him as Herr Handsome. Alice calls him Hans Gruber and says she'd happily give him access to her vault. I had to watch *Die Hard* before this made any sense to me.

She makes a beeline for me as soon as I enter the room. 'I'm so disappointed. You know those men on Tinder who have pics of themselves hugging mountains and hanging off climbing walls by one finger? He's one of them. He just spent ten minutes telling me that he's spending Christmas in the Black Forest, doing some cross-country ski-jumping shit, and I had to look impressed.'

I open the fridge and remove the green super-juice I placed in there this morning, casually eyeing him up.

'Well, you don't think he got a physique like that from sitting on his ar—'

'What the fuck are you drinking?' she interrupts, looking horrified.

I look at the bottle. 'It's a smoothie thing. Green shit and pineapple. It's surprisingly good. Toby let me try some the other—'

'Oh, sweet Jesus, is there anyone in this room who isn't a closet health freak?'

I nudge her in the direction of Gwyneth Conroy, head of social studies, who's wearing some tinsel round her neck and spoon-fucking a jar of Nutella at eleven a.m.

'I love that woman,' Alice utters. 'Now, tell me – how is the great big fat Christmas lie coming along? You should consider giving Evan laryngitis. All he would have to do is nod for four days.'

'I'm sorry I told you,' I reply as we sit on the couch. 'You make me feel guilty and ridiculous, all at the same time.'

'Well, technically, you didn't tell me. I overheard you talking in the hallway—'

'Overheard?! You eavesdropped!'

'That's not important. What is important is that you both have your stories straight.'

I nod, gulping down my juice. 'He knows to answer to Robert . . . and we're driving up in an appropriate car. He assures me that he can bluff his way through any market-ing-based job questions and refrain from—'

'No.' She stops me. 'I meant that you've been dating for eight months, right? Does Evan know where Robert took you for your first date? Which side of the bed you prefer? What your parents do for a living? If you snore or not? Who your best friend at school was? What's he getting you for Christmas?'

I stop drinking. I freeze.

'Does he know what films you like, what makes you laugh, how old your siblings are? These are all things that he should know after eight months.'

'OK, I get it!' I reply, just as the bell rings. 'I'll talk to him when I get home.'

My palms feel sweaty. I'm in full panic mode. I want to rip that jar of Nutella from Gwyneth's hand and com-fort-eat myself into a coma. Evan knows where we went for my birthday, but he doesn't know when my birthday is. Fuck! We're never going to pull this off.

Alice sees the panic on my face and squeezes my arm. 'Hey, relax. Look, I'll see you back in here at half one and I'll help you make a list. Just remember, not only does he need to know everything about you, but also everything you know about Robert.'

'Yes.'

And you only have until Thursday ... Tick-tock, tick-tock ...' She smiles mischievously at me before heading back to class.

Ugh, she's the devil.

I stop off at Waterstones on my way home to buy books for everyone for Christmas, except for Patrick, who thinks reading is a waste of his gaming time and has requested vouchers instead. Once inside, I remove my scarf and slowly wander around, browsing the displays and feeling like I'm among friends. So many authors who inspired, shaped, shocked and delighted me in one place and not one of them is aware of the impact they had on my life. If the Brontë sisters were still alive, I'd be fangirling the shit out of them.

I buy Iona the new Harper Lee; Mum gets Brian Blessed; for Dad, Frederick Forsyth; Patrick's wife gets Jon Ronson and I buy myself *The Year of Yes* by Shonda Rhimes, which I will lovingly wrap and Evan will give to me on Christmas morning, along with the unopened bottle of Chanel Kara brought me back from her honeymoon. For appearances' sake, he can have the Armani shirt I bought for Robert and intend to return when we get back to London.

An hour and several impulse purchases from Paperchase later, I admit defeat and declare my Christmas shopping finished for another year. It's dark and cold as I trek back to the flat, bags in hand, and I can't help wondering how things would have gone if Robert hadn't been married – how genuinely excited I'd be about our first Christmas together. Instead, there is an ever-increasing sinking feeling in the pit of my stomach because we only have one day left. One day to get our story straight. One day to perfect our happy faces. One day to become the perfect couple.

'Emily, we've been at it for four hours. I need a break.'

Evan stands up and stretches his legs, while I sit on his bedroom floor, surrounded by Post-it notes, flash cards and Starburst wrappers. 'Take five, then,' I say grudgingly. 'But we still have lots to cover.'

'Fucking teachers,' he mumbles under his breath, then leaves to get us some drinks.

Evan's room is not what I expected. For a start, it's tidy: clothes hung up, bed made, no underwear strewn all over the floor. Most surprisingly, there are no posters of half-naked glamour models, no football colours, no beer-can towers – nothing. He's a disgrace to all students. Our rooms are identical, down to the en suite, but, where I have a loveseat, he has a large desk with an expensive-looking desktop computer complete with LCD television screen and various games consoles. Now, that I *did* expect.

'Nice computer,' I remark when he returns. 'And your room is surprisingly un-student-like. Where's the bong? Where's the crusty clothing pile?'

He hands me a bottle of Stella. 'Emily, I'm not a student. I'm twenty-nine, for God's sake. I left uni years ago.'

'Oh. I'm sorry,' I reply, slightly confused. 'I just assumed . . . I mean, you live with students, you're never dressed like you have a proper job and, well, you're noisy as fuck when everyone else is trying to sleep.'

He shrugs and passes me the bottle opener. 'Who do you get your judgemental side from, then?'

I laugh. 'My mum. My sister is worse than me, though. Be thankful you're not pretending to go out with her. So, what *do* you do for a living? That's some computer set-up. Are you a hacker? Are you Mr Robot?'

He sits on the floor beside me. 'Let's focus on what Robert does. If I tell you, you'll be overwhelmed with admiration and forget why we're here.'

I smile. He's obviously embarrassed by what he does, so I don't force the issue. 'Fine. OK, I think you have the marketing spiel down – very impressive, by the way. I have no idea whether it's bullshit or not, so that's a good sign.'

He raises his bottle.

'OK. Quick fire. When is your birthday?'

'Thirty-first of February.'

'Evan . . .'

'I'm kidding! The twenty-first.'

'When is my birthday?'

'Halloween. You're thirty-eight.'

'Correct. Who is my favourite singer?'

'That depends on your mood; though, at the moment, you are loving Sia.'

'Corr—'

'Because she is odd, like you.'

'Shut up. Next question: who is my best mate in the whole world?'

'Caroline.'

'No. KARA!' I scroll through my Facebook friends and show Evan her picture. 'Look at this face. We all had lunch together in the summer. I've known her since high school.'

'Pretty. Is she single?'

I punch him on the arm. 'Take this seriously!'

'Ouch!' He laughs, rubbing his biceps. 'OK, fine. Next question.'

'What annoys you about me?'

'Everything.'

I glare, hard.

'Your snoring and the fact your feet are always freezing.'

'What do you do that annoys me?'

'I work too much and I consider flowers to be a waste of money.'

I punch the air. 'I think we are done.' I hold my bottle up so he can clink me, but he's shaking his head.

'Hug me instead.'

'What? No.'

He stands up. 'I am your boyfriend. I bought you perfume and a really interesting book for Christmas. I put up with your icy feet. You're going to have to hug me sooner or later.'

I stand up to face him. 'Fine. But that's it. Nothing else. I won't be making out with you in front of my parents, so there's no need to practise that.'

He holds out his arms and I carefully step into him. His head goes to the left of mine and his arms wrap around my shoulders while I face away from him and gently pat his back with one hand. We stay like this for approximately three seconds before he pulls away, laughing.

'And this is what I was afraid of. You have hugged before, right?'

I shake myself off. 'Well, I wasn't prepared! You've turned a hug into a *thing*, now. You made me nervous.'

'If we do that awkward fucking shambles of a hug in front of your family, they'll never let you live it down. You should be giving me running-jump hugs, not whatever the hell that was.'

'Agh, I know! OK, hug me again,' I insist. 'We're going to hug until it comes naturally.'

'Emily, you're moving around like you're getting ready to defend your heavyweight title. It *should* come naturally. It's just a cuddle.'

We move in again and this time we interlock arms and heads properly. He squeezes me a little and my entire body is pressed against his. I start to pull away, but he's still squeezing.

'Stop squirming, Emily. Hold your position, soldier. When it doesn't feel weird anymore, we can stop.'

We stand in silence.

'Evan, I can smell your skin.'

'Yeah, all right, Miggs. Are you implying that I stink?'

'No. You smell like soap. We're just closer than I had anticipated.'

'Well, your hair smells like onions,' he replies, sniffing my head. 'You smell like a hot-dog van.'

'Sorry. Toby was frying them at dinner.'

'It's not entirely unpleasant.'

I start sniggering. A snigger that turns into a full-body shudder.

'What are you laughing at?' he asks.

'Miggs.'

He starts to laugh too. To be fair, the *Silence of the Lambs* reference wasn't even *that* funny, but the sheer ridiculousness of our situation has made us mildly hysterical.

When we eventually calm down, I move my head and rest it on his shoulder. I snuggle in a little. This isn't so bad, really, I think to myself. Weird, perhaps, but not entirely—

'I think we're good,' he suddenly announces, in a slightly broken voice. 'We have mastered the hug.' He pulls away sharply and checks his watch. He isn't wearing one, so he looks for his phone. 'It's almost midnight. Let's call it a night; I have to pack.' His face is flushed and he looks uneasy.

'Sure; fine,' I reply, grabbing my things from the floor. 'The car is being delivered at eight a.m., so be ready before then.'

'Yep, I'll see you then. Night, Emily.'

One minute we're hugging and laughing, and the next I'm back in my flat with a fistful of Post-it notes. Bloody hell, does my hair smell that bad? He couldn't get me out of there quick enough.

I brush my teeth, flannel my face until it squeaks and get into bed. Unlike Evan, I'm organised. My case is packed, presents are wrapped, phone and iPad are currently charging and my comfy travel clothes are laid out over the back of my snuggle chair. All I have to do in the morning is wash the onion smell out of my hair and I'm good to go. Given that tomorrow is the first day of our four-day farce, I feel unexpectedly composed – apprehensive, perhaps, but not the panic-stricken mess I thought I'd be. Maybe, just maybe, we can make this work.

CHAPTER TWELVE

DAY 1

The next time I see Evan, he's sitting on his suitcase in the hall, like Eva fucking Peron, drinking coffee from a travel flask.

'All set?' he chirps. 'I've brought some snacks for the journey.' He lightly kicks the carrier bag beside his foot, drawing my attention to the stash of crisps and sweets he's either bought or nicked from Tesco. 'Oh, and I made a playlist for the car. You can't have a road trip without good music.'

'Evan, you're not going on your bloody holidays. We're not Thelma and Louise! This journey up will be the perfect opportunity to go over everything again; we're not wasting it singing power ballads.'

'They're not power ballads . . . Well, not *all* of them . . .'

I reach back into the flat and pull out my suitcase, closing the door behind me. 'The car will be here in a few minutes,'

I inform him. 'We'd best go downstairs and wait for it – you know how arsey people get about double-parking.'

I bend over to sort the zip on my case, aware that my recently washed jeans feel stiff and tight. I probably should have worn my cargo pants.

'I like your trainers,' he compliments. 'Converse?'

I nod. I love these trainers. They're like comfort food for my feet.

He looks at them again. 'I thought throwback Thursday was limited to social media, but it appears I was wrong.'

'Evan, I've had quite enough of men having any kind of opinion on my footwear.'

He laughs. 'Oh, I forgot about that. I imagine Robert wasn't wanking over your high-tops, though . . .'

'Leave my trainers *alone*, you little twerp!' I storm over to the lift and press the button. If he's going to taunt me for the next four days, only one of us will be driving back.

Evan follows me over and stands beside me. He buttons up the front of his jacket. It's a very nice jacket. It's a navy, woollen pea coat and it suits him. My fake boyfriend has taste; that's one thing less for my family to mock. He gives me a gentle nudge. 'You know I'm only winding you up, don't you? Your trainers are great. You suit them.'

'Can we talk about something else, please?'

'Sure . . . OK . . . Er, do you want to take the first driving shift or shall I?' he asks. 'We should swap halfway. York, maybe?'

'I'll take the first half,' I answer. 'I'll get us through England.'

'Why can't I go first?' he whines, as expected. He wants first shot of the car. Boys are so bloody predictable.

'Because your driving skills might be shite,' I reply. 'If you're going to crash and kill me, I'd rather it was in Scotland, with my people.'

The doors open and we wheel the contents of our lives for the next four days into the lift.

'I'd rather be haunting the Scottish countryside than the M1,' I add, pressing the ground-floor button. It's sticky. Why the hell is it sticky? Seconds later, I'm hunting in my case for a wet wipe.

'Christ, that's morose,' he replies. 'I'm adding "ghastly in the morning" to the list of things that annoy me about you. I have a feeling this list may be in the hundreds by the time we get to Scotland.'

'You can add whatever you like, but only if I can add "uses the word *ghastly*" to yours. Oooh ... ghastly. You sound like my mum.' Finding a facial wipe in my toiletry bag, I speedily clean the stickiness from my finger and close my case.

'Funny. Does your mum also use the word "zip it"?'

'No, because that's two words.'

An amused Trevor watches us emerge from the lift, still squabbling as we park our suitcases beside the front door. I pop outside to see if our car has arrived, but there's no sign, so I hurry back inside, out of the cold, overhearing

Trevor saying that he's never been to Glasgow and we should have a nice time. Confused, I thank him as Evan comes over to stand beside me.

'Glasgow?' I whisper. 'You know we're not going to Glasgow, right?'

He leans in. 'I just told Trevor that because I couldn't remember the name of your hick village,' he teases. 'What's it called? Melba? Mellow? Mel—'

'Melrose!' I despair. 'And it's a town. They filmed some of *The Da Vinci Code* there.' I smile as I remember Mum telling me that she'd gone down to Melrose Abbey, trying to catch a glimpse of Tom Cruise. She stood there for three hours before she realised it was Tom Hanks.

I stood there in the pissing rain for Forrest bloody Gump. Never again.

Evan steps aside to let Mrs Holborn and her leaking terrier pass, before replying, 'Ah, yes. Melrose. But you do live on a farm, right?'

I furrow my brow. 'No? Why on earth would you think that?'

'You said you grew up in a farmhouse!'

I roll my eyes. 'Yes, but that's entirely different from growing up on a working farm. Jesus! Do I look like I have a clue about agriculture?'

He grins. 'Well, how was I supposed to know? When I think of the Scottish Borders, I think farming and hills and hayrides. I imagined you all chopping wood and stepping over cowpats – maybe burning a wicker man or six before breakfast.'

He thinks we're country bumpkins. My sister might just eat him alive.

'Sweet ride alert!' Evan yells, peering out the front door, and, sure enough, parked outside on the street is our car. Our big, gleaming, black Mercedes. I instruct Evan to bring the cases, while I go and sort out the paperwork. A cheery man in a beanie hat asks us both to show our photo ID, sign on the dotted line and, after a quick tour of the car, we're handed the keys.

I climb into the driver's seat as Evan loads the cases in the boot, allowing myself to get secretly excited by the pretty car while he's not looking. I've been in Robert's car loads of times, but it's different being in the driving seat. Everything is swish. The leather is soft, the headrest is moulded and there's not a Nickelback CD in sight. While I'm busy stroking the dashboard, Evan jumps into the passenger seat, slamming the door behind him.

'You did me proud, Emily,' he gushes. 'This is definitely the next car I'm going to buy. I was torn between this and the BMW 5 series.'

I start up the car, hearing it purr. 'Sure it was. And I was torn between a Lamborghini and a private jet. Put your seat belt on.'

I reach over, switch on the satnav, which quickly loads, and type in my parents' postcode.

Distance: 411.3 miles. Driving time estimated: 7 hours, 19 minutes.

I sigh. With traffic jams and service-station breaks, it's going to take closer to nine hours. Still, I guess I can sleep while Evan drives, or catch up on some reading. I buckle my seat belt as he activates the car's Bluetooth, ready to connect to his playlist, which no doubt consists of every guitar band from the nineties and a few obscure groups I won't have heard of and will definitely hate. I hold my hand up, halting his progress.

'Woah! Not so fast. We need some rules.'

He stops scrolling. 'What rules? Don't go all teacher on me, Emily. I'm a grown-ass man!'

I do my best not to smile at his rubbish American accent. 'When I'm driving, I want my music. Not yours. I don't want to have to endure the entire Oasis back-catalogue while I'm behind the wheel. When you take over, you can play what you want. Deal?'

He reluctantly agrees, putting his phone away for later, while I connect mine and press *play*.

'I have a horrible feeling you're going to make me listen to –' the music starts – 'Christmas songs. I fucking knew it.' He throws his head back against the seat as Bing Crosby softly croons out a winter wonderland.

'They'll make us feel festive!' I inform him gleefully, putting the car into first gear. 'But, don't fret, there's some Sia, some Kate Bush, Adele, a whole lot of random pop, some dance, and I've even thrown in some Proclaimers – just for you.'

'Oh, kill me now. I'm not even kidding. Just push me out and run me over.'

'Too late,' I declare. 'We're out of here.'

I pull away from the side of the road and turn right at the end of the street, as per the satnav's instructions. It's eight twenty-five a.m. and we're about to leave London behind us. I have jingling bells in one ear and a sulking man, asking for a quick death, in the other.

Here goes nothing.

CHAPTER THIRTEEN

'Jesus Christ, Evan – do you have to sing along to *every* song?'

For a man who started this journey hating my music library, Evan's been vocally destroying every track that's come on. I mean, how the hell does he know every single word to 'I Heard a Rumour' by Bananarama? He's doing this on purpose.

'I know you're secretly impressed by both my singing ability and my musical knowledge,' he says, resting his arm against the passenger window. 'I'm more surprised by your lack of participation. You've barely hummed a note since we set off an hour ago, unless that ridiculously high-pitched sneeze counts?'

Normally, I am the queen of the singalong, especially on car journeys, but I don't trust this man enough to fully relax in front of him. I cannot sing for shit and I can definitely do without being ridiculed by a man who's just eaten strawberry laces for breakfast. Besides, belting out tunes hasn't exactly been my top priority. I've been too busy concentrating on navigating the streets of London in a car I'm not used to driving. I'm just grateful I haven't stalled, crashed or knocked down a cyclist.

'I've been focusing on things like not driving under the wheels of a bus,' I reply solemnly. 'Let's hope you're as considerate when we swap over at York.'

'Man, you're chilly this morning,' he moans. 'I'm switching your heated seat on; it might defrost you a little.'

I sniff nonchalantly and continue behind a line of slow-moving traffic on Islington High Street. In front of us is a light-green people-carrier with a huge Alsatian staring at us from the back seat, seemingly transfixed by Evan's current enthusiastic rendition of 'Uptown Funk'. I lean over to my bag and take out a bottle of water – one which appears to have been sealed shut with superglue. I motion to Evan to help me open it and he obliges.

'I'm so strong,' he boasts. 'See – without me, you'd have been stuck, staring back at the dog, all alone and thirsty.'

I take a long drink before placing it in my cup holder. 'No, Evan,' I reply. 'I'd be on a train, reading my book, possibly in first class, where they have complimentary coffee and quiet, boy-free carriages.'

'Um, I don't think they do.'

'It's my fantasy; they'll have whatever I say they have.'

'That dog is creeping me out,' he says, giving a shudder. 'Your parents have a dog, don't they? Is it like Cujo, there?'

'It's a Great Dane called Pacino,' I reply, throwing a

'back off' look at the driver who's trying to cut in front of me. 'He's a sweetheart, but awfully clingy. If he loves you, he'll follow you everywhere, even to the bathroom . . . HEY, PRICK FACE! INDICATING DOES NOT MEAN YOU HAVE RIGHT OF WAY!'

'Great Danes are huge!' Evan announces, peering past me to frown at the obnoxious driver. 'Cool name, though. We never had animals growing up; our house was too small, even for a cat.'

'You grew up in London?'

'No, Brighton. Not the rich part, though – Whitehawk.'

'Never heard of it. Rough area?'

He shrugs. 'It gets a bad rap, but I was happy there as a kid. When you're young, you don't consider it better or worse than anywhere else – it's all you know.'

'Your parents still there?' I enquire, trying to contain my road rage. 'Won't they miss you over Christmas?'

He gives a grunt. 'Nah. I haven't seen either of my parents in years. They were pretty useless. Mum stayed at home, Dad was a school caretaker. He kept his wages and she kept her mouth shut. I don't remember much, but I remember that they liked their drugs and booze . . . My gran raised me.'

'Your gran? Is she still around?' I ask.

'No, she died in 2004. I came to London the following year.' He turns away and looks out of the window. 'I don't talk about it much.'

'Oh. Right,' is all I can say. I'm not sure how to react. This was not the upbringing I imagined Evan to have had. I pictured weary but loving parents, who put up with his tantrums, encouraged his laddish behaviour and funded his gap year in Bali or Bondi Beach.

'I hear Dad was arrested for armed robbery a few years ago. Turned over a local bookies. Shot a policeman in the leg.'

'Bloody hell!' I gasp, throwing him a shocked look. 'Are you serious?'

He slowly answers, 'Nope . . . Not at all. Well, my gran did die in 2004, but my parents raised me. They're both doctors. Emigrated to Canada two years ago. I'm going to visit in February, actually – it's ski season.'

'Oh, you little shit!' I exclaim. 'I almost felt sorry for you.'

He reaches into his bag and pulls out a bottle of Ribena. 'Sorry for me?' he says, turning the cap. 'The look on your face was more horrified than pitying. Worried that you might be taking home some working-class criminal's son, eh?'

'Says the man who thinks my family practises pagan burning rituals . . . You must have a low opinion of me. I couldn't care less what your parents do for a living.'

'I'm guessing that your family care, though,' he replies. 'Otherwise, you wouldn't have made me memorise the fact that Robert's parents both attended Cambridge.' He puts on a fake plummy accent. 'Mummy studied theology and Daddy studied linguistics. I studied business, of course, because they paid for it and there wasn't a shoe-shagging course avai—'

I slap him on the arm and he laughs at my reaction, looking very pleased with himself. I can't help but laugh too.

'My family don't care about any of that!' I insist. 'Well, my brother and my dad don't. My mother has her moments and my sister ... well, yes, she's a tad elitist, but ... oh, fuck it – it doesn't matter, anyway. They're not judging you; they're judging Robert. Just don't be *you* and you'll be fine.'

I didn't intend for that to sound as cruel as it did, but he doesn't react, so neither do I. Instead, I turn up the Waitresses on the stereo and continue pushing forward through the traffic.

Eventually, we hit the M1 and I start to relax a little. It's a bright morning – clear skies all around and straight roads from here to Scotland, with no bike riders wobbling perilously into my path. Plus, there's the added fancy-car bonus of cruise control, which makes me feel like Knight Rider. Evan has been quiet for a while now, gazing out of the window, deep in thought, most likely preparing himself mentally for the next few days.

'There's a service station in about twenty miles,' I say, snapping him out of his daydream. 'I could use some coffee.'

He nods and yawns at the same time, which in turn makes me yawn too, but I try to stifle it, making my face contort and my ears go all funny inside. I cannot give in to the yawns yet – I'll catch some zeds when Evan takes the wheel. It seems he has the same idea.

'Just give me a nudge when we're there,' he requests, balling up his jumper to lean against. 'I'm knackered.'

I don't protest. I'm happier not forcing conversation with someone who just makes shit up, anyway. Book-maker-robbing caretaker father, indeed. Next he'll be telling me that he's a special agent for the FBI, or his best mate is James Franco, or that his legs are made entirely from bacon. Anything is possible.

I exit left after junction eleven and drive into the service-station car park. A premature stop, perhaps – we still have miles to go – but I underestimated my need for caffeine before I left this morning. Evan is snoozing against the window and doesn't stir until I yell, 'WAKEY WAKEY!' into his right ear. He tries to swot me like a fly.

'For God's sake!' he yelps. 'I nearly wet myself.'

'Come on, Sleeping Beauty,' I chirp, 'you can buy me a latte.'

He pulls on his jacket. 'Yes, ma'am. Anything else? A pastry? Sausage roll?'

'Yeah, maybe. Something buttery.'

'*Last Tango in Paris* buttery, or—'

'Yes, Evan.' I sigh, rolling my eyes. 'That's exactly what

I want. It's like you read my mind. Can you tell what I'm thinking now?'

'Get the fuck out?'

'Well done.'

We exit the car and head inside, passing a family with four small children, who all look as miserable as each other. We make our way over to Costa Coffee and I grab a grubby-looking table while Evan goes to order. We've only driven forty miles, but it feels like more. Kara and I drove back to Melrose a few years ago and it was a hoot. We didn't annoy each other. We didn't make inappropriate, Marlon-Brando-based sex jokes. We sang in harmony to every track on Madonna's *True Blue* album and played sweary I spy, where every answer was, 'A fucking car.' That journey was fun. This is anything but.

'One latte and one almond croissant.' Evan slides the tray on to the table and smiles at me. I immediately become suspicious. 'Why are you smiling? Did you spit in my coffee? Evan, did you lick my pastry?'

'Dammit, Emily, I've only just got the butter image out of my head.'

'Oh, grow up. Not everything is a bloody innuendo.'

He takes the lid off his coffee and stirs. I can smell the hazelnut syrup. 'To answer your questions – no, I haven't done anything sinister to your food, and I'm smiling because I have a plan.'

'Oh?' I reply, taking the lid off my latte. His smells

better than mine. I wish I'd asked for syrup. 'What plan is that, then?'

'We're still far too awkward with each other,' he begins. 'At a push, we could pass as friends, but not as a couple – you agree?'

'Yeah . . . So . . . ?'

'So we need to get to know each other. Not just the crap I've memorised; I mean *really* feel comfortable with each other. We need to be able to make each other laugh. We need to be able to look at each other like we've shared our most intimate thoughts and secrets.' He motions behind him. 'We need to look like that couple by the door.'

I move my gaze in the direction of his head bob and see a couple, late forties, having breakfast. He's laughing loudly while she speaks and is looking at her like she's the most enchanting creature he's ever seen. Glancing down, I see her legs are stretched out towards his and their shoes are touching, reassuringly brushing against each other every now and again. These are two people who adore each other.

I take a bite from my croissant and slowly chew.

'See their feet?' he asks. 'They could be saying nothing and you'd know they were into each other. That's the look we need to convey.'

I know he's right, but I'm in no hurry to let him know that I know that.

'And you can stop that, for a start.'

'What? Eating?'

'No, that *attitude*. And those *fuck off* eyes you make at me. What's your problem? You don't like me, I get that, but you're going to have to start acting like you do.'

I put down my coffee, trying to keep my face as neutral as possible. 'OK. What's the big plan, then? How do we fix this? I'm not playing footsie with you in public, sunshine.'

'Well,' he begins, with a mischievous look on his face, 'I thought we could play a game.'

'A game?' I reply, my face squinting in confusion. 'Is the game called *shut up*? Because I like that game. You go first.'

'I was thinking more of truth or dare.'

'You're not serious?'

'Totally. By the time we reach Scotland, we'll know *and like* each other just enough so that you won't overreact, or even blink an eye, when I do THIS!'

He whips the pastry from my plate and takes a huge bite.

'Give me that!' I say, trying to grab it back.

'Couples share food.' He laughs, fighting me off. 'You see, this Chinese burn you're giving me – ouch! – isn't indicative of someone who's in love with me.'

People are starting to gawp at us, so I reluctantly sit myself back down on the plastic chair, allowing Evan to finish my pastry. I never took any of this into account when I asked him to participate in this stupid plan. I thought he'd have to pretend to be Robert and I'd just be me, but his analysis of the situation is correct. I'm going to have to be fake in love with the fake Robert.

I take a deep breath, then ask, 'Truth –' his face lights up – 'or dare?'

He throws his head back and laughs. 'I'm so happy right now! OK . . . Truth.'

I haven't played this game since my early teens, when questions revolved around whether you'd ever been felt up and who you fancied most at school. What exactly do adults ask each other?

'Have you ever stolen anything?' is my first question. Pathetic, I know.

'Of course,' he replies. 'I'm dangerous. My most recent theft was a carrier bag from Sainsbury's.'

'So you didn't pay the 5p bag charge. Wow, it's like I'm sitting across from Al Capone.'

'Fine – same question to you, smart-arse.'

I take a sip of coffee. 'Most recently? Food from my room-mates, but they do the same to me. In my younger years . . . A bracelet from a shop in the high street, when I was twelve. I never wore it, though, in case my mum asked where it came from.'

He applauds. 'The most pointless crime ever. Well done.'

I bow my head in thanks. 'OK. Truth or dare?'

'You're enjoying this now, aren't you? I'll take another truth.'

I drum my fingers on the side of my cup. 'What's your most embarrassing moment?'

'Just today, or in my entire life?' He pauses and thinks for a moment before taking off his coat. 'To be clear, we keep whatever we say private, yeah?'

'Of course,' I reply. 'Ooh, now I'm intrigued.'

He runs his hand through his hair. 'I was nineteen, dating this girl, Clara . . . Clara Ferguson, who was amazing and completely out of my league. Anyway, one night I got horribly, *horribly* drunk and I pissed the bed.'

My eyebrows sink. I was expecting something much more humiliating. 'That's it? I've known loads of men—'

He holds up his hand to shush me. 'Yes, but we were in bed together at the time. I had my leg wrapped around her . . . She practically slapped me awake, she was so livid.'

I begin to snigger. 'You peed on your sleeping girlfriend? That's disgusting.'

He nods sheepishly. 'She never spoke to me again. It was pretty humiliating.'

I raise my cup towards him. 'Credit where it's due, Mr Grant. There aren't many men who would admit to being such a disgusting beast . . .'

He raises his cup to meet mine. 'I wouldn't get too smug, if I were you,' he replies. 'Same question to you, Miss Carson.'

Bollocks. I'm avoiding that question at all costs.

Flashbacks from the Glastonbury pooing incident of 2003 appear in my mind. Agh, go away!

'Hang on . . . Um . . . You didn't say truth or dare!' I say in a panicked tone, trying to stall. 'I mean, rules is rules.'

He rolls his eyes. 'OK. Fine. Truth or—'

'But before you do, I'm getting another pastry.'

I dash quickly to the counter and pretend to browse the overhead menu. There is no fucking way I'm admitting my most embarrassing moment. As far as uncontrollable bodily functions go, mine beats his hands down. Or should that be 'pants down'? Because I, Emily Carson, shat myself at Glastonbury. Even the thought of saying it out loud to another human being makes me sweat. I'll need to take a dare; there's nothing else for it.

I buy a toasted crumpet from a sullen-looking barista and return to the table, ready to bite the bullet. He gapes at me while I spread on some butter and jam, but I don't make eye contact. I'm hoping he'll just vanish into thin air and all of this will be over.

'Truth or dare, Emily? I'm waiting . . .'

'Dare.'

He bangs on the table and laughs. 'I knew you'd say that! The whole point of this game is to be completely truthful, remember that.'

'Yes, I know.'

'And to open up to me . . .'

'Yes. Still "dare",' I reply.

'You can't say "dare" forever. You're going to have to tell me a truth eventually.'

I don't say anything else. I just munch on my crumpet while he silently schemes. I can hear 'Fairytale of New York' begin playing over the speakers and feel sorry for the staff who will be forced to listen to it on loop all day long.

'I dare you . . .'

I steel myself.

'And you have to do this. No backing out. Promise?'

'Sure. Whatever . . . This coffee is amazing. I wonder what roast it —'

'Sing along to this. Out loud. Publicly.' He moves his hands around in the air in time to the music.

I nearly choke. 'What? Uh-uh. Nooooo way . . . Anyway, I don't know the words,' I lie.

He claps his hands in delight. 'Oh, even better!'

I shake my head. 'I'll be doing exactly none of that.'

'Now, Emily.' He frowns. 'I took my turn. You chose dare. Don't be a chicken. You can do this . . .'

'B-but I'll get thrown o—'

'Standing, please.'

I bite my bottom lip and have a quick scan around the café to size up my blissfully unaware audience: the loved-up couple at the door, solo man in a checked shirt at the counter, family of three at the table to my right and a woman on her phone, who has just walked in. Oh, surely he's not going to make me do this? My pleading looks are ignored as he relaxes back into his chair and watches me squirm.

I rise slowly from my chair, head down, staring at my feet. Evan leans forward as I begin to sing along to the Irish folk beat, my cheeks burning to the point of combustion.

'I can't quite hear you,' he says, holding his hand to his ear.

What an arsehole. I scowl back and clear my throat, which makes an even louder off-key note leave my mouth and float towards the unsuspecting family of three. First to turn around and look is the small boy, who pulls the sleeve of his dad's Christmas jumper and points at me. His father, obviously assuming I'm either drunk or mentally unwell, turns his son back around, but now the mother is staring and I'm ready to crumple. I smile weakly at her in an attempt to quell her justifiable fears that I might just freak the fuck out and murder everyone, but now it looks like I'm serenading her. Oh, God, here comes the chorus again; does this song *ever* end?

My pain is obvious; my humiliation, evident – but this isn't enough for Evan. Evan told me his piss-the-bed story and now he wants me to suffer.

'What were the bells doing?!' he shouts, louder than necessary, and with that, it's all eyes on me. Staff, happy couple, woman on phone, lone man, family – everyone.

Just when I'm about to see if it's possible to commit suicide with half a crumpet, I spot the man in the checked shirt approaching me. I almost breathe a sigh of relief because, if he asks me to shut my face, I'll have no choice but to end this dare and scamper back to the car. But he doesn't look annoyed. He's smiling.

He's singing.

I throw a look at Evan, who's swaying in his chair, gesturing wildly for me to seize the moment.

And, right there, in the middle of the coffee shop, I duet with a stranger holding a straw as a microphone. He sings the Shane MacGowan part with such enthusiasm, it's hard not to follow his lead. And we go for it, big time, gradually bewitching those around us – the small boy is dancing, the mother is laughing and the woman on her phone is still ignoring us all, but I'm sure, deep down inside, she's with us. Had this been at any other time of the year, we'd have been forcibly removed and barred from the premises, but, at Christmas, fleeting moments of insanity are welcomed.

As the song ends and the stranger stops twirling me around, the couple applaud and everyone goes about their business like nothing happened. I sink back down into my chair, while Evan beams at me, like a proud parent.

'What the hell are you grinning at?' I snarl, feeling rather stunned by the whole event. My hands are shaking. I think I need a drink.

'That was amazing. I have literally never been happier.'

'You're easily pleased. Can we just—'

'You cannot sing. At all.'

'Shut up.'

'I'm sorry.' He's not, though. He's still smirking.

'I'd like to leave now,' I insist, taking my coat from the back of my chair. 'And never, ever return.'

He drinks the last of his coffee while standing up and follows on behind me as I make a quick escape, towards the main bathrooms. They're very bright, very cold and stink of cleaning products – a harsh change from the cosy, coffee-aroma-filled café I've just left. I lock myself in a cubicle and give a little delighted squeal. And then another. For someone who can't even do karaoke without a tequila drip, I've surprised myself. As I wash my hands and stare at myself in the mirror, I understand why Evan was smiling at me. Sure, making a fool of myself is a big part of it, but perhaps it also has something to do with how surprising I am. Perhaps I am just a little, teeny bit extraordinary, after all . . .

CHAPTER FOURTEEN

'You did not lose your virginity at twenty. What are you? A nun? You're such a liar.'

'It's true! I swear!' I insist. 'Danny Bradford, in his parents' room—'

'With the candlestick?'

'And it was the most underwhelming experience of my life. A bit like that joke.'

Two hours on and our truth-or-dare game is still going strong. So far, I've learnt that Evan lost his virginity at fifteen, has an irrational fear of bluebottles, can do a reasonably good impression of Christopher Walken, would like at least one child, preferably a girl, and designs computer games for a living.

'What, like *Super Mario*?' I ask, before pausing. 'Is that even still a thing?' I start humming the familiar tune. 'Once upon a time, I had an Atari, you know.'

He smirks. 'It is. I can see you're up to date on your gaming . . . Not a big fan?'

'I'm one hundred years old, so no,' I reply. 'My brother likes his games, though. He does something computery for a living too . . .'

'Does he? Like what?'

'I have no idea what he does and, to be honest, the less I know about my brother, the better. I recently discovered he phones people while he's naked in the shower. I'm sure you'll have loads to talk about, though . . . Joysticks and Lara Croft . . .'

'Um, well, *I* would have loads to discuss with him,' he replies. 'But would Robert? I don't think Mr Big-Shot Marketing Director would spend his free time gaming. He's probably too busy having posh wanks and playing polo.'

Robert. Duh. Of course. Strangely enough, I haven't thought about him in a while. I wonder if he's miserable. 'You're right,' I reply firmly. 'I'm losing my focus, here. I need to get back on track. You're Robert. *You* are *Robert*!'

I see signs for Hull ahead and get in lane. The further north we go, the more my stomach starts to churn. It's a mixture of excitement and nerves. I'd be lying if I said there wasn't part of me looking forward to seeing my family, because, despite all their infuriating habits, no one hugs you quite like your clan. I'm eager to make good time, but it's lunchtime and we'll need to stop again to let Evan take over the driving duties. I swear, if he turns out to be a boy racer, he'll be continuing the rest of the journey from inside the boot.

*

Evan makes a dash for the toilets as soon as we arrive at the next motorway services and I do the same before wandering off to peruse the horribly overpriced sandwiches and snacks available for lunch. Everything is pre-packed and somewhat pathetic-looking, but I'm so hungry I could eat a buttered monkey, so my food fussiness is at an all-time low. I pick up a packet of prawn mayo sandwiches, meticulously checking the sell-by date, before joining the checkout queue. I'll get some tea for the car journey before I go.

There are three people in front of me, all looking underwhelmed and road weary. The man directly in front has decided that the ham salad baguette is the food least likely to kill him and the woman in front of him has chosen to buy six packets of crisps, making her my soulmate.

I feel my phone buzz in my pocket. I bet it's Evan, to tell me he's in Burger King.

We've just arrived. Are you and lover boy en route? What's taking you so long?

I sigh. Unlike me, Patrick chose to stay closer to home after university; in fact, no one thought he'd ever move out. He's the type of man who can handle complex computer coding problems, but is incapable of working a washing machine.

Distance is what's taking so long, Patrick – you only live down the bloody road. We'll be there soon.

I estimate that 'soon' will be at least another zillion hours because I still have to wait for Evan to reappear, eat food, put petrol in the car and drive the remaining hundred and fifty miles. I'm now next in the queue, so I send Evan a quick text to find out where he is and put my phone in my pocket.

'Six pounds forty, please.'

'For one sandwich?'

I grudgingly hand the cashier a ten-pound note, wondering what magical ingredients were used to make such an expensive, small sandwich. Maybe the bread was baked in a diamond oven. Maybe the prawns were hand fucking picked by King Triton himself. Who knows? It's a mystery. The cashier hands me my change and smiles, telling me to have a lovely Christmas, and I force a smile back in return. Christmas at the Carsons' is never lovely – it's just compulsory . . . and if the man who's currently walking towards me, wearing a Burger King crown, can convince my family he's not an utter twat, I'll be happy.

'Truth or dare, Evan,' I ask as he slides up beside me.

'I haven't taken a dare yet,' he replies. 'Go on.'

'I dare you to take that hat off and pretend you're a grown-up,' I growl through gritted teeth. 'I look like your fucking carer.'

I'm not entirely sure if his hurt face is real or not, but he whips his crown off his head and throws it into a nearby bin. 'You really have no sense of fun.' He sniffs, petulantly. 'And the capacity for silliness is what separates the good guys from the wankers. Remember that.'

We head back to the car and drive across to the petrol station, where Evan fills up the car and I go to pay. The snow is beginning to fall again as I climb into the passenger side and buckle myself in, praying that Evan won't drive like a tool the rest of the way and give me heart failure.

But, thankfully, his driving is fine – good, even – and I feel relaxed enough to close my eyes and try to get some shut-eye before we get to Scotland. The motion of the car is soothing and I start to drift off, listening to the low hum of the engine.

'Oh my God, Emily – we're going to CRASH!'

A small scream flies from my mouth as I sit bolt upright in my seat. Evan's laughter doesn't stop for quite some time.

I whack him on the side of the arm. 'You shit. You utter shit. What the hell is wrong with you?!'

'I couldn't resist,' he replies between laughter sobs. 'Aw, mate – your face, though . . .'

'I nearly had a fucking heart attack. You could have been driving my corpse home for Christmas.'

'You were seriously going to sleep the rest of the way?' he asks, finally controlling his laughter. 'I provided hours of in-car entertainment and I expect the same from you. I expect singing, joke-telling, soul-bearing and—'

'You fell asleep too!' I quickly interrupt. 'And I have given in to all of your demands: the car, truth or dare, sharing food . . . everything. Don't forget that I'm paying you to be here.'

I turn my head towards the window and close my eyes again.

'I feel wounded,' he says quietly.

'You'll get over it,' I reply, eyes still closed.

'And cheap. I feel cheap again.'

'Whatever.'

'I bet this is how Julia Roberts felt in *Pretty Woman*. Not only am I Robert, I'm also Vivian.'

I start to laugh and close my eyes again.

I'm allowed a few more moments of silence before 'It Must Have Been Love', by Roxette, starts blaring from the speakers.

'Ha ha! FINE. You win!' I exclaim. 'Just turn this off. I don't even want to know why this is on your playlist.'

'I have a romantic side,' he replies. 'The ladies love a good ballad.'

'Please, stop talking.'

'I'm kidding. I have Spotify. I just searched for it while your eyes were closed.'

'Oh, God – that's as bad as texting and driving.'

He skips to the next track. 'We're really going to have to work on this uptightness.'

'I'd shift down a gear,' I interrupt, leaning forward. 'Oh, and get into the left lane, we're taking—'

'Will you relax?' he says. 'I'm driving! I have eyes to

read road-signs *and* a satnav giving directions! God, you're such a control freak!'

'I might be a control freak, but at least I don't text and drive!' I yell back.

'I *wasn't* texting!'

'Yeah . . . ? Well . . . "uptightness" is not even a real word.'

We carry on like this for the next few miles, arguing over absolutely nothing, until we make our final service-station stop before home. We both exit the car in a foul mood, heading in the same direction, but without saying a word. Everything is going wrong. How are we going to stand each other for the Christmas holidays if we can't even manage a car journey?

I reapply my make-up in the bathroom, because my mother will find it deeply suspicious that I'm bare-faced or less than perfect in front of my boyfriend. She's the type of woman who wears a full face of make-up to pick up the morning papers from the local shop, run by a man in his eighties with cataracts.

I know you're not bothered about wearing make-up, darling, but it's not for you. It's for the people who need to look at you.

Mum never has this issue with Iona because Iona always looks like a lawyer from *Dynasty*: power suits, blunt bobbed hair, red lips, and suspicious eyes peering at you from under many coats of black eyeliner and spidery lashes. She doesn't miss a trick and she's going to be the hardest one to fool. Christ, if Evan and I carry on like this, even the dog will know we're not a real item.

As the bathroom door swings behind me, I look around for Evan and see him standing outside by the main entrance, looking fed up. His expression doesn't change when he sees me walking towards him.

'Calmed down yet?' he asks. 'Or shall we just have a fist fight and get it out of the way?'

'I'm sorry,' I say, giving him a playful nudge as we walk towards the car. 'I'm just stressed.'

He nudges me back. 'Apology accepted. Although, if I was your real boyfriend, I'd be expecting at least a cuddle to appease me.'

We reach the car and I glance at him as he unlocks it and opens the driver's side.

'Well, seeing as our last attempt at a cuddle was a disaster,' I say, coyly, 'I guess another try wouldn't hurt.'

He holds the door and smiles over at me. 'You sure?'

'I am. In fact, I dare you to hug me again. For at least a minute.'

'How is that even a dare?' He laughs, watching me walk around to his side of the car.

'Because you obviously found it hideous last time; I could tell by the way you practically kicked me out of your flat. This time, you're stuck with me for another three and a half days.'

He shakes his head, but pulls me in close, squeezing

hard, and I give a little giggle. The warmth of his body is welcoming and, for at least a minute, we cuddle the hell out of each other as the snow settles around our feet. No awkwardness remains; we're just two people, hugging in a car park at Christmas.

'Your phone is ringing,' he says softly into my left ear.

'I hear it,' I reply. 'But my arms are comfy like this. I'll phone them back later; it's probably just—'

But before I can finish, Evan reaches into my coat pocket and yanks out my phone. 'Unknown number. Exciting.'

'Give me that back!'

I grab for my phone, but he holds it above his head, swiping the *answer* key.

'Hello? ... Ha ha! Get off! ... Hello, Emily's phone ... Hello? ... This is Robert; who's this? Who?' He hangs up the call and throws the phone on the driver's seat. 'Oh, shit.'

We both stare at the phone. 'Evan? What the ... ? Who was it? What happened?'

The phone starts to ring again. Unknown number.

'You might not want to answer that,' he says, his face now very pale, but I pay no attention, reaching in to retrieve it from the driver's seat. After his reaction, how can I *not* answer it?

'Hello?'

'Emily, it's Robert. Don't hang up. I came to the flat, but your flatmate said you'd already left for Scotland. Who answered the phone? Who's with you?'

'That's none of your business. Don't call me again.'

I hang up and place the phone back into my pocket, then make my way around to the passenger side. I buckle my seat belt in silence and wait for him to start the engine. We move off and join the motorway again to begin the last leg of our journey.

'Sorry,' Evan says awkwardly a few minutes later. 'I did say not to pick up. Please don't let this upset you.'

'Upset me?' I say, before laughing so hard it feels like my face might collapse in on itself. 'You . . . told . . . him . . . you . . . were . . . *him* . . .' The tears are streaming from my eyes now; I'm hysterical.

'What? Stop laughing. I can't hear what you're saying.'

I wipe my eyes on my sleeve. 'He was all, "Who dis?" and you were, like, "This is Robert." Ha ha ha ha ha ha!'

Evan starts to laugh too. 'Stop it! I have to drive.'

'I can't. It's too perfect.'

'I know,' he replies. 'What a head fuck. He sounded really surprised when he heard his own name, never mind another man's voice . . . Hang on . . . Are you crying?'

I sob and nod at the same time, burying my face into my hands.

'Wow,' he says. 'That escalated quickly.'

I try to form some intelligible words between my sniffing and blubbering. 'I don't want to speak to him,' I howl. 'But I need him to know just how much he's hurt me. He needs to see what a mess he's made.'

'He doesn't need to see this,' Evan says gently. 'You shouldn't allow him access to one more second of your life.'

'I know,' I sniff. 'But I just want him to see what actually happens to a person when you fuck with their heart.'

'Does he have Snapchat?' Evans asks. 'I could totally send this to him.'

I giggle-sob.

'Though, you might want to wipe your nose first,' he continues. 'Unless you want to show him both the emotional and the mucus-y mess . . .'

I whack him on the leg and look for a hanky in my bag.

I don't calm down fully until we're fifteen miles shy of the Scottish Borders. I pull down the sun visor, checking under my eyes for mascara stains.

'What do you think he wanted?' Evan asks as I swipe under each eye with a tissue. 'To grovel?'

'Who knows? He probably thinks he can talk his way back into my good books. He forgets that I'm not twenty-one anymore. I don't have years to waste on the wrong person.' I sigh and flip the visor back up. 'Before he dropped his bombshell, I was planning for my future . . . with him. Admittedly, I might have been getting ahead of myself, but I was hopeful. Hope is good. Now, I have no clue what the future holds and whether that future is even in London.'

'You are where you need to be right now,' Evan replies,

staring at the road ahead. 'It's amazing how one moment, or thought, or encounter can change everything. The thought of knowing *exactly* what my future holds is depressing. I want life to surprise me – good or bad.'

'But you must have some idea of where you want to be by the time you're, say, fifty?' I say, turning to face him. 'Unless living with your delightful room-mates forever is your life goal?'

He laughs. 'Hell, no; I've already planned to move from there after New Year! Our company has just finished a big project, so I'm free to roam anywhere.'

'Maybe you'll be in Canada?'

'Why Canada?' he enquires, looking puzzled.

'Didn't you tell me your parents lived there?'

'Yes. Sorry; my brain's on a go-slow. I'm getting tired. Anyway, who knows where I'll be at fifty? Maybe married? Divorced? Living in a penthouse in New York? Maybe broke and working in a bar in Walthamstow, paying child support for three kids? Who knows? Who cares!'

I don't know whether I want to applaud him or shake him.

I lean my head against the window and silently watch the scenery whizz by. It's a little after five p.m., dark now, and the snow is coming down around us. Evan is concentrating hard on the road and looking somewhat anxious, but I have the feeling that it's not the driving conditions making him feel this way.

'So, quick rundown of your family, then,' he says. 'What should I expect?'

'Hmm. Good question,' I reply, turning down the music. 'Let's see. They're all pretty full on. Believe it or not, I'm the laid-back one of my family. I'm the peacekeeper – never the instigator. Anyway, Dad lives for a party and will insist you eat, dance and drink, even if you don't want to. Iona, the lawyer, will get pissed and will tell you confidential shit about her clients. Patrick still lives to torment his twin sister, and his wife, Kim, will come across as quiet and reserved until the booze kicks in, and then they're both like teenagers on a spring break. Seriously, we caught them shagging in Dad's shed last year. Mum, like Dad, loves to party, and, despite knocking back a gallon of gin, she's always the last one standing.'

'I think I can handle that.' Evan smirks. 'Could be worse.'

Bless him. He thinks I'm finished.

'You do need to be aware of something, though,' I continue. 'Despite the fact that my family is desperate to see me paired off, they will put you through your paces. They won't accept you as one of us unless they feel they've met their match. Not only do you have to be good enough for me, you also have to be good enough for them.'

'That's ridiculous,' Evan replies.

'It is,' I agree. 'Put it this way, my parents weren't too enthralled by Kim, when they first met her, and didn't make a secret of this, saying that her face "just didn't fit in". Then, about three years ago, at Christmas, Kim waited until everyone had passed out, and stuck pictures all over the house of herself giving the middle fingers. I'm not even lying. When we lifted the toilet lid, there she was. They were everywhere: bathroom mirror, inside the fridge, cupboards, dog's basket and even one over Santa's face, by the front gate. She'd planned this with precision. She then walked home, thinking that this would be the last she'd ever see of anyone, including Patrick.'

'Holy shit!' Evan exclaims. 'What happened?'

'They all thought it was genius, including me. Here was a girl who had told an entire family to fuck off in the most original way possible. They made Patrick go and bring her back and welcomed her with open arms.'

Evan decreases the windscreen wipers' frequency as the snow begins to ease. 'I can't wait to meet her. She sounds like a blast.'

I nod. 'It's weird. Kim is very gracious, straight and serious – the complete opposite of Patrick, who is a fifteen-year-old in the body of a grown man. But one too many units of alcohol and all hell breaks loose ... Oh, God – we're almost there.'

I'd been so busy recounting tales from Christmas past, I hadn't noticed that we'd exited the motorway a while back and were now heading directly along an unusually quiet and snow-covered Melrose High Street.

'Well, this is pretty!' Evan says, admiring the Christmas fairy lights as we drive through. 'It looks like a postcard.'

It does. But, growing up, it bored me. I wanted to live anywhere but here. I wanted to experience the world outside of my small-town existence. Now, when I come back to visit, I can finally appreciate its charm and I sometimes wonder why I left. The anonymity of London has certainly lost its appeal over the years.

'See that street, up to the left?' I say, pointing past the roundabout. That's where Patrick and Kim live. The houses look deceptively small from the outside, but inside they're bloody massive.'

'But they're staying at your parents' house?' he asks. 'Why, when they live so close?'

'Because it's tradition that everyone stay under the same roof. We must eat, sleep and breathe each other, or it doesn't count as quality family time,' I reply. 'Escape is not an option.'

Evan indicates right and we drive away from the town towards my parents' house, turning up the old country lane at the side of the church, a road I know like the back of my hand. The snow has almost completely stopped, now, and the view ahead of us is clear. Half a mile up the hill, I spot the familiar large oak tree I played under as a kid and where we buried my first dog, Roy. As we reach the top of the hill, the car's headlights illuminate the small grey brick wall which runs around the property, lots of overgrown hedges and trees, and, of course, the grinning face of Santa.

'HOLY FUCK!' Evan yelps, hitting the brakes. 'What in the hell is that?!'

I giggle. 'Evan, meet Santa.'

Evan peers closely through the windscreen. 'What is wrong with his face?'

I sigh. 'Everything. Age. Weather conditions. Demonic possession ... He's had a hard life ... Just drive up the road ahead. We're here. Use your full beam, though; it's not well lit.'

We continue through the gateposts and I hear Evan give a little gasp as the farmhouse comes into sight. 'You're kidding, right?' he says, looking at me in disbelief. 'You grew up here?!'

I nod. 'Yep. This is home.'

'Farmhouse, my arse,' he mutters. 'This is like an effing stately home.'

From the old grey stone walls covered in ivy, to the renovated dark wood barn, which adjoins the main bungalow, the place is undeniably impressive. However, it's the garden area at the back of the house which still blows my mind: large landscaped grounds, surrounded by trees which go on as far as the eye can see – home to deer, fox, umpteen bird species, and the occasional twat looking for magic mushrooms or fairies. There's a clear, sparkling stream running along the side of the garden, a wooden dining gazebo, a conservatory and, most importantly, there isn't a disruptive neighbour in sight. Well, except the one sitting next to me.

The snow-covered gravel crunches under the car tyres as Evan pulls into a space in front of the house, setting off the security lights and the low bark of an old Great Dane.

The engine's hum finally comes to a halt and we sit in silence for a moment, until Evan says, 'I feel a bit sick.'

'Me too,' I reply, staring at the front gate. 'Evan . . . are you sure you're up for this?'

'Well, it's a bit late to back out now!' he replies. 'And you'd better start calling me Robert.'

I take a deep breath and laugh nervously. 'Right, *Robert*. Open the boot and let's get our stuff inside. They'll be hanging out the windows to get a peek at you any moment.'

'Pikachu? Like Pokémon?'

'Huh? No . . . A *peek* at *you*! Not Pikachu!'

He grins. 'I fucking love the Scottish accent.'

We step out of the car and into the cold, crisp night and Evan takes a deep breath. 'Man, I had forgotten what clean air smells like,' he remarks, lugging the first case out of the boot. 'It hits you right in the chest.'

'Think that's good? Look at the sky,' I say, smiling. He puts down the second case and tilts his head back.

'Beautiful, eh?' I say, closing the car boot.

Evan gazes in wonder. 'It's so . . . black! The stars are

incredible . . . and it's so quiet. You can practically hear the stars.'

'Jesus Christ, Evan, that's poetic,' I tease. 'I'll be bringing you back in January to address the haggis.'

'Address the what, now?' he asks, glancing down at me.

'The haggis. Burns night?'

'I've never had haggis. It frightens me.'

'Well, prepare to be a brave soldier,' I reply. 'Dad makes a mean haggis stuffing. Now, we should prob—'

'Darling! You made it!'

Evan nearly jumps out of his skin and we both spin around to see Mum on the doorstep, waving her arms in the air. Oh, God. Not only is she wearing fluffy white mule slippers, she's got new Christmas antlers. She wears them every year. Last year's were plain brown ones – silly but inoffensive. This year, she's upgraded to massive red ones, which flash intermittently, like some sort of warning signal. Her insanity is escalating.

'Hi, Mum!' I reply, plodding over to meet her, while Evan carries the bags. 'You're a feast for the eyes.' As she pulls me in for a hug on the doorstep, I can smell her hairspray and the faint, recognisable odour of gin and bitter lemon. I cuddle her back just as tightly as she cuddles me.

'And you must be Robert. The mystery man.'

Evan smiles widely and holds out his hand. 'I am indeed. Robert Shaw. Pleasure to meet you, Mrs Carson.'

Mrs Carson shakes Evan's hand and returns the smile,

but it's the inappropriate leer of a woman who's just briefly considered leaving her husband for her daughter's new boyfriend.

'Please, call me Jenny . . . Well, aren't you an improvement on the last one!' she says, giggling. 'Let's hope you've brought your sense of humour with you.'

'MUM!' I nudge her back to reality. She still hasn't let go of Evan's hand.

'Oh, I'm only messing with you. Lighten up. Now, please, come in, both of you. Get out of the cold. The dog's going crazy in there; I'll get Iona to put him in his run for an hour and tire him out.'

She grabs one of the bags at my feet and carries it into the large, brightly decorated hallway, yelling, 'Everyone! Emily's here! She's brought Ryan Gosling with her.'

Evan snorts and I cringe. We bring the other bags in and I close the front door behind me, while Mum heads across the hall and back into the living room, yelling at Pacino to calm down.

I remove my coat and hang it on the coat stand, advising Evan to do the same. Feeling crumpled and dishevelled after the long drive, I smooth down my top and brush the hair from my face before taking a deep breath.

'Ready for this?' I whisper.

Evan winks at me and takes hold of my hand.

It's game on.

CHAPTER FIFTEEN

The first thing I see when we enter the living room is Dad on a ladder, messing around with the fairy on top of the tree. He's wearing a plum-coloured woollen jumper, which is nearly the same colour as his face. He stops and wobbles precariously when he sees me.

'Emily! You made it!' he bellows. 'Good timing – we're just getting the drinks sorted.'

You made it. Why does everyone keep saying this? As if *not* making it was ever an option. I spot Kim and Patrick at the back of the room.

'Hey, guys! Merry Christmas Eve! Bloody hell, Dad – be careful up there; you look like you're about to have a stroke . . . So, who is taking pride of place this year?'

He angles the fairy slightly to the right and starts to climb down the ladder. 'Well, your brother made Justin Bieber the fairy this year, but we've decided that Donald Trump is much more deserving, so I'm just changing the photo . . . And you must be Robert.'

'Want a Bloody Mary, Em?' Patrick yells, holding up a bottle of Tabasco.

I shake my head. 'Maybe later; just a G & T for now, ta.'

Evan, looking completely bemused, shakes my dad's hand – who, in turn, gives him a whacking great thump on the back. 'Nice to meet you! Emily will fill you in on the tree situation. Let's get you a drink. You look like a rum-and-Coke man. Correct?'

Evan laughs. 'I'm a happy-to-drink-whatever-you-have man; thank you.'

And, with that, Dad strolls to the bar at the other end of the room to join Kim and Patrick, leaving me to explain what the bloody hell is going on.

I usher Evan over to the couch. 'Every year, we pick someone who's worthy of having a jaggy branch up their arse and stick a photo of their face on to the fairy. Last year, it was David Cameron. This year . . . well, you can see.'

We both look over and admire the large silver fairy with the smug face of Donald Trump. Dad's even stuck some fluff on the top, for hair.

'Makes total sense,' he replies, before taking a gander around the room. 'This place is awesome . . . Hang on . . . Didn't your mum come in here? Is there a portal?'

I laugh. 'She did. See that door behind the bar? That leads on to the kitchen and the garden. She'll be in there with Iona, sorting the dog.'

Kim, wearing a black sparkly playsuit, saunters over with our drinks, kindly wishing us both a merry Christmas Eve. I can see Evan secretly sizing her up, wondering if this quietly spoken redhead will turn into the 'fuck you' picture lady any time soon.

'Same to you, Kim,' I respond, giving her a hug. 'How's life treating you? Patrick behaving himself?'

'Somewhat,' she replies bashfully before quietly acknowledging Evan and removing herself from the conversation by sitting on the opposite couch.

I take a sip of my drink and sit back, admiring the living room in all its splendour. Mum's theme this year is blue and silver; bells, tinsel and pretty ornaments hang all around, including some strategically placed mistletoe that I'll advise Evan to avoid and a big pile of presents, all lovingly wrapped by someone at John Lewis. The fire is roaring, Fleetwood Mac is softly playing in the background and, just for a moment, a sense of calm washes over me. Perhaps this year will be different.

'Get your finger *out* of the hummus, you fucking *CHILD*!'
Perhaps not.

Iona stomps in from the kitchen, her Prada heels sounding like military boots on the wooden floorboards. 'Don't eat the red-pepper hummus,' she instructs, placing some breadsticks on the coffee table. 'Patrick just contaminated the whole lot with his grotty little hands. Honestly, men are the fucking wor—'

'Iona,' I interrupt, before she has the chance to verbally annihilate the entire male population, 'this is Robert.'

Evan stands up to shake her hand and she reciprocates, but not before giving him a good old eye-judging.

'You're Robert?' she asks, taking a step back to have another look, then throwing a glance in my direction. 'You're not what I expected. At all.'

'Very pleased to meet you,' he replies. 'Emily's told me lots about you.'

'Has she, now?' she replies coolly, looking him straight in the eyes. 'I wish I could say the same. My sister kept you quiet for months. Perhaps the age gap bothered her. What are you – twenty-five? You do realise my sister's twenties are a distant memory?'

I almost choke on my G & T. 'Iona, stop being so bloody rude! You promised!'

'I'm twenty-nine,' Evan replies, 'and it's all right, Emily. Your sister has the right to ask. If I'm being completely honest, Iona, I don't notice the age gap. Your sister's qualities are far greater than the sum of her years.'

A smile creeps over Iona's face. 'All right, Robert. I'll buy it, for now. I like a man who can think on his feet.'

I breathe a quiet sigh of relief. Round one to Evan.

'Anyway,' she continues, 'now that we're finally all here, we can get started. Mum! Bring through the bubbly!'

I tug Evan's sleeve and he sits back down beside me, the tiniest bead of sweat appearing on his forehead. 'Fuck me!' he whispers. 'She's genuinely terrifying. I thought she was going to hook me up to a lie detector.'

'There's still time.' I sigh.

'Can you show me where the bathroom is? I think I need to compose myself.'

I nod and motion for him to follow me. 'Back in a sec; just showing Eva—'

Evan nudges me and coughs loudly.

'*Robert* where the bathroom is.'

I grab Evan's hand and scurry into the hallway, cursing as I go. I drag him into the bathroom and hurriedly close the door behind me.

'Fucking hell, Emily!' he exclaims. 'That was close.'

'I know, I know!' I reply, pacing across the floor. 'Oh, God. There's a very real possibility that I am going to fuck up tonight – especially after a few drinks. I don't think they heard. Do you think they heard? Oh, God – what if they heard?!'

He runs his hand through his hair. 'I don't think so, but you need to be careful. It's unlikely I'll be referring to myself in the third person, so I'm afraid this is all up to you.'

I perch myself on the edge of the bath and try to figure a way around this. 'It's cool. I'll just not use your name. I'll call you a pet name. Couples do that.'

He considers this. 'That could work. I respond best to "bae".'

'Oh, shut up.' I giggle. 'How about "hun"?'

'Like Attila?'

'OK, fine . . . "Baby"?'

He shakes his head. 'Ugh! Too American. Isn't there a Scottish term of endearment?'

'C∗nt?'

His laugh echoes around the bathroom. He thinks I'm joking.

'Look, just call me whatever springs to mind because, right now, I really have to pee and, well, you're standing here.'

'Oh, sorry; of course!' I reply, hurrying out to give him some privacy.

As I leave, I hear him mumble, 'Jesus, this bathroom is bigger than my flat.'

Reluctant to go back into the living room just yet, I decide to move our cases from the front door into my old bedroom while I wait for Evan to finish. Lugging them over to the door, I push it open and, as I turn on the light, I'm hit by the persistent stench of dog. Oh, for God's sake, I know Pacino sleeps in here, but they could have at least burnt a candle. I position the cases against the wardrobe and close the horrific floral curtains Mum has decided to hang instead of my wooden blinds. In fact, Mum seems to have given the entire room a Laura Ashley makeover since I was last here, because my bed now appears to have an entire fucking meadow sprawled across it, complete with matching runner and scatter cushions. It's still the same light and airy, spacious room it was when I lived here, but long gone are my posters, patchwork armchair, bookshelves and the giant white fluffy rug I used to stand on barefoot, curling my toes.

I hear the toilet flush and walk out into the hall to meet Evan. 'All right?' he asks, turning out the bathroom light. 'Been back in yet?'

I shake my head. 'Not yet. I just stuck our cases in the bedroom. I needed a moment to regroup.'

'We both need a drink,' he asserts quietly, ruffling his hair. 'Let's just get back in there and be the best fake couple Melbourne has ever seen.'

'It's Melro— Oh, forget it. I don't have the energy.'

Just then, the living-room door opens and Mum trots out carrying two glasses of champagne, antlers now in full flickering disco mode. 'Everything all right?'

'Fine, Mum. Just doing a quick tour of the house . . .'

'Oh, you can do the tour later, Emily,' she says, handing us each a glass. 'We want to get to know this man of yours!'

She walks behind us and pushes us forward up the hall, saying, 'Kim has just taken her first sly shot of tequila. Things are about to get interesting.'

CHAPTER SIXTEEN

Everyone has now gathered in the seating area: Patrick and Kim on the duck-egg blue couch nearest the fire, Iona on the couch we'd previously occupied and my dad in his favourite lounger, feet up and drink in hand.

Mum ensures everyone's glass is topped up, while Evan and I reclaim our seats as she asks Patrick to bring Pacino back inside.

'I've just got comfy,' he moans. 'Can't someone else do it?'

Mum gives him one of her 'stop bloody moaning and just do it' looks, which is all that's required to make him slink off through the kitchen door.

'Well, isn't this marvellous,' Mum says, beaming at everyone. 'I do love this time of the year . . . Emily, I forgot to say – old Mrs Peacock finally popped her clogs. I met her son, Dominic, at the tennis club. He's divorced, you know. Good head of hair.'

I squirm uneasily. Evan is sitting three inches away from

me and she's *still* trying to set me up with eligible men. She doesn't even realise she's doing it anymore.

'Was Mrs Peacock the old racist who lived near the football ground?' I say, deflecting the topic away from her son.

Mum shakes her head. 'No, that was Mrs Babcock. Mrs Peacock was the one who owned the big hotel and restaurant near Innerleithen. Dominic just inherited the lot, Emily. Worth a fortune, now.'

Evan gives me a sideways glance, trying not to laugh. Thank God he's not really my boyfriend; I'd be mortified.

'I remember her!' Kim chimes in. 'She was sharp as a tack, even in her nineties. Remember when George Clooney was staying there incognito a few years back and she put on the "I'm just an old, senile, doddering woman" act, persuading him to take a picture with her for the office wall?'

Mum roars with laughter. 'Oh, God, that's right – and, after he checked out, she exploited the hell out of the picture and the fact he'd stayed there. Her business went through the roof.'

We all giggle, expect for Iona, who's staring at Evan, tapping the side of her champagne glass with her perfectly manicured acrylic nails.

'Emily tells me you work in marketing, Robert,' she says, in a serious tone. 'What's your take on that – from a marketing perspective? Smart move?'

I feel myself tense up. It's obvious that Iona is going to

put Evan through his paces this evening. I step in to try and lighten the mood again. 'Come on, let's not get bogged down in serious—'

'It could be viewed as that,' Evan replies confidently. 'Her actions certainly raised the profile and brand awareness for both of them. Her business is now known as a place where celebs not only frequent, but are willing to have their photo taken with the owner. And Mr Clooney looks like a kind, down-to-earth, normal man, who takes selfies with grannies. His fans will eat that shit up.'

'But?' Iona asks. 'On the flip side?'

'On the flip side, if he's specifically asked for privacy, then she's broken and exploited that confidentiality and trust. It'll deter future celebrities from staying there. It's a very fine line to tread. But my guess is he didn't publicly complain, because no one wants to be the guy who jeopardises the family business run by the poor sweet old lady in the photo . . .'

'Clever man you've got there, Emily,' Mum gushes. Iona looks content enough with his answer, so I just smile and nod. If I didn't know better, I'd totally believe that Evan knew what the fuck he was talking about. He's killing it.

From the corner of my eye, I see Pacino lumbering through to the living room, followed by a shivering Patrick.

'You could have left him out there,' he chatters, rubbing his arms furiously. 'His kennel is warmer than in here.'

'He needs company,' Mum replies, talking directly to

the dog in a baby voice. 'You know he doesn't fare well on his own.'

Pacino gives her a gruff, throaty response before trotting over to Evan and me.

'PACINO!' I cry, stroking his back and floppy ears. 'How are you, boy? I've missed you.'

Within seconds of my greeting, Pacino has raised himself up and plonked his front legs on to my lap, before going in for the face-lick of death.

'Jeez!' Evan flinches, making it obvious that he's never been around large dogs before. 'God, he's like a horse. He's friendly, right?'

I can hear the others laughing. 'He's a big teddy bear,' I reply, gently stroking his soft, smooth black fur. 'Aren't you, boy?'

Evan, still keeping his distance, watches as Pacino drops to the floor and rolls on to his back, demanding a belly rub. I sink to the floor beside him and oblige.

'He won't bite, *honey*,' I assure Evan. 'He's too lazy to be hostile.'

Evan, aware that being nice to the family dog is a good way to curry favour with your potential future in-laws, places his drink on the table and cautiously lets Pacino sniff his hand.

Pacino gives a quick sniff, but remains motionless on the floor, while Evan gently rubs his belly. The look on Evan's face is quite triumphant, so I let him have his moment. I don't have the heart to tell him that Pacino would sprawl out in front of Charles Manson if a belly rub was on the cards.

Iona gets up and strolls towards the bar. 'So, people, what is the drinking game *du soir*?' she asks, reaching for the tequila. 'I'm not playing charades again; last year, everything Patrick did was *Game of Thrones*-related and all Emily did was name obscure literature that no one had heard of.'

Kim rolls her eyes. 'Totally agree with the *Game of Thrones* comment. I cannot stand that bloody show.'

'That's not true about me, though!' I retort. 'Totally unfair. You lot must be the only people in the world who haven't heard of Gaiman's *American Gods* or *Asking for It* by Louise O'Neill.'

'I did see that *Tattooed Dragon Girl on the Train* book you were talking about,' Mum responds, reaching for the breadsticks. 'I didn't fancy the look of it. Too dark.'

Why is this my life? I nod at her in acknowledgement, but in my mind's eye I'm fashioning a noose from Christmas tinsel.

'Iona's comment about me was fair,' mumbles Patrick. 'But I love *Game of Thrones* and I'm not sorry.'

Kim rolls her eyes. 'You're on your own with that one; I cannot stand it.'

'What about alphabet celebrity? We played that once.'

Kim groans. 'I hardly know any famous people – you all have an unfair advantage. What do you suggest, Robert?'

Evan stops playing with the dog to find seven pairs of eyes staring at him – including Pacino's, who's wondering why the patting stopped.

'Me? I haven't played a drinking game in a while . . . Um . . .'

I butt in. 'I know! We could—'

'Let him answer!' Mum interjects. 'Emily's last boyfriend was a bit of a damp squib when it came to party games. I'm sure you'll be much more enthusiastic.'

Not one to back down from a challenge, Evan smirks and says, 'Truth or drink? The rules are simple: you either answer the question or you have a drink. In fact, Emily and I played a similar game on the journey up here. Without the alcohol, of course. Very enlightening.'

I recoil in horror, shaking my head furiously. 'Oh, no . . . no, no, no. I think I speak for everyone when I say—'

'Fuck, yes!' Iona interrupts, placing a silver tray on the table, which holds a bottle of tequila, seven small shot glasses, some lime segments and a salt shaker. 'Now, *that* could be fascinating.'

The family whoop like idiots, while I seem to be the only person who thinks this is a horrible idea.

'Are you crazy?' I ask. 'This will be beyond awkward! No good can come of this!'

'Nonsense,' Dad replies. 'Honestly, Emily, sometimes I think London has turned you into a bit of a drag. Do you know, Robert, when Emily was twenty, she took magic mushrooms in her bedroom and spent fifteen hours talking to her poster of Monica Belluci and declaring that everything finally made sense. We sat with her the entire time, in case she freaked out.'

I throw my face into a cushion, utterly mortified at the disclosure.

'Emily, darling, is this true?' I hear Evan ask. 'Did you trip in front of your parents?'

I throw the cushion to the side and grumble, 'God, why can't you be the kind of parents who are appalled at this? Fine! Yes, it's true. Happy?!'

Everyone cheers and applauds. 'Then the game has begun!' Evan declares. 'Now, it's your turn.'

I'm stunned by what's happening here; my family is playing well with the new boy. They're smiling, laughing and hanging off Evan's every word. Even Iona looks like she's lowered her threat level to moderate. It's working. My new boyfriend is a hit. As far as my family is concerned, I finally have my ducks in a row; I'm no longer the woman who just can't quite seem to get things right. I should be enjoying this.

'OK, fine,' I submit, rising to my feet. 'We'll play this, but first let's get some party music on. Let's show Robert how we really do Christmas.'

CHAPTER SEVENTEEN

'Doggy or missionary?'

Patrick almost spits out his drink. 'KIM! You can't ask my mum that!'

'Course I can!' Kim laughs. 'She's not *my* mum!'

This game is going exactly as I expected. Kim has opted to drink more than she's answered, Iona has only answered questions that portray her in a favourable light, Patrick has drunk even when he's answered a question and my parents have answered questions they weren't even asked. Evan has very sensibly kept his drinking to a minimum, as have I. One false move and the game could be over – in more ways than one.

Patrick is covering his ears, murmuring, 'Please choose drink, please choose drink,' while Mum ignores him and answers, 'Neither, as it happens. I prefer spoons. Much easier, at our age.'

'MUM!' Iona and I both yell at the same time, but she doesn't give a shit. She's too busy high-fiving Kim.

'Oh. OH! This is my song!' Dad pulls the lever on his recliner and sits forward. 'It's dancing time.'

I watch as he starts shuffling around the floor in his comfort-fit chinos and loafers, his hands moving in time to the beat, like little drumsticks. It isn't long before Mum has joined him, doing the kind of bouncy dance only mothers can do.

Evan leans in and whispers, 'Your dad's jam is "Cake by the Ocean"?'

'My dad's jam is anything with a beat. He'd dance to a car alarm,' I reply, giggling. 'You thought my playlist was cheesy? You haven't seen my dad's.'

Iona opens the door for Pacino, who has obviously had enough excitement for one night and wants to go to bed. My bed. Every year, I ask that he sleep somewhere else, and every year, I'm ignored. It also means that I have to leave my bedroom door open so he can use the dog flap in the kitchen, which leads into his kennel and open-air run, if he so desires. I'm surprised they don't give him his own fucking key, pocket money and the use of my old car.

I see Kim drag Patrick up by the arm, demanding he dance with her, while Iona stumbles slightly against the Christmas tree, making Donald Trump wobble comically. She turns her stumble into a shimmy and manoeuvres her way in-between Mum and Dad.

No one has noticed that Evan and I are relatively sober, and they therefore cannot understand why we're still seated, yelling at us to hurry up and join in. I assure them we will – normally, I'm equally as eager as my dad to strut my stuff – but, right now, I'm apprehensive. Things have gone somewhat smoothly so far and we're so, so close to completing a successful first evening. The sight of us dancing clumsily together could show us up for the frauds we are.

Evan puts his arm around my shoulder and leans in to whisper in my ear: 'Your sister is watching. Play along.'

I don't look at her; instead, I plaster a smile across my face, giggling like he's just said something funny. 'Quick question – can you dance?' I ask, still smiling. I can feel the slightest brush of his stubble on my cheek. 'You need to warn me if you're shit, so I don't act surprised or horrified.' I place my hand on his knee, because otherwise it would look like he's one step away from putting me in a chokehold.

Now he's laughing at the imaginary joke. 'We danced in your room,' he replies, 'the night you split with Robert. I have moves – many of them.'

'I'm serious,' I say, squeezing his knee tightly to let him know that his conceit isn't appreciated at this moment. 'Just don't spring any break-dancing bombshells on me – my family will torment you relentlessly.'

To be fair, my family won't give a shit whether he has moves or not – to them, any dancing is better than no dancing – but he doesn't need to know that.

Kim, now wild-eyed and shoe-free, freestyles her way across the floor. 'I know you're all loved up and shit,' she says, prizing us apart, 'but there's only twenty minutes left until Santa comes. Get dancing.'

'Not the Santa outside, I hope,' Evan replies, but she can't hear him, what with the sound of her own voice warbling along to Bruno Mars. Just like Patrick, Evan is dragged by the arm towards the makeshift dance floor.

I bite the bullet and swiftly down a shot of tequila, the familiar burn jolting me into action. Only twenty minutes until we're officially into day two. I can do this. *We* can do this.

I can barely bring myself to look at Evan as I enter the bopping swarm of Carsons, choosing instead to attach myself to Iona, who's completely smashed and greets me like she hasn't seen me in ages.

'EMMMY! Everyone! It's *Emmy*!'

When Iona was younger, she couldn't pronounce 'Emily', and it appears that nothing has changed.

She twirls me around by my hand to face in the other direction and I see that both Kim and Mum have abandoned their husbands in favour of dancing with Evan.

I do my best to keep my jaw above floor level as I watch him. He wasn't lying. The boy has moves. It's all rather understated – nothing too cheesy or flashy – and he's confidently captivating his female admirers without breaking a sweat.

Iona is tapping me on the arm with what feels like her fist.

'Easy!' I say, rubbing my triceps. 'That hurt!'

'I have to know. How the fuck did *this* happen, then?' she slurs, looking at Evan. 'He's *my* age. Is he like a crisis? Like a midlife crisis? Like a May-to-December deal?'

'Fuck's sake, Iona!' I reply, doing my best to keep up with everyone's dancing. 'I'm not that old.'

'But he's not even your type,' she continues. 'I don't get it. There's something not right, here.'

Dad is the next one to bump into the Christmas tree, sending baubles scattering and breaking Iona's concentration for a moment while she laughs. Dammit. Even a bucketload of booze can't throw Iona off the scent. She's perceptive, though. Every boyfriend I've ever had has been dark-haired, with a demeanour far more serious than mine. I always choose men of that ilk, thinking that their brooding nature will offset my flighty one, hoping they'll be the yang to my yin.

Dad incorporates bauble-kicking into his dance routine, as Dead or Alive blare out through the speaker system. I shift away from Iona, hoping that she'll let this drop, finding myself in-between Mum and Evan. Mum is doing her special 'Pan's People' moves, her antlers flashing intermittently as she gyrates.

'You haven't even kissed him yet!' my sister yells over at me, like a foghorn.

Oh, fuck off, Iona. I do my best to ignore her, but she's caught everyone's attention.

'What are you yelping about?' Patrick asks, catching his breath. We all stare at Iona, who, unlike the rest of us, hasn't stopped dancing.

'Just an observation,' she replies. 'Doesn't anyone else find that a bit odd?'

Slut drop. She just did an actual slut drop.

'Of course I've kissed him,' I hiss back at her. 'I just choose not to slobber all over my boyfriend in front of my family.'

'You slobbered all over Tomas,' Mum says, resuming her swaying. 'Or he slobbered all over you. Either way, there was definite slobbering.'

'Tomas was a Spaniard, though,' Patrick reminds her. 'They're passionate people.'

Mum and Kim murmur in agreement, while Dad moves over to where Evan is standing and no doubt wishing he were anywhere else.

'I'm sure Robert is just being respectful,' he insists, giving him another slap on the back. 'Besides, English men are far more reserved when it comes to showing their women affection. Scots, like the Spaniards, are far less inhibited. It isn't his fault.'

I scowl at my dad. He's trying to get a rise out of Evan. Iona is grinning from ear to ear, as she knows his game.

'You can all behave yourselves,' I reply, keeping my cool. 'Now, I'm going to get some more drinks. Robert, would you like to help me?'

Evan agrees and follows me to the back of the room. He can't see me mouthing a plethora of swear words, but I know he's aware I'm doing it.

'Deep breathing,' he says as we get to the small bar area. 'Just keep smiling.'

I remove a bottle of champagne from a cooler while Evan sets up some glasses. We both stand and stare at my family, who look like they're about to launch into a haka.

'What are they—?'

'No idea,' I interrupt. 'Best not to ask. Can you pop this?' I hand him the wine bottle. 'I'm scared of cork-popping.'

He takes a tea towel and covers the cork. 'You don't like surprises, do you?' he says, keeping his voice low. I flinch as I hear a muffled pop, watching him place the bottle on the bar, completely unaffected by the whole event.

'It's not surprises, per se,' I reply, picking up a champagne glass. 'It's more loud noises. You should see me trying to burst balloons. I have to close my eyes and cover my ears and then I can't even see what I'm doing. It's a mess.'

'So loud noises are a no, but surprises are a yes?'

'That's an odd question, but I guess—'

He kisses me.

It's very light and tender, his lips soft and warm. I feel my cheeks flush as his bottom lip brushes against mine and a shiver runs gently down my spine.

But then he kisses me again and this time it's much bolder. Much firmer. It's the kind of kiss that resonates through every part of my body, and this time I feel it in my bones. My legs begin to wobble, as does the champagne glass, which slips from my fingers, smashing instantly when it hits the floor.

I pull away and take a step backwards, the sensation of his lips on mine still lingering. I feel a little giddy. My eyes widen, asking the question, *What the hell was that?!*

Evan just shrugs. 'Surprise?' he mouths.

'That must have been some kiss,' Dad says, laughing. 'I'll get the Dyson.'

I break Evan's gaze to see Patrick, Kim and Mum all applauding, while Iona stands with her hands on her hips. I can tell that she's still not convinced by the whole *Robert*-and-me situation, but that's not what is bothering me. What's bothering me is that, for ten knee-trembling seconds, I was utterly convinced. I bought into the whole charade, hook, line and sinker. Christ, am I really that pitiful?

Get a hold of yourself, Emily. You've paid him to do a job – stop being so pathetic.

I sink to my knees behind the bar, carefully picking up the larger pieces of glass, while Evan towers over me. Patrick turns up the music to ASBO level.

'Get down here,' I whisper, pulling on the leg of his jeans.

He obeys, hunkering down to look for shards.

'You could have warned me,' I whisper, retrieving part of the glass rim, which had slipped under the bar. 'But I

think it worked! Job done. They got their silly kiss and . . .
Oh – shh – here comes Dad.'

We both stand up, wrapping the glass we've collected
inside a sheet of newspaper. Evan tugs on my sleeve. 'Look,
I didn't do it for—'

His words are drowned out by the sound of the Dyson
moving towards us, being operated by a man who's three
sheets to the wind. I wait for Evan to finish his sentence,
but he doesn't. Instead, he returns to the party, boldly
asking Iona if he can have this dance.

I move aside to let Dad hoover, getting another glass
and carefully setting it beside the others. A couple more
drinks and I'm calling it a night. I can't afford to have any
more surprises this evening.

By one thirty a.m., the fire has burnt down to a dull
glow and the mood is less energetic. Patrick has abandoned the dancing and has regressed into a six-year-old
boy, rummaging through the presents under the tree and
begging to open just one. Iona is spark out on the couch,
snoring heavily, and Kim has disappeared into the garden
to take up smoking again.

'We're off to bed,' Mum announces, being inelegantly
twirled around by my dad. 'Stick the Christmas lights off
when you turn in, will you?'

I nod and hug them both goodnight, while Evan politely
thanks them for a fun evening. As they stagger off down
the hallway, I hear them saying goodnight to Pacino. Ugh
– I'd forgotten about him.

Evan looks a little lost, waiting for me to advise him of our next move.

'We'll need to get Iona to bed,' I say, tiredly rubbing the back of my neck. 'That couch will kill her back.'

'Aww, what a good big sister you are,' he says, before looking over at Patrick, who has now decided to nap under the tree. 'And him?'

'Oh, Kim can sort him out,' I reply. 'My sisterly nature only stretches so far.'

Iona, half awake and groggy, allows us to help her walk to her room. We place her on top of her bed and I remove the one shoe that remains on her foot.

'You text . . .' she slurs into the pillow. 'You text each other, but you're with each other. It's fucking weird.'

'OK, Iona – night night,' I reply, clueless as to what she's babbling on about. 'See you in the morning.'

'I saw your phone,' she continues, eyes still closed, with half her face hidden under her hair. 'His message. Real men say they love you with their voices. Not texts.'

Evan and I give each other confused looks as we softly creep out of her room, making our way back into the hallway.

'Huge room,' he comments, giving a little yawn.

'Yep,' I agree. 'Patrick's room is the same.'

'You didn't tell me your family were rich.'

We reach my bedroom door. 'No, I didn't,' I reply. ''Cos it doesn't matter.'

My room is illuminated by a soft glow from my lamp, which makes the floral explosion a tad more bearable. There, slap bang in the middle of the bed, is Pacino, sprawled out and calmly staring at us.

'He's not going to move, is he?' Evan says.

'Oh, he'll move . . .' I reply, taking out my earrings. 'But only to the end of the bed.'

'I'm too tired to care,' he responds, kicking off his shoes. I watch him zip open his case and bring out a T-shirt and pyjama bottoms. He then starts to remove his top, exposing his bare chest.

'Hey, hey, HEY!' I proclaim, turning away. 'I do not want to see any of *that* while you're here.'

'Any of what?' he asks, looking down at his body. 'Am I supposed to magic my PJs on?'

'Well, no, but you can change in the bathroom,' I reply, firmly. 'And we're putting pillows between us. Lots of pillows. I'm just making sure you don't get the wrong idea.'

Carrying his pyjamas and toothbrush, he calmly walks back towards the door. 'I'm confused as to whether you have a low opinion of me, Emily,' he says, 'or a high opinion of yourself.'

Ouch. That's me told.

I sheepishly take my own pyjamas from my case and pull them on in record speed, just in case Evan returns sooner than expected to chastise me further.

I've brought along my blue-and-white striped jammies,

which are a tad old-fashioned and not something I'd normally wear, but my creased T-shirt and pants ensemble would allow Mum to voice yet another opinion on something that doesn't matter.

I give Pacino a quick pat on the head while I pick up my phone and he gives a little contented sigh in return, nuzzling his face into my leg.

Pressing the *home* key on my phone, it quickly powers up, revealing an unread message on the home screen.

I love you. Robert xx

Suddenly Iona's drunken ramblings make sense.

You text each other, but you're with each other . . .

Fucking Snoopy McSnoopface has been in my room, having a good old peek at my phone. I've never been more grateful for the invention of fingerprint passcodes, otherwise she'd have read Robert's previous grovelling messages and my heated replies.

I close my eyes and cringe. Why is this happening? Not only has Robert filled up my inbox with pointless apologies and declarations, now he's inadvertently filled Iona's head full of nonsense. There's no way she won't tell everyone about this tomorrow. As well as pretending we're in love, we're going to have to be the kind of dysfunctional, overly entwined couple who text each other when we're in the same room. The kind of couple who make finger love hearts at each other and hashtag their feelings on Facebook.

Still sitting upright, I pull the duvet from under Pacino and over my head. It's not a fort, but it'll have to do. I sit there, motionless, like a flowery bed ghost, just as Evan returns to the room. I feel the bed sink under his weight as he sits down. 'What are you doing?' I hear him ask. 'Oh, God – you're not sulking, are you? I never took you for a sulker.'

'Look at this,' I reply, my arm stretching out from under the duvet to hand him my phone. 'It'll all become clear.'

'OK . . . hang on,' he replies, shortly followed by, 'This is what's bothering you?! A message from Robert? It can't be a huge shock, surely? Shoe boy was always going to . . . Oh. OH! . . . Shit.'

'Yep.'

'Your sister thinks I sent this. *That's* what she was talking about.'

'Bingo.'

'Oh, God, now I'm that guy . . . Now we're *that* couple . . .'

I slowly peel back the duvet. 'This is not good!' I wail. 'This is *almost* as bad as knowing what sexual position my mum prefers.'

He hands me back my phone. 'Iona was pissed, though – drunk as a fart. Come tomorrow, she might not even remember.'

I laugh. My sister remembers things she doesn't even know yet.

'Let's just get some sleep,' he suggests, attempting to

push Pacino away from his side of the bed. 'We'll deal with it tomorrow.'

I nod in agreement. 'Fine, but I'm going to brush my teeth. The taste of indignity isn't a pleasant one.'

When I return, Evan has placed several pillows down the middle of the bed. He stands to face me, hands by his sides. 'Berlin Wall complete and ready for inspection, sir,' he jokes, saluting me. 'Permission to speak freely?'

'Permission granted.'

'Cool, 'cos I was just wondering which member of the Golden Girls was kind enough to lend you those pyjamas, because—'

'Permission revoked.'

Evan continues finding himself hilarious while I climb into bed and turn off the lamp, sending the room into darkness, except for the small chink of light coming from the hallway.

'Does the door have to be half closed?' he asks. 'Is it for the dog?'

'I prefer to think of the door as half open,' I reply, sleepily. 'I'm an optimist. And, yes – otherwise Pacino will feel boxed in and attack you while you sleep.'

'What?!'

'Goodnight, Evan.'

I close my eyes and drift off with the theme tune from *The Golden Girls* playing over and over in my head. Damn him.

CHAPTER EIGHTEEN

DAY 2

I'm not sure if it's the sound of 'Ding Dong Merrily on High' being played loudly through the house or the commotion Pacino is causing because he can smell bacon frying that awakens me first on Christmas morning, but, regardless, I lie there wishing they'd both shut the hell up. My hand reaches out from under the covers, clumsily grappling for my phone on the bedside table, and I focus just long enough to see that it's ten twenty-five a.m. I hear the muffled sounds of Iona talking to Dad while she collects the dog's lead from the hallway and the squeak of her trainers as she walks back through to the kitchen. I wonder if she's remembered about Robert's text, yet.

I can picture Mum in her mint-green dressing gown, pouring yet another cup of tea from her owl-shaped teapot while Dad makes breakfast for everyone. Patrick and Kim will stay in bed until they're forced to move at gunpoint, but nothing can keep Iona from her morning run, even on Christmas Day.

On the other side of the pillow barricade, Evan snores softly, seemingly able to sleep through the ruckus which is quickly taking over the house. I consider scaring the shit out of him in retaliation for his *Golden Girls* joke, but that would mean moving from my comfy position. I just don't think I'm ready for that kind of commitment yet. As I lie beside him, the events of last night start racing around in my mind. The drinking, the truth telling, the dancing, that kiss . . .

I stop to replay it over in my head again.

And again.

And. Again.

While I know that it was part of the act and I'm aware that it meant nothing, it still doesn't stop me taking a moment to remember just how lovely it was. I was kissed properly and fervently by a man who has no intentions of breaking my heart and no intentions of leading me on, and for me, at this moment, that's enough.

I unlock my phone and immediately delete Robert's text. He almost ruined Christmas once; I won't let him try it again. I send Kara a quick 'Merry Christmas' message with a gif of a drunken Santa falling over in a car park, followed by the exact same one to Alice and Toby, because I'm an abhorrently lazy friend. Unable to doze off again, but unwilling to get up, I scroll through my Twitter and Facebook feeds, randomly wishing people a merry Christmas and grudgingly writing *Congratulations!!!!* under the bejewelled-hand selfie of a girl I went to school with who just got engaged.

I manage to lie through renditions of both 'Hark! The Herald Angels Sing' and 'Little Drummer Boy' before I admit defeat and decide to give in to the smell of the bacon, leaving Evan alone in my bed while I stealthily creep to the bathroom.

The sight of myself in the mirror isn't exactly a pleasant one, but at least my hair has remained flat for once in its miserable life. Knowing that I'll be diving into the sunken bathtub after breakfast, I give my face a quick wash and head through to the kitchen.

'Merry— *Fuck's sake!*' I say as I stub my toe on the kitchen door and hop over to the table. 'Christmas. Merry Christmas. Is there tea on?'

'Merry Christmas, darling!' Mum leans in to hug me before inspecting my toe. 'You've been doing that since you were two,' she informs me. 'You'll need a plaster.'

'Merry Christmas, Emily,' Dad says, kissing the top of my head. 'Bacon or square?'

'Both, please,' I reply, lifting off the tea cosy and grabbing a mug from the middle of the table. 'And a tattie scone on the square, if there's any going?'

'Aye, there is. Sauce?'

'Red, thanks,' I reply. 'I like your mugs, by the way.

They're huge. Like bowls. I'm glad someone has finally invented a bowl of tea; it's been long overdue.'

'I like your pyjamas,' Mum says, looking me up and down. 'They look well made. Good long-length top.'

I know, I think to myself. That's why I wore them.

Mum smiles approvingly. 'They're very flattering for your shape.'

To the untrained ear, that comment could be considered a compliment. However, after thirty-eight years' worth of training, I know a sly dig when I hear one.

'My shape? And what shape is that, then?'

Dad coughs nervously and starts to whistle the tune to *The Great Escape*.

'What? Oh, don't get all defensive, darling,' Mum says. 'You have a lovely shape. In Brazil, your backside would be a national treasure.'

'Oh my God! So – what? Outside of South America, it's best hidden under long clothing?'

'Look, don't shoot the messenger. Blame your father, dear; you inherited your arse from his side of the family.'

'Now, Jenny . . .' Dad begins, but Mum dismisses him with her hand.

'It's true, William. Your mother was like the back of a pantomime horse. Nice woman, but it was like trying to contain two space hoppers in a goldfish net.'

'Pay no attention to her,' Dad says reassuringly. 'There's not a scrap on you.'

Before I have the chance to maim my mother, there's a loud whack against the patio doors. We all turn to see Pacino with a massive branch in his mouth, trying to get into the kitchen. Iona is close behind him, yelling for him to 'DROP IT', which proves futile, as he bangs against the glass again. Dad, being the massive softy that he is, opens the door for the dog and lets him in, branch and all, which Pacino takes to his old chewed bed at the back of the room.

'I had to remove his face from my pillow *twice* last night,' I announce, looking around for the milk jug. 'You have to do something about his breath.'

'Oh, good – you're up,' Iona says as she sits down beside me at the table, sweaty and flushed, taking out her ear buds. 'Merry Christmas, sis! I won't hug you yet; I'm a tad sweaty.'

'Merry Christmas to you too,' I reply, grateful that there's no mention of Robert or the text. 'Mum's just been telling me how big my arse is. How's the head?'

'Fine, as it happens,' she replies, grabbing an identical mug to mine. 'Dad, I'll just have whatever's ready. I'm starving. I didn't have that much to drink last night, but it hit me like a ton of bricks.'

'I noticed.' I snicker. 'Robert and I had to help you to bed.'

She thinks for a moment. 'Nope; no recollection of that whatsoever. Speaking of Robert, where is he? Still asleep?'

I nod. 'I let him lie in for a bit. I can only imagine how exhausting it must be meeting you lot for the first time.'

'Well, wake him up!' she insists. 'You know we all eat breakfast together. And tell Patrick and Kim to shake a leg, while you're at it.'

'Man, you're bossy!' I moan, rising from the table as she pours herself some tea. 'I'm the oldest sibling – that's my job . . . but, fine. I need a plaster for my toe, anyway.'

She looks over at Mum. 'Did she stub it on the door?'

Mum nods.

'There's a shocker, eh?'

I roll my eyes and slouch off to round up the remaining sleepyheads so we can all begin Christmas.

First stop is Patrick and Kim, who are sleeping in Patrick's old room in the first converted barn. It's a bright, cream-coloured space with exposed wooden ceiling beams, two arched windows and a sliding door, which connects to the main house. It also has heated floors, a walk-in wet room and a beautiful brick fireplace that Patrick is banned from using without adult supervision. Iona's room is exactly the same, only she's allowed to make fire.

I knock respectfully on their door twice, announcing that breakfast is ready, but I'm met with silence. My third attempt is less polite and more of a continuous banging and yelling until Patrick appears, looking the worse for wear.

'We're up, we're up,' he insists, rubbing his eyes. 'You can stop that now.'

'Merry Christmas, you two!'

I hear a muffled 'Merry Chrissmiss!' from Kim, who's still under the duvet.

'And how is my baby brother?' I continue, knowing full well that he's feeling more than fragile. 'Hungry? There's sausage on the go. And eggs. Lots of runny, undercooked egg and slimy—'

He shuts the door in my face. I wait a couple of minutes and then bang on the door again, knowing that they'll have tried to go back to sleep. The sound of something heavy being thrown at the door means my work here is done.

Before I wake Evan, I hunt around in the bathroom cabinet for some plasters. I find Bic razors, a box of aspirin, some cotton buds, antihistamine, one rubber glove and, finally, a box of Disney Princess plasters that have been there since Iona was a kid. Oh, come on – where are the grown-up Band-Aids? Why is nothing ever straightforward in this house? Feeling pressed for time, I wrap Snow White around my little toe and throw the box back into the cupboard.

Moments later, I charge into my bedroom, ready to shake Evan awake, but the bed is empty. He can't be in the bathroom – I've just come from there. Dear God, has he made a run for it? I look out of the window, but the car is still parked where we left it.

'Honey?!' I yell, as I stand in the hallway. 'Hoonnneeeyyy!' I listen for a reply, but all I can hear is 'O Little Town of Bethlehem' floating through the hall. But then I hear something. It's my mum laughing, but it's not her usual belly laugh – it's the laugh she uses when she's around handsome men. A twinge of panic sets in. He's up. He's up, he's in the kitchen with my family and he's alone and unarmed.

Ignoring the dull ache from my princess toe, I sprint through the living room and throw open the kitchen door. Everyone's sitting around the table and Evan is holding court.

'. . . I was rushing back to the office, so I sent over a drink and my number on a business card. It's disgustingly lame, I know, but I just had to get her attention before I left.'

'Honey!' I interrupt, my eyes wide and fearful. 'I didn't hear you get up! I would have been here sooner.'

'Oh, don't worry,' he replies, taking a sip of coffee. 'Your family have been looking after me. I'm just filling them in on how we met.'

I smile nervously and take a seat beside Dad, as Mum and Iona have occupied the seats beside Evan. Everyone is still in their sleepwear, including Evan, who appears to have borrowed a dressing gown from my dad, who's passing out the breakfast rolls.

'I didn't know if you wanted bacon or square, so I just made both,' he says, handing Evan the plate.

'Square?' Evan asks. 'Square what?'

'Sausage,' I explain. 'Lorne sausage is about as Scottish as haggis, which, incidentally, my darling *Robert* has never tried.'

Not Evan. Robert. Ha! Nailed it.

Everyone playfully gasps in horror, but not Iona. Iona just sighs. 'What is it with Scottish folk and haggis? Why do we turn into twee, nationalistic idiots whenever it's mentioned?'

'Um, because it's delicious,' Patrick replies, with a mouth full of bacon. I see his appetite has returned.

'We only eat it once or twice a year,' she continues. 'I'm pretty sure Robert doesn't turn into an arse when someone mentions that they haven't tried cockles or jellied bloody eels.'

'Well, he'll be trying haggis later,' Dad confirms, 'because it's already been shoved up the turkey.'

'Aren't cockles associated more with Dublin?' Kim asks, stirring her tea. She seems to have turned back into her quiet, passive self. 'They're quite nice,' she continues. 'Salty.'

'They're a London delicacy too, though; right, Robert?' Iona replies and, without waiting for a response, yells, 'MUM, why on earth is this holy-choir shit still playing! Every year, you play this. We're not even religious!'

Mum isn't listening. 'William! Will you stop feeding that dog so much bacon? He'll have a heart attack. Won't you, boy? Come here.'

I sit back and eat, while observing the chaos that is my

family. Patrick and Kim are stealing kisses and sharing food, Mum is now kissing the dog, Iona is telling Dad that her shower isn't working properly and Dad is suggesting we all have a hair of the dog before lunch. In the midst of the madness, I catch Evan's eye as he munches on his first square-shaped sausage. 'Is it a winner?' I ask, skilfully dodging a toast crust that Iona throws at Patrick when he declares that she can't use his shower.

'It is,' Evan replies. 'I'm most impressed.'

'Callaghan's the butcher,' Mum interrupts. 'He makes his own. Emily always takes some back with her, when she visits. Do you visit your parents often, Robert?'

'I do,' Evan replies, glancing at me for reassurance. 'In fact, Emily and I will be spending New Year with them in Surrey. Didn't Emily tell you?'

No, Emily didn't, I think to myself, because you just fucking made that up on the spot.

Mum slaps me lightly on the arm. 'This one is making a habit of keeping things to herself.'

'And what do your parents do for a living?' Iona asks casually, which, roughly translated, means, How much money do they earn?

'They're retired now,' Evan replies. 'They were both professors.'

'Interesting,' she says. 'I always thought Emily could be an English professor, but she seems to enjoy the lower end of the education pay scale.'

'Oi! Snobby! Shut it,' growls Patrick, who is now on his third breakfast roll. 'You'll have to forgive my sister, Robert. She forgets that not everyone can be a partner in a law firm her *husband* owns, living in a house her parents paid for. Without him, she'd be doing legal-aid divorce cases and will-writing . . .'

'Ha!' she responds, sneeringly. 'Without *your* wife, you'd still be living here with Mum and Dad, pretending that your lowly IT job is an actual career and not just a step up from data entry. And Mum and Dad bought your house too, fuck-face.'

'Oh, enough, the pair of you,' Mum snaps. 'You're making Robert uncomfortable and that's the last thing I want.' She turns to Evan and smiles. 'Now, Robert, I want you to feel welcome here. If you have any problems while you're here, or even if you just want a wee chat, my text-message inbox is always open . . .'

The kitchen erupts with the sound of laughter. 'Oh, you complete bastards!' I exclaim, thinking that this will be the moment Evan declares he's had enough of me, my family and my oddly shaped sausages.

But he's laughing. In fact, he's laughing louder than anyone else. He holds his hands up. 'You got me,' he says playfully. 'You all heard the story about the business card, right? What can I say? I'm horrible at romance, but I meant every single word of that text.'

They're not laughing anymore. Now they're *aww*-ing and

ahh-ing and telling me how lucky I am. Evan takes hold of my hand and gives it a little squeeze. I smile and squeeze back twice as hard. '*Honey*, you're embarrassing me.'

'Can we just do the bloody gifts now?' Iona asks, throwing looks of disgust around the room. 'And I'd like to get showered at some point today . . .'

'Well, you're a bundle of fun this morning, aren't you?' Dad remarks. 'I'll take a look at the shower after we do gifts – I have a feeling that I forgot to switch on your immersion heater.'

Mum stands up and starts to clear away the dishes. 'Living room in fifteen minutes, please,' she instructs. 'And if Santa hasn't brought me something from Yves Saint Laurent, there will be blood.'

We all start to pile out of the kitchen, feeling full and rather sluggish, but still managing to retain a small amount of Christmas cheer. Evan and I go back to my room, me dragging along my sizeable arse and Evan humming 'Do You Hear What I Hear?' in time to the choir.

Door closed, I throw open my case and remove each gift, carefully stacking them in a pile, ready for carrying.

'This is your present to me,' I say, handing him the expertly wrapped book and perfume, tied together with silver ribbon.

'But it looks exactly like all the others.'

'So?' I reply, zipping my case back up. 'What's wrong with that?'

'Well, it looks like you've wrapped your own present.'

'Oh, shit – so it does.' I panic. He's absolutely right. Each gift has the same ribbon work and gift-card placement. 'Just take off the ribbon and scrunch it up a bit. Make it look like a careless boy wrapped it.'

Evan obliges, taking seconds to undo all my hard work. 'All set?' he asks.

I nod. 'Remember, this black shirt I'm giving you must *not* be worn. It's going back to the shop.'

'I might really like it, though.' He ponders. 'It might suit me.'

'Well, it'll go well with the black eye I'll give you if you ruin it.'

'Ugh. So angry,' he teases, reaching into his bag. 'Where's all that Christmas cheer gone?'

'I must have left it in the car. What have you got there?' I ask as Evan produces four white envelopes from his bag. 'Did you bring cards for everyone?'

'Yes,' he replies. 'I'd have felt like a cheapskate showing up empty-handed. Besides, it makes you look good, and the whole reason I'm here is to make you look good. Right?'

'Indeed,' I say. 'But it's still a nice gesture, though. They wouldn't have expected anything from you. They're unhinged, but they're not unreasonable.'

Evan's token of goodwill has left me feeling all warm and fuzzy inside, and I smile to myself as I gather the presents from my bed.

'Can you just open that window before we go?' I ask. 'It still smells like dog.'

He does as I ask, letting the gentle, cold breeze blow through the room.

'Did you know I have a massive arse?' I ask him, obviously unable to let this go. 'Mum told me. Apparently, I inherited it from my gran on my dad's side.'

'Your gran left you her arse in her will?'

'Something like that.'

'Well, the answer is no . . . and yes,' he replies. 'I mean, it's not gargantuan, by any means, but it's not small either. It's ample. It's like an arse from the 1950s.'

'I have a retro arse?' I ask, completely delighted. 'I can live with that.'

'Do you take everything your mum says to heart?' he asks, opening the bedroom door. 'Because you shouldn't, you know. Nine times out of ten, people's negative comments come from their own insecurities.'

'Is your mum judgemental?' I ask, stepping out into the hall. 'You haven't really told me anything about her.'

'All mums are the same,' he replies. 'My mum probably thinks I have a fat arse too.'

In the living room, everyone is sprawled out in various stages of breakfast bloat, chattering away like oversized budgies.

'Do we have any Bloody Mary mixture left?' Dad asks, still clinging on to his previous hair-of-the-dog suggestion.

'Everything except celery stalks,' Patrick answers, 'which is no great loss.'

Dad claps his hands. 'Anyone want a little pick-me-up, before we begin?' He's already up on his feet and dashing towards the bar before anyone answers.

The consensus is an overwhelming yes, with everyone convincing themselves that Bloody Marys don't really count as booze because the tomatoes cancel it out. While Dad prepares the drinks, we all hand our gifts to each other, ready to rip them to shreds when he finally sits down. Evan watches in amusement as we grab, throw, inspect and arrange our presents in front of us, delighted when he receives one from my mum and dad to place on top of his unwearable shirt.

'Come on, Dad!' Patrick yells, impatiently. 'We have work to do!'

'Patrick, you asked everyone for vouchers,' I remind him, fiddling with a red bow on one of the gifts. 'You know what you're getting . . . or did you ask for a pony again?'

He blushes, throwing a scowl in my direction. 'I was three, Emily. Let it go.'

'Seven!' Dad shouts across the room. 'You were seven and you wanted a white pony.'

'I remember that!' Iona exclaims. 'I wanted the board game, Mousetrap, and you wanted an effing pony!'

Mum starts to reminisce about how Patrick had bonded with a Highland pony called Jackerby, from the local riding school, and how he might just die if Jackerby didn't come and live with us.

'We couldn't bring ourselves to tell him that Jackerby had a gammy leg, was blind in one eye and was headed for the glue factory at any moment – it would have broken his wee heart. So we told him that Santa really wanted him to have a Game Boy instead.'

'So we can blame you and Dad for his unhealthy interest in technology,' Iona says, clearing the table for the incoming tray of drinks. 'Honestly, I don't understand grown men being so obsessed with gaming. YouTube is filled with emotionally stunted men, filming themselves playing *Minecraft*, and they give themselves idiotic names, like Tweetypie and Markoplayer—'

'It's PewDiePie . . . and Markiplier,' Kim corrects, staring into space. 'Markiplier . . . He's so hot.'

'Oh, hell – not you too, Kim! I'm so disappointed.' Iona helps Dad put the tray on the table, looking thoroughly disgruntled, as does Patrick, who obviously had no idea his wife fancied a vlogger.

'What about you, Robert? Are you an amateur gamer when you're not strategising or managing budgets?'

'Iona,' he says, placing his right hand on his chest. 'I can honestly say, hand on heart, that I'm one hundred per cent *not* an amateur gamer.'

I give him a quick foot-nudge. This is getting a bit too close for comfort now. We need a diversion. 'OK, people!'

I say, louder than necessary. 'Raise your glasses! Merry Christmas, everyone!'

Despite our inability to be civil with each other for more than a few minutes at a time, the room rapidly fills with the sounds of well wishes, laughter and glasses clinking, before the unwrapping frenzy begins. Pacino sits patiently, watching everyone like a hawk, ready to pounce on anything edible or stick-shaped. This is only his third Christmas, but he's aware that one of these brightly wrapped parcels is for him.

Evan begins unwrapping his first box, revealing the shirt originally meant to make Robert love me even more than I stupidly thought he did.

'Wow,' he says, holding it up in front of him. 'Now, that's a damn fine-looking shirt. Thanks, Em.'

'My pleasure,' I reply, giving him a hug and hoping that he doesn't put it anywhere near his Bloody Mary. 'Open your other one.'

He tears into a squishy red parcel to reveal a pair of sheepskin gloves and a stripy scarf. He grins at my parents. 'That's very kind of you. I love them.'

'You're welcome, lad,' Dad says, giving him a nod, while Mum plants a smacker on his left cheek, leaving a bright-red lipstick mark. Yes, my mother wears lipstick, even in her dressing gown.

'You're very welcome, Robert,' she says. 'It can get bitter out there. You'll need them if you go out walking with Emily.'

Kim has also received some winter accessories from her in-laws and is already wearing her new chocolate-coloured Cossack hat, which looks stunning against her red hair.

'You look like a Bond girl,' Patrick tells her. 'How the hell did I get so lucky?'

She smiles shyly and opens her next present. '*Star Wars* earrings? You got me *Star Wars* earrings?'

A hush falls over the room while we wait for Kim to repeatedly punch her husband into a galaxy far, far away.

She leaps on him. 'NO! *I'm* the lucky one!' she squeals, kissing his face. 'They're unbelievable!'

I go in for a closer look as she hooks them into her earlobes. Two large silver oval shapes, one with a picture of Princess Leia, saying, 'I love you', and one with a picture of Han Solo, saying, 'I know'. Evan high-fives Patrick, while Iona is genuinely lost for words.

'Look, everyone! Robert got me the book I wanted ... and Chanel!' I hold both of them aloft so they can remark on how wonderful he is. It might not be *Star Wars* earrings, and, sure, I had to buy one of the gifts myself, but it's better than sitting here alone, getting pitying looks from my family.

Iona, struggling with the Sellotape on her second gift, looks at Evan's offering and screws up her face. 'Surely that's not all you got her?!'

Patrick throws some wrapping paper at her. 'What's wrong with that?! You're so bloody obsessed with the value of everything! What did you expect him to give her? An island?'

Evan looks around awkwardly. 'Well, of course it's not *all*—'

'Are you saying that our sister doesn't deserve an island?'

'You're missing the point, Iona. And what did Graham get you? Something diamond-encrusted to make up for the fact he's not here? A new car? A voucher for new tits?'

'We're doing presents when he gets back,' she growls. 'But, yes, it'll be something you can't purchase off Etsy . . .'

I take the Chanel out of the box and begin spraying them like a pair of annoying mosquitoes. 'I'm very happy with my presents. Move on.'

I hear Mum give a little shriek of excitement. 'The Sac de Jour handbag! Oh, William, darling, I adore it. Look, Iona! Look at the craftsmanship on that.'

Mum and Iona are like peas in a pod. They enjoy anything with a large price tag and a designer name. Admittedly, Mum's snobbery has mellowed somewhat over the years, but she still gets genuinely overwhelmed at the sheer magnificence of a £1,800 Yves Saint Laurent handbag. She kisses my dad, thanking him like she had no idea this was coming, when, in reality, she sent him the link to the handbag in September.

I look at Dad thumbing through his Frederick Forsyth memoir, a look on his face that portrays both happiness and annoyance that he has to spend time with us when he should be reading this. 'Wonderful, Emily,' he proclaims. 'Just wonderful.' Dad doesn't give a shit how much his present cost. He only cares that you put some thought into it.

Pacino, feeling ignored, barks at us all impatiently, snuffling around the wrapping paper for something dog-related.

Mum reaches under the tree and produces a large bone-shaped parcel. 'Here you are, boy,' she says, scratching behind his ear. 'I wouldn't forget about you, now, would I?'

She holds the present in her hand while Pacino begins unwrapping it with his teeth, eating small pieces as he wags his tail excitedly. Finally, he reaches the bone and takes it gently from Mum; he turns around in a little circle before resting beside the fire, gnawing happily.

While the last present is being unwrapped, Iona is passing round a box of tiny chocolate Christmas trees. 'God, I really need to shower. Are we all done now?'

'You haven't opened Ev— *Robert's* cards yet,' I stutter. Dammit. That was close.

'Oh, of course – how rude of us,' Patrick says, lifting his from the floor. 'Sorry, mate.'

'No, honestly, it's fine,' Evan insists awkwardly. 'You can open them whenever you like. Quite frankly, I'm a little embarr—'

'Too late!' I announce, tearing the envelope open. 'Everyone loves a Christmas card! I like the funny ones with . . .'

My mouth falls open. The rest of the family quickly

follow suit. This isn't a funny Christmas card. In fact, this isn't a Christmas card at all.

'Holy shit!' Patrick declares, showing the card to Kim. 'Are you serious?!'

Mum gives her 'surprised at my handbag' shriek again – only this time she means it.

Please enjoy a weekend stay in one of our luxurious suites at a time to be arranged at your convenience. Your stay includes full use of the spa facilities, swimming pool and golf course. All meals are provided. We look forward to welcoming you to Wallace Hall.

'Well, well, well!' Iona exclaims. 'This place is *at least* a grand a night. Who the hell do you do marketing for? Saudi Arabia?'

I start to laugh nervously. 'Guys, I think this is Robert's idea of a joke,' I say, nudging him playfully. 'I'm not entirely sure what the punchline is, but there's no way—'

'No joke,' Evan says, shaking his head. 'No punchline. Just call the hotel to arrange—'

'Hotel? It's more like a castle!' Mum interrupts. 'Isn't that the place Madonna got married?'

'No, that was Skibo Castle,' Dad corrects. 'Wallace Hall is where the Clintons stayed last year.'

'Darling, can I speak to you alone for a moment?' I say, rising from the couch.

'Of course, sweetheart,' he replies. 'Lead on.'

He follows me into my bedroom, where he barely gets a chance to close the door behind us before I demand to know exactly what he's playing at.

'This isn't funny.' I scowl, being careful to keep my voice lowered in case Iona has her ear pressed against the door. 'It's one thing to lie to my family for me; it's another thing entirely to lie to their faces and pretend you've paid for a fucking weekend stay in Wallace Hall. They'll be so disappointed when you tell them it's bullshit. Goddammit, I'm the only one who's allowed to disappoint my family!'

'I'm really not lying! I promise!' he insists. 'Look, I didn't mention it earlier in case I got here and something went wrong, like we blew our cover immediately or your family were inhospitable wankers or something.'

'But it doesn't make sense,' I continue. 'You don't have bags of cash to chuck at my family. I paid you £650 to come up here! You rent a room in a high-rise, for God's sake!'

'Look, sit down and I'll tell you everything,' he says, directing me towards the bed. I comply, still baffled by the whole situation. We both sit and, after a moment, he takes my hand, which I immediately withdraw.

'Stop that.'

'Ha ha, I'm sorry. Aw, you don't have to sit on your hands; I won't try it again.'

'Just hurry up.' I scowl.

'The truth is . . .' he begins, looking tense. He gets tiny little wrinkles between his eyes when he's tense. 'The truth is that I'm a secret millionaire! Like in the television show. But not.'

'Oh, for fuck's sake; I thought you were going to be serious,' I reply, giving him a shove. 'Christ, if my family think you're a millionaire, they'll disown me when I announce that Robert and I are no longer together. Like to try again?'

He smiles. 'Fine. I know a guy who works there. The catch is that they can only use them in February, when most of the hotel is closed for refurbishment. It's basically a free room on a building site.'

There's a faint knock on my bedroom door. It's Dad. 'Emily? Robert? Are you coming back through? Would you like some coffee?'

'Yes, please! Be right there!' I yell, jumping up from the bed. I swing around and grab Evan by the shirtsleeve. 'Total dick move,' I announce, pulling him up. 'But here's what's going to happen: you're going to graciously accept their thank yous, tell Iona you don't like talking about money when she inevitably asks you how much you earn per annum, including staff bonus, and carry on being Robert, better than the actual Robert could have done himself. Deal?'

'Deal.'

'OK. Good,' I reply, straightening my pyjama jacket. 'I'll

just have to play dumb when they try to book it. Are you going to spring anything else on me, while we're here? Any more scams? Any secrets I should know about? Witness protection? Alien abductions? Porn movies?'

'Hmm, that depends. Just watching? Or performing in?'

'Performing in!'

'Ah. Then, no to all three.'

We dash back into the living room, where coffee has been served and the choir music has finally been turned off. Instead, Wham's 'Last Christmas' is melodiously floating around the room.

'You took your time,' Iona says, raising an eyebrow. 'Trouble in Paradise?'

'Quite the opposite,' I reply, giving Evan a squeeze. 'I was just thanking Robert properly for my presents.'

'Ah, young love,' Mum coos, handing me a cup. 'Well, one of you, anyway.'

I'm almost glad to hear her last remark. It shows me that nothing has changed and no one has called the hotel while we were out of the room.

'What time is Christmas lunch?' Patrick asks. Surely he can't be hungry already?

'Quarter past three,' Mum replies. 'After the Queen's speech. The same time it is *every* year.'

Not only does Mum become religious on Christmas Day, she also becomes a royalist. The other 364 days of the year are entirely choir- and Queen-free.

'I'll nip off and look at your shower, now,' Dad says to Iona. 'If it doesn't work, you can use ours, Patrick's or Emily's, so there is really no reason to have that perpetual scowl on your face any longer.'

He has a point. Iona's known for her stroppiness, but it's pretty spectacular at the moment, even for her. Maybe she's missing her hubby? Regardless of what she says, there's no way she's not feeling at least slightly miffed that she has to contend with the family at Christmas, solo. Maybe she's finally getting a small taste of what it's like to be me?

CHAPTER NINETEEN

We all disperse in a mannerly fashion to get showered and changed. Mine is the only bedroom in the house which isn't en suite, so I get the main bathroom all to myself, which has a tub and separate shower cubicle.

Evan lies down on the bed, while I close the window, then hang up my red velvet skater dress and sparkly tights on the wardrobe door.

'Just going to run the bath,' I inform him. 'I intend to soak in there 'til next Christmas.'

'Shall I just use the shower while you're in the bath, then?' he asks, admiring his new gloves.

'Um, no. You can shower when I've finished.'

He leans up on his elbows, his T-shirt clinging to his stomach. Where does he keep his fat?

'I don't want to be waiting all bloody year to get clean, and, by the sounds of it, the rest of the bathrooms are in use. Come on – two birds and all that. No need to be shy.'

He's suggesting this like it's the most normal thing in the world.

'In case you've forgotten, we're not actually a couple,' I remind him, gathering up a bath towel. 'There is no reason in hell for us to be undressed in the same room.'

'Well, it looks a bit weird if we're doing everything separately,' he moans. 'I bet Kim and your brother aren't arguing over who gets to wash first.'

'Probably not, but the answer is still nope,' I reply. 'No one will even notice; you're thinking too much into it. I won't be too long; you can read my book or try on my shoes or something.'

'Yeah, I'm not taking over Robert's role completely, you know . . .'

I laugh. 'Technically, he never wore them, as such . . . He just . . . Oh, never mind.'

I walk across the hallway and into the bathroom, which is cosy warm and smells like mum's favourite black tea and vetiver room fragrance. I open the hot water tap and let it run while I inspect the various bubble baths on the shelf: peach . . . Radox . . . floral (of course) and wild raspberry, which I declare to be the winner. For the first time since we got here, I begin to relax properly. It's just me, my bubbles and Iona standing right behind me.

'AGHH! Where the hell did you spring from? God, I nearly had a heart attack.'

'Dramatic,' she replies, standing with a towel in her

hand. 'I need to use your shower. Mine is definitely broken and Mum and Dad's smells like Deep Heat Rub.'

'I'm just about to get in the bath,' I say, indicating the running water. 'And Robert will be using the shower after me, so you'll have to wait.'

She puts her hand on her hip. 'Why can't Robert use the shower while you're in the bath? Then you'll both be finished and I can get in.'

'Because I want five minutes to myself!' I reply. 'Why is everyone trying to get in here with me?'

'What are you wittering on about?' she asks impatiently. 'Look, I'm not going to stand here and bicker with you. There are seven people who need to get showered and ready before lunch.'

'Fine,' I say. 'You can use the shower first. Robert can wait.'

'Oh, don't be silly. I don't want to see you stark naked while I'm in the shower, and I imagine the feeling is mutual.'

'How are my girls?'

Oh, good – now Mum's here. What a treat.

'I left my shampoo in here,' she says, walking over to the shower cubicle. 'I'll be out your way in a second.'

'Mum, Emily doesn't want her boyfriend to shower while she's in the bath,' Iona says, sticking her tongue out at me. 'She'd rather see my naked arse than his. I find that very odd.'

'Oh, God. Are you grassing on me now? Really?'

'Well, in Emily's defence, it must be quite intimidating having someone who looks like Robert see you naked, I'd imagine,' she muses, picking up her shampoo. 'But he is your partner, darling. He loves you just the way you are.'

'How do you manage to be so hugely critical and supportive in the same sentence?' I ask, checking my bath water. 'It's a gift. A really, really terrible gift.'

'Don't be so sensitive. I was only saying that it must be daunting being an older woman with such a handsome younger partner. It wasn't a criticism.'

'Oh, for Pete's sake. You're both getting on my nerves now.' I fling open the bathroom door, yelling, 'ROBERT! . . . ROBERT! Come and shower with your elderly girlfriend. Hurry up, before I fall and break a hip.'

Aware that impulse reactions seem to be my speciality these days, I panic like hell on the inside, while appearing calm and collected in front of Iona and Mum. I walk over to the bath and turn off the water. Dear God – please don't let Evan wander in here naked.

Thankfully, he appears fully clothed, carrying a razor and shaving gel, with a towel under his arm. He stops in his tracks when he sees Mum and Iona, who don't look like they're in a rush to leave any time soon.

'Oh, good – we're all here,' he says, throwing his towel on to the floor. 'Emily warned me that there might be some kind of weird, naked bath-time initiation ceremony. Shall I go first?' To my horror, he pulls up his T-shirt as if to undress, and I pounce on him, yelling that he's being highly inappropriate, while Mum creases up with laughter. Even Iona cannot contain her giggles.

'Out!' I insist, pointing at the open bathroom door. 'Both of you.'

Evan grins and picks his towel up off the floor as the two giggling idiots make their way into the hall.

'I will call you when we're done,' I inform Iona. 'Oh, stop laughing, Mum; it wasn't that funny.'

I slam the door shut behind me and rest my head against it for a moment, trying to think of how I can get out of this. There is no way I'm stripping off in front of him. Mum's comments, although uncalled for, aren't that far from the truth. Would this be as much of an issue if I still resided in my twenty-five-year-old body?

'Here's what we'll do,' I dictate, pacing back and forth. 'We'll just have to make sure we're facing away from each other at all times. My bubbles will camouflage most of my body, so . . .'

I hear the shower door creak and the sound of fast running water. Then singing. Lots of singing. He's already in.

'A little warning might have been nice!' I hiss, but he can't hear me.

'Oi! Which way are you facing?' I ask, a little louder. No reply.

I crank my neck to the side, trying to gauge which direction he might be facing, and catch a brief glimpse of his bare bottom through the increasingly steamy glass pane. Good – he's facing the wall. Now, if I can quickly strip off and jump in, he won't see me and ... I'm still staring at his bottom.

My head shoots back to its original position and I physically try and shake the image out of my brain while giving myself a little pep talk.

It's an arse, Emily; it's just an arse. A peachy-looking one, admittedly, but you're an adult ... an adult who's letting her bath go cold because she's too busy thinking about arses.

Oh, forget this. I'm getting in. Head down, I turn and scuttle over to the bath, removing my pyjamas like they're made of bombs. Then I'm into the water and up to my neck in bubbles before Evan even has time to finish his chorus of 'Santa Baby'. I settle back, feeling relieved that my strategy worked and, should Evan turn around, all he'll be able to gawp at is my head. However, there is one slight problem. Now, I'm facing the shower cubicle directly and there's a very real chance I'm going to witness the reason Cassie made all of those weird squealing noises. Swiftly, I dunk my head under the water, feeling the bubbles cover my face and go up my nose. It's not pleasant, but at least there's no chance of seeing a cock under here. As hard as I try to hide out underwater, I last a whole thirteen seconds before a misjudged sniff means I'm spluttering and coughing my way to the surface, complete with bubble beard and foamy toupee.

'Do you need arm bands?' I hear Evan ask as I wipe the soap from my eyes. 'A snorkel, perhaps?'

'I'm glad you find this amusing,' I reply, moulding myself a bubble-bath bra while I reach for the shampoo and quickly lather my hair. 'Just keep facing the wall until I've washed my hair, please – that's all I ask.'

I grab the detachable shower-head and rinse off the shampoo – and my makeshift bra, in the process. This has been the most stressful bath of my lifetime. Evan appears to have kept to his word and, thankfully, the steam from the shower has finally masked his naked frame. Now for the tricky part.

I lean over and grab my towel from the floor. 'I'm getting out now, Evan,' I inform him. 'If you turn around before I'm decent, I swear, I will cover your testicles in hair-removing cream while you sleep.'

He laughs. 'You're threatening me with personal grooming. Some men pay for that . . . but, fine – I *swear* I won't turn around.'

Trusting him to keep to his word, I spring from the bath, wet feet slipping precariously as I drip all over the tiled floor. 'Nearly done,' I inform him, wrapping my towel securely around me. 'Just need to brush my teeth and then I'll be—'

'HURRY UP, PLEASE!' Iona yells from the hallway. 'IT'S NEARLY FUCKING NEW YEAR.'

'Be out in a min!' I yell back, squeezing the last few drops of water from my hair into the bath. I grab a second towel and wrap my hair into a turban.

'Time's up,' Evan says, turning off the shower. 'I'm coming out. Brace yourself.'

I turn to face the back wall, while he steps out of the shower.

'You know, this part would run a lot smoother if you weren't wearing my towel on your head.'

Ugh – he's right. 'Nothing about today has run smoothly,' I grumble, throwing the towel behind me. 'Why should this part be any different?'

Moments later, we're side by side at the sink – me brushing my teeth, and him in mid shave – both aware that Iona is stalking us from the hallway, getting ready to storm the bathroom and shoot on sight.

'What's your tattoo of?' he asks, running his razor under the tap. 'The one on your thigh; it's a gang tag, isn't it?'

'You looked! I spit into the sink furiously. 'You promised you wouldn't turn around! You *promised*!'

Iona bangs on the door again and I tell her we'll be right out.

He holds his hands up. 'I didn't turn around, I swear! I didn't need to. The glass at the back of the cubicle . . . Well, it's very, erm, reflective . . .'

'You spied on me! You're a liar! A liar and a big, dirty, spying pervert!'

'Come on!' He laughs. 'This is the real world! I defy you to find any straight man who wouldn't do exactly the same . . . and it was only for a moment, anyway, because the glass steamed up.'

'Bullshit reasoning,' I reply.

'*You* were the one who made me come in here!' he says, checking in the mirror to see if he's missed anywhere. 'Stop acting like I'm some sort of deviant! Besides, I saw you having a look at my bum, and you don't see me getting all outraged. In fact, I quite like you looking at me.' He rinses his razor and places it back on the sink.

'Not as much as you like looking at yourself, I imagine.' I draw his attention to his own physique, wrapped in a little white towel at the waist. 'I mean, look at you. Is that contouring? You must spend hours in the gym . . . and your skin . . .' I run my hand across his cheek. His skin if softer than mine. 'Do you exfoliate? Man, I bet you own more skincare products than I do.'

Before I have the chance to remove my hand, he puts his on top of it and holds it there against his face.

'What are you doing?'

'This,' he replies, pulling me in closer, towel touching towel. He smells fresh and clean and I breathe him in. It gives me a tingling sensation that starts at my toes and floods my entire body, from those areas of exposed flesh to those hidden only by my flimsy white towel.

'That night in my flat,' he begins, my hand still on his cheek. 'The night we had our first hug and you accused me of kicking you out—'

'Well, you did—'

'I know, I know, but it wasn't because I didn't like hugging you. Quite the opposite; it was because hugging you felt like this.' He takes my hand from his face and places it on his chest. 'Feel that?' he asks. 'It feels like it's going to beat right through my skin.'

I take a breath. There was a time when a girl like me would have done anything for a boy like him. A time when superficial lust and sex were just as important and valid as true love. But time has given a girl like me a woman's perspective.

As our eyes lock, I can tell what he's thinking. He's thinking that this is the part where we kiss.

There's a split second before two people kiss that changes everything. It's that moment where eyes meet, breath is held and everything stops making sense, in order to make perfect sense. This is not that moment.

'A book.'

My words jolt his thoughts away from my lips and back to reality. 'Huh? What?'

'The tattoo. On my thigh. It's a little book. Robert would know this, so you should too.'

'Right. OK . . .'

'And this . . . whatever this is,' I begin, taking my hand

off his chest, 'isn't going to happen. Seriously, you thought I'd be that easy?'

I brush past him to leave, but he pulls me back. 'Hey, slow down. I don't understand. I thought—'

'Yes.' I laugh. 'I know what you thought because I thought it too! But, unlike you, I thought past the sex part and kept on thinking, and thinking . . . finally stopping when I came to the inevitable, pathetic conclusion. Jesus, Evan, I *paid* you to be here, but you're not a male escort. I don't need some pity fuck from a twenty-nine-year-old guy who'll forget about this the moment we return to London. I've already been the mistress cliché this year, don't turn me into an even worse one.'

When I push past him this time, he doesn't stop me.

'It's all yours!' I yell at Iona, making my way into the bedroom. Evan follows, slamming the door behind him.

'Easy, there!' I say, taking my underwear out of the case. 'You nearly took the door off its hinges!'

'Fuck you, Emily,' he says, marching over to his side of the bed. 'I'm so pissed off with you right now.'

I open the wardrobe door and stand behind it, blocking Evan's view as I pull on my knickers. 'Why?' I ask. 'Because I wasn't seduced by your whole routine?'

'It wasn't a seduction, Emily. I was trying to tell you how I feel.'

I pop my head round the side of the door. He's still

sitting on the bed in his towel. 'Feel? How can you feel anything? We hardly know each other.'

I retreat back behind the door and put my bra on, confused that he genuinely seems wounded by my response. I stretch my arm around the door to retrieve my dress, but I can't quite reach. Damn.

'Would you hand me my dress, please?' I ask, fully expecting him to say no, but thankfully I hear the bed springs expand under him when he stands up and walks over. 'Thanks,' I say, holding out my hand. I hear the sound of the coat hanger being taken down, but no dress appears.

'Are you really telling me that you feel nothing? That this is all one-sided?'

'Evan, are you holding my dress hostage?'

'Until you answer me, yes.'

'Fine. Yes, I'm telling you that it's all one-sided.'

He pushes the door closed, leaving me exposed in my underwear.

'I don't believe you,' he replies. 'When I kissed you last night . . . the way you kissed me back . . . that wasn't nothing. Why can't you just admit that you're attracted to me?'

I grab my dress from his hands and attempt to cover whatever is left of my modesty.

'You kissed me because you had to!' I reply, getting exasperated. 'Because Iona had brought the fact that you hadn't kissed me to everyone's attention! And so what if I fancy you?! It doesn't mean I have feelings for you, because, if I felt something from a kiss that meant nothing, what does that make me? I'll tell you what it makes me: fucking pathetic. Tragic, even!'

He shakes his head. 'Iona may have brought the subject up, yes, but I kissed you because I wanted to; let's get that straight.'

'But why?! Why are you so determined to go off script?! First, the hotel gifts, then the kiss and now this. Why can't you just pretend to be my arsehole boyfriend, like I'm paying you to?'

'Wait. You fancy me? You just said you fancy me, right?'

I sigh and pull the wardrobe door open again, letting him know that this conversation is over.

'Fine,' he replies, admitting defeat. 'I give up. We'll just pretend like nothing is happening here – if that's what you want.'

'All that is happening here is two people are getting ready for lunch,' I say, pulling on my tights. 'Nothing else. Let's move on, shall we?'

I don't hear another peep from him while we dress.

You did the right thing, I think to myself. You've only just broken up with real Robert; now is not the time to be recklessly shagging the fake one in your parents' house . . . Besides, in a few days you'll be back in London, back in the classroom and back to reality.

'I'm good to go,' I hear him say. 'What do you think?'

I look from behind the door and stare. He's wearing the shirt I bought for Robert.

'Oh, for God's sake,' he says. 'Relax. I'll pay you for the shirt. Close your mouth.'

I'm not staring because he's wearing the shirt. I'm staring because he doesn't just look amazing in it, he makes me want to erase everything I've just thought and replace it with, You fucking idiot. Look at him! For £650, you could have at least been felt up.

'It's fine,' I say, clearing my throat. 'Keep it. Looks good.'

'Whatever. I'll wait in the living room for you.'

Half an hour later, my hair is dry and my make-up applied, and I'm still kicking myself for not at least kissing him again. I need some moral support here, and I certainly won't be getting it from my family. I call Kara.

'Merry Christmas, Emily!' she shrieks down the handset. 'I was just thinking about you!'

'How's your day going so far?' I ask. 'Get anything good?'

'Morning sex.'

'I meant Christmas prezzies, but thanks for sharing.'

'Oh, yes; I got loads of stuff, as it happens. New bag, new coat – both of which I picked out myself – and a pair of stunning emerald earrings, which I'm wearing right now. My mother-in-law got me a cookbook and a thirty-two-piece kitchen-utensils set.'

'I think she's trying to tell you something.' I laugh.

'Yes, she's trying to tell me that she's an arsehole.

Anyway, how's it going there? I hope no one is making you feel bad about Robert. He's the loser here, not you.'

'I didn't tell them anything about the break-up,' I reply. 'I'll keep hold of that nugget of disappointment until after Christmas.' I don't have time to fill her in on the Evan / Robert situation. She'd think I was insane, anyway. 'Anyhow, I need to run. The Queen will have finished her speech by now. Just wanted to say hi, my lovely.'

'Take care, Em,' she says. 'And keep your chin up! Give my love to the family!'

I hang up and call Alice, but she doesn't answer. 'It's me,' I tell her answering machine. 'He tried to get it on with me in the bathroom. And I wish I'd let him. I'm having a crisis. Phone me back when you can. Oh, and my family don't suspect a thing, so we might just pull this off ... His arse, though ... Remind me to tell you about his arse.'

I hang up and place my phone in its charger. I suppose I'd better show my face before they come looking for me. Spraying some Chanel, I take one last look at myself in the mirror before heading through for Christmas lunch. I can hear them all laughing; I bet Evan's telling them about my bubble-bath beard.

CHAPTER TWENTY

'Dad, you've outdone yourself this year. Everything looks delicious.'

Iona, seemingly in a much better mood, *oohs* and *ahs* over the Christmas feast Dad has been preparing since yesterday. The smell of rich turkey gravy and roast potatoes almost makes me weep with joy.

'I second that, Dad,' I say. 'Are those honey-glazed parsnips? What a genius you are.'

'Oh, it's nothing,' he replies modestly. 'The oven does most of the work. Go and grab a seat, everyone; it's almost ready.'

I sit between Evan and Iona and across from Kim and Patrick, while Mum and Dad take opposite ends of the table, which is already groaning under the weight of the feast. Mum starts pouring everyone champagne, whether they asked for it or not.

'Emily, have you shown Robert the garden yet?' she asks, picking up my glass. 'You'll love it,' she insists. 'A little bare in the winter, but in the summer it's quite exquisite.'

'I will,' I reply, pinching a parsnip from the serving tray. 'Or maybe tomorrow. It'll be dark after we've finished eating.'

When Mum and Dad have guests over for dinner, they use the dining conservatory, a large white and gold room which seats six well-behaved adults under a heavy gold chandelier and overlooks the garden fountain. However, when *we* all come to visit, we eat at the kitchen table, which is a far less formal environment and far more suited to our unceremonious ways. Growing up, I was always astounded by the way my friends and their families ate together. It was always very polite, very calm and very uneventful. In our house, it was usually bedlam: ten different conversations between five people, food-throwing, uncontrollable laughter, under-the-table kicking and occasional weeping. Things really haven't progressed much.

'Patrick, I swear to God, if your fingers touch any of this food directly, I will cut your balls off,' Iona threatens, swiping a dish of pickles away. 'There's a fork in there. Use it.'

'"There's a fork in there. Use it,"' he mimics back at her.

'Do you realise that you two have been having the same pointless fights for the past twenty-eight years?' I say. 'And they're not even proper fights; they're just squabbles. You're both adults, with jobs and responsibilities and spouses! Can't you even just pretend to like each other?'

'Who says we don't like each other?' Patrick asks, seriously. 'What on earth gave you that idea? I think she's ace!'

'Um, everything I just said . . .'

Iona laughs. 'Seriously, Emily?! I adore Patrick – he knows that – but we're twins. We've been fighting each other since the womb. It's what we do.'

'You wouldn't understand,' Patrick condescends. 'It's hard to explain to an only child.'

'An only . . . ? Patrick, you know I'm your sister, right? Mum, you did explain this to him?'

'Oh, you know what I mean.' Patrick laughs, while Mum gives him a playful clip round the ear. 'You didn't have anyone to fight with when you were younger.' He lifts a cracker from the table and holds it out for me to pull. It goes off with a whimper, but the other eleven are loud enough to make Pacino gruff at us in annoyance.

'Dig in, everyone,' Dad says, putting on his green paper hat. He gives Evan a nudge. 'We don't stand on ceremony here, lad; just dive in.'

'So, Robert, do you have any brothers or sisters?' Iona asks, putting sprouts on her plate. 'Emily really hasn't given us any background on you at all.'

'Spoken like a true lawyer,' I grumble. 'He's not a case file, Iona.'

To be fair, it's a perfectly reasonable question, but it's not one that we've rehearsed, so I'm stalling for time.

'I don't, I'm afraid,' Evan replies. 'Just me. Although, seeing you all together, it makes me wish I had.'

'Well, if you and Emily decide to tie the knot, you'll have sibling in-laws . . .'

'Mum, please.'

'I'm just making conversation, Emily; I'm not prying.'

Patrick seems to feel my pain and tries to steer the conversation away from reasons to marry me. 'So, Mum, what did old Lizzie have to say, then? Good speech?'

'It really was . . . I do admire the Queen, you know. She's knocking on a bit, but she still soldiers on, going through the motions . . . She must be sick of it by now. She must be ready to hang up her crown and let someone else deal with all the shite . . .' She stops and looks at Evan's plate. 'Robert, you haven't taken any haggis stuffing. William, get Robert some stuffing, will you?'

'And here we go again with the bloody haggis,' Iona moans. 'You don't have to eat it, you know. It's not mandatory.'

But it is. I think, when you come to Scotland, you try the haggis. Everyone knows this – I bet even the Queen wouldn't get a royal haggis pardon.

Not one to refuse a challenge, Evan takes a huge forkful of stuffing and eats it while we all rudely stare at him. He chews, he swallows and then he declares that it's bloody marvellous, much to the delight of everyone – well, everyone except Iona.

'Really great, Mr Carson. A unique taste, but I enjoyed it. I imagine a good malt would complement that.'

Fucking hell, he really did sound like Robert, there. That was spooky.

'What do you get if you cross Father Christmas with a duck?'

Oh, good, it's shitty Christmas-cracker joke time. We all look at Kim, who's waiting for our answers.

'Christmas crackling?'

'Crackling comes from a pig, Jenny.'

'Father Duckmas.'

'That doesn't even make sense, Patrick. No, the answer is a Christmas Quacker!'

'My turn,' says Dad, over the groans. 'What do snowmen have for breakfast?'

'Ice Krispies?'

'Good try, Robert, but it's not right.'

'Snowflakes?'

'YES! Well done, Emily. I think I liked Robert's better, though. Your turn, Emily.'

I take a bite of turkey and pick up my joke. 'OK. Why is a foot a good Christmas present?'

'A flute?'

'No, Mum, a foot. F-O-O-T – foot.'

Everyone puts up their hand and waits to be picked.

Evan chortles. 'Do they do this every year?'

'Oh, yes.' I sigh. 'The teacher joke never gets old in this house . . . OK, fine. Mum – your answer?'

'What was the question again?'

'Why is a . . . Oh, forget it. Too late. Iona? Your guess?'

'Because you get a kick out of it?'

'I wish that was correct because then this game would be over . . . Anyone else? No. Well, the correct and completely hilarious answer is because it makes a great stocking filler.'

I crumple the joke up and throw it at Patrick, who's picking at the pickles again. 'What's the plan for tonight?' Kim asks. 'Do we have one yet?'

'I vote for karaoke,' Patrick declares. 'Although Emily may have to get drunk first, but that shouldn't take long.'

'I think Emily's overcome her fear of public singing,' Evan interjects, giving me a sly smile. 'We worked through it together.'

'But is she still tone deaf?' Iona asks, leaning past me to get some carrots.

'Oh, yes.'

'Excellent. I'm in.'

'But I wanted to watch *Love Actually*,' Mum whines, stabbing a roast potato. 'It's not Christmas without *Love Actually*.'

'She makes a good point,' I agree. 'It really isn't Christmas unless you watch a man being caught doing creepy close-ups of his best-friend's wife . . .'

'Oh, shush,' Mum replies. 'You love that film just as much as I do.'

'So we'll do both,' Dad dictates. 'Cocktails and karaoke first, then the film, for those who are still sober enough to watch it. Agreed? Good. It's settled, then. Now, who wants trifle?'

CHAPTER TWENTY-ONE

While Kim belts out a very unique rendition of 'Fire-starter', Iona and I mix up the second batch of pina colada, the first batch having been devoured at record speed.

'This is too delicious,' Iona remarks, swaying unsteadily on her feet. 'I don't know why we don't have this for breakfast – you know . . . instead of food.'

I pour the mixture into the blender and push the *on* button, screwing my face up as it whizzes noisily. 'I approve of this message,' I reply, watching the ice turn to slush. 'You should make this into a law. Like, a real law. You can do that, right?'

I'm officially one drink away from becoming a burden on society and, by the looks of things, I'm not the only one.

'Yes!' Iona asserts loudly. 'I can make shit happen. I can use my powers for good, you know.'

Kim has head-banged herself back on to the couch, helped by Evan, who at some point during the evening decided to wear Mum's antlers. He passes the microphone back to Dad – compère extraordinaire.

'Right, ladies and gentlemen, next up tonight we have Patrick! Round of applause for Patrick, please.'

Iona and I make whooping noises from behind the bar while Patrick takes to the floor. As the first few bhangra beats from 'Get Your Freak On' play, everyone hollers in support, especially Kim, who seems determined to prove she's the hip-hop queen of Melrose.

Mum bops her way on over to help us carry the drinks, her tinsel scarf hanging skew-whiff around her neck. 'Best Christmas Day yet,' she declares. 'Great music, great company and, I have to say, Emily, great taste in men. Robert is a delight!'

I grin in agreement, haphazardly pouring the creamy mixture into glasses so huge we have to use two trays. 'Yes, he's quite something.'

'Doesn't it bother you that, when you're almost sixty, he'll just be turning fifty?' Iona asks. 'I mean, young men like older women, that's no big secret, but it's the reverse when *they* get older. He's not going to be wanting some wrinkly old bird on his arm. No offence, Mum.'

Mum frowns at Iona, but she doesn't disagree. 'Men are fickle like that,' she muses. 'That's why an unplanned pregnancy is generally a wise move, while you're still able. If he's going to leave you, you may as well get something out of it.'

'What is wrong with you two?' I snarl. 'Seriously? One minute I'm making pina coladas, and the next I'm knocked up, sixty and single!'

'We're just being pragmatic,' Mum says, taking a tray from my hands. 'Practical.'

'I think the word you're looking for is "psychotic",' I reply, making sure Evan isn't within earshot. 'Let's just drop it, shall we?'

I carry the second tray of drinks over and sit down beside Evan, who's flipping through the karaoke songbook.

'I can't decide between "Tiny Dancer" or "Seven Years". Any suggestions?' he asks.

'Yes: let's make a run for it. They're so drunk, they won't notice we're gone for hours.'

'Ha! What's happened now? Ugh – do they hate me? Are they giving you a hard time?'

I down half a glass of piña in one gulp. 'Yes, but not because they hate you – because they're convinced that you'll leave me when I hit sixty.'

'Years or miles per hour?'

'And I can't protest too much because, when we split up, they're going to be all, "We told you so".'

He lifts his drink and contemplates for a moment. 'They must think I'm a capricious little shit, if they truly believe I'd piss off for something as silly as that.'

'Nah,' I reply, 'they just think you're a man.'

'It's pretty unfair, though,' he continues. 'For all they

know, I could be madly in love with you. Like marry-me-and-have-my-children besotted.'

'Oh, speaking of children, I'm supposed to get knocked up by accident too. Just so I won't be lonely and childless when you eventually dump me.'

'What? Who *are* these people?'

'Welcome to my world, darling.' I clink my glass against his. 'Just be grateful you get to leave this behind in a couple of days. I have to wait until they're all dead.'

Dad launches into a slower number, with Mum swaying drunkenly in front of him like a teenage fangirl. Evan scribbles down his song choice on a scrap of paper.

'What did you choose?' I ask, watching Mum spill some of her drink on Dad's shoes. 'Dad's singing Elton, so you might have to rule that one out.'

'You'll see,' he says with a sly smile. 'Prepare to be dazzled.'

'Dazzled?' I panic. 'What do you mean? There really is no need for any kind of dazzling.'

Dad, basking in the rapturous applause for 'Goodbye Yellow Brick Road', invites Evan up to sing next.

'Thank you,' he says, taking the microphone. 'I just want to say that the song I'm about to sing is inspired by you, Emily.'

The jukebox in my mind starts playing Puddle of Mudd's 'She Fucking Hates Me' and I try not to laugh.

'This song was playing the first night I came to your flat,' he continues. 'And even though it pains me to perform it in public – this one's for you.'

I look across at the television screen. *Everybody (Backstreet's Back) – The Backstreet Boys.*

'Oh! I'm so excited for this!' I exclaim. 'I can't believe you remembered!'

I clap my hands in glee, laughing as he attempts to do his finest boy-band member impression – and, peculiarly, it works, even when wearing Mum's antlers. And it's not only me who's impressed – by the first chorus, everyone has joined in. Patrick (who seems to know the routine a little too well) even tries to teach Mum how to do a shoulder brush.

'But that looks silly.' She frowns. 'It looks like I'm brushing off dandruff.'

'But imagine that dandruff is worry! You're brushing off your worries . . . and your haters . . .'

'I think I might have dandruff.'

'Oh, forget it.'

Meanwhile, Dad and Kim are doing something which resembles line dancing, but with less coordination, and Iona is singing loudly at the dog. My heart feels happy. Nothing makes me gladder than a room full of people being silly and, in my elated state, I forget myself, planting a huge smacker on Evan's lips – a gesture he counters by kissing me back twice as hard and with an urgency I haven't felt for a long time, maybe ever.

It's only when I hear Patrick jokingly say, 'Dude, get off my sister,' that I hurtle back to reality, breaking a kiss that can only be described as *hell, yes!* A dumbfounded Evan endeavours to start singing again, stumbling through his words while I pretend to go and get some water from the kitchen.

I'm not sure exactly how long I've been in the kitchen, but Pacino has wandered in to play a game of silent staring, which I'm more than happy to participate in. I hear the commotion continuing in the next room, with everyone booing Mum's song choice, while she, in turn, yells that 'Windmills of Your Mind' is a perfectly acceptable Christmas party song and to give her the bloody mic. I feed Pacino some turkey scraps while I try to block the noise out and gather my thoughts.

It would be easy to read too much into this, for many reasons, but mainly because I'm shit-faced. Shit-faced and festive. This is the reason so many office Christmas parties get out of hand. 'Don't ever get a desk job,' I tell Pacino. 'No good can come of it.'

'Film time!' Patrick announces as he walks into the kitchen. 'Not sure Kim will last, though; she's pretty tanked . . . You all right?'

'Of course!' I lie. 'I'm just giving Pacino some life advice. I'll be right through!'

As Patrick leaves, Evan enters, minus the flashing antlers.

'Do we need to talk about this?' I ask. 'Because I do not want this to create a hostile working environment.'

'How drunk are you?!' he asks, smirking.

'Some.'

'No, I don't think we need to talk about it,' he replies. 'It's Christmas. People get drunk. People kiss. No biggie.'

'Good,' I reply, getting to my feet. 'That's the right attitude to have . . . But that kiss was, like, *BLAM!* There were sparks and fireworks and shit.'

'Let's just see if you remember it tomorrow; we can talk then, if you want to . . . Are you up for watching the movie?' he asks, offering me his arm. 'You look a little unsteady, there . . .'

'Oh, I'm just peachy,' I chirp. 'This film is ace . . . I love Ralin Ickman, don't you?'

'Alan Rickman was a fine actor, yes . . . Eek! Mind your foot on the do—'

'Fuck's sake!' I look down to examine my toe. 'I just plastered that . . . Maybe I do need a hand, now.'

Evan helps me hobble into the living room, the alcohol dealing with the majority of the pain for the time being. The lights have been dimmed and everyone is now in various states of snuggle. Patrick and Kim are on the big blue couch, with Mum, half asleep at the end. Dad's in his recliner, as always, and Iona's on the grey velvet tub chair, her legs swinging over the side. Evan sits on the smaller couch and I nestle into him, like couples are supposed to do.

'Are we all ready, then?' Dad enquires, his finger hovering over the *play* button on the remote. There's a gentle hum of agreement and Iona switches off the standard lamp, making the Christmas tree twinkle even brighter in the darkness.

Twenty minutes into the film, Pacino appears, choosing Iona as the person he'd most like to sit on. 'Can someone get this beast off me?' she moans, trying to peer past his large frame. 'He did one of his silent farts and it smells like turkey. Ugh! Seriously, it makes me want to boke.'

I expect to hear Patrick suggest that it's probably Iona who smells like turkey, but when I glance over I see that he's asleep, his head resting on Kim's lap while she strokes his hair. I feel a little pang of envy. Sure, I might be precariously leaning against an extremely handsome man who smells like a mixture of Dior's Sauvage and pina colada, but it's nowhere near the same as snuggling up to someone who adores you enough to buy you *Star Wars* earrings.

Still, it could be worse. I could be here alone, surrounded by ghostly dog farts and wishing my life was more like a Richard Curtis movie.

'Can anyone else hear "Down Under"?' Kim asks. 'You know, the Men at Work song. I keep hearing it!'

'Alice!' I proclaim. 'It's my phone!' I leap off the couch. 'Be right back.'

I scoot through to the bedroom and answer before it switches to voicemail. 'Hello! Hello! I'm here!'

'I've rung you three times already!' she tells me. 'You can't leave me a voicemail like that and then not answer!'

'Sorry,' I reply. 'Phone's been charging in my room all day. Merry Christmas! You having a good time?'

'Yeah.' She giggles. 'Toby decided to stay in London, so we're making margaritas.'

'Ah, that well-known Christmas cocktail.'

'Never mind about that, though; I need the arse gossip you promised me!'

I step over to the door and kick it closed with my foot. 'I saw him in the shower. I didn't mean to look, but it was just *there*.'

'Fuck, Emily – are you showering with the guy? I know he's supposed to be your boyfriend, but – wow – that's a bold move.'

'No, it wasn't like that,' I explain. 'It wasn't planned. Long story. But *then* he was beside me and smelled so good and I could totally tell he wanted to kiss me.'

'Toby, I'll be there in a sec! Stop whinging! Sorry,' she says. 'He can't find any clean glasses. Look, cut to the chase – did you shag him?'

'No!' I exclaim. 'Oh, tell Toby there's a box of glasses in the cupboard beside the sink . . . I did *nothing* with him!'

'And why not?' she asks, before relaying my message to Toby. 'Oh, would your parents have heard?'

'It's not that,' I reply. 'It's just . . . it wouldn't have felt right.'

'I'm sure it would have felt great . . .'

'No, I mean, it would have made things awkward and we'd be acting all weird in front of my family afterwards. Besides, I feel pathetic enough having a fake boyfriend, never mind sleeping with him.'

'You're mad,' she informs me. 'Utterly bonkers. I'd have been cowgirling that fella into New Year.'

'I know you would.' I laugh. 'Listen, we're watching a movie; I need to go.'

'All right, but just remember that you're single. And single women are allowed to sleep with anyone they like, even their fake boyfriends. Catch you later!'

When she hangs up, I notice yet another unread text from Robert. I tap on the icon.

Please call me, Emily. I have some news and we need to talk. I'll drive up there, if I have to.

'Ha!' I laugh to myself. 'You don't even know where . . .' Oh, shit. He does. I texted him the address at dinner, didn't I? He knows exactly where I am.

In my panic, I quickly reply: *Don't even think about it. You are not welcome here and I have a very large, very angry brother who will kick your teeth in if you show up.*

If he won't take no for an answer, maybe the threat of violence will make him think twice before coming up here. In reality, Patrick couldn't knock the skin off a rice pudding, but it was all I could think of.

I return to the living room just as Hugh Grant wiggles

his way across the hallway of 10 Downing Street. 'Isn't he handsome, Emily?' Mum remarks with a look of lust in her eyes. 'He reminds me of your father. Strong jawline.'

'I can dance better, though,' Dad says. 'He looks ridiculous.'

I park myself back down beside Evan, who looks relieved to see me. 'How's the mad Australian?' he whispers. 'Getting up to no good with pretty boy?'

'You cannot call Toby a pretty boy when you are also one,' I reply softly. 'Ryan Gosling – remember?'

He starts to laugh. 'You must be mistaken; I am rugged and manly. Like a lumberjack.'

'He's threatening to come up here,' I mumble.

'Ryan Gosling?'

'No . . . *Him*,' I reply, through gritted teeth. 'He probably won't . . . but what if he does?'

'He won't,' he whispers. 'What's he going to do? Pretend he's nipping out for milk and drive four hundred miles? He's full of shit.'

'Keep it down, you two.' Mum scowls. 'She's about to ruin Colin Firth's book.'

I glance over at Evan, who doesn't look back, but instead gives my thigh a little reassuring squeeze. He's right, of course. There's no way Robert's going to abandon his family at Christmas to drive up here and get an imaginary kicking from my brother. He's selfish, but he's not stupid. *Relax*, I tell myself. We're winning here. We've made it through day two. We might be pissed, injured and faintly traumatised, but we made it.

Putting some distance between Robert and me has made it easier to clear my head. I'm not missing him half as much as he obviously thinks I am, in fact, at this very moment, I'm not missing him at all.

CHAPTER TWENTY-TWO

DAY 3

'We are getting out of here this afternoon,' I announce, looking out of my bedroom window, while Evan lies in bed, thumb-tapping out a message on his phone. 'We're going to have a pub lunch, maybe take a walk in the countryside – anything, as long as it's away from here.'

It's only half past nine in the morning and I've already had enough of this place for one day. I can hear Pacino barking at some birds while Dad yells at him to be quiet, and Mum is playing Phil Collins on an endless bloody loop.

'Sounds good,' he replies. 'Though, my footwear isn't exactly appropriate for countryside walking.'

I look over at his brown soft-leather chukka boots in the corner. 'Hmm. Dad or Patrick might have a pair of something more suitable. What size are you?'

'A ten.'

'I think Dad's a ten. He'll have some old boots some-where.'

I join him on the bed and check my own phone. There's a message from Alice – *Happy Boxing Day!* – with a photo of Toby fast asleep on the kitchen floor, the word *cock* lovingly written on his forehead in marker.

There's also a message from Kara asking if I know any good hit men.

I smile and put my phone back on the bedside table, turning to look at Evan, who's all dishevelled and sleepy.

'Whatcha doing?' I ask, trying to peer at his screen. 'Who's that? Who's that?'

'Nosey,' he replies, turning his phone away. 'I'm just chatting with a friend.'

'A *girl* friend?' I gasp. 'Are you cheating on me? Does our fake relationship mean nothing to you?!'

He laughs and continues typing. 'It means everything to me. Truly. But, yes. You've withheld your passion for too long and Gillian, here, seems really keen to – how does she put it? – see my massive, throb—'

'HA! Enough!' I yell, giving him a shove towards the edge of the bed. 'I don't want to know.'

'I'm playing with you.' He laughs, showing me his phone. 'I'm talking to my mate, Vikram – a guy I work with. He's just bought himself a BMW.'

'I have a BMW,' I reply. 'It's in the garage, here. Not a new one, but it's still my baby.'

Evan closes his screen. 'Really? Why is it here and not in London?'

'Where would you suggest I park it in London?' I ask. 'Unless you want to buy me a permit for the next few years?'

'Can I ask you something?' he says, while I moan about London parking. 'Your family have money, obviously. Why aren't you using it to your advantage? Most people would.'

I shrug. 'I'm not most people. Look, I left a huge house and a pretty car to live in a shared flat and teach at a state school – that's how much I care about money . . . Besides, it's their money – not mine.'

'Yes, but it's no crime to ask for help if you need it.'

'True, and they do help me out now and again, but no more so than any other family. Patrick's very similar to me. He doesn't like taking handouts. Well, except for his house, but that was a wedding present, so he thinks it doesn't count.'

'And Iona?'

I laugh. 'Iona would be distraught if her bank balance contained anything less than six zeros. She married into money too, just in case she's cut out of the will.'

Evan chuckles, then rolls over to face me.

'Don't get too close,' I warn him. 'I have morning breath.'

He stretches backwards to reach his jeans, which are on the floor, producing a packet of chewing gum from his pocket. 'Here, stinky. I've already had some.'

I take a piece of gum and hand him back the packet.

'So, you're the odd one out,' he says. 'You're the martyr.'

'Hardly. I just didn't want to live my life spending someone else's money or to choose to love someone based on what they earn.'

'But there's a flaw in your story,' he replies, 'because Robert was loaded. It must have had something to do with your decision to go out with him.'

'It didn't! Honestly! Robert is the only wealthy man I've ever dated. From an early age, Mum would always say, "It's just as easy to love a rich man as it is a poor man," and it annoyed the hell out of me – I dated a lot of unambitious losers based on that. It was misguided rebellion. And, Robert ... I dated him because he was completely different from anyone I'd dated before. Sure, it was nice having someone take me for expensive dinners and it was a pleasure staying over in his swanky apartment, but I went out with him because he made me feel secure. I don't mean financially; I mean he was very stable. Confident. I thought that was what I wanted.'

'And now?'

'Now? Now I realise that you cannot rely on someone else to make you feel a certain way. And also that he is a fud.'

'A what?'

'A fud. Scottish insult. Can mean "dickhead" or, also, "vagina".'

'I'm totally using that when I get back.'

'But don't use it when you're with a girl – like, saying she has a lovely fud or something. It doesn't work that way.'

'Noted.'

We lie and look at each other for a bit. It's amazing how, a few days ago, I couldn't even hug him without feeling awkward, and now I'm comfortable enough to just lie beside him and gaze. That kiss last night, though . . . Neither of us has mentioned it.

'While we're on the subject of money,' he continues, 'I refunded your £650. I never had any intentions of keeping it – I just wanted to see how serious you were about me coming to Scotland. And to punish you for Cassie.'

'You did? Thank you!' I feel myself blush. 'Yeah, I did go a bit over the top with her. Sorry.'

'It's all right,' he replies. 'Besides, I consider us mates now. I wouldn't take money off a mate.'

'Oh, God – we're bonding, aren't we?' I laugh. 'This is new.'

He chuckles. 'I guess we are, in that you haven't told me to fuck off for at least fifteen minutes and you only stuck two pillows between us last night, instead of six. It's progress.'

'About last night . . .' I begin, psyching myself up to discuss the kissing elephant in the room. 'We should probably clear the air.'

'Ah, yes.' He nods. 'I was wondering if you were going to bring that up.'

'I just don't want you to get the wrong impression. One minute, I'm telling you to back off, and the next I'm kissing you. It's unfair.'

He smiles. 'Forget about it. It's not the first drunken kiss I've had, Emily. It looked good in front of your family, though – that's the main thing. You're making a big deal over nothing.'

Nothing? I'm embarrassed now. Yesterday, I was making his heart beat out of his chest and now he feels nothing?! I feel a sulk coming on. Why is he being so blasé about this? Did he not *feel* that spark?!

The sound of tyres on the gravel drive draws my attention back to the window. I jump out of bed.

'It's the marquee,' I say despondently. 'Another reason to avoid this house like the plague this afternoon.'

'I thought the party wasn't until tomorrow night?'

'It isn't,' I reply, 'but it takes ages to set up. They have a proper, heated marquee with a dance floor, posh toilets and everything.'

We watch Dad and Pacino greet the driver, who's instructed to bring everything through the side gate. I can tell that this is all fascinating and weird for Evan, like watching a reality television show that both intrigues and disgusts you. But, for me, it's normal. It's part of the Carson family tradition, going back generations. It's rumoured that Dad was conceived at the Christmas do in 1950, when my ample-bottomed gran got frisky with her distant cousin, whom she married quickly after.

'Let's grab some breakfast before this place turns into even more of a circus,' I say, knotting my hair into a pleat. I have no desire to probe him on kissing-gate any further. 'Then we'll haul ass. I hope you like fish soup.'

'Oh, fuck that,' he replies. 'Fish soup? Like, actual fish, floating in soup? Do you know who likes fish soup? *No one*, that's who! I'd rather eat that haggis crap again.'

'But you told Dad you loved it!'

'You're really having a go at me for lying to your dad? The whole point of me being here is to lie to your dad, and everyone else.'

'I hate that you make a good point. Now, hurry up. If we're quick, we'll be able to eat before Iona comes back from her run and pouts all over the toast.'

Wearing Dad's old hiking boots, which look like Pacino's been having a gnaw at them, Evan pulls on his jacket and throws his new scarf around his neck, looking very pleased with himself. 'I've got this countryside-living lark nailed.'

We step out into the morning air, which nips at our cheeks and noses. 'It's bitter, but it's bonny,' I say, feeling the hardened snow cracking under my boots.

'Off for a stroll?' Dad asks as we pass the marquee truck. He sees Evan's rosy cheeks. 'It's bitter out, eh?'

'Aye, but it's bonny,' Evan replies.

Dad chortles. 'We'll make a Scotsman of you yet, Robert.'

'I thought I'd take Robert to the Bumbles,' I say, squinting in the sunlight. 'Introduce him to Cullen skink.'

'Who's he?' Evan asks. 'Is he the one who's going to make me eat fish soup?'

Dad laughs so loudly, I fear the snow might avalanche off the roof and bury us all.

'Cullen skink is the *name* of the soup,' I reply, watching Dad wipe the tears from his eyes. 'And you realise that everyone is going to make fun of you when we get back?'

'Yep.'

'Brilliant. Oh, before we go, I'll show you my car. Is the garage open, Dad?'

'Aye, my side is.'

We walk around to the side of the house, where a large double stand-alone garage sits.

The right side is open, displaying Dad's Land Rover and two rusty-looking bikes.

'You'd need a good off-roader, up here,' Evan remarks. 'Especially in the winter. Does your mum drive that too?'

'Sometimes,' I reply, making my way around the car, 'but Dad does most of the driving. She gets nervous behind the wheel . . . And there you have it. This used to be my pride and joy.'

My BMW is still in pretty good shape for an older car; clunky, compared to the newer models, but it runs well.

'Ah, you never forget your first.' He smiles, peering through the windows. 'You know, get a decent stereo system in here and it'd be a pretty respectable motor. Or you could just trade it in for something from this century.'

'This was my eighteenth birthday present,' I inform him. 'I felt like a superstar driving around in this. It holds a lot of good memories.'

'I hear ya,' he replies. 'I've held on to my first PlayStation. After playing *Final Fantasy* and *Resident Evil*, I knew I wanted to design games.'

'So you didn't ever want to get a proper job, then?' I tease. 'I mean, I liked driving my car, but I never wanted to do Formula One.'

'It is a proper job! God, you sound exactly like my guidance teacher in sixth form. She was a wizened old bag too.'

'Ha ha! Fuck you. I bet your guidance teacher didn't have a convertible, though.' I stroke the roof, lovingly. 'Goodbye, car. I'll come back for you, one day . . .'

Leaving the garage, we wave goodbye to my dad and start to walk down the path to the main gate, passing Santa.

'Yeesh, I had forgotten about him.' Evan stops to get a close look in the daylight. 'I'm not sure if he's smiling or grimacing,' he says, 'but I'm pretty certain he's killed before.'

'Funny you should mention that,' I say, pulling my hat down over my ears. 'Before we had Pacino, we had a dog called Byron – a beautiful chocolate Labrador, used to follow me everywhere; a really kind-hearted, loyal dog. Anyway, every Christmas, without fail, Byron used to bark and whine at Santa whenever we took him out for a walk – I mean, this thing really freaked him out.'

'No wonder,' he agrees. I can see Evan's breath forming little clouds as he cautiously prods at Santa's grotty beard.

'So, the Christmas before I moved to London, I took Byron out on his walk – same route we've just taken – and everything was fine until, suddenly, something made him freak out. I mean, he went apeshit. Byron was a really placid dog – had never attacked anyone, never even chased squirrels – but he attacked Santa with a force I'd never seen before. Ripped his jacket to shreds. See here –' I point to where the shabby red coat has been badly ripped – 'and here, on the leg, where it's all damaged. I had to drag him off.'

Evan studies the coat and the marking on Santa's leg. 'Wow. That's creepy. What made him flip out?'

'We never found out because, the next morning, Byron was dead.'

'NO!' Evan yells in surprise. 'What happened?'

'Vet said it was heart failure,' I reply sadly. 'Like something just made his heart . . . stop.'

Evan's rosy cheeks have suddenly become very pallid.

'But the weirdest thing about it was, when Christmas was over, Dad went to bring Santa back into the shed and got the fright of his life. Santa's expression had changed. Before that day, his mouth had never been visible beneath the beard, but now . . . there he was . . . smiling . . .'

Evan takes another look at Santa. 'Please, tell me you're joking,' he says meekly, taking a step backwards. 'Because that might be the freakiest fucking thing I've ever heard.'

'Sometimes, at night,' I say softly, 'I swear I can hear footsteps coming up from the gate . . . crunching on the gravel . . . crunch . . . crunch . . . BOO!'

Evan jumps at least three feet into the air, before sliding spectacularly on to his backside, while I laugh until I can't see.

'Oh my God!' I gasp, in between laughs. 'Your face . . . I cannot deal . . .'

Evan is still on the ground. 'You were kidding? But his torn clothes . . . ? The marks on his leg . . . ?'

'His coat got caught on my bike when I was a kid,' I answer. 'We didn't even *have* a dog! Ha ha ha ha!'

Evan scrambles to his feet. 'Oh, you're in trouble now,' he warns, gathering a huge pile of snow in-between his gloves. I screech and run for cover, but it's too late. A huge snowball whacks me on the back and I'm floored. Now, it's his turn to laugh.

For the next few minutes, we batter each other with snowballs, each one making us giggle more than the previous, until my final snowball catches Evan square in the face. He screams in pain and falls to his knees.

'Oh, shit! Are you OK?' I ask, rushing over to see him. 'Oh, God – was there a stone in there? Is it your eye? Let me see!'

I slowly help him remove his left hand from his face, preparing myself to see a big, dangly-eyed, mushy-faced horror show staring back at me. Instead, all I see is the snowball in Evan's right hand as it makes contact with my own face.

'I do believe I am the winner,' he gloats as he pins me to the ground. 'Now, repeat after me: I, Emily Carson.'

'Evan, I have snow up my nose, can I just—'

'Don't make me tickle you.'

Eek. I hate tickles. 'I, Emily Carson.'

'Do solemnly swear.'

I shake my head, trying to dislodge some snow. 'Do solemnly swear.'

'That I will remember how much fun I can be when I'm not being an uptight fud.'

'You remembered!'

'Just say it.'

I sigh. 'That I will remember how much fun I can be when I'm not being an uptight fud.'

He releases his grip on my arms. 'Then you are free to go.'

I sit up, feeling exhausted but exhilarated. 'I'm soaking now,' I say, brushing the snow off my jacket.

'I love it when you talk dirty.'

'You're easily pleased.'

'I meant what I said,' he affirms, helping me brush the snow from my back. 'I like this version of you. I mean, I've seen glimpses of the new version – the overly dramatic Cassie performance, the woman who builds forts . . . who cries at *Love Actually*—'

'He cheated on Emma Thomson! She was devastated!'

'Who sings in service stations . . . who farts in her sleep—'

'I do not!'

'Oh, you do. Last night, it was like the opening bars of "Tijuana Taxi".'

I bury my face in the snow again.

'All I'm saying is, perhaps this is the real you, because, as hard as you try to be sensible, the very real . . . very silly . . . very gorgeous you keeps making an appearance.'

'Gorgeous?' I laugh, turning to face him. 'I have snow snot right now.'

He shrugs. 'You are. I just want you to know that I think Robert is a tool of the highest order. He didn't deserve you.'

'I agree,' I reply. 'The highest order. If he were a knight, he'd be Sir Lies-a-lot.'

Evan stands and helps me to my feet. God, my bum is freezing now.

'If he were a Scottish king,' Evan says, 'he'd be Robert the Wuss.'

'Oh, OH . . . You're good at this,' I declare, stopping to

fist-bump him. I link my arm with his as we make our way down the slippery hill. 'Let's go and eat.'

'If Robert were a food, he'd be fish soup . . .'

'Stop it, now.'

'Where is this place, anyway?' he asks, sniggering at his own joke. 'And why isn't there a Tube station anywhere near here? It's all very uncivilised, you know.'

'About three miles that way,' I reply. 'Should take us an hour or so.'

'See, this is why Scotland has never really caught on.' He sniffs. 'No one wants to walk for three miles just to get some soup. In London, someone will bring you the soup and pour it into your mouth without you even having to get off the couch.'

'True, but a three-mile walk will ensure an enormous appetite *and* you won't see *that* from your bed.'

I point towards the tops of the trees ahead, where a large bird is gracefully soaring.

'What *is* that?' Evan asks, trying to shield his gaze from the sun. 'Is it an eagle?'

'A buzzard, perhaps,' I reply. 'Can't really tell from here.'

He seems impressed. 'That's very cool. You get a point for that. Two points if you can find me a deer.'

'Oh, we see lots of deer round here,' I say. 'And rabbits. In the spring and summer, we have loads of bunnies in the garden. It's very cute.'

'Did you ever see *Watership Down*?' he asks, following me

further down the hill. 'That killed me. I cried for about a week after.'

'Yeah. I read the book too. Harrowing stuff for a kid.'

I hear him mumble something softly and I halt our walk.

'Hang on . . . Did you just say . . . "Rabbits are brave"?'

He looks embarrassed. 'Maybe.' He starts walking down the hill again, avoiding my gaze.

'You did! Oh my *God* – you are too *cute*!'

Saying nothing, he picks up the pace.

'NO! Wait!' I yell, trying to catch up to him. 'I really think we need to talk about this.'

Damn, that man can walk fast when he needs to.

We reach the Bumbles, a small pub located about half a mile from Melrose, in good time, choosing to sit in the main bar, close to the crackling log fire. From the outside, it looks like a posh country-house hotel, covered in climbing honeysuckle and clematis plants, with a well-kept beer garden at the back and a car park out front. But, inside, it's cosy and informal, with comfy leather couches in the bar and old wooden tables in the dining area. The decor throughout is eclectic, to say the least, with large quirky Matylda Konecka prints on every wall, deer-antler candelabras, untidy bookshelves and a running yellow-and-black theme throughout.

Evan takes off his coat and rests it on the back of his chair. 'I am so ready to eat,' he informs me, picking up the menu. 'The Bumbles,' he mouths, looking at the gold-foil lettering. 'Funny name – Bumbles.'

'As in bumblebee . . . This place used to belong to bee-keepers,' I inform him. 'There's a lane out back which leads on to the old apiary. Everyone bought their honey from here.'

'Emily! Nice tae see you back, hen!'

I turn to see a stout woman in a Penguin jumper smiling down at me.

'Rosie!' I exclaim, standing up to give her a hug. 'You're looking well! Yep, home for the holidays, once again. How are you? How's the family?'

'Och, fine,' she replies. 'The bairns are both off to university now, so it's just me and Campbell rattling roon the auld place. Who's yer pal?'

'Sorry! Evan, this is Rosie, the owner here. Rosie, this is Evan.'

Evan's head darts up from his menu, as we both realise what I've just said. It's too late to take it back. It's out there.

'Nice tae meet ye, Evan,' Rosie replies, obviously oblivious to the mammoth error I've just made. 'I've known this one since she was knee-high tae a grasshopper. You've done well there, son.'

'Oh, I agree,' he replies, 'and your pub is wonderful. I've heard great things.'

'Aye, we like it,' she replies, grinning from ear to ear.

'Oh, there's the phone – I'll need to run. We're awfy busy, this afternoon. I'll send Abigail over in a couple of minutes to take yer order.'

She dashes off towards the bar, leaving Evan and I to look over the menu.

'She'll have forgotten my name already,' he says, seeing the look of panic on my face. 'Don't worry.'

'I guess so . . . but what if she doesn't? My parents eat here . . . Patrick eats here . . .'

'Then you just say she was busy and must have misheard you. Really, stop worrying.'

I agree that he's probably right and try to relax. 'Any thoughts on what you're having?' I ask. 'The chef here is great. His hand-made ravioli is delish.'

'There's a Yorkshire pudding filled with black pudding and gravy that I have my eye on,' he replies. 'Although, the ravioli does sound good.'

'I'm having the soup and bread, followed by some pâté and oatcakes,' I decide, closing the menu. 'I could eat more, but I really don't fancy trying to walk home with the weight of a steak pie in my stomach. You'd have to carry me and that wouldn't end well.'

'Does this place always look like this?' he asks, scanning the room.

'Like what?'

'Like a set from a Tim Burton film?'

I laugh. 'It does, doesn't it? Rosie likes to surround herself with things that make her happy, and those things tend to be on the quirkier end of the spectrum. It's a very cool place, though. Once a month, she has board-game night, where people come and drink and play backgammon and Monopoly or chess . . . there's even an Operation set.'

'Damn, that sounds fun,' Evan replies, as Abigail arrives to take our orders. 'I would definitely be up for that . . . Sorry, yes, can I have the Yorkshire pudding and just some curly fries and onion rings on the side? I'll take a pint of Guinness too, thanks.'

'No bother. And for you?'

'Cullen skink, please,' I say, 'with extra bread, and then the pâté, please. You can just bring it all together. Oh, and I'll just have some water.'

She scurries off to fetch the drinks, almost tripping over a toddler who's trying to get undressed in the middle of the floor, much to his mother's dismay.

Evan nods in their direction. 'See, when *he* does that, it's cute. When *I* do it, the police are called.'

'Do you think being a parent is as awful as it looks?' I ponder, watching the tiny boy reduce his mother to a frazzled wreck. 'I mean, I'm sure it has its merits, but I teach older versions of that boy and it isn't pleasant.'

'I guess, if it was *that* horrendous, the human race would have died out years ago,' he replies. 'I think I read somewhere that children emit some sort of weird hormone only their parents can detect. It hypnotises them, or something.'

'Yeah, I'm pretty sure you just made that up.'

Abigail brings our drinks, while the mother scoops her child up, taking him away from the table and leaving the weary father to rub his own forehead until it bleeds.

'So what happens on Boxing Day night, then?' Evan asks, admiring his Guinness. 'What's been planned?'

'What makes you think anything's been planned?'

'Call me crazy, but, from what I've seen so far, your family like to ensure that they squeeze as much into the four days as possible.'

'Quiz night,' I reply. 'Bloody quiz night.'

For as long as I can remember, we've done quiz night on the twenty-sixth, and no one takes it as seriously as my family. One year, they even made team T-shirts.

'I knew it!' he exclaims. 'Do you join in with the one on telly, or do you have your own?'

'My dad pays a guy to do it for us. No, seriously, his colleague, Edward – creepy little bloke – makes up the quiz on fucking *PowerPoint*, sticks it on a USB and we play it through the television.'

I thank Abigail as she starts placing down our food dishes.

'It's all in sections, too – music, sport, entertainment, general knowledge, the lot!'

I lose Evan for a second while he stares at the food being laid out in front of him. 'That Yorkshire pudding is the size of my head.'

'And just as dense, by the looks of it.' I rip off some sourdough bread and dunk it in my Cullen skink, while Evan looks on.

'When you said, "fish soup," I pictured fish heads sticking out and mussel shells floating around. That doesn't look too bad at all.'

'Try some,' I offer, pushing my bowl towards him. 'It's basically haddock, leek and potato soup.'

'Does that mean I have to give you some of my Yorkshire?'

'Definitely.'

He takes a spoonful of soup and makes a face before he's even tried it. I bet that toddler makes less of a fuss over a bowl of bloody soup. Finally, he takes a deep breath and puts the spoon in his mouth, like a big boy.

'That's pretty incredible,' he declares, taking a second spoonful. 'Seriously good.'

'I know,' I reply, 'that's why I ordered it. Now, hand over your Yorkshire.'

'Can I just finish this?'

'Not if you want to live.'

He slides his plate over and I cut off a chunk of Yorkshire and black pudding, making *nom* noises as I eat. Quickly, our separate meals descend into one big sharing platter, each of us congratulating the other on choosing well and wondering if we'll have room for dessert.

'So, is there a prize for the winning quiz team?' he asks,

dabbing bread on the dregs of the soup. 'Is there a cash reward? A shiny trophy?'

'Not quite,' I reply. 'It's more of a forfeit for the losers. The losing team has to perform chores or duties for the winners. Like, last year, I was on the losing team and we had to give everyone foot massages. The year before, Iona's team had to bring everyone breakfast in bed – even Pacino. Stuff like that.'

He sits back in his chair and laughs. 'The more I hear about your family, the more I like them.'

'And yet you hardly mention your folks,' I reply. 'What are they like?'

He sits upright again, looking uncomfortable. 'They're just normal folk. Anyway, we agreed not to talk about my actual life, remember? You don't need to be getting Robert and me mixed up. I'll be happy to tell you all about my life and my family when we get back to London – if you still want to know about it, that is.'

Before I get a chance to reply, Abigail comes to clear the plates. 'Tea or coffee?'

'Americano with milk, for me, please,' I reply. 'Ooh, and some tablet, if you have any.'

'Same,' Evan says. 'And I don't know what tablet is. Do I want some?'

Abigail grins. 'It's butter, sugar and condensed milk.'

'You'll want some,' I interject. 'Trust me.'

'I'm drawing the line at deep-fried Mars bars, though,' he says, handing Abigail his glass. We both groan.

'Nobody actually eats those,' I say, rolling my eyes. 'It's a myth – like Nessie.'

He narrows his eyes. 'So you'll eat sheep offal and buttered sugar, but you draw the line at deep-fried chocolate?'

Abigail giggles at Evan, her teenage cheeks flushing pink. Oh, for God's sake, is there anyone this man can't charm? Oh, yes. Iona.

I manage to get my hand on three small pieces of tablet before Evan devours the lot in a sugar-fuelled frenzy.

'I think I deserve a Scottish passport now,' he proclaims, patting the crumbs with his fingers. 'All I need is a kilt and some bagpipes.'

'Scottish passport? Well, I'm sure, if we ever become an independent country, you'll be the first to get one . . .'

I'm reaching into my bag to get my purse, when my phone begins to ring.

'Hi, Mum . . . Yes, we're just finishing . . . No, I haven't forgotten about the quiz . . . Yes, I'll tell Robert to get his thinking cap on . . . No, I haven't seen my brother . . . OK . . . See you soon. Bye.' I place my phone on the table. 'We do this quiz every year,' I say. 'How on earth she thinks I'll forget is—'

The phone rings again. I throw Evan a frustrated look and answer.

'Mum, we're on our . . . What do you want, Robert? Why are you calling me?'

Evan, seeing my face change from frustrated to

wounded, stops slouching and leans forward, mouthing, 'Just hang up.'

'No, I'm not interested in what you have to say and I have nothing to say to you ... Well, it's none of your business who I'm with ... Don't call me again.'

I calmly put my phone back in my bag and continue searching for my purse.

'You all right?' Evan asks. 'No, put your purse away; I've got this.'

'I'm fine,' I reply briskly, 'and perfectly capable of paying for my own meal.' I take my debit card from my purse and start tapping on the table. 'I mean, really – the fucking nerve of him! I don't know what's more insulting – that he thinks he has the right to call me, or that he thinks I actually want him to call!'

'Um ... I—'

'He truly believes that he's some sort of fucking prize! Does he think I am so fragile, so *needy* that a married man is the best I can do? That my self-esteem is so low, I'd just forgive and forget?'

Evan is looking a little apprehensive. 'I don't know what his intentions are, but if you'd just lower your—'

'Have I once said that I want him back? That I think we still have a future? *No*, of course I haven't. *And* he has the audacity to ask who I'm with! Because obviously I must have hooked up with someone else! There must be some other mug filling my metaphorical void—'

'Shall we just take this conversation outside?' Evan has already paid for the meal, left a tip and is now putting on his jacket. 'I'm listening,' he assures me. 'I just think this rant might be better suited to wide open spaces – you know, somewhere you can fully express your rage.'

At first, I think this is a stupid idea because, well, he suggested it, but when we step out into the fresh air and start to walk towards home, I suddenly have the urge to scream. Not just a frustrated yelp – a full-blown, ear-shattering, throat-burning roar. I want to scream until every last drop of bitterness, anger, sadness and disappointment has left my body. I want to scream myself clean and, when we're half a mile from the pub, it happens.

Even though this was Evan's suggestion, I doubt even he is prepared for the noise which flies from my mouth. Or the swearing. Or the foot-stamping. Probably not even the random air-pummelling which follows, but he observes it all, keeping a sensible ten feet away at all times.

'What's the matter with me?' I yell, hacking away some ice with my boot. 'Why do I seem incapable of getting my fucking act together? I'm two years away from forty and yet, here I am, having a bastarding tantrum in a field!'

Evan takes a step closer to me as I stamp some snow to death. 'You seem pretty together to me,' he says tentatively. 'Well, maybe not at this exact moment, but, you know, in general.'

'Are you kidding?' I ask, finally running out of steam. I

decide that now is a good time to sit. 'Evan, I'm still living the same fucking life I was living fifteen years ago! People are supposed to evolve, yet I'm still trying to please my parents, still working in the same school, still living in a shared house ... still getting fucked over by men I've chosen to date for all the wrong reasons.'

Evan plonks down beside me on the snow. 'So what's stopping you changing things? What's holding you back?'

'The simple answer is *me*,' I reply. 'I'm the one that's been holding me back. I left here at twenty-four with a plan: to make a life for myself in London. It was a good plan. It worked.'

'But?'

'But the things I wanted at twenty-four are not the things I want now. I didn't plan on needing a new plan.'

'You're like the Riddler.'

'Maybe. But I understand myself. I've been desperately trying to cling on to a life I've already lived. It's time for a new plan.'

'Oh. OK. I think I—'

'But that plan may be ... not to have a plan.'

Evan puts an imaginary gun into his mouth and pulls the trigger.

I laugh and lie back in the snow, staring up at the evening sky. After a moment or two, Evan decides to join me. The sunlight has already started to fade and those stars I love so much are beginning to push through.

'So what would this non-plan look like?' he asks. 'Have you thought about it?'

'I have,' I reply, moving the hair from my face. 'A lot. Move back to Scotland. Own a whole house. Reclaim my car. Teach at a new school.'

'You'd leave London?' he asks. 'I don't think I could ever do that. London is way too much fun to leave.'

'I'm ready for a different kind of fun,' I reply, gazing at the stars. 'And besides, Scotland is my home. London was just my fling.'

We lie quietly for a moment, enjoying the silence. It's like we're the only two people on earth.

'I think I made things worse for myself, bringing you along,' I say, putting my hands into my pockets.

'How so? It's going really well! Your parents like me! Wasn't that the goal, here?'

'It was,' I reply. 'But I thought they'd just tolerate you; I didn't bank on them actually *liking* you.'

'What does that mean? Oh, please, don't make me get my gun again.'

I laugh. 'OK, I'll try and explain. Their only single child – me – is now seeing someone they consider worthy. This person is literate, handsome, funny and financially stable. In their minds, especially Mum's, they'll be planning the wedding, grandkids, limitless boasting to their friends – the whole shebang.'

'I'm following, so far.'

'And, in a week or so, I'm going to tell them that we broke up, thus shattering their dreams and making myself look like the idiot who thought age difference wouldn't matter. We've given them hope and now I'm going to piss all over their bonfire.'

'What if we came clean?' he suggests, shifting around beside me.

'What are you doing? Are you making a snow angel?'

'Uh-huh.'

I begin to join in.

'We could . . .' I reply, feeling the snow beneath me shift into neat little piles. 'I could tell them that you're not really a marketing manager called Robert, who drives a flash car and gives hotel stays for Christmas, and that you are, in fact, my not-even-remotely-wealthy neighbour, who plays video games and was paid to pull the wool over their eyes for four days.'

'I think they'd forgive me if I were stinking rich, though,' he says, fanning his arms. 'That might help ease the blow.'

'Well, it's a redundant argument, but, truthfully, I think they'd be wary of you. Why would a rich twenty-nine-year-old be interested in a thirty-eight-year-old teacher? Because that's exactly what I would be wondering. So, you see, there is no positive outcome here.'

He sits up and brushes the snow off his coat. 'There is another option to consider,' he says, helping me move from my frozen position.

'I know, but murder isn't legal and your gun isn't real,' I reply. 'God – my legs are completely numb. Shall we start heading back now? It'll be dark soon.' I shake my legs off, trying to restore blood flow.

'What if we don't finish?' he says, rubbing his hands together.

'Finish what?' I ask, making my way back on to the footpath.

'This,' he replies. 'Emily, can you stop walking for a moment? Please?'

'I want to get home!' I moan. 'We can talk and walk, although I'm not sure what you're asking me.'

'I'm asking . . . what if we keep seeing each other? What if, for once, you don't give a flying fuck about what anyone else thinks or feels and we keep this going – properly?'

My chattering face turns to look at him, expecting him to laugh, waiting for the punchline. Either his face has frozen solid or he's being deadly serious.

'You're not joking, are you?'

'No.'

'But we're not seeing each other! How can we keep something going that never started?'

'Goddammit, Emily, why do you do that? Why do you keep trying to deny that there's something going on here? That kiss!'

'The one you said meant nothing?' I reply bluntly. 'Or the one you did on Christmas Eve, for show?'

'Of course it didn't mean nothing; I was saving face,' he

replies. 'I didn't want to be the guy who reads too much into a kiss.'

'Well, I didn't want to be the woman who does that, either! Why are we arguing the same point?'

'I don't know!'

We both retreat to our corners and take stock.

He stamps his feet up and down on the spot, trying to keep warm. 'All I know is that, when I'm with you, it feels like that's where I'm supposed to be . . . and when I kiss you . . . it's like . . .'

'"Hell, yes"?'

He laughs. 'Exactly.'

I don't remember giving my legs permission to walk towards Evan, but they're doing it regardless. I feel like I'm being pulled along by a tractor beam.

'I'm not ready to fuck up everyone's Christmas,' I say, crunching my way through the snow. 'We only have a couple of days to go. It wouldn't be fair.'

'So, we're just keeping going as we are?' He looks disappointed. 'OK. If that's what you want.'

'Well, I didn't say *that*,' I reply, approaching him slowly. 'All I said was that I didn't want to tell my family right now . . .'

'So we're going to—'

'Oh, I very much hope so.'

I grab him by the jacket and pull him towards me, our faces only inches apart. Now it's my heart that feels like it might explode.

CHAPTER TWENTY-THREE

It would have been great to return home full of the joys of sex, but sadly the weather meant that our third kiss was less than spectacular.

'I can't even feel my lips, never mind yours.'

'I'm frightened to touch anything in case it snaps off.'

When we do eventually make it home, Iona is there, ready to pounce. 'Jesus! We thought you two had died from exposure,' she barks, ushering us into the living room. 'Dad was worried we'd be two players short for the quiz.'

Ah, shite. The quiz.

'Give me a second to get my jacket off,' I insist. 'Maybe get a cupp—'

'No time, Frosty,' she replies, thrusting pens and paper at us. 'We're about to begin.'

I take our jackets and dump them in the hall cupboard, while she drags Evan to join the others in the living room. My head is spinning. How the hell am I supposed to concentrate on a quiz when all I want to do is Evan?

'Three teams,' Patrick says as I enter the room. 'Two teams of two and one of three.'

'No! Two teams,' Iona suggests. 'Boys against girls. What do you think, Emily?'

I think that I'm struggling to give a fuck, here. Evan's giving me the same look he gave to that plate of tablet earlier, and we all know how that ended. 'Battle of the genders,' I reply, trying to move things along. 'Winners, which will be us, get French toast and bacon in the morning.'

'With syrup,' Kim adds. 'Lots of syrup.'

'I like French toast,' Dad replies. 'Especially the way Emily makes it. Right, Jenny, go and sit with the losers on the blue couch; Patrick, Robert – you're with me.'

'But they have four members,' Patrick complains as he's forced to move seats. 'Unfair advantage.'

Dad pats him on the back. 'Son, the other day, your mum asked me which continent Africa was in. I think we'll be all right.'

Evan's laughing soon stops when I ask him how his Scottish passport is coming along. The battle has begun.

We're forty-eight questions and two rounds of drinks into the quiz, with the final two questions coming up. So far, I'm pretty positive about the outcome, with Kim answering two tricky maths questions, which, to me, may as well have been written in Klingon.

Dad clicks on to the next slide.

Question 49: General Knowledge.

What is the term given to a group of goldfish?

Both teams huddle up to discuss quietly.

'It's a shoal, right?' I say in a whisper, looking at the group for confirmation.

Both Iona and Kim are nodding, but Mum is shaking her head. 'No. Wait. Last year, when I was looking into getting fish for the outside pond, the guy mentioned to me that a group of goldfish is called a troubling.'

'Was he messing with you?' I ask. 'I've never heard that term in my life!'

'No, it's true. Your dad wasn't with me, so I doubt he'll know this one.'

I don't think any of us are entirely convinced this is true, but Iona writes it down anyway.

'Last question coming up,' Dad announces. 'And it's literature.'

Everyone on my team high-fives because I'm bound to know this. The boys' team just collectively groans.

Westeros is a fictional continent in which series of novels?

Mum, Iona and Kim all look at me, hoping I know the answer. What they don't realise is that I'm looking back at them with the exact same hope.

'Well?' Iona asks. 'What am I writing?'

'I have no idea! Westeros? I've never heard of it!'

I turn to look at the boys, who are huddling again and giving nothing away.

'A book series, set on a fictional continent,' I repeat to

myself. '*The Hunger Games*? *Discworld*? Oh, stop looking at me like that; I like to read, but I haven't read *every* fucking book.'

'I've seen one of *The Hunger Games* films,' Kim informs us. 'Don't remember anything about Westeros. Kind of sounds like that mean Baptist-church group.'

Just then, I notice Patrick's face. He's smiling. In fact, it's more than just a smile – he's *smug*. He knows the answer.

'*Game of Thrones*!' I whisper quickly. 'Put *Game of Thrones*.'

'TIME'S UP!' Dad announces. 'Swap papers, please, and let the marking commence.'

By the time we reach number forty-seven, the boys are one point in front, because apparently Lonnie Donegan sang 'My Old Man's a Dustman' and not George Formby, like Mum insisted.

Question 49: A group of goldfish is called a troubling.

And Mum redeems herself, big time. Iona puts a big cross next to the boys' answer – *school* – teasing them as she does it.

It all comes down to the final question.

'Get ready to make my breakfast, biatch,' Patrick tells Kim, as Dad reveals the final answer.

Question 50: Westeros is the fictional continent appearing in the series A Song of Ice and Fire *by George R. R. Martin.*

'YES!' Patrick yells, jumping up from his seat. 'So close, ladies, but *Game of Thrones* is a book from the series, not the name of the series. We win, lads! Victory dance!'

With cries of 'FIX!' and 'BOLLOCKS!' from the losing team, Dad puts on 'You're the Best' from the *Karate Kid* soundtrack and we're forced to watch them slide around the floor in their socks, wiggling and gyrating, until we give up protesting and join in.

I laugh as Evan tells me, 'Sweep the leg,' when Patrick waves his winning scorecard in my face.

'It's fine,' I reply. 'I'll tell Kim to make sure Pacino licks the bacon before it goes on his plate.'

Patrick frowns at me, lowering his answer sheet. 'I bet you didn't realise how evil my sister was, until now,' he says to Evan. 'Hell hath no fury like a woman being beaten at a quiz. I'd sleep with one eye open tonight, mate.'

Evan moves across to me and whispers, 'I don't intend on getting much sleep later, anyway. Do you?'

As his hand brushes lightly against the small of my back, a tiny, involuntary purring noise escapes from my throat. 'Garden. Now,' I demand.

'We're just going to let Pacino out in the garden for a bit,' I tell Mum as we walk towards the kitchen door.

'No!' she insists. 'He'll wreck the marquee. He's fine using his run until morning.'

Dammit. 'OK, well, I'm just going to show Robert the marquee, then,' I reply, but again she's all about the noes.

'The lights don't work yet. It's too dark and cold. Just stay put. Plenty of time to see it tomorrow.'

Evan walks over to the door frame and removes some mistletoe. 'I'm just going to kiss the face right off your daughter,' he announces matter-of-factly. 'We'll be back shortly.'

'Well, why didn't you just say so?' Mum asks me. 'Honestly, Emily – you're a grown woman; you don't need to sneak around.'

Evan pulls me by the hand into the kitchen before I have time to argue. Sliding the patio door open, a huge gust of cold air blows through us.

'No chance,' I say, sliding it back again. 'I've had enough chattering bones for one day.'

So, instead, we stand by the closed door, mistletoe held above us, and kiss the way we wanted to earlier. Slowly, at first – lips brushing gently against each other, bodies barely touching – just innocently finding a rhythm to ensure that each kiss that follows is as perfect as the one before.

And we don't know when it'll happen, but we know that, eventually, one of those kisses will feel different – less innocent, less gentle – and that kiss will become the catalyst that leads to the mistletoe being thrown to the floor, while hands urgently try to make contact with skin under clothing, every touch confirming that what's about to happen will be nothing short of breathtaking.

'Oh, sweet Jesus, I don't need to be seeing *that*.'

Evan pulls his hand out from under my top, while I scramble to make myself decent.

'Patrick! Fucking hell! Don't you knock?'

'To come into the kitchen? Not usually.'

Evan starts to tuck his shirt into his jeans, but, on closer crotch inspection, decides to leave it where it is. Instead, he calmly takes one step behind me, where I can shield Patrick from any further trauma.

'Be thankful it wasn't Dad,' Patrick remarks, getting some ice from the freezer. 'I'm not sure the sight of his daughter being dry-humped over the worktop is something he'd be able to erase from his mind.'

'Can you just bugger off, now?' I ask, smoothing down my ruffled hair. 'We'll be through in a minute.'

'I'd give it five,' he smirks, pointing to Evan. '*That's* not going anywhere any time soon.' He leaves before I have time to find and throw something sharp at him.

Evan, looking suitably mortified, starts laughing. 'I feel about fifteen. Getting caught messing about in your parents' house – I thought I was past all that.'

'We should go back through,' I say, wiping my lipstick from his mouth. 'He'll be making it sound worse than it is. Dad will be out with the shotgun soon.'

He puts his hand on the back of my head and pulls me in for one last kiss. 'We're finishing this later,' he insists. 'That was insane.'

'*You're* insane, if you think we're doing it in my parents' house!' I reply. 'Not now!'

'But—'

'But nothing! Imagine if they heard us! Fuck – I feel ill at the thought of it.'

He adjusts himself and takes a deep breath. 'Fine. We're getting rid of the pillow divider, though – yes?'

'I don't know if that's a good idea,' I say, taking steps towards the door. 'It might stop wandering hands . . . or spooning . . .'

He sighs. 'Oh, come on. You can trust me, for God's sake. I'll keep my distance; you have nothing to worry about.'

'Oh, you're so sweet!' I say, pushing the door open. 'But it's not you I'm worried about.'

I'm not certain whether Patrick has told everyone what he saw in the kitchen, but I'm definitely getting a what-have-you-been-up-to-young-lady? vibe from Mum. However, I refrain from acting like I've done anything wrong, because I haven't. Christ, she's the one who suggested getting knocked up on purpose, a few hours ago; she can shove her moral high ground up her arse.

'So, what's happening tomorrow?' I ask, subtly checking that I'm not sitting there with nips like bullets. 'Everything organised?'

'Aye,' Dad replies, sipping on a whisky. 'Usual crowd have been invited, food and booze are sorted – it should be a good party.'

'Who's doing the music, Dad?' Iona asks. 'It's not that nitwit from Galashiels who did it last year, is it? It was like being at Butlins.'

'You've never been to Butlins,' Mum remarks.

'Exactly – and this is why. When he played "Agadoo" – well, I just wanted to hit him.'

'Iona, you did hit him,' Dad replies. 'Luckily, he was more pissed than you were and couldn't remember who'd given him his black eye.'

She smirks. 'So I did . . .'

'It's a guy called Niall. He was the DJ at Tabitha Ralston's wedding. Comes very highly recommended.'

'Tubby Ralston got married?!' Iona asks in disbelief. 'Bloody hell! There's hope for everyone, then – eh, Emily?'

Tabitha Ralston was Iona's nemesis in high school. She was taller, thinner and acne-free – unlike Iona, whose face erupted several times a day. However, time passed, and the clearer Iona's skin became, the more Tabitha's waistline expanded, hence the nickname. We were all convinced that Iona had done some clear-skin deal with the devil and cursed Tabitha. Normally, I wouldn't approve of Iona's mean comments, but, with Tabitha, I'll make an exception. She was a mean-spirited, stuck-up little bastard, who was especially cruel to my baby sister.

'I hope her inevitable divorce is very painful,' I reply, raising a glass to Iona. 'Long story,' I murmur to Evan. 'She's a horror.'

'Remember we're getting our hair done at eleven a.m.,' Kim says. 'At Studio J.'

'This is the first I'm hearing of it!' I exclaim. 'When was this arranged?'

'Ages ago,' Mum replies. 'I thought I'd told you ... Ah, well – never mind; you could do with a trim. Get some of that weight off the sides.'

Christ, even my hair is overweight.

I shake my head. 'Sorry; I've already planned to spend the day with Robert,' I say, nudging him. There is no way I'm leaving Evan unattended – it's too risky.

'Nonsense,' Dad interjects. 'He could use a bit of man time. You've had him on a pretty tight leash, we've all noticed. Give the poor man some space.'

I turn to Evan, looking for backup, but he just pats me on the knee, saying, 'It's fine. Go and get your hair done.'

'Aww,' Iona chimes in. 'Don't worry, Emily; if he misses you, I'm sure he'll text you ...'

'That's settled, then,' Mum decides. 'How lovely. Just me and my girls.'

'Yes,' I reply. 'Lovely.' Only it isn't lovely – it's nerve-wracking. Those three vultures are going to quiz me about Robert relentlessly and Evan's going to get the same treatment here. One slip of the tongue, one ad-lib too far, and we'll have a lot of explaining to do.

Slip of the tongue. Oh, God, now I'm thinking about the way Evan kisses, the way he felt ... how hard he felt when he pressed against me ...

'Emily! Are you with us?'

'YES! Who? What? What was the question?'

'I was asking if you'd drive us?' Kim repeats. 'Tomorrow.'

'Yes. Of course!' I reply. 'You don't mind if I take your car, honey, do you?'

I give Evan's leg a squeeze, but it's not a mild-mannered, reassuring squeeze – it's a sensual, almost erotic squeeze, combined with a look that tells him I am completely fucking aroused and it's all his fault.

'You look a bit unwell,' he says. 'Are you feeling all right?'

It appears that my look conveys sickness rather than arousal.

'I'm pretty tired,' I say, removing my can't-flirt-for-shit hand from his knee. 'I might hit the hay.'

'But it's only ten o'clock!' Iona exclaims. 'I was going to put a film on ... You know we always watch a scary film after the quiz!'

'No, we don't,' I reply. 'We did it once. Last year. That's hardly always ...'

'Now, what was the name of the one we watched, Patrick?' Mum asks. 'The one where they videotaped the ghosts.'

'*Paranormal Activity.*'

'Ah, yes!' she continues, turning towards Evan. 'Honestly, Robert, I've never heard a grown man scream like Patrick did. It was hilarious.'

'It was a scary film!' he despairs. 'Emily was terrified too; it wasn't just me.'

'Hey, don't bring me into it!'

'I'm sure Robert wants to watch with us,' Iona continues. 'I've brought *The Babadook*. Stick it on, Dad.'

Any hopes I had of getting Evan to my room are disappearing rapidly. He's too polite to decline and I'll look like a party pooper if I bow out early. Maybe this is a good thing, I tell myself, because getting Evan back to my room and *not* sleeping with him might be far more torturous than sitting through two hours of jump scares and my shrieking brother.

As the credits roll, I voice, very clearly, my desire to go the fuck to bed, and this time no one has any objections. Saying our goodnights, I sleepily make my way to our room, with an equally exhausted Evan trailing behind me.

Pacino is already sprawled across the middle of the bed, so any attempt to install a barricade would be futile. He's already there. The room is pitch black, but I don't turn the light on; I want everything to remain dark and quiet and geared towards my imminent coma.

Without thinking, I undress in front of Evan, throwing my clothes in a pile on the floor. I don't even bother putting on my pyjamas, instead choosing to sleep in my underwear. The lack of vocal appreciation for my half-naked form means that Evan either hasn't noticed or is asleep already.

Sitting on the edge of the bed, I realise I have about five inches of free bed space before I hit dog.

'I swear, Pacino, if you don't move the hell over, I'm

going to make it my life's work to ensure you never get to play with another stick again.'

I know he can't understand me, but I still feel a pang of guilt for saying it. Sticks are Pacino's favourite thing in the whole wide world. He does, however, move to the bottom of the bed, allowing me to crawl in.

I sigh as I lie against the warm bed-sheets, my head hitting the soft pillow, which moulds around me.

'I feel like I should tell you something,' Evan murmurs in the darkness. 'Y'know, before we go any further.'

'Tell the dog,' I mutter. 'He can give me the highlights in the morning.'

'I'm serious, though. It's important.'

I turn my pillow over to the cool side. 'Evan, unless you're going to tell me that you're dying or that we're related, it can wait.'

I hear him mumble something else, but his words are lost on me now.

'Tomorrow,' I reply softly. 'Tell me tomorrow.'

CHAPTER TWENTY-FOUR

DAY 4: The Home Stretch

I feel the weight of Evan's arm draped over me and his chest pressed against my back, slowly rising and falling. I haven't woken up like this in a very long time and it's perfect. Robert didn't do sleep cuddles, or spooning. In fact, Robert didn't enjoy anyone on his side of the bed, unless they were fully awake and naked.

Eyes closed, I grind down into him a little, ensuring our bodies are flush against each other, feeling a little rush of excitement. He's not wearing any underwear. He's stark bollock naked and, in a few seconds, I could be too. We're in the perfect position. We could easily have slow, sleepy morning sex and no one would be any the wiser. He could reach under the covers and pull down my underwear, while he kissed my neck and . . . Dear God, Evan, please wake the fuck up!

'RISE AND SHINE, EMILY! You're on bacon duties!'

Iona's voice thunders down the hall and into my ear, not only reminding me that we lost the quiz last night, but also that I have zero chance of getting away with a sly shag.

'BE THERE IN A SEC!' I yell back, feeling Evan stir beside me.

'Morning,' he says, still pressed up against me. 'Can you not shout, please. Like, ever again.'

'Sorry,' I reply in a softer tone. 'Iona was just reminding me that I'm on breakfast duties.'

'OK, but this is comfy,' he says, nuzzling into me. 'Just one more minute.' Eventually, his brain finally catches on to the fact that we're spooning.

'Hang on ... Are you just in your underwear?' I can feel his breath on my neck as he slides his hand under the covers to check. Finding my underwear, his hand soon moves over my thighs and my stomach. 'Breakfast can fuck off,' he says, quite seriously. 'You're going nowhere.'

I take his hand and move it on to my bra, my body giving a little shudder. 'I have to,' I reply. 'Iona will come in here and drag me out by the hair.'

'Nope. Not happening. Fuck, Emily – you smell like vanilla.'

Now his hand is inside my bra and I can feel, pressed against my back, exactly how much Evan likes the way I smell. I reach behind and grip him and he moans while his hand starts to peel off my knickers.

'Hurry up,' I breathe, helping with my underwear. 'Just hurry.'

'Come on, for God's sake, the French toast will ... Oh ... Sorry; am I interrupting?'

Iona gets halfway across the floor before we even spot her. Then it's a scramble to pull the duvet over our heads, while she stands there.

'What is the matter with you?!' I yell from under the covers. 'Get the fuck out!'

'Well, it's your own fault,' she sniffs. 'I gave you plenty of warning. God, first the kitchen and now here? Can't you control yourselves? This isn't *Geordie Shore*.'

I knew Patrick had spilled the beans. This is so embarrassing. I wait for her to leave the room.

'Has she gone?' I ask Evan.

He shrugs.

'Have you gone?'

'Yes. Get up.'

'IONA.'

Finally, I hear her walk out and the door close behind her. The duvet comes down and Evan starts laughing. 'I guess it just isn't meant to be.'

'Perhaps not. Well, not here, anyway.'

'It was close, though.' He smirks. 'I'll be thinking of that all day long ... Not the part where your sister walks in, though, obviously.'

I pull my pyjama top over my head. 'I shall return

momentarily, with breakfast,' I inform him. 'And possibly Iona's head on a stick.'

I march through to the kitchen, where Mum is having some tea, Kim is cracking eggs into a large clear bowl and Iona is putting coffee grounds into the percolator.

'Finally,' she mutters. 'Bacon is in the fridge.'

'Morning, everyone,' I say, throwing a dirty look in Iona's direction. 'Are we all looking forward to the party?'

'I will be once they've finished hammering on that bloody marquee,' Mum replies. 'Thank God we're out of here for a couple of hours. I need a head massage.'

'I think I'm going to get my hair straightened,' Kim says, whisking up the eggs. 'Take a wee break from the curls.'

'But your curls make your hair look thicker, Kim,' Mum says. 'You can see your scalp quite clearly when you straighten your hair.'

'What about you, Emily?' Kim asks, ignoring Mum's comment. 'Going to do anything different?'

'Shaved,' I say, taking the pack of streaky bacon from the fridge. 'Maybe just leave a tiny fringe at the front. I'm not sure.'

'You don't have the right skull shape for a shaved head,' Mum remarks, still sipping her tea. 'You really need a petite head – you know, like Sinead O'Connor.'

'I wasn't serious, Mum,' I reply. 'But it's nice to finally know how you feel about my skull.'

Iona laughs, turning on the coffee machine. 'I think I'll just get my bob trimmed and blow-dried. There isn't much else I can do with this.'

'I'll be sad when you're all gone tomorrow,' Mum says. 'I do like a full house. The noise reminds me of when you were all young.' She takes some plates out of the cupboard and lays them on the worktop.

'That's a really old-person comment to make, Mum,' Iona says, helping Kim with the French toast. 'That's something your old grey-haired granny would say.'

'Well, hurry up and make me a grandmother,' she retorts. 'And then it won't seem strange when I say it. I mean, there's three of you and not one baby between you. It's ridiculous.'

My mum is something else. In the space of five minutes, she's managed to insult my skull and Kim's thinning hair, and has berated all three of us for not having children. I wonder what she'll do for an encore.

I place three slices of bacon beside Evan's French toast, plus an extra piece for my mouth, and carry it through to the bedroom.

'Voila,' I say. 'Breakfast is served.'

'That smells amazing,' he replies. 'Where's yours?'

'I ate it while I was cooking,' I reply. 'Now I'm going to have a quick shower because we're out of here shortly to get our hair done.'

He looks at his plate and then at me. 'I am willing

to sacrifice this breakfast if there is *any* chance of getting you back on my lap.'

'Afraid not,' I say, making a sad face. 'Besides, you know that the moment you become hard again, someone will appear and ruin it.'

'What do you mean, "get hard *again*"? It never stopped.'

And, true enough, there is still significant bulge appearing through the duvet.

'Oh, my . . . We are going to come back to this later. Who knows, we might be able to find a quiet spot while everyone's at the party.'

'I'm going to hold you to that.'

So I leave Evan and his bulge to enjoy breakfast while I jump in the shower. Let's just hope that neither of us fucks up today and ruins it. We're on the home stretch now, and tomorrow we'll be driving back to London. And, for once, I intend to be the one making the noise on his side of the wall.

We barely make it out of the driveway before the interrogation begins, and they don't even try to pretend it's anything else.

'Do you *really* see this going anywhere?' Mum asks. 'He's a very nice boy and all, but almost ten years is quite a significant age gap.'

I turn on to the main road and drive carefully through the melting snow. 'I bet Madonna, or Jennifer Lopez, or Demi

Moore don't have to put up with this shit, or, you know, *any living man*. Seriously, if Robert was forty-eight, you'd be telling me what a catch he is. Why can't I be the catch?'

'Because all of those celebrity women have plastic surgeons on hand to stop them ageing. And men, well, it's just more acceptable, isn't it?'

'And if he can afford to send us to Wallace Hall, why are you driving around in a hire car?'

I scan the dashboard, looking for clues as to how Iona would know this. Then I spot it in the rear-view mirror: a small car-rental sticker on the back windscreen.

'Because his car is in the garage, stupid.'

'And there's something a bit off about you two,' Kim chimes in.

Get fucked, Kim, I think to myself. Who told you you could play? But, out loud, I say, 'Really? Do tell.'

'I know you've only been dating a few months, but it's like you're so polite and restrained around each other. There's nothing personal there. I mean, Patrick and I squeeze each other's spots, and I haven't even seen you hold hands.'

'Oh, I can confirm that there is definitely something *personal* there,' Iona reveals, laughing to herself. 'Let's just say that this morning there was nothing restrained about what I witnessed.'

I bite my tongue as Iona is doing a fine job of convincing Mum and Kim that we're into each other.

'And Patrick caught them in the kitchen,' she continues, talking like I'm not even here. 'It's almost like you're having an affair.'

Mum gasps and clutches the glove box. 'Emily! Is this true? Are you having an affair with Robert?'

I start to laugh, and once I start, I can't stop, tears blinding me as I drive. It's too perfect. It's too ironic. By the time I finally park up outside the salon, I've given myself a stitch.

I dab the tears away from my eyes and turn to face everyone. 'I can guarantee you, one hundred per cent, that I am not having an affair with that man, or any other man, for that matter. Now, if there's nothing else, I'd quite like to get my hair done.'

'Welcome to Studio J, ladies! How are we?' asks the man behind reception, giving us all a bright-white toothy grin. 'Cheryl – coats!' he snaps at a young girl with a pixie cut. 'How are you, Kimmy, darling?' he asks. 'Hubby good? Greeaaattt. Now, let's get you all looking fabulous.'

The rest of us are greeted by our stylists, while *Kimmy* is led away by the one she calls Julian, to what I assume is the 'special' chair. I've been assigned a woman called Izobel-with-a-zed, who fluffs up my hair until I look like a toilet brush, while asking me what I want her to do with it.

Well, you can stop doing that, for a start, you fucking maniac.

'Oh, just a trim, thanks,' I reply, watching my mane get bushier and bushier.

She shakes her head. 'You see all this?' She's waving my own hair at me. '*This* is weighing your face down. I think you need to take at least two inches off, thin it out ... maybe some long bangs to soften the edges.'

'YES!' shouts Mum from across the room. 'That's what *I've* been telling her.'

Sometimes I feel sorry for Mum. She truly believes that I'm one good haircut away from transforming into a Kardashian. She's pinning all her hopes on a big reveal that will never come.

I agree to everything, except the bangs. Not only because it's called a *fringe*, but also because the last time I got a fringe, I looked like someone who was clearly working through some emotional issues.

Cheryl washes my hair in something which smells like oatmeal and then gives me a head massage while my conditioner performs its magic. I like Cheryl. She never once asks me what I'm doing that evening, where I'm going on holiday next year, and she calls Julian a 'skinny prick' under her breath when he snaps his fingers at her for the umpteenth time. She's getting a huge tip for that.

Cheryl gets me a sparkling water from the fridge, while everyone else takes advantage of the Prosecco. I'm all right with this. I've done enough drinking over the past few days to last me a lifetime, and there's still tonight's party to get through.

Kim ignores my mother's advice, getting her long red

hair straightened to within an inch of its life. She looks incredibly glamorous; I have no idea why Mum feels the need to pick everyone apart. Iona, as usual, rocks her sleek dark bob and is finished way before the rest of us. Mum gets her dirty blonde hair blown right back into the eighties: soft feathered waves at the side, followed by backcombing for root lift and maximum staying power.

When I'm finished, I'm surprised at how good my hair looks. She's managed to keep my Helena Bonham Carter messy vibe I like so much, but it's all much softer and sleeker and defined. I know Mum will still feel a burning desire to attack it with that comb she carries everywhere, but, to me, it's imperfectly perfect.

As this is part of our Christmas gift, Mum whacks the whole lot on her credit card, while I tip Cheryl twenty pounds and tell her to buy something her mother wouldn't approve of. We then all hurry back to the car in an attempt to protect our shiny new hairdos from the elements. The questioning on the way back home is far less intense, but of a far more probing nature.

'So, how is he?' Mum asks, checking her hair in the passenger-side mirror. 'You know, in bed? I remember your father at that age. It was all over quickly, but he was up for round two, seconds later.'

'You do realise that Patrick is the same age as Robert?' Iona remarks. 'Making this line of questioning disturbing, to say the least.'

'I'm just curious!' Mum exclaims. 'There must be some reason that she's seeing him; I'm just trying to get to the bottom of it.'

I pull up to the traffic lights as they turn red. 'So, it couldn't be because he makes me laugh or that he's handsome and intelligent and kind?'

Kim, who has been quietly stroking her new flat hair, gives a little chuckle. 'Yeah, right, Emily. You're with him for his *personality* . . .'

They all find this hilarious when, in fact, I *do* like Evan for all of those reasons, and we've never actually slept together. So, technically, the joke's on them, but they'll never know. The lights change and I move off.

'Fine,' I reply, driving towards the back roads. 'He's incredible in bed. Very eager to please.'

'Does he shave his chest?' Iona asks, now suddenly interested. 'He looks like he does.'

'No!' I exclaim. 'When I first met him, I took him for a shaver too. Funny, that.'

'Do you hope to marry him?'

Aha! The ultimate question – one that I knew Mum would ask eventually. One that's more important to her than it is to me. Not having the heart to say anything negative, I reel off all of the silly wedding ideas I'd formulated in my head about the real Robert – like the double-barrelled surname, the wedding in Kew Gardens, the honeymoon in Barbados – everything. The sad fact is I've got to know and like Evan more in the past couple of weeks than I ever did with Robert, even after months together. But I made these plans because I saw Robert as a feasible marriage prospect. Do I see Evan that way? The answer is no.

Feeling a tad gloomy about this realisation, I let everyone else chatter about my future for the rest of the car journey, nodding and agreeing occasionally so as not to rouse suspicion. I park at the front of the house and let everyone out first, taking a moment to myself before I go in.

This morning I'd left the house excited about seeing Evan when I came home, but now I'm wondering if my feelings are going to do more damage than good. Sure, it's early days, but if I know, almost immediately, that he's not the marrying kind, are we just starting something that's doomed before it's even really begun?

CHAPTER TWENTY-FIVE

Evan, my dad and Patrick are all sat round the kitchen table, having a beer and watching the workmen finish up the marquee.

'Well, don't you all look gorgeous,' Dad says, kissing Mum on the cheek. 'We haven't bothered with lunch yet, love. Thought we'd wait for you.'

Evan turns to me and smiles. 'Hair looks good,' he remarks. 'Shiny.'

I graciously thank him before pulling up a chair across from Patrick. 'So, what did you lot do while we were out?' I ask, trying to gauge whether Evan confessed everything the moment we left.

'Not much,' Patrick replies, picking at the label on his beer. 'Gave the lads a hand bringing some stuff out to their van, made sure the heating was working, that kind of thing. Just guy stuff . . . Hey, doll face – sexy hair.' He pulls Kim on to his lap and squeezes her. 'I'm going to have to run home and pick up my suit. You coming?'

'Nah,' she replies. 'I'm going to get a nap in. That Prosecco at the salon has gone straight to my head.'

'OK, babes; don't mess your hair up, though,' he replies, shifting her off his knee. 'That's my job, later.'

'Does anyone want some lunch?' Mum asks, examining the fridge contents. 'There will be plenty of food at the party, but I can fix a salad or an omelette or something.'

Kim declines and toddles off to lie down.

'I'm all right, thanks,' Evan replies. 'I might give that nap thing a go as well . . . unless you need any help here, of course?'

'What a thoughtful man you are,' Mum declares, lifting out the salad bowl. 'But no, we're fine. You go and have a lie-down with Emily.'

So, I'm having a lie-down too? I was hoping for a mushroom omelette.

Once inside the bedroom, Evan closes the door while I lie on the bed with every intention of remaining fully clothed. My body language makes him uneasy. 'I do just want a nap,' he says. 'You can stop rolling yourself up in that duvet.'

'Sorry,' I reply. 'Things are just feeling a bit odd at the moment.'

'I have no idea how we got here either,' he remarks, trying to pull some cover out from under me. 'But there's no pressure. Let's just get today over with, shall we?'

We hear yet another van pull up outside the house, and it appears to contain several swearing men.

'Toilets,' I inform Evan, who's straining to see out of the window. 'Like posh Portaloos. Mum would rather people piss in a large box than have them trailing in and out of the house all evening.'

'Why exactly do they have this party tonight?' Evan asks. 'Surely it's more of a New Year event?'

'It is,' I agree, 'but Mr and Mrs Sloan do the New Year's party every year and it's equally as grand as this. Having it tonight is purely for selfish reasons. We used to hold the party on Boxing Day, but it became overrun with children who were visiting their relatives, and there's nothing Mum and Dad hate more than a room full of adults watching their language and their alcohol intake.'

'You sure they won't need help setting up?' he asks. 'You know – with food and stuff. I feel a bit guilty just lying here.'

I laugh. 'The caterers will be here around five and Mum will shoo them away before the guests arrive at eight, so she can pretend she did it all herself. The serving staff will be here at seven and we'll all be ruined by midnight.'

He stops watching the toilet men and lies down flat beside me. 'Remember I said I had something to tell you?'

'Did you?'

'Yes. I said it was important, but you made a joke about us being related and fell asleep.'

'Ah. Yes. And you want to tell me that important thing now?'

'I think I should. We're in a weird place and I think it's only fair to be honest.'

I plump my pillow under my head and get comfortable. 'OK, shoot.'

'Where to start?' he says, sitting himself up. He looks anxious. 'A lot of what I've told you about myself isn't exactly true . . .'

I feel a twinge of uneasiness creep over me.

'Only, a lot of it is.'

'What does that even mean? Oh, God – you'd better not be on a register.' I brace myself for his answer. Jesus, aren't there any men in my life who don't have bloody secrets?!

He shifts uncomfortably on the bed. 'OK, OK . . . First of all, the stuff I said about growing up in Brighton and being raised by my gran? Well, that's all true. My parents don't live in Canada. I have no idea where my mum is and my dad really is in prison for armed robbery.'

'Shit! For real?'

'For realz . . . I know. I'm the son of a crook. It's embarrassing. Secondly, I am rich.'

'Oh, not this bullshit again. Can you—'

'Will you just listen?!' he whisper-shouts. 'Admittedly, I wasn't wealthy until very recently – until the day of the carol concert, actually – so I can understand your confusion. I'm still getting used to it myself. Saying that, you don't act like you come from money.'

I think back for a moment. 'What happened on the day of the carol concert?'

'Those guys I was with? They're my business partners. We're game developers. Horror games, to be exact – mainly Kickstarter, crowd-funded beta applications for iOS and Android. You know, basic RPGs, survival horror, which . . . OK, I see from the look on your face, I've lost you . . .'

'Games. Got it. Move along.'

'OK, in a nutshell: once upon a time, we designed a game. It was well received and we struck a deal with a major publisher for exclusive rights, plus the sequel.'

'So you got an advance on your game? Like a book?'

'Yes – well, we got an advance a year ago. It paid off my student loan and I went to Japan on holiday, but that wasn't why we were out celebrating. On the day of the carol concert, we received our royalties.'

'That's based on sales, right?'

'Right.'

'So how many did you sell?'

He scrunches up his face like he's about to tell me something awful. 'Around fourteen million.'

'What? Noooo!'

Evan quickly puts a hand over my mouth and shushes me before I make any further racket. His hand smells like Pacino.

'Fourteen million?' I repeat through his hand. '*Million?* So you're a millionaire?'

'Yeah . . . Kind of . . . But only a little one.'

I take stock for a moment. This has to be nonsense.

'Why are you doing this? What are you hoping to achieve?' I say, pulling his hand away. 'I mean, that's a fucking *huge* lie – and for what? To impress me? You should know me well enough by now to understand that money is the thing that impresses me the least!'

'It would be a pretty fucking stupid lie to make up,' he replies. 'I'm not trying to impress you; I'm trying to be honest!'

'So what's the game called?' I laugh. 'This cash cow of yours? *Resident Evil*? *Pac-Man*?'

'*Trauma*,' he replies. 'Although, I'm guessing you've never—'

'*Trauma*? The zombie one?'

'So you have heard of it!'

'Of course I have! I'm a teacher surrounded by game-playing teenagers all day. They never shut up about it. You didn't make that. You couldn't have.'

'Google me,' he says, handing me his phone. 'Our company name is G. O. D. Games.'

'God Games? Really?'

'No. G-O-D. It's our surnames. Just google it.'

I take the phone and do as instructed, clicking on a Wikipedia page.

G. O. D. Games was founded in 2009 by London-based developers Evan Grant, James Ostler and Vikram Darsha. Achieving moderate success with indie point-and-click horror games Bedtime *and* The Hospital, *G. O. D. Games went on to develop survival horror game* Trauma, *with sales reaching over 14.2 million.*

This can't be real. I click on Evan's name, which takes me to his personal Wikipedia page.

Evan Grant (born 10 April 1987) is an English video-game designer and founding member of G. O. D. Games, best known for . . .

I stop reading and look over at Evan, who's sitting quietly, awaiting his fate.

'There's no picture of you,' I say, holding up the open page on his phone. I'm pretty much lost for words. 'If this was you, wouldn't there be a photo?'

'I don't really have a lot of photos online to—'

'Fourteen million.' Those words are pin-balling around in my head. 'Why didn't you say something sooner?'

He retrieves his phone from my hand, which seems to be suspended in mid-air.

'I did try to test the water a few times,' he replies, closing his phone. 'Look, I had no reason to tell you straight away. Initially, you hated me, and although I wanted you to like me, I didn't want to give you fourteen million reasons to suddenly have a change of heart. I wanted you to like me . . . for me. Besides, I wasn't here to be me – I was here to be Robert.'

'This is a head fuck,' I say, sitting up. 'So, the hotel gift cards . . . ?'

'Oh, they're real,' he admits. 'No building sites included . . . and I acknowledge that was a dick move. I did think it was something Robert would have done, but I was also just showing off. I wanted to impress everyone, especially you.'

'And now that you've told me?'

'Well, in a roundabout way, I still have the same problem,' he replies, furrowing his brow. 'Because, now, you like me, but I'm scared I've just given you fourteen million reasons to go back to hating me.'

'You don't literally have fourteen million quid, though, do you?'

'Nah; there's three of us and tax and legal fees . . .'

'Well, however much it is, it wouldn't make me hate you,' I reply. 'What that money does do, however, is open a lot of new doors for you, and I'm thrilled about that . . . but your doors will be very different from the ones I'll be opening.'

'I don't like where this is going.'

I laugh and light-heartedly nudge him. 'Don't be so glum. We're just on different paths – as we should be. I'm pretty sure those paths will cross once or twice, though . . .'

I hear Pacino barking at the vans as they pull out of the driveway.

'Let's just enjoy tonight,' I tell him. 'We'll drink, we'll dance, we'll no doubt get caught kissing in the bathroom and we'll celebrate the last night that you have to pretend to be Robert. You'll get your own name back.'

The truth is, I'm feeling as disappointed as he is, but I know I'm right. The world has suddenly opened up for him and I can guarantee that settling down, in any respect, won't be on the cards for him.

'Can I just say two things?' he asks. 'First of all, I'm really happy that you asked me to come for Christmas. Not only did I get to spend time with you, I felt like I was part of a real family – a deranged one, admittedly, but they're all brilliant. It means a lot.'

'You're very welcome!' I reply. 'I'm glad you came.'

'And the second thing . . . About tonight's kiss – does it have to be in the bathroom? Because I was thinking—'

I lift a cushion and hit him in the face. 'If you're not careful, you'll be kissing old Mrs Penman.'

'Mrs Who, now?'

CHAPTER TWENTY-SIX

'Mrs Penman! So glad you could make it!'

Mrs Penman adjusts her creased stocking at the ankle before lifting a heavily bejewelled hand up towards Dad's face.

'Oh, William,' she says, patting him on the cheek. 'You're looking more and more handsome every year. If I were twenty years younger . . .'

'You'd still be too fucking old,' Patrick mumbles, keeping his distance. 'Keep her away from me, Em; last year, I swear she tried to grab my knob on the dance floor.'

No one is entirely sure how old Winnifred Penman is, but what we do know is that she's been married five times, widowed twice and has outlived all but one of her five children. She still lives in the cottage she shared with her late husband, Kenneth – a large B-listed building with a chequered-floor hallway, old-fashioned morning-room and perfectly manicured lawns – but now she's looked after by her dutiful daughter, Clarissa, who is her constant companion. Clarissa must be in her fifties, and is unlike her mother in every respect. Never married, never flashy and very rarely seen without her beloved poodle, Humphrey. But there's something about Clarissa, something hidden behind that dowdy, shy persona – something perhaps only recognisable to someone who also has an overbearing mother.

'There's a seriously unhinged deviant under all that frump. You watch – the minute she gets her hands on the family fortune, she'll be putting the dog down, dressing in leather and fucking the gardener.'

Yep, Iona gets it.

When she's finally finished touching my father's face, Mrs Penman hands her coat over to the cloakroom assistant and is escorted by Clarissa down the walkway and into the marquee, which is already filling up with guests.

Iona and I leave Patrick and Dad in the reception tent, making our way into the main marquee, where we spy Evan and Kim having drinks.

'Not dancing yet?' I ask Kim, who shakes her head.

'I will need many more of these before you'll catch me dancing to whatever this is.'

'It's "The Ballroom Blitz".' Iona laughs. 'One for the middle-agers. I'm going back to the house to find the tequila. Anyone care to join me?'

Evan and I decline, but Kim doesn't need to be asked twice.

I pull Kim's chair round and sit beside Evan, who, as it happens, is looking delicious in his white shirt and waistcoat. He listens intently as I fill him in on the weird and wonderful lives of our party guests.

'The man with the dark-green cravat – he owns the Golf Club. Pretentious twat and complete coke-head. His wife left him for their plumber and it's easy to see why. Oh, and the woman in the maxi dress, next to him – she's a former accountant with Dad's firm who recently started doing stand-up. She's hilarious. Oh, and the elderly woman dancing proactively near the waiter – *that's* Mrs Penman; now, there's a proper cougar. She'd eat you for breakfast . . . but she'd need to put her teeth in first.'

Evan slides his hand around my waist. 'Did I mention how frickin' sexy you look?' he says, eyeing up my white slinky evening dress. 'You're the hottest woman in here – well, not including Mrs Penman, of course.'

I laugh. 'Aww, you have to say that because you're my fake boyfriend.'

His hand slips down to the small of my back. 'I'm going to get us a drink and then I'm going to return and admire you some more.'

I give an excited giggle as he walks off to find some champagne.

From the corner of my eye, I spot Mum at the buffet table. She's wearing her new red velvet evening dress and is casually rearranging some hors d'oeuvres, making it appear that she's been in charge of cuisine all along, when really she was watching *House of Cards* on Netflix and painting her nails while the caterers were busy setting up.

'Emily!' she says, waving me over urgently. 'Quick word.'

I leave the comfort of Kim's warm chair and make my way over to her.

'Did you see? Bill and Steph brought their son, Donald, the pilot, with them. He's over there, by the DJ. Not bad at all. I mean, nothing a low-carb lifestyle wouldn't fix.'

'Mum, look at me. I am with Robert. I am physically here with Robert. You can stop being on the lookout for potential boyfriends. I'm all set.'

She moves my hair from behind my ears and positions it to her liking. 'Darling, Robert is a very nice chap, but would it hurt to keep your options open? Just in case?'

'What if Robert was worth millions, Mum? Would I still have to keep my options open?'

'Emily, dear, if he was worth millions, he'd have some Playboy bunny on his arm and we wouldn't be having this conversation.'

'Wow,' I say, laughing in astonishment. 'So a young, handsome millionaire would have no interest in me. Thanks, Mum.'

'Oh, stop being so oversensitive. I'm saying that a young, handsome millionaire wouldn't be interested in anyone other than himself!' She spies two of her friends from her gardening club and waves. 'There's Annie and

Maureen. I mean, what am I supposed to tell them? That my daughter has a toy boy?'

'No . . . Tell them I paid him to be here,' I snarl, shoving a goats' cheese tartlet into my mouth. 'I'm going to sit down.'

Reclaiming my seat, I catch Clarissa's eye and give her a smile of solidarity. She smiles back politely, and then I watch her down a glass of champagne in one. I know exactly how she feels.

An hour into the party, I've managed to keep my distance from Mum and guzzle four glasses of champagne on a stomach containing only one tartlet. Evan is proving quite the hit with the ladies and I take great drunken pleasure in ensuring they all know he's taken.

'You're rich as fuck,' I tell him as we slow-dance to Al Green. 'What are you going to do with your life now?!'

'That's a very big question to be contemplating on a dance floor,' he replies. 'I have no idea. Buy a bigger flat. Keep making video games. I don't know.'

'Ah, the man who doesn't like to know what the future holds.'

'That's me.'

'You're going to marry some top Swedish model and she'll have lots of kids and still be thin,' I say. 'And I'll be like her –' I motion to Clarissa – 'still single, overweight from my antidepressants and looking after Mum while she tells me that my hair is fat.'

'Would it be inappropriate to laugh at that? Because I really want to.'

'Meh,' I say, resting my head on his shoulder.

'I still want to see where this goes,' he says softly into my ear. 'My crash course in you has been a blast and I'd like to get to know the rest of your story at a proper pace. So you're older than me – so what?! Ten years is fuck all, Emily, and I'm certainly not going to let a stupid thing like maths dictate who I should be with.'

'Can you kiss me now?' I ask. 'Because I really think that you should.'

He holds my face in his hands, pressing his lips against mine, and that familiar feeling returns. The feeling that starts at my toes and floods through my body, making me feel completely weak and utterly fabulous.

'I think we should take this outside,' he says, glancing at the guests around us. 'I don't want to be the half-time show, here.'

He takes my hand and leads me off the dance floor and towards the walkway. A blast of cold air suddenly hits my bare arms and I shiver.

'Wait here for me,' I say. 'I'm going to pop to the house and grab a coat. I'll be right back.'

Stealing one last kiss, I scurry through the reception tent, run round to the front of the house and in through the front door, where I stop to catch my breath. I feel woozy. I really need to eat something before I'm face down in the snow, covered in my own vomit.

I grab my coat from the hall cupboard and make a detour to the kitchen. I need something to soak up the booze. I open the cupboard where the bread lives, hoping that Patrick hasn't snaffled it all, like he used to when we were kids. The noise from the party suddenly becomes louder when the patio doors slide open.

'Emily, there you are,' Mum says. 'There's someone here to see you!'

Pulling my head out of the cupboard, I turn around and freeze to the spot, my heart dropping from my chest into my stomach. Standing five feet away from me is a well-dressed, snow-covered, smiling Robert.

'Hello, Emily. Merry Christmas.'

I can't speak. I can't move. My eyes dart over to the open patio doors, in case Evan appears, but there's no sign. Oh, God – this can't be happening.

'Aren't you going to introduce us?' Mum asks, glaring at me. She knows. Oh, *she knows* who he is, because their conversation would have gone something like:

Hi I'm looking for Emily.

She's inside! Hi, I'm her mum – and you are?

I'm Robert. Her boyfriend.

'Robert,' I say feebly. 'Mum, this is Robert Shaw.'

She barely flinches. 'Hmm, and if this is Robert,' she continues, 'who exactly is that man in the marquee? The man who's been staying with us for four days? Emily, who the hell did you bring home with you?'

Robert, totally confused, looks at Mum and then me. 'Emily? You're here with someone?'

This situation can now go one of two ways. I can either backtrack, and deny all knowledge of the man standing beside Mum, demanding he leave before I call the police, or I can confess everything and look like the most pathetic idiot who ever lived.

'EMILY! EMILYYYYY! LIGHT OF MY LIFE! Hurry up and get your sexy arse out here! I'll see you on the dance floor!'

Or a third option, which involves Evan drawing attention to himself and Robert stomping off in that very direction.

'Robert! Wait!' I yell, but he's already gone through the patio doors and out into the garden. I need to reach Evan first. So I run. I run through the kitchen, past Robert, through the smokers and finally into the back entrance of the marquee, where Evan and the stand-up comedian are dancing to Calvin Harris, surrounded by several other guests.

'There you are!' he bellows, beckoning me over. 'You took ages, so I decided to dance.'

I politely push my way through to reach him. 'You have to come now,' I demand. 'It's serious.' Suddenly, I see Robert enter the marquee from the back, looking around. 'Now,' I growl. 'Let's go.'

'Jesus! Did someone die?' he asks as I drag him out.

'Not yet,' I reply. 'Just keep your head down.'

We scarper through the front entrance and back into the kitchen, where Mum, Dad, Iona, Patrick, Kim and even Pacino have gathered. I hear Robert enter the house behind us. We're trapped.

'You'd better start explaining,' Dad begins, but I'm too busy saying 'Fuck!' repeatedly to answer.

'Emily, what's going on?' Evan asks.

'Look behind you,' I reply, and he does.

'Oh,' he says, staring at Robert. 'Fuck, indeed.'

'You? Why are you here, you little twerp?' asks Robert, slightly out of breath.

'Twerp?' Evan replies. 'That's the word you're going with? Well, seeing as you ask, I was invited. The question should be, what are *you* doing here?'

'I was invited too.'

'Emily?'

'I sent him the address,' I say, sullenly. 'Ages ago. At dinner. Where he sat there and lied to my face.' I point to the kitchen table. 'Everyone, please, sit . . . No, not you, Pacino.'

They all comply, looking at each other in disbelief. Once everyone is seated, I begin pacing up and down beside the table, trying to find words to form coherent sentences.

'Where do I even start, here?' I mumble, rubbing my brow. 'OK, as you've probably now gathered, this is Robert. The real Robert. The one I told you all about.'

'Then who the hell are you?' Patrick asks Evan, who's sitting quietly. 'And why are you pretending to be him?'

'This is Evan,' I say. 'Evan is my neighbour.'

'I *knew* there was something going on between you two,' Robert sneers. 'I knew he wasn't gay.'

'Oh, shut up, fuck-face,' I hiss at Robert. ' I haven't even begun with you yet.'

'Are you gay, Robert? I mean, Evan?' Mum asks. 'I did wonder. I thought that's why you weren't very openly hands-on with Emily.'

'MUM!' I yell. 'Can we focus, here?!'

'You're Evan Grant,' Iona says, drumming her nails on the table.

We both look at her like she's some sort of witch.

'How the ... ? How long have you known?' I ask, dumbfounded.

'Oh, I didn't know anything until now,' she replies, crossing her legs. 'But I called Wallace Hall yesterday to make sure the invites were genuine and they told me it was arranged by an Evan Grant. I just assumed it was his assistant or something.'

'Assistant?' Robert scoffs. 'I'm not even sure this little twerp has a real job.'

'And there's that word again ...'

'Oh, shut up, the pair of you.'

Just then, Mrs Penman and Clarissa wander into the kitchen. We all hush up.

'Wonderful party, Jenny! Just looking for the powder room!'

'Mum, you know where it is. You've used it a hundred times before,' Clarissa says under her breath.

'Into the hall, Winnie,' Mum replies. 'Third door on the left.'

'Righto!'

We all patiently wait until she leaves before we continue.

'I'm lost,' Dad says. 'Totally lost. Why would you lie to us?'

'Because this fuckwit is married!' I exclaim, pointing at Robert.

'Separated,' he interjects. 'I've left her, Emily. For you.'

'You've what?!' I can't believe what I'm hearing. 'Say that again.'

'I've left her,' he repeats. 'My life is with you, now, Emily. If you'll still have me?'

The room falls silent. I need to sit down.

'Emily, you're not—' Evan begins, but Iona hushes him.

'Robert, I don't know what to say . . . I'm stunned.'

He smiles and walks over to me. 'You're my girl,' he replies, taking my hand. 'I'm just sorry I didn't do it sooner.'

Everyone is waiting with bated breath, their gaze firmly fixed on me while I try to take all of this in – except Evan, whose gaze is fixed upon Robert's hand, holding mine.

'I'll wait in the bedroom,' Evan says, rising from his chair. 'You guys obviously have stuff to discuss.'

Seeing Evan's dejected face makes me pull my hand away from Robert. After everything we've been through,

Evan deserves his place at this table. He isn't the one who'll be leaving.

'Sit where you are,' I insist sternly, turning to address my family. 'Dad, I can see you're still confused, so let me explain. You see, when I found out the truth about Robert, it seemed easier to pretend that Evan was him, rather than admit that the great guy I'd been bragging about was nothing but a cheating little weasel of a man. You'd never have let me live it down. *Poor Emily, alone again . . . Poor, gullible Emily – will she ever get it right?*'

'Nonsense!' Mum declares. 'We'd never have done anything like th—'

'Yes, you would,' Iona interrupts. 'We all would have, because that's what we do.'

Again, we remain quiet while Mrs Penman and Clarissa make their return journey.

Once she's back outside, I turn to Robert. 'You're so arrogant. I told you I wasn't interested, but you continued to call me. I told you not to call, so you texted. And now you show up here? Why on earth would you think this is appropriate? It's fucking creepy! When a woman says she wants nothing to do with you, it doesn't mean that you have the right to ignore her wishes and hound her.'

Robert shifts uncomfortably in his seat. 'Look, Emily, what I did was wrong, but you wouldn't listen to the whole story. Can we just go and talk? Please? I've driven all this way.'

'But I'm not looking for an explanation. I don't need one. Now, read my lips: WE ARE FINISHED. Get back in your car and go!'

Everyone stares as he stands up and straightens his jacket.

Iona holds her hand out and takes mine, squeezing it gently. 'I'm sorry you had to go through this,' she says. 'We should have been supportive, because what a normal, supportive family would do is to *tell this piece of shit to get the hell out of this house!*'

'You dumped your entire family at Christmas?' Mum snarls. 'You stupid man. Do you think I'd let my daughter anywhere near someone who's capable of doing that?'

'The other Robert seems like a right prick, Emily,' Kim tells me. 'I much prefer this one.' She gives Evan a nudge and he grins.

'Oh, for God's sake!' Robert bellows. 'If you'd rather waste your time on some kid who doesn't have a penny to his name, be my guest. But let's face it – when you're approaching fifty, he won't be around. Men prefer their women younger.'

'That's enough.' My dad stands up. 'Emily's made her feelings perfectly clear. Now, lad, off you fuck before I set the dog on you.' He claps his hands on his thighs and Pacino stands up and barks. This is all Robert needs to move and he's out of there like a flash, while every single person at the table wants to roar with laughter because that's the only trick Pacino knows to get a biscuit.

I sit down beside Evan and slowly start banging my head on the table. What a disaster.

'Graham left me.'

I lift my head to look at Iona, who's sitting back in her chair, taking out her earrings.

'He's not on business. He's fucked off with Zara Brown-Gifford, who owns a publishing house we represent. They're in New York for Christmas and I'm divorcing him.' She turns to me and smiles, her heavy lashes blinking away her tears. 'We all pretend to be happier than we actually are, Em.'

Mum and Dad turn to look at Patrick and Kim.

'What?' Patrick asks. 'I have nothing to declare! We're fi—'

'He has a low sperm count,' Kim interrupts. 'We've been trying to get pregnant. He has a low sperm count and I have a lazy ovary. So, when you make offhand digs about having no grandchildren, Jenny, it hurts.'

Mum and Dad just sit there in silence. This was definitely not what they had in mind for their annual shindig. Outside, the music is blaring and people are starting to wander towards the house in search of more booze.

'I'm going to get some more wine from the garage,' Dad announces. 'But before I do, I just want to say something: I'm extremely proud of all of you and if we've ever made you feel like you couldn't come to us with a problem, then that's on us. I promise you now, that won't happen again. We love you, no matter what.'

He starts to walk towards the door, but stops and turns back. 'And, Evan, you might not technically be Emily's boyfriend, but, I have to say, I don't ever think I've seen her smile so much as she has this Christmas. So, if you're not dating – well, maybe you should.' And, with that, he continues on his mission to find more wine.

Mum's sitting very quietly.

'You OK?' I ask her.

She shakes her head. 'Kim, I'm so sorry. In fact, to all of you – I'm sorry. And, what your dad said – that goes for me too. You're all wonderful; don't ever doubt that for one moment. I love you all to the moon and back.'

There's a few moments of hugging and sniffling before Iona says, 'Right, can we just go and drink now? I'm suddenly disgustingly sober. Robert ... Evan ... whatever your name is – come and do shots with me. I'll tell you some shit about Emily that'll make your hair curl.'

I watch everyone disperse back into the garden while I sit a bit longer at the table with Mum.

'I feel awful,' she says. 'Believe it or not, my mother was a very critical woman. Your dad's mum might have had a fat arse, but she was kind – like you are.'

'It's OK,' I reassure her. 'We all need to start being a bit nicer to each other. This is a good thing.'

And, with that, Mum leans in and hugs me so tightly I fear she might break me.

*

Twenty minutes later, the party in the marquee is still going strong. While Dad brings in more wine for the servers, Kim, Patrick and Mum strut their stuff on the dance floor. I sit this one out, watching Iona and Evan deep in conversation. If she tells him about Glastonbury, I'll fucking kill her.

I always knew my family weren't perfect, I just didn't realise how human they were, and it took a huge lie to finally get everyone to start telling the truth. We're all as messed up as each other.

Dad joins me at the table, handing me a glass of champagne. 'Robert's car's away,' he informs me. 'Now that I've met him, I have to say, I'm very glad you didn't bring him home. What a complete and utter London twat.'

I laugh and cheer my dad. 'He really is. But he's in the minority. London is full of some of the best people I'll ever know. I'll miss it when I leave.'

'You're moving?' he asks. 'When?'

'I'm not sure exactly,' I reply. 'Lots to sort out. But soon.'

'Are you coming home?' he asks. 'Your mother would be thrilled, you know.'

'*Do not* mention anything to her yet,' I plead. 'She'd never let it lie. If I do come back to Scotland, it won't be to the Borders. Glasgow, maybe . . .'

'And what about Evan?' he asks. 'Where does he fit into all of this?'

I turn and watch Evan laughing with my sister. 'I'm not

sure he does, Dad. He loves London, his job is going well and we're on very different paths right now.'

Dad leans over and gives me a hug. 'Well, if you did ever decide to bring him back, he'd be most welcome. And forget about the age difference. When you love someone, you love them.'

'Woah! Easy, Dad!' I laugh. 'Who said anything about love? I've only known him for five minutes.'

'It took me roughly the same amount of time to fall in love with your mother,' he replies. 'Just saying . . . Now, come and dance with your old man. I've asked the DJ to play some Shakira.'

We pull Iona and Evan on to the dance floor with us as 'Hips Don't Lie' begins and is met with a roar of approval from a predominately over-fifties crowd. Evan takes his turn dancing with everyone before finding his way back to me.

'You all right?' he shouts over the music. 'Not too freaked out?'

'I have no idea what you're saying.'

He grabs me by the hand and pulls me away from the noise. 'I was just checking you were all right. You know, after Robert and everything afterwards. It's been quite a night.'

'I'm more than fine,' I reply. 'I was just telling Dad about my plans to leave London. I feel excited about the future.'

'So you're still leaving, then? I thought that, you know, you might stick around. See what happens with us.'

'Well, I'm not leaving tomorrow!' I reply. 'Of course I'm willing to give us a go; I'm just not putting all of my eggs in one basket! And you have to promise me that you won't do that either.'

'OK,' he replies. 'Let's just leave it up to the universe.'

'I like that,' I say. 'No pressure.'

We walk back to the dance floor, hand in hand, ready to see what the universe decides.

CHAPTER TWENTY-SEVEN

'Glad to be home?' Evan asks as we step into the lift. 'It feels a bit odd being in a confined space now. I'm missing the countryside already.'

'I'm exhausted,' I reply, pressing the button. 'In fact, I think I might be past sleep and possibly somewhere into the future.'

The lift starts to ascend. 'So, in the future,' he asks, smiling, 'are you asleep in your bed or mine? Be nice to know in advance.'

'Mine!' I reply. 'And, in the future, no noise comes from your room. It's very peculiar, but also a fact.'

He wraps his arms around my waist. 'Come and sleep with me. We've still got that spooning game to finish; I think I was in the lead.'

I shake my head. 'Tempting as that is, I just want to pass out in my own bed. I'll see you tomorrow, though. I'll have lots of that vitality stuff I've heard so much about.'

We get out on the top floor, dragging our cases behind us.

'Well, you know where I am if you want me. Need me. Miss me. Whatever.' He kisses me on the forehead, then disappears into his flat.

I take my keys from my pocket and open the door, expecting to hear Alice's dulcet tones insulting Toby. But it's quiet. It's calm. They must be asleep. I close the door and move along the hallway as stealthily as possible, happy in the knowledge that my bed is only moments away. Turning the handle, I step into my room to see Toby fast asleep in bed. I'm so tired that, for a moment, I think I have the wrong room and step back into the hallway, softly apologising. Two seconds later, the light is on and I'm back in the real world.

'TOBY! What are you doing? Get out of my fucking bed!'

A red-faced Toby scrambles from my bed and begins gathering up his clothes from the floor, clumsily stepping in a plate of some ungodly vegan-looking fare he'd left lying around.

'Bollocks. Sorry, Em; I didn't mean to fall asleep again.'

'Again? Have you been squatting in my room since I left? What's wrong with your bloody bed?'

'I only slept here last night. My bed kind of . . . well, it broke,' he replies, grinning. 'Don't ask.'

'And you couldn't have stayed in Alice's room?' I ask, frowning at the plate of squashed brown mess. 'I imagine she's a contributing factor to your bed situation.'

'She wouldn't let me,' he responds, crossly. 'Period stuff, or something. I think she just doesn't like sharing her bed.'

'Well, that makes two of us!' I open the door and point in the direction I wish him to disappear. He shuffles off, tail between his skinny legs.

I flop exhaustedly down on my loveseat, kicking off my shoes, and gaze around my room. Even though I've only been away for four days, it feels longer. Everything feels different. I feel different. I have arrived at a fork in the road, where both roads appear to be less travelled. In one direction lies a brand-new life back in Scotland – new house, new job, new plan – and the other road leads directly to a man named Evan Grant, who just might be the best, most surprising thing that ever happened to me.

'When did you get back?!' Alice flies into my room, throwing herself on to my bed. I grunt at her in response. 'Are you tired?' she asks. 'Or just really, really Scottish, because I have no idea what you've just said.'

'Oh, for God's sake, now *you're* in my bed!' I exclaim, throwing a cushion at her. 'Tell me, am I going to have to burn these sheets?'

'Never mind about the sheets,' she replies, hurling the cushion back at me. 'What about him next door?! Did you do it? You did it, didn't you? Did you have to gag him so your parents didn't hear?'

'We certainly did not *do it*,' I insist, aware that I sound like a frigid old school mistress. 'We kissed, yes, but—'

'AHA! I knew *something* had happened. Seriously, you'd better start talking before I implode all over your nice duvet.'

'In the morning,' I promise. 'I'll tell you everything then. Now, please, let me get some kip.'

'Deal!' she replies, getting off the bed. 'And don't worry about the sheets – unless Toby's been knocking one out, they'll be fine.' She springs back up and leaves as quickly as she arrived.

I sigh and start stripping the sheets from my bed. As much as I love Toby, I'm aware that all boys are beasts and cannot be trusted. I'm also not looking forward to telling Alice I'm thinking of leaving London. Not one bit. I didn't consider that people might miss me when I leave.

Five minutes later, the bed is changed and I'm finally ready to sleep. I don't think I've ever been so happy to see a bed in my entire life. I strip naked on the spot, then close my eyes and trust-fall, face first, on to the pillow.

Thirteen hours of sleep does a lot for a person. I wake up feeling rejuvenated, hungry and eager to see Evan. I shower and dress before nipping over to see if he wants to grab some food.

'He's not here,' his delightful room-mate, Stephanie, barks. 'No idea when he'll be back.'

'OK, no worries; I'll text him. Actually, when he comes b—'

She closes the door.

Jesus, if I lived with her, I'd permanently be out.

I wander back into the flat, where Alice is making tea.

'Morning,' she chirps. 'Feeling better?'

'Much,' I reply. 'Make me a cuppa too, would you? I'm parched.'

She drops a tea bag into my pink cup. 'Just at Evan's house, were ya?' she asks. 'Just an early-morning call, was it?'

I laugh. 'I wanted to see if he was up for some breakfast, that's all. But he's out. It's no big deal.'

'So . . . you guys got along, then?' she asks, bringing over my tea. 'Which is all good and well, but I'm really far more interested to know whether you saw more than just his arse.'

'Sadly not,' I reply, adding my milk. I smirk, as she looks genuinely disappointed. 'I did *feel* quite a bit more, though!'

I'm convinced Alice's squeal of delight can be heard by Trevor downstairs.

'No . . . No! You shagged him, didn't you?'

'*No.* Well, not quite, but we—'

'Oh, you lucky bitch. I need the details! Hang on, I need some toast too.'

I watch her buzz around the kitchen enthusiastically while I describe my Christmas to her. I leave out the part about him being loaded, however; I think she's had enough excitement for one day.

'I cannot believe Robert turned up,' she says, digging her knife into some peanut butter. 'What a fucking cheek! I bet he thought he was making some grand romantic gesture, when, in fact, he was just being an intrusive little goblin.'

I shrug. 'Well, whatever he hoped to achieve didn't work. He got told where to go by everyone, so all he really did was waste his own time and petrol.'

'But *Evan!*' she continues. 'So, are you dating or what? Can Toby and I double-date with you and we can all behave like insufferable arseholes?'

'Maybe . . . I don't know. Look, we've only had a couple of intense fumbles – it's complicated.'

'No, it's perfect. He's hot as hell, he lives next door and you have plenty of time to see where it goes.' She chomps down on some toast, happily jiggling from side to side on her seat.

'Well, as it happens,' I begin, 'I'm thinking of moving back to Scotland.'

She shakes her head. 'Terrible idea. None of us are there.'

She's waiting for me to agree with her, but instead I sit quietly and sip my tea.

'But you can't!' she insists. 'Didn't you hear me? *None of us are there!*' Suddenly, she doesn't seem to be hungry anymore.

I think this is why Iona avoids the whole 'making friends' part of life, because this part sucks.

'It's just an idea at the moment,' I reply. 'We'll see.

Besides, you and Toby have got your own thing going on here. Soon you'll want the place to yourselves, or you'll move, and I'll be left here looking for new flatmates. I'm too old for flatmates!'

'Just you wait,' she says, digging her heels in. 'You and lover boy will get your happy ever after and you'll end up moving *him* in. I have foreseen it.'

'Soothsayer, now, are we?'

'Damn straight. I know things.'

'That's interesting, but what's *more* interesting is that you didn't instantly dismiss my comments about you and Toby getting your own place.'

She grins widely. 'What can I say? He gets me. I'm happy.'

'Oh, I believe you. It must take an awful lot of happiness to break a bed . . .'

She's about to launch into the sordid details when there's a loud thumping at the front door. We both sit quietly, hoping that Toby will get up and answer it, but a second thumping means he's staying put and refusing to encourage our laziness.

Evan is standing on my doorstep, armed with a huge box of Krispy Kreme doughnuts and a smile.

'Spending your fortune wisely, I see.' I invite him in. 'Ooh, there's an apple pie one. I bagsy that.'

I lead him into the kitchen, where Alice is now at the sink, washing her plate.

'Evan brought doughnuts,' I say, presenting the box like a game-show hostess. 'I do believe more tea is in order.'

'Oh, good job, neighbour!' Alice exclaims, peering inside. 'I can see why Emily is so fond of you.'

I feel myself blush and Evan smirks. 'She's fond of me, is she?' he replies. 'Tell me more.'

'TOBY! Doughnuts!' I yell over the top of their voices, as Evan takes a seat at the table. Toby arrives ten seconds later, wearing Alice's purple and pink dressing gown, and I put the kettle on.

'All right, man,' he says to Evan, taking a chocolate-filled doughnut from the box. 'You good?'

'I'm well, thanks,' Evan replies, putting his jacket on the back of the chair. 'Had an awesome Christmas. Did you know that Emily's family live on a massive estate? They had a garden party, with a marquee – like the Queen does.'

Alice nods. 'Emily invited me there last year during the summer school break. It's quite something. I love her parents, though – they're mad!'

'Must have been difficult pretending to be Robert,' Toby says, licking his fingers. 'Did they ever find out you weren't really him?'

I glare at Alice, who shrugs. 'What? Like I wasn't going to tell him? How do you *not* share that kind of gossip with your boyfriend?'

Two doughnuts later, Toby leaves to get ready for work

and Alice makes herself scarce, giving Evan and me some alone time.

'You're coming with me to a party tonight,' he says, wiping his hands on a piece of kitchen roll. 'Actually, it's more of a gathering.'

'I am?' I reply. 'What's the occasion?'

'Part house-warming, part royalties celebration. Just friends . . . and some gaming folk. It's at James's new flat in Soho.'

'A house-warming? Should I bring something? Like a plant?'

He laughs. 'No. I have some champagne; I think he'll appreciate that more. Knowing James, that plant would be dead within two weeks. I'll call round at eight?'

'Sure, sounds great.'

I swear to God, if I'm the oldest one there, I'm going to scream.

Evan's business partner, James, has chosen to rent a two-bedroom apartment in Soho, with underfloor heating and a private roof terrace, which is where we find him, among clouds of cigarette smoke. He's the one I saw cleaning his glasses on a scarf at the carol concert.

'Evan! How's it going?' he asks, wafting the smoke away from us. 'Glad you could come.'

'This is Emily,' Evan says, giving his friend a hug.

James reaches over and shakes my hand. 'Nice to meet

you, Emily,' he says, throwing Evan a sideways glance that I cannot decipher. 'When Evan said he was bringing someone, I was expecting one of his gigglers.'

'*One* of his gigglers? How many are there?'

'Pay no attention to him,' Evan replies. 'Emily's a teacher over in Acton.'

'I wish my teachers had looked like you,' James responds, nudging Evan.

'Shall we get a drink?' Evan asks, giving me an apologetic look that's very easy to recognise. 'See you in a bit, mate,' he says, taking me by the arm and leading me back into the flat.

With barely any furniture, it's obvious that James has literally just moved in, but as it's not a huge space, it's probably just as well. There must be close to a hundred and fifty people here, who all seem to know each other, flitting from one room to the next, dipping in and out of different conversations with ease.

'Gigglers, eh?' I say as we reach the living room. 'Do I not look like I giggle, then? Is that another way of saying I'm a po-faced sod?'

'Ugh – I'm sorry about James,' Evan says, cracking open a couple of beers from a cool box. 'He's not even drunk; he just thinks he's funnier than he is.'

We prop up the side wall, swigging from our beers while the party begins to escalate. The dancing has started to ripple from the middle of the floor outwards, from groups of girls perfecting their shoulder wiggles, to wallflowers finding their three-drink bravado. Everyone here is trendy, loud and under thirty, and I am definitely the only one here who wishes there was somewhere comfy to sit down.

Evan waves over at two guys who've just come through the door. 'The one on the left is Vikram,' he tells me. 'He's much more normal.'

Vikram makes his way over to us, taking off his gloves. 'How are you?' he asks, giving Evan a manly hug. 'This place is wicked, yeah?'

'Vik, this is Emily.'

I hold out my hand, but Vikram bypasses it in order to give me a cuddle. 'Great to meet you,' he says. 'You're the photographer, right? Evan says you're very talented.'

'Emily's a teacher,' Evan interjects before I can correct him myself.

Beside me, a girl wearing ridiculously high heels goes over on her ankle, pulling one of her friends down with her.

'Oh, sorry,' Vikram replies, with one eye on the pile-up happening beside us. 'You know Evan! I can never keep up ... Paula Green is here? Wow – James kept that one quiet. Back in a sec.'

I watch Vikram manoeuvre through the crowd towards a girl wearing a white string vest and harem pants.

'Well, this is embarrassing,' Evan says, taking a swig of beer. 'My friends make me sound awful.'

I turn to him and grin. 'Are you kidding me? This is hilarious. I know you're not a choirboy, Evan. We share that wall, remember?'

'Doesn't stop me wanting to make a good impression, though,' he replies, smirking. 'At the moment, I'm coming across as a total dick.'

'Oh, I don't know,' I say, stroking his back. 'I'm impressed your friends know your girlfriends' names and, to be honest, I'm wondering what noises I'll make from the other side of that wall . . .'

He leans down and whispers, 'You read my mind. Want to leave?'

'Oh, yes.'

We place our bottles on the worktop in unison and manage three steps before Vikram appears. 'You're not leaving, are you?'

Evan scratches the back of his neck. 'Yeah, I'm not feeling too good. So, erm . . .'

'Did he tell you about the festival? It's going to be so sweet.'

'We really have to get go—'

'Festival?' I ask. 'A music festival?'

'Nah, man; it's a gaming festival that tours all over the country. We're doing four cities in the UK and then two in Europe. Remember to get your passport sorted for next week.' Vikram slaps Evan on the back and shoots off towards the stairs.

'That sounds amazing!' I say heartily. 'You must be thrilled.'

'I was going to tell you,' he replies, looking downcast. 'It's just for a few months. We need to promote our new stuff, do meet-and-greets, that kind of thing.'

'Stop looking so sad!' I reply, never letting the smile leave my face. 'I'm happy for you. It's exciting!'

He perks up and begins chattering about the festival as we walk out of James's apartment and look for a taxi, going into detail about the gaming industry, and all I can think is, I knew this would happen. He's a young guy, with a sack full of cash and no ties. This is exactly where he's meant to be and exactly where I'm not. However, the final blow comes when we bump into Cassie and two of her friends on the street outside.

'Very thoughtful of you, Evan,' she says, looking me up and down. 'Taking your mum for a night out. What a good boy you are.'

They all start to giggle.

'Oh, God – you're the gigglers!' I say, laughing. 'I wondered what James was talking about.'

'Shut the fuck up, granny.'

'You're a lot less adorable without your bear hat, Cassie,' I respond. 'I can't believe I actually felt sorry for you.'

'Evan is the one I feel sorry for,' she snarls, 'having to deal with your dried-up old cooch. Had fun listening to us through the walls?'

'Cassie, that's enough,' Evan snaps at her. 'Let's go, Em.'

'It's true, I've heard you through my wall,' I say. 'All that squealing. Very unattractive. But do you know what I didn't hear? I didn't hear a peep from Evan. That's the difference between me and you, sweetheart. I know what the fuck I'm doing. And – Jesus, girls – unless the "chimney sweep" is the look you're going for, lay off the contouring.'

And then it happens. Cassie pushes me, her perfectly manicured hands bouncing off my new coat, making me stumble back. I'm stunned. I haven't had someone try to square up to me since high school.

Evan's about to jump in when I launch myself at Cassie, take her by the coat collar and say, quietly, into her ear, 'Get yersel' tae fuck before I slap the shadow right aff yer body. Don't believe me? Just try me. I double fuckin' dare you.'

She pushes me off and picks up her handbag. 'She's fucking crazy,' she says nervously, sorting her coat collar. 'Let's just go.'

We finally get a cab and clamber in, giving the driver the address. We sit silently for a minute or two. Evan can't tell, but inside I'm relieved that Cassie didn't actually take me on, as I cannot fight to save myself. Also, she implied I had an old dried-up fanny and that hurt my fucking feelings.

'Is it wrong that I found that hot?' he asks, staring straight ahead. 'What did you say to her?'

I smile. 'Let's just say there's nothing like an angry Scot to make you consider your next move very carefully.'

'Did you go all *Trainspotting* on her? You looked like a really sexy Begbie.'

I start to laugh.

'And you're right, you know. What you said about me not making any noise.'

'Oh, I know,' I reply, placing my hand on his leg. 'And, in any case, we're about to find out.'

By the time the taxi pulls up outside the flats, Evan is wearing the majority of my lipstick. He pays the driver and drags me by the hand into our building. Trevor says a polite 'Good evening' as Evan leads me towards the elevators.

'Hi, Trev,' he yells back, rapidly pushing the *up* button. He's like a man on a mission. Once inside the lift, he has me up against the wall, his mouth on mine and one hand up my skirt. It's like the stuff you see in movies, only we're in a rickety lift that smells like ageing dog.

'My flat or yours?' he asks breathlessly, as we stumble out of the lift and into the hallway. 'Or here? We can do it right here; I don't care.'

'Yours,' I reply, as he nuzzles into my neck. 'Alice and Toby are in.'

'Did I mention we could do it here?'

I push him towards his front door while he takes his keys from his pocket. Once he finally gets me into his room, he doesn't even bother turning on the lights. We move towards his bed, ripping at each other's clothes and kissing desperately, until finally I'm at the other side of my wall and I'm in charge.

My mouth makes him moan first, followed by my tongue, then my hands and finally just the culmination of every single sweaty, filthy, uninhibited thing we manage to do, until I finally call a timeout before we break each other.

'That thing –' he says, catching his breath – 'with your tongue and your mouth. Holy shit.'

'I know,' I reply, moving my hair from my face. 'But that thing, when I'm on my stomach . . .'

'Holy shit,' we say in unison.

From the other side of the wall, someone called Alice or Toby bangs loudly, followed by clapping and cheering. I bang back *fuck off* in my own style of Morse code.

'You are never allowed to leave here,' he insists, pulling a pillow under his head. 'We are going to do this until the paramedics need to get involved.'

'You underestimate my endurance,' I reply. 'You'd miss your gaming festival.'

He turns on his side to face me. 'To be honest, I wish I didn't have to go, now. You're pretty amazing, you know. I could quite happily stay in bed for the next month.'

'It's a nice thought,' I reply, smiling.

'Can I ask you something?'

'Sure.'

'Are you still thinking of leaving London? Because I'd really like you not to do that.'

I turn and stare at the ceiling.

'I'll be finished with all this work nonsense in a few months. Then we can—'

'We have bad timing,' I say, my heart sinking. 'We need to be honest about this. I'm done with London. I'm done with the room-mates and the crowds and seeing the same faces at work every day. I'm done, Evan, but you're just beginning. This is where you need to be.'

'So you'll move in with me. I'll buy us a house and—'

'Evan, we're in very different places right now,' I say firmly. 'And let's be realistic. You're rich, you're handsome and you are going to meet some games designer or computer whizz who will be young and beautiful, and she's going to knock your socks right off. I don't want to be older, saggier and living in a house that *you* bought when that happens.'

He sighs and sits up, turning on his bedside lamp. 'So that's it, then?' he asks. 'We just go our separate ways?'

'No, we just live our lives,' I reply. 'We can keep in touch.'

'OK,' he says, putting his arm around me. 'Let's do that.'

As we lie in bed, cuddling, we both know that's unlikely to happen.

CHAPTER TWENTY-EIGHT

'All right, everyone, settle down, please.'

I watch my fifth-year students reluctantly take their seats.

'Aww, Miss, you're not going to make us work today, are you?'

The rest of the class groan in agreement.

'Yes, Adam, I'm more than aware that we're finishing up for Christmas break today, unless you think wearing reindeer antlers is a normal occurrence for me. But today is still a school day and I'm obliged to follow the curriculum.'

More groans. And a disgustingly wet sneeze. God, children are awful.

'So,' I continue, handing Johanna McBride a hanky, 'you can either waste time sulking, or we can spend this period productively – eating chocolate and watching *Ant-Man*.'

I let them have their cheers. I may have only been teaching at Mearns Secondary for ten months, but I know I'm already their favourite.

I close the blinds and dim the lights while chief moaner, Adam McKerral, starts the film. Trying to ignore my Paul Rudd crush, I walk up and down the class placing handfuls of sweets on everyone's desk, except for Johanna McBride, who has a nut allergy; she gets a bag of giant chocolate buttons all to herself because I did my research and also I'm a thoroughly decent human being.

Returning to my desk, I unwrap a miniature Fudge and eat what I'm certain will be the first of thousands of chocolates between now and January. I open the top drawer and start removing anything I don't want to go missing over the holidays, but it's all junk: breath spray, deodorant, tampons – if anyone's desperate enough to pinch this, they obviously need it more than I do.

I'm emptying the contents of my electric sharpener into the bin when I hear my phone buzz. It's a text from Kara:

Mother-in-law isn't coming to us for Chrimbo this year. I actually punched the air when John told me and now he's sulking. Totally worth it. Call me later x

I try to text her an emoji of a happy smiling lady, but my thumb slips and I end up sending her a man in a turban instead.

'I thought you weren't allowed phones in class, Miss Carson,' says a smug voice from the back of the room.

'That's right, Nicole, you're not,' I reply, still staring at my phone. 'And you're also not allowed food. So, if you want to go down this road, I'll be happy to put my phone away, while you remove the sweets from everyone's desk. I'm sure they'll thank you for being such a stickler for the rules.'

She doesn't respond.

'Mm-hmm,' I mumble. 'Didn't think so . . .'

The teachers' lounge in Mearns Secondary is much smaller than the one in Acton Park, but what it lacks in size it more than makes up for in coffee quality. Gone are the days of shitty generic freeze-dried granules, for here we have a proper electric one-hundred-cup percolator, which requires no effort whatsoever and makes everyone's day that little bit brighter. In fact, there are lots of reasons why this school outranks my old one. Not only does it take me just twenty-five minutes to get to work, but I get there by car. Sadly not my BMW convertible, which failed its MOT and would cost more to fix than the value of the car, but my new little white Mazda, which never breaks down and is very cheap to run. I did think about getting another convertible, but then I remembered that this is Scotland and we only get three days of sunshine a year.

However, Acton Park does have one thing that this school is sadly missing . . . and that's Alice. I know she's missing me too, judging by her text this morning:

Kenneth Dawson keeps sitting beside me in the break room. I will never forgive you for leaving.

In this school, the Christmas decorations are put up by someone from the woodwork department, with spirit-level straight tinsel stapled to the walls in carefully measured rows of two. We also have a tiny fibre-optic tree, which sits near the window, unplugged and unloved – nothing like the chaotic splendour Alice used to create. I take a photo and text it to her with the caption, *Don't you think I'm being punished enough?*

Coffee in hand, I take a seat at the table nearest the pigeonholes, sorting through any important staff notices I've chosen to ignore all year. It turns out that being head of English is a lot duller than it sounds, with a lot more paperwork.

Another text comes through from Alice, with a selfie of her giving me the finger in front of a garland of rainbow tinsel, stuck to the wall in swirls, captioned, *See you on Friday, mofo!*

I grin. I'm looking forward to my flying visit this weekend. Their new flatmate, Mila, will be back in Holland for Christmas, so I'll get to sleep in Alice's old room, as she moved into mine twelve seconds after I left. I'm sorting through some paperwork when Dave Calgie, the PE teacher, pulls up a chair beside me.

'What're your plans for Christmas, Emily? Just you and the hubby?'

I cannot stand this guy. For a PE teacher, he's the weediest-looking drip of a man I've ever seen. The girls all call him 'Creepy Calgie' and I fully support this.

'I'm not married,' I reply, watching his stained teeth

bite into a mince pie, but he already knows this. He knows this because a) I don't wear a ring, and b) my title is Miss, and c) he fucking asked me to my face when I joined the school, shortly before trying it on with me. Dick.

'I'll be spending it with my family,' I continue. 'What about you? Just you and the wife?'

He gives me a dirty look and moves seats, while I laugh. I know he's not married because a) he doesn't wear a ring, b) he's divorced, and c) the reason his wife divorced him is because he's a fucking dick who tries it on with his co-workers.

After the last bell, I pop in to see Gordon, my old school friend and current head teacher. He looks like he's been making his coffees Irish all day.

'You off?' he asks, typing away on his laptop.

I sit down on the seat in front of his desk. 'Yep, I have a million things to organise. What are you doing over Christmas? Quiet one?'

'I wish,' he replies. 'Brenda's sister and her two kids are coming in from Manchester later, so it'll be bedlam.'

'Your boys will love that, though,' I say. 'But – I know – families at Christmas can be hard going. We just have to grin and bear it.'

'You go back to the Borders for Christmas, don't you?' he asks, leaning over to grab a sheet of paper from the printer.

'Usually,' I reply. 'This year we're trying something different.'

'What's that?'

I scrunch up my face. 'They're all coming to me.'

I have this idea in my head that if I only eat pre-prepared foods before everyone arrives on Sunday, then my kitchen should remain in its current spotless state. So, with this in mind, I pick up a pizza from Domino's on the way home. Keep pizza in box, eat pizza from box, put box in bin. Simple.

When I get home, I park in my driveway and carefully lift the pizza from the front seat. I still haven't got used to owning my own driveway yet. It's quite special. I feel like I'm announcing myself every time I come home. What I have got used to is having my own place. I've been sharing a home my entire life, first with my family and then with a stream of flatmates; I'm beyond ready to take on the role of single female homeowner. I was born for this role. The first couple of nights were nerve-wracking because obviously every unfamiliar creak or groan from the house meant I was about to die horribly. At least in London I knew exactly what every bloody creak and groan meant. But now I'm used to them, and I've even stopped sleeping with a kitchen knife under my pillow. Progress.

I've managed one slice of my stuffed crust when my phone begins to buzz in my bag.

'Kara!' I say, trying not to chew too loudly. 'I was just going to call you!'

'How are you?' she asks. 'Glad to be finished for the year?!'

'I am! And you must be glad that you're mother-in-law-free,' I reply. 'Is John speaking to you yet?'

'Ha ha, yes. He can never stay angry at me for too long – especially when he knows I'm right. What are you eating?'

'Chicken. Stuffed crust.'

'Ah. Evan's not been in touch, then?'

'That has nothing to do with my dinner choice,' I reply, ready to tell her about my excellent clean-kitchen plan.

'Oh, it has – more than you realise. You'll have gained fifty pounds by the time you've stopped pining.'

'I haven't heard from him in months,' I say despondently. 'He didn't even tell me that he'd moved away – Alice sent me a photo of the movers taking his stuff down to the van.'

'It probably just wasn't meant to be,' she replies. 'I know I've said this before, but you were right to move back to Scotland, and you had just split with Robert. Jumping head first into another relationship was the last thing you needed.'

'But he just cut me off,' I whine. 'I'd have been happy keeping in touch!'

She sighs. 'I'd have done the same thing. Someone I'm into moves miles away and just wants to be friends? He probably has enough friends.'

'Ugh, that's harsh,' I reply. I take two huge bites of

pizza in succession. 'So, are we still on for Friday?' I ask, steering the subject away from Evan. 'I'm getting the half nine flight, so I can meet you for lunch.'

'Definitely!' she replies. 'There's a new Asian-fusion place near Covent Garden. Their tempura is exquisite.'

'Sounds like a plan. I'll text you when I get to Stansted.'

We say our goodbyes and I throw the phone on the couch, continuing with my new mess-free, fork-free lifestyle. I think this could catch on.

An hour later, the pizza is gone and the hole still hasn't been filled. So maybe I do miss Evan, but that's OK. For a brief moment, we shared something lovely, and I don't regret a thing. Fifty pounds, though? I hope she's kidding.

CHAPTER TWENTY-NINE

As I pack my overnight bag with everything I'll need for my visit to London, I begin to think about how much has changed in the last year. Iona decided to start her own legal practice, investing the money she squeezed out of Graham during the divorce and taking a lot of his clients with her. I talk to her on the phone much more often these days, as well as Patrick. He and Kim are looking into alternative fertility options in their attempt to make Mum a granny. And Mum – well, she's still Mum.

Gone, however, are the weekly Sunday-at-six-p.m. check-ins, because Mum now plays poker with her friends instead. Poker! Dad tells me she's quite the shark. So I have been bumped to Thursdays at seven p.m., which is the new time I allow her judgemental voice to travel the considerably shorter 92.5 miles from the Scottish Borders to my new house in East Renfrewshire.

'Hello, Mum; how are you?' I ask, popping some travel shampoo into my toiletry bag.

'I'm fine, Emily, just fine,' she replies. 'How's the new job?'

'Well, it's not so new anymore,' I reply. 'I'll have been there a year in February.' I can hear Dad whistling 'Do You Know the Way to San Jose' in the background.

'Gosh! A whole year! How times flies! Are the staff nice?'

'They are, Mum. I've told you this several times. Everything's great at work.'

'And your neighbours – how are they?'

This is the same conversation we had last week. I think poker has messed with her cognitive function.

'I don't see them that much, Mum. I'm out all day and they're quiet.'

'That's wonderful.'

'Wonderful's a bit strong . . .'

'So, tell me . . .'

Here it comes.

'Have you met anyone nice?'

I'm laughing before she's even finished the question.

'Oh, for God's sake, Emily. I haven't asked you that in months! I'm trying, here, but we haven't heard you mention anyone since you moved. Have you even been looking? You know, dipped your toe in the pool up there?'

I lie down on my couch. 'No, Mum. No toe-dipping here. No dipping of any kind, in fact. I've been far too busy.'

'Have you heard from Evan?' she asks. 'He was such a nice boy.'

'Mum, you spent the entire time, last Christmas, telling me how being with Evan wasn't a good idea. Stop back-tracking now – it's too late.'

'Iona agrees with me, you know. And Dad. We all think he was good for you.'

'Well, we both agreed that it wasn't the right time for us. Que sera, sera . . .'

'Oh, nonsense,' she retorts. 'You sound like your granny – "what's for you won't go by you" . . . Complete twaddle. Life doesn't owe you anything; you have to put the work in.'

'Which granny? Dad's mum or yours?'

'Oh, your father's, of course. That's the reason her arse was so big. She sat around on it all day, waiting for things to happen.'

'All set for next week?' I ask, changing the subject. 'You're still sure you want to have Christmas here?'

'Absolutely. It'll be nice to have someone else cook for us.'

'Yes,' I agree. 'Mrs Marks and Mr Spencer look forward to feeding you.'

'OK, darling, I have to run, but we'll see you on Monday! Love you!'

'Love you too, Mum.'

I hang up the phone and throw some clean underwear

into my travel bag. I don't need much. Lunch with Kara, then overnight with Alice and Toby, before flying back home to tackle my first ever Christmas lunch.

I catch the Stansted Express to Liverpool Street and let Kara know I've arrived. It feels like I've never been away. The snow hasn't fallen this year, but it's still grey and damp, with a glimmer of sparkle from the Christmas decorations. I buy a coffee and take a seat in the courtyard, waiting for Kara to let me know where to meet her. As I watch the world go by, I'd be lying if I said I didn't feel glad to be back, even if it's just for the night.

Finally, Kara texts: *Just jump on the Tube to Holborn. I'll meet you there in half an hour.*

'I love your hair!' she exclaims when she catches sight of me walking towards the entrance. 'It's so bouncy!'

'I got some highlights, darling,' I say, swishing it over my shoulder. 'New me and all that.'

We hug beside the news-stand as the rain begins to patter down on us. Kara takes her umbrella from her bag. 'Quick,' she says, motioning for me to follow her. 'It's just up here.'

Kara's idea of 'just up here' involves a ten-minute walk in the rain, but thankfully we're only mildly soggy when we reach the restaurant. Kara shakes off her jacket and hangs it on the coat stand, taking a seat near the window.

'Sake, please,' she informs the waitress, 'and two prawn tempura bento boxes. Thanks.' She snaps her chopsticks down the middle and turns to me. 'You're going to love this,' she insists. 'There's no point in ordering anything else – this is the bomb.'

'Do they do those little mochi desserts here?' I ask, picking up a menu. 'I love those.'

'You're looking so well,' she says. 'Must be all that decent Scottish tap water.'

'I feel well,' I reply as the waitress sets down our sake. 'I'm settled in, things are going well at school, I even joined a gym!'

'What?!' she exclaims. 'I can't imagine you doing spin classes and weight training.'

I laugh. 'I said I've joined; I didn't actually say I'd been.'

Our bento boxes arrive quickly and Kara is absolutely right.

'I think this tempura was made by angels,' I say, examining it between my chopsticks.

She nods in agreement, too busy eating to reply.

'Christ, this sake is strong,' I say, my face crumpling. 'I'll be pissed before I even get to the flat.'

'Good,' she replies, clinking my cup. 'It's Christmas. Time to let that highlighted hair of yours down.'

At three p.m., we say our goodbyes and I catch a taxi to my old flat, texting Alice to let her know I'm on my way. I'm not drunk, but I am merry – merry enough to tip the driver ten quid. As I clamber out, he thanks me and wishes me a happy Christmas, making some stupid joke about the Scots not being as tight as everyone says.

I'm glad to see that Trevor is still behind the concierge desk. He gives me a wave.

'Emily! Very nice to see you!'

'You too, Trevor!' I reply, walking towards the lift. 'Just back for the night!'

It seems some things have changed, however, as the left lift now smells clean. No eau de dog-remains, just the faint smell of air freshener and cleaning fluid. I guess the dog finally crossed the rainbow bridge, or fell off it, or whatever the hell pets do when they die.

As the lift doors open on the seventeenth floor, I can't help but glance over at Evan's door. I know he moved out months ago, but there's still a tiny part of me that wishes he was behind that door.

'Hey, lady!' Alice calls. 'Get your butt in here! Toby made flapjacks for you. Fucking *flapjacks*!'

I stride over to the door, where Alice awaits me. 'Welcome home!' she says, helping me with my bag. Her Christmas jumper is impressive – it's got a robin in a Santa hat and he's standing beside his perplexed-looking penguin friend. There's a lot going on.

We go through to the kitchen, which has been given a new coat of mint-green paint in my absence, and, as usual, the fridge is covered in Christmas cards, including the pop-up Santa one I sent last week. As Toby welcomes me in, I see I'm not the only one with a new Christmas 'do'.

'Toby! Your hair! Where has it gone?'

He lays a plate of what I assume are flapjacks in the middle of the table. 'Alice pulled a Delilah on me,' he says. 'Cut it off while I slept.'

'Oh, you liar!' she exclaims, laughing. 'I did not. He had to cut it for some photo shoot.'

'Marc Jacobs,' he says, pulling a model pose, before grinning from ear to ear.

'I'm so proud!' I reply, giving him a hug. 'No more pet shop?'

'Not for four months now.'

I congratulate him again before sitting at the table and kicking my boots off.

'The hamsters sent him a Christmas card,' Alice says, pointing at the fridge. 'They miss him terribly.'

'That's from the *owner*, not the hamsters,' he responds quickly.

'No shit, Sherlock; I was making a joke.'

As they begin to squabble, I sit back and smile. I'm glad to see that they haven't changed, not one little bit.

As the evening progresses, we get through three bottles of Prosecco and some Baileys. Toby's flapjacks lie uneaten in favour of the three tubs of Pringles Alice bought in especially for me.

'I'm taking Toby to Oz in January,' Alice informs me. 'He's meeting my parents.'

'Well, that's big news!' I reply, draining the last of the Prosecco. 'Do not cancel on her,' I say to Toby, wagging my finger. 'Because then she'll be forced to pay someone to be her boyfriend.'

'He was in the paper the other week, you know,' Alice says. 'Opened a gaming café in Piccadilly, or saved some orphans or something. Can't quite remember. Did you know he was filthy rich?'

I nod. 'I found out last year.'

'And you're sitting here with us, instead of whatever yacht in the Caribbean he's spending Christmas on? You could have been pushing out an heir to his millionaire throne by now.' Alice shakes her head. 'You and your bloody good moral character. I thought I raised you better.'

I laugh. 'Oh, I'm sure he's got some perky twenty-year-old earmarked for that job.'

'Bullshit,' Toby says. 'You're too hung up on the age thing. I mean, look at you – you're a super intelligent, funny, gorgeous woman. Evan wouldn't have given two shits about your age, I guarantee.'

Alice claps in agreement. 'Samson has a point.'

I shrug. 'It doesn't matter now, anyway, but I promise you both, if I'm ever pursued by a handsome, younger man, I will not let the age difference be an issue and will approach the relationship with wild and reckless abandon.'

'Well, unless he's a pupil,' Alice interjects.

'Good point.'

'Now that we have that sorted,' Toby says, 'will *someone* please try my fucking *flapjacks*?!'

I leave the following morning, armed with a Lush Christmas gift set, a necklace Alice borrowed two years ago without telling me and a small Tupperware box full of flapjacks, which, as it turns out, are delicious.

'We'll come and stay at Easter,' Alice promises, kissing me goodbye. 'Unless you burn your house down cooking Christmas dinner.'

'You know that might actually happen, right?' I reply. 'Thanks for the Lush stuff. I hope Santa's good to you!'

'Oh, do me a favour and give this to Trevor,' she says, handing me a Christmas card. 'He goes off on holiday today, but I can't be bothered getting dressed to do it myself.'

I take the card and put it in my pocket. 'No probs. I'm sure he'll be touched by the half-arsed gesture. Will call you soon.'

I walk across to the lift and press the button before double-checking that I have my passport. Once downstairs, I head over to Trevor, who's wearing a Santa hat and humming along to carols.

'Leaving us again?' he asks, turning down his little radio.

I smile. 'Yep. Just wanted to give you this! It's from Alice and Toby.'

He takes the card and thanks me. 'Do you need a taxi?' he asks, tearing open the envelope. He smiles at the puppies on the front of the card.

'That's OK,' I reply. 'I've ordered one. Thanks, anyway, and have a nice Christmas!'

I'm standing at the main door, phone in hand, waiting for my Uber, when a large blue BMW double-parks on the pavement outside. I scowl, knowing that he's blocking traffic, and, more specifically, my Uber.

'Move your bloody car!' I yell as the driver opens the door. 'You can't park h—'

'Emily?' Evan closes the car door and takes two steps towards me. 'What are you doing here?'

He's wearing that pea coat I love so much, but his hair is different. He's ditched the Brylcreem.

'I could ask you the same question,' I reply, trying to hold my nerve.

'A parcel came here for me,' he says, pointing towards Trevor. 'You?'

'Just visiting Alice,' I reply, as my Uber arrives behind his car. I give the driver a wave. 'That's my taxi.'

Evan's head shoots around to see the car waiting patiently for me. 'You're leaving now?!'

'Yes, I'm flying home tonight.'

'But . . .'

The driver honks his horn. 'I have to go,' I say, picking up my bags. 'Was nice seeing you, Evan.'

'But . . .'

'I'm sorry.'

He steps in front of me. 'No way,' he replies. 'Not again. Fuck this.'

I watch him run over to the Uber and hand the driver something, before rushing back to me. 'Stay right here. One minute, I promise.'

Now he's flying through the doors towards Trevor, who hands him a parcel, and then he's back beside me, slightly out of breath.

'I paid the Uber driver to piss off,' he says, package in one hand, car keys in the other.

'What?! You can't! I need—'

'Remember when we said we'd let the universe decide?'

'Yes, but—'

'Well, it has!' he exclaims. 'You think us both being here on the same day at the same time is just some weird coincidence?'

'I do, actually, but, even if you're right, I'm still up there and you're still down here. Nothing's changed!'

'Then we'll make it change. All I know is that I'm not losing you again over something as stupid as geography. Dammit, Emily – I've missed you. I've missed us. Tell me you don't feel the same?!'

'Of course I've missed you,' I reply, my eyes beginning to fill with tears. 'I've missed you every single day.'

'Then get in the car.' He takes my bags and walks over

to his BMW. The traffic is already starting to back up behind him.

'What are you doing?' I say as he opens the boot. 'I have a plane to catch!'

'I know,' he replies. 'I'll drive you. And if, by the time we get to the airport, you aren't ready to admit that this, *whatever this is*, is worth holding on to, then I'll accept your decision. Agreed?'

The cars continue to honk their horns as he holds open the door for me.

'Pretty soon they're all going to get out of their cars and murder me, Emily. Please get in.'

'OK,' I reply, 'but on one condition.'

'Name it.'

'I get to choose the music.'

He grins. 'I haven't missed you *that* much . . .'

CHAPTER THIRTY

I'm up bright and early on Christmas Eve, preparing to panic-shop before everyone gets here at five p.m. I'm very glad they've chosen to leave on Boxing Day, so they can get back for Pacino and still indulge in their party, because I have no idea where I'd put everyone for the full four days. Still, I'm excited. I have a feeling that this Christmas might be the best one yet.

I zoom around Asda, picking up extras, since I've already made my way through most of the festive nuts and crisps I bought last week. As usual, I don't appear to be the only one who's eaten half of their Christmas food shop before Christmas, because everyone south of the River Clyde is, at this very moment, standing in front of me at the checkout. I watch a woman try to take a full trolley into the ten-or-less section, and then I watch her flee when she's caught breaking the golden rule of checkouts.

'Get tae fuck wi' yer big shop. It's *ten or less*.'

'Oi! Can you no read? Well, whit part of "ten or less" is no clear?'

'That's outrageous. Can someone get security?!'

There is no good will to all men at Christmas. It's every man for himself.

I'm home by half two, leaving me plenty of time to hoover the bedrooms once more and try to figure out the best way to tell Iona she's sleeping on the fold-down couch. Also, everyone sharing one bathroom isn't going to be pretty. I should have thought this through more. Giving the place one last spot check, I collapse on the couch, intending to power-nap for twenty minutes. But that twenty minutes turns into eighty, and I wake up in a dark living room to the sound of a car pulling up outside.

It's them. My already nervous tummy does a massive summersault, followed by what feels like a very wonky landing. I pull back the blinds and peer out into the darkness. They're here! For the first time in thirty-nine years, I'm the one hosting Christmas for my entire, badly behaved family, and I have couch-head and drool on my cheek.

I open the door and watch their figures emerge from the Land Rover. Only it's not their old Land Rover – it's much fancier.

'Dad? Did you finally upgrade the car?' I yell. He grunts something in return, but I can't quite hear him.

First to charge towards me is Iona, who locks me in a

massive hug before pushing me back into the house. 'Well, let's see it, then!'

'OK . . . but let me just help Mum and—'

'Patrick will do it; he'll let us know if he needs a hand.'

She's pushing me down my own hallway, demanding a tour.

'Where am I sleeping?' she asks. 'Is it bigger than it looks from outside?'

She walks into the front bedroom and I hear her gasp.

'Emily, my wardrobe is bigger than this. How on earth did you get a bed in here? Is it inflatable?'

'Emily, can you give us a hand, please?'

I leave Iona, who's now demanding to see what other bedrooms are available, and help with the cases.

'How was the drive, Dad?' I ask, lugging a huge black suitcase into the hall.

'Fine,' he replies, giving me a big hug. 'Roads were pretty clear.'

'Darling! How are you?!' Mum exclaims, bag-free and pushing past Kim and Patrick. 'I must just use the bathroom.'

'Last door at the end of the hall, Mum,' I reply, taking a case from Kim. 'Merry Christmas Eve, guys.'

With Mum in the loo and Iona now snooping in my room, yelling, 'Christ, Emily – is every room a shoebox?' I usher Dad, Patrick and Kim into the living room.

'Your house is fab!' Kim says, admiring my tree. 'It must be great to finally have your own place.'

'It is!' I reply, as Dad chooses his seat for the evening. 'A little small for all of us, but for me, it's perfect!'

'What is Iona blethering on about?' Patrick asks, taking his coat off.

'I think she's asking what hotels are nearby.'

'Ignore her,' Dad says. 'She's annoyed that we made her sit in the boot.'

'What?'

He laughs. 'Not in the boot, exactly. It's a seven-seater. She sat at the back.'

Once everyone has moaned, peed and had their first drink, the evening begins to run smoothly.

'Well, Miss Hostess,' Mum says, knocking back a gin and tonic. 'Once you've finished checking your phone for the millionth time, would you like to tell us what our Christmas Eve game is?'

'I thought we'd do charades.'

Everyone groans.

'BUT, if no one guesses what charade you're doing, you have to do a shot.'

'Tequila?' Kim asks, suddenly perking up.

I grin. 'What else?'

'*Skyfall*?'

'Falling Over . . . no *Falling Down*!'

'*Jumpin' Jack Flash*!'

Just as no one guesses Patrick's charade for the sixth time, I hear my doorbell.

'Are you expecting someone?' Mum asks, her nosiness radar now at DEFCON 1. 'It's after ten. Isn't that a bit late?'

'It's probably the neighbours complaining about Patrick's *umpteenth shitty charade attempt*,' Iona snarls.

'Be right back,' I say, but no one is listening – they're all too busy shouting random film answers at Patrick, who's trying to mime out a song.

I close the living-room door and quickly check my make-up in the hall mirror, removing a small crumb of Bombay mix that's attached itself to my chin. Taking a deep breath, I open the door.

'You made it!' I squeal.

Evan steps into my house and into my arms. I hug him like someone's going to take him away at any moment.

'Do they know I'm coming?' he asks, squeezing me back.

'Nope,' I reply. 'They have no idea.'

'So they don't know we're madly in love and will have sex for an entire month when they leave?'

'Did you just tell me you loved me?'

'Yes, but I also implied that you love me back.'

I squeal again.

'Emily!' Mum yells. 'Who's at the door?'

'IT'S RYAN GOSLING.'

I grab Evan's face and kiss him.

'Are you ready for this?' I whisper. He winks at me and takes hold of my hand.

It's game on.

ACKNOWLEDGEMENTS

I'd like to both thank and high-five the following people for their help and support:

Kerry and Ella at Susanna Lea Associates, Kathryn and the entire team at Quercus, Celine Kelly, my friends, my family (for being nothing like the Carsons) and my daughter Olivia who gives the best cuddles ever.

I'd also like to say a huge thank you to anyone who's ever read, reviewed, bought or borrowed one of my books. I'm forever grateful.

If you enjoyed *The Most Wonderful Time of the Year*, why not try Joanna's other novels?

The List:
A Year of Adventures in Bed

Phoebe Henderson may be single but she sure doesn't feel fabulous. It's been a year since she found her boyfriend Alex in bed with another woman, and multiple cases of wine and extensive relationship analysis with best friend Lucy have done nothing to help. Faced with a new year but no new love, Phoebe concocts a different kind of resolution. **The List**: ten things she's always wanted to do in bed but has never had the chance (or the courage!) to try. A bucket list for between the sheets. One year of pleasure, no strings attached. **Simple, right?** Factor in meddlesome colleagues, friends with benefits, getting frisky *al fresco* and maybe, *possibly*, true love and Phoebe's got her work cut out for her.

I Followed the Rules
Dating by the Book

Rule 1: Never ask him on a first date.
Rule 2: Laugh admiringly at all his jokes.
Rule 3: Always leave him wanting more. . . *wtf?!*

Have you heard of *The Rules of Engagement*? It's a book that promises to teach you to find the man of your dreams in ten easy steps. Unsurprisingly, I don't own a copy. What is it, 1892? But I'm a journalist, and I've promised to follow it to the letter and write about the results. Never mind that my friends think I'm insane, I'm stalking men all over town and can't keep my mouth shut at the best of times. My name is Cat Buchanan. I'm thirty-six years old and live with my daughter in Glasgow. I've been single for six years, but that's about to change. After all, I'm on a deadline. I Followed the Rules and this is what happened.

Motherhood and Writing

Joanna Bolouri writes about how motherhood
inspired her in unexpected ways

When my daughter was two, I lost my job and became a single parent. This was the defining moment in my life. I had a choice; I could sit alone night after night, worrying that our lives would always be a struggle or use this this time to try and do something to change them forever.

As with most single parents, free time was scarce so I'd sit up at night and write while she slept, catching naps with her during the day to keep me sane. I put everything else in my life on hold, not allowing myself to consider that my work might not actually be any good. I couldn't. It was all I had. It was exhausting, it was lonely but it was the best decision I ever made. Almost a year later, I'd written my first novel, *The List*.

My daughter is almost ten now and in the eight years I've been writing and raising her, I've come to realise that being a mother and a writer are actually two very similar callings. Both require discipline, a sense of humour, a well-stocked booze shelf and most importantly, patience.

I still worry about the future and things are still a struggle but I have managed to raise a bright, kind, funny girl who knows how loved and important she is.

As cliché as it sounds, my daughter motivates me to be a better writer. I see the world and myself very differently, since she arrived. I'm stronger, more resilient and able to express myself in ways I found impossible before.

I want her to be proud of me. I want her to know that every book I've ever written was because she inspired me to find my voice.

Motherhood gave me something that I never expected. It gave me my muse.